THE MARTINI SHOT

THE MARTINI

PETER CRAIG

SHOT

A NOVEL

WILLIAM MORROW AND COMPANY, INC. · NEW YORK

Library of Congress Cataloging-in-Publication Data
Craig, Peter.
    The martini shot : a novel / Peter Craig.
        p.   cm.
    ISBN 0-688-15658-4
    I. Title.
PS3553.R229M37   1998
813' .54—dc21   97-41898
                          CIP

Printed in the United States of America

First Edition

1 2 3 4 5 6 7 8 9 10

BOOK DESIGN BY DEBBIE GLASSERMAN

www.williammorrow.com

FOR AMY

A C K N O W L E D G M E N T S

I'm grateful to Lisa Bankoff, my agent at ICM, for her advice, encouragement, and resolve; my editor, Zachary Schisgal, for his thoughtful and attentive work; Ben Anastas for his friendship and his help over the years; and Connie Brothers. Thanks to Claire Wachtel for setting the wheels in motion; and to Anne Cole and Randee Marullo for their contributions throughout the process. I'd also like to thank the Michener-Copernicus Society for their generous support. And, of course, thanks to my family, who are my best friends, confidants, critics, and supporters.

—P.C.

CONTENTS

PART ONE

EXHIBITS

A

THR●UGH

Z

Ava worried that her father had forgotten their plans. Sitting in the far corner of the patio where the hedges shielded her from Ocean Avenue, she leaned back and tried to stay out of the candlelight. Her three-year-old son tore up bread rolls and dropped crumbs into his water. The waiters kept glancing at the mess. Ava checked her reflection in a spoon: her hair was frizzing from the damp wind that blew off the ocean and across the bluffs, tousling the tall palm trees aligned as straight as the parked cars below. Behind her she could hear engines idling in the valet parking driveway, and she listened for the distinct sound of her stepmother's heels striding out of their Range Rover.

Her son was fidgeting. So Ava dug through her bag for a coloring book and pens, collecting them again when he began to scribble on the tablecloth. "We're going to play a game, Chris. We're going to try to impersonate grown-ups. Okay? So far I'm winning."

Charlie West had invited her to dinner that day from his car phone. He had said, "Ava, it's your father. I've been doing some very serious thinking." Then he drove into a tunnel, so that she could hear only a blast of static. When he emerged he was at the climax of a fiery speech about wanting to get reacquainted. He longed to know his grandson. He needed to strengthen his sense of family. The urgency sounded rather staged to Ava, but she assumed that he had built to this crescendo while in the tunnel. Just as he was naming the restaurant, she heard a blaring horn, a screech of tires, and a crunch.

Her father shouted, "Oh, you're *kidding* me."

He dropped the phone and all she could hear was shouting in the distance and the tidal sound of passing cars. To a distant murmur she heard her father respond, "Well, that's nice of you to say anyway. No, no, it wouldn't be any trouble. What's your son's name?"

"Dad, you're scaring me. Please pick up the phone."

He returned and said, "Get me the hell out of this town. So, where were we? Dinner. Right. You and Chris, eight o'clock. Ivy on the Shore—it's Barbara's favorite place. We can fax the directions to you if it's a problem."

"Dad, are you delirious? Do you need me to call an ambulance?"

"No, no. Some idiot sideswiped me and then he wanted a damn autograph. I'm fine, though. You'll be there, I hope. Eight o'clock."

Now she had waited at the table long enough to notice changes in the weather. The city lights colored the underside of an expanding marine layer. She struggled to put a jacket on Chris while he made his arms limp, then she ordered herself a Bloody Mary and lounged back, trying to relax amid all the movement— passing trucks, a low-flying jet, a medley of car alarms. Chris was now stuffing whole slices of bread into his glass. He pulled on the sleeve of Ava's workshirt and said, "Mom, Mom, Mom. Look. Bread soup."

"That's just wonderful, Chris. We'll order some onions. Then you can make French onion soup."

A waiter came and asked if she'd like to go ahead and order. Ava took a sip of her drink and held it in her mouth while she tried to recall the space left on her credit card. She swallowed and said, "They're just chronically late. I promise they'll be here."

At last, in the driveway an engine idled louder than the rest. Two doors slammed, one creaking with a dent. Moments later her stepmother's voice came from behind the hedges. "It's just infuriating, Charlie. I don't see why you always have to make it out like it's *my* doing. I'm the good guy here." With hustling steps like a ticking stopwatch she rounded the corner and headed into the restaurant.

When her father stepped onto the patio, Ava noticed he was wearing tiny rectangular glasses on his broad pink face. His graying blond hair, the color of soapy water, had been blown loose by the wind and was long enough to hang against the tortoise-shell rim and spill over one of the lenses. It was a haircut for a teenage boy. He was an inch shorter than his wife, despite the clopping boots he wore, and his stockiness—so mammoth and imposing in his movies—made him appear small and square in person. Ava was troubled that she remembered him most vividly from the way he appeared on-screen. But the terrible affectation of those reading glasses, as if the menu script might catch him off guard, was most disconcerting. They looked in danger of being broken as he greeted friends at tables along the way. Every gesture he made was exaggerated—the way he grabbed an entire arm when he shook hands, the way he patted the shoulders of seated colleagues so hard that they nearly lost mouthfuls of food. Over the din of voices Ava could hear her father describing a recent flying lesson, and when his friends did not seem entirely captivated, he stretched out his arms to imitate the wings, chopping one hand into a busboy. His wife, Barbara, kissed the cheeks of women rising from their chairs, napkins clutched in their hands. When her husband began to speak too loudly, she grabbed his lapel and cut him off, telling the group that she'd already heard this story a thousand times.

They turned and began slaloming through tables toward Ava, Barbara wearing baggy white pants that billowed with each step. A sleeveless beige sweater displayed her toned shoulders. Something about the dim lights made her blond hair appear to have a greenish tint. She said, "Ava. I am *so* sorry to keep you waiting. It's a long story, but your father is impossible." When they touched cheeks, Ava noticed a scent of chlorine on her. Barbara then reached across the table and mussed Chris's hair. He was putting pepper on top of the floating bread.

The hostess pulled out a chair and waited as Charlie mouthed something to a table across the patio. She sighed and tapped her foot and held his menu until Charlie had finished pantomiming a message to a man with a napkin tucked into his collar. Ava remembered a time when a restaurant's staff would tolerate anything from her father. She worried that this new mood of irritation was a bad sign. "Oh, thank God," Charlie said as he finally sat down. "Let me catch my breath for a second."

"Run run run," said Barbara. "Never a dull moment."

The hostess still held out the menu. Charlie told her, "I think we already know what *we* want. Barb?"

"We would like two green salads with the dressing on the side, and then a half portion of the sea bass with none of the sauce—and no butter—on a bed of rice pilaf. To drink I'll have a Chardonnay and my husband will just have a Pellegrino and lime." She looked up at Ava and said, "Have you two already ordered?"

"We haven't decided yet."

"Mom! *Onions.*"

"Oh. My son would like a plate of onions, please."

The hostess nodded and said that she would send a waiter back for the rest of the order.

Barbara smoothed her napkin on her lap, then in a cartoon voice said, "Well, look at you, Mr. Chris. You've gotten gigantic." When Chris didn't answer, she asked Ava, "What are you feeding this great big boy?"

"I think the current fad is cream chipped beef on toast."

Chris slid the glass across the table and said, "This is soup."

"Well, it looks delicious," said Barbara. "But I don't want to spoil my appetite. I'll just leave it here and have some later. Okay? Mmmm."

"So here we are. The entire extended family," said Charlie. "God, I feel a hundred years old."

"You look great, Dad."

"Cryogenics. Come see me in a week when I thaw out."

"Charlie, we're about to eat here," said Barbara. "Don't mind him, Ava. They've moved up the release date of this film and

THE MARTINI SHOT

6

they've already got him running all over the place. *And* they've gone a week over on the new one—*The Last Stand Three*—so he's got a whole extra week of shooting. But this one coming out, Ava: it's a major change. You won't recognize him. Just drop-dead touching. I mean, it's an action picture, of course, but it has this *something*. This sensitivity."

"Are you nervous about it, Dad?"

"About the end of my career?"

"He's thrilled. Don't listen to him. He just pouts over there to get attention. I saw the rough cut, Ava, and you won't believe it. You really get to see what kind of an *actor* he is. I get goose bumps just thinking about it."

"I'm getting the hell out of this town forever," said Charlie.

"And you would go stark raving mad. Two days and you'd be climbing the walls."

"I'm already climbing the walls."

"Oh, Charlie. We better get some food over here fast. Your blood sugar is plummeting."

For Chris, Ava ordered a virgin strawberry daiquiri and a plate of ziti; for herself, a pot of bouillabaisse.

"I can't wait for your metabolism to slow down," said Barbara. She talked for a while about Charlie's film and what a success she was sure it would be. She saw the amount that he had invested in it emotionally, and had faith that the public would agree. Barbara said that she understood the public better than Charlie did. "I grew up in a very normal household." She scanned the table for reactions. "I didn't know anything about all of this—*craziness*."

Throughout her speech Charlie became more distracted. He slumped in his chair, mumbling to himself. Beyond the hedges a Ferris wheel churned at the pier and Charlie looked hypnotized by it. Finally he joined Chris in putting chunks of bread into the water glass. Chris watched him, fascinated, then said, "Drink it!" Charlie cradled the glass like a brandy snifter, smelled it, then took a swig. A trail of wet pepper clung to his lip. Ava was still listening to Barbara, but her son repeated, "Mom, Mom, Mom," until she turned and said, "I *saw* it, Chris. I saw him drink it."

When the food came, Chris refused to eat because he thought the noodles were weird. Ava said, "Baby, they're the same damn thing as spaghetti. They're just hollow." He started to blow through them, wiggling on his booster chair and pretending to play a tune. Charlie took one and both whistled through the noodles.

"We've got a reed section over here," said Barbara.

"Dad, try not to encourage this."

"We're playing the national anthem, I think."

"How patriotic," said Barbara.

Ava made a deal with Chris: every noodle that he blew into had to be eaten immediately. She told him they would whistle in his stomach all the way home.

"Do you just love being a mother?" asked Barbara.

Watching her son suspiciously, Ava said, "Ask me again in a little while."

"We've talked about having a baby. But we're both just so insanely busy these days. We'd have to really set aside the time. I mean, practically all of our friends are having babies. Everyone is really oriented around *family* these days. So are we. I just don't know if I could manage to be pregnant anytime soon."

"That's what the black market is for," said Charlie. "Ava, would you like a Romanian brother?"

A spray of tomato sauce splattered onto the tablecloth around Barbara.

"Chris! Don't blow through the ones with sauce in them, please."

Charlie asked, "Ava, are you *working* again? I have no idea what you do with your life these days."

Chris blew another cloud of spray and Ava sighed. "You're just going to torture me all night, aren't you? What, Dad?"

"How are things going?"

"Right now things are going all over the table." Chris blew a noodle out of his mouth and it landed in the candle. "I should've had these stuffed with Ritalin."

"Does he have attention deficit disorder?" asked Barbara, resting her chin on her clasped hands.

"No, he has gimme more attention disorder."

Chris aimed the ziti at Charlie, giggling.

"Chris, if you blow that noodle at your grandfather, I'm going to be really upset. I'm warning you right now. I don't think it's cute. He's just *nervous* about something. This is the way he copes with stress."

"I should try it," said Charlie.

Charlie stared at his grandson with a beleaguered expression. Chris was smiling and keeping the eye of the tube pointed at him.

"Let me share a secret with you, kid," said Charlie. "Never soil the person who's paying for your meal."

"That's a good piece of advice, Mr. Chris."

The standoff continued: the boy with the ziti, and the actor, who was now holding up a napkin like a matador.

"Chris, I mean it. There is going to be hell to pay. Don't test me."

He blew his hardest. Sauce splattered across Charlie's napkin and shirt. Ava burst out of her chair, seized Chris around the waist, tucked him under her arm, and hauled him across the restaurant. She groaned at his weight. Chris screamed. As he wiggled his feet and fought, she staggered between tables, the guests going silent as his kicking legs swam past.

In the ladies' room she sat him down next to the sink. He was shouting and Ava said, "Quiet. Quiet, Chris. Just stop it and listen to me. Oh, boo-hoo-hoo, the world is so horrible, isn't it? You can't just spit on anybody you want. What suffering you must be going through. Stop crying or we're getting into the truck and I'm not taking you to a restaurant again until you're thirty."

In the mirror behind him she saw that her blouse was streaked with sauce. Her cheeks were flushed. Her red hair, which earlier had been sprayed into neat curls around her forehead, was now a fossilized splash.

"This is not cute, Chris. You're not a two-year-old anymore. You have to control these impulses. You think I don't want to shoot sauce onto everybody? You bet I do. I'd like to pour that whole bowl onto my stepmother's head. But then somebody would have to carry *me* to the bathroom, and you'd be stuck out there with Barbara, pulling noodles out of her hair. She'd probably be worrying the calories would filter in through her scalp. So I *restrained* myself. That's how civilization works."

Chris stopped crying and wiped his chubby face with the back of his hand.

"Most of those people out there keep their kids locked up in a big rec room. They have au pairs running around with *Game Boys* dangling from their necks and gum ball dispensers on their backs. You should be thankful that I saved you from all that. You'd be handcuffed to a bumper-pool table if it wasn't for me."

He looked at her. Big eyes blinked, tears on his lashes.

"It's bad enough that everybody assumes I'm your nanny. Now they all think I'm a bad nanny. An evil nanny. They're all out there saying, '*Why on earth don't they just fire that evil nanny?*'"

"No, Mom."

"Yes. These people fire their own families. These people are sharks. With big fangs." She hung her fingers over her mouth to show him the fangs. "Grrr," she said. "Big fangs and a giant silicon fin." She made the shape of the fin on her head with praying hands. She ducked and bobbed around the room, then came toward Chris beside the sink, humming the theme song from *Jaws.*

She swam at him and Chris said, "No-o, Mom."

"We're in infested waters. It's their main feeding ground. And what do you do when there's a shark around? You have to be *very* still. Or it sees you." She bobbed at him.

He giggled and said, "No-o."

"Uh-oh. He's moving!" She surged up and grabbed him as he squealed. She started to tickle him. She lifted his shirt and blew a raspberry onto his belly. "What a surprise. He tastes like marinara sauce."

Beside the valet parking driveway Ava waited with her father as Barbara helped Chris twist the top off a bird-of-paradise. When

Barbara tried to wedge the huge flower behind the boy's ear, Charlie fretted and yelled, "For God's sake, Barbara. He doesn't need flowers in his hair."

Ava tried her best to appear nonchalant about the earlier episode, despite the fact that she was now carrying a take-out carton of tinfoil sculpted to look like a duck. Charlie wanted to know about her work. As a car alarm went off nearby, she told him about the sets she'd been designing at a small community theater. She still took courses in design and lighting, and for a few years she had done some of the drafting and construction for a theater in Pasadena. At first Chris would play all day on a blanket at center stage while Ava hammered and used Skilsaws and swept a clean moat around him in the drifting sawdust; but as he grew older he ran around the aisles and fiddled with nails and stepped into buckets of flameproofing liquid and covered his head with crepe paper snow. Now Ava's mother was helping take care of Chris at home. Ava tried to work in the garage, driving to the theater every other day, but a year ago she'd started losing jobs to other designers.

Charlie said, "You know, Ava, life is so strange and unpredictable, you just have to keep fighting. It's the struggle that counts. Let me give you an example from *my* life. There was a time when I had my troubles, back in my crazier days, and I couldn't get arrested in this town. I'm speaking figuratively, of course. I had been typecast as an absolute buffoon. Just the biggest jerk you ever saw. I went in to read for parts and people laughed me out of the building. But you see, I didn't give in to it. I didn't stop *fighting*."

"That's wonderful, Dad." The wind blew her hair over her face, and with the tinfoil duck occupying one hand and the bag of toys in the other, she needed to tilt her head to shake it off.

"I wasn't going to be denied. Of course, I had my problems, but I was always focused on my work. I just put my neck out there and I said, 'Go on. Chop me, you bastards. I dare you.'"

"That's true. I'm very proud of you."

"That's the kind of spirit that you need to have, Ava. You can't listen to the world. There were a lot of people who doubted me. But you know what I said?"

Her nose itched and she tried to scratch it against her shoulder. "You told them to go jump in a lake."

"Well, in far more dramatic terms. But yes. Did you use the valet parking? Let me give you money for a tip."

"It's okay, Dad. I've got money."

"Well, just let me loan you a few dollars, then. I've got so much on my plate right now, I don't know when we're going to be able to get together again." He didn't look at her when he spoke, but at something over her shoulder, far in the distance. "Think of it this way: I'm buying one of your sets. Some piece of stage furniture. I always need furniture. I'm living in a damn museum." He glanced at Barbara. She was holding on to Chris's jacket to keep him from crawling into the hedge.

"What do you need?"

"A chair. A nice chair to sit in, where I can watch my career fall apart."

He unfolded a few bills and held them out in his cupped hand. Ava put down the duck and took the money without looking at it. There was an abrupt formality to the way their hands brushed.

"I can always get you a job too, Ava. Say the word."

"Thank you," she said, and gestured to Chris with her chin. "It's more complicated than just that."

When the Range Rover pulled up, Barbara climbed into the passenger seat and gave a twinkling wave to Chris. After strapping himself in, Charlie rolled down his window and said, "And give your mother my love, of course. Remember. I want a chair fit for a king."

"I know just the one." When they were safely out of sight, Ava took her son's hand and they walked around the corner to her pickup truck, which was sitting beside a meter. The windmill palms swayed high above, dropping fronds and debris onto the street. She strapped Chris into his seat and noticed that the bottom of his shirt was drenched with sauce. His pockets were full of spare noodles. He was beginning to doze as she fastened him, so she whispered, "What a guy. Plan ahead for breakfast."

The long drive back to Altadena was meditative. She considered working for her father, which she had done once while in college on a big-budget mob picture called *Wise Crackers*. She didn't grow up with her father and didn't know much about the actual production of movies, so she had assumed she would work as a lackey in either the art or property department. That was what she had been studying and the only experience she had. Maybe she would nail down props in a studio speakeasy, running around with a tool belt amid flappers.

She had told her father that she was studying design, which he had mistaken for fashion design. He found her a job in the wardrobe department. When Ava told him that she could barely match her socks, he corrected the error by getting her hired as a production assistant. Ava needed the money and enjoyed the atmosphere, but she couldn't figure out exactly what she was supposed to be doing. There were nine production assistants for this movie, each the son or daughter of a more prominent member of the crew, and because of the surplus, they became too difficult for the assistant directors to organize. At the end of the first week, they were told simply to take care of their own parents.

The PAs had their own walkie-talkie channel. All day long it was jumbled full of voices saying, "Teddy, your mom wants you again"; "Yo, Reed. Your dad is freaking out. He forgot his thyroid medication"; "John, we got a project. Your old man locked his keys in the car."

A team of PAs surrounded the car armed with coat hangers. They pried and poked at the windows until finally they unlocked it with great cheering and dancing followed by a sudden disappointment: *What do we do now?*

Ava had the most vital assignment: she took care of the star. In the morning she ran across a sweltering asphalt plain to a glaring silver wagon, where she ordered her father a vegetarian burrito. It was her most clearly defined task, so she did it with great enthusiasm. Some days it was followed by ten, twelve, even fourteen hours of dead time, during which Ava's main job was to be one of two dozen people who screamed "*Quiet, please*" after a bell rang.

Mostly the PAs loitered around the craft service table with their radios mumbling. They had long, cynical conversations with their mouths full of Fig Newtons. Ava enjoyed their company: they were articulate, witty, well educated. But she grew tired of their diatribes about Hollywood and society, always delivered with lips smacking and Popsicle stains on their collars. Everyone wanted to earn enough money to "get the fuck out of this town and maybe even this country." When they grew weary from complaining, they would try to stump each other with obscure movie titles.

Charlie's Winnebago driver was a man named Tom Sloan, whom everyone referred to as "Sasquatch" because of his shaggy beard and disheveled hair. Sloan had lived for almost ten years with Ava's mother—acting as a common-law stepfather to Ava—and during that time he had become Charlie's driver. When he was first hired, Ava was too young to understand the details, but once on the set it seemed to her that Charlie hired legions of people he met through relatives and friends. Perhaps, she thought, her father was not comfortable with anyone who was not dependent upon him.

Sloan was a relentless salesman, pitching one scheme after another, and in the late eighties he had convinced Charlie to buy a mobile home instead of using one provided by the studio. His argument was that it could then be equipped for all of Charlie's *specific needs,* whatever those were. But Sloan wound up living in it himself for several years.

Sloan was the only person who did less than Ava. He was a scuba fanatic, and he wandered around the trailers telling stories about reefs and spear fishing and nitrogen bubbles in the brain. Ava imagined shoals of fish trapped in his beard. Since they were working mostly on a sound stage, Sloan rarely needed to move the trailer. His responsibilities included keeping Charlie's favorite sodas in the refrigerator and occasionally arranging a platter of Charlie's favorite fruits. One day rumor spread that Charlie was in a bad mood, and Sloan sidled up to Ava and asked, "Do you know how your old man feels about kiwi?"

"I think he has a love-hate relationship with it," she said, squinting into the blast of sunlight off the awnings and asphalt. "Just stay the course with the peaches and apricots."

THE MARTINI SHOT

14

Long hours of heat and inactivity made them giddy and emotional. Sloan hugged Ava by the snack table that day and said that he had always loved her like a daughter. Ava couldn't respond because her mouth was full of Wheat Thins.

But the air of delirious camaraderie never quite seeped into Charlie's mobile home. All the radios sounded like a NASA transmission the moment he emerged into the sunlight. "He's on his way to the makeup trailer. We've got him right here. He's in the chair. He's getting a touch-up. Okay: he's out of the chair and he's sixty yards from the set. Flying in. ETA about thirty seconds."

Charlie was stern and professional. He could inject a feeling of urgency into the most inane tasks, like when he was *deeply* disappointed that Ava forgot his "specific lactose-free instructions" and put butter on his asparagus.

"What would your fans say if they knew you couldn't digest butter?"

"They would say '*Bravo*.' And then they would ask me why I hired such a smart-ass daughter."

"It's not arsenic. I'll wash it off."

"That isn't the point. I don't have time to wait around while you hose off my dinner. Thousands of people want these jobs, and I bet every one of them would get the order right."

"I'll get you some more."

"You're not following me. There are no small jobs, Ava. Whether it's ordering dinner or focusing the camera, everything is important, and a lapse of concentration like this just isn't acceptable. I have a specific diet."

"I will go on a public campaign tomorrow, Dad. To promote awareness of lactose intolerance."

Sloan met her outside and wanted to know every detail of the conversation, fearing that he had been mentioned. "He didn't say a word about the peaches," said Ava. "So you're safe for now."

As the production wore on, most of the crew spoke about Charlie with a hint of fear, like he was an irritable circus bear who at any moment might turn volatile and attack them. They also believed they were superior and resented having their livelihoods tied to a creature of limited intelligence. When Charlie told the makeup artist that she was using too much base—making him look like Charo—the entire makeup and wardrobe crews conspired between trailers. "You think he knows my job better than me? That man has never been to a day of school in his life, and I've got a friggin' MFA."

Charlie needed to be guarded. The second assistant director panicked if Charlie ever tried to do anything by himself. "We can't have him on the loose, Ava. If he needs to go somewhere, you come and tell me." Ava escorted her father to the set inside the cavernous sound studio with its pockets of cool air, and the crew would clear a path for him. The boys around the sound cart tested the pitch of his voice but never spoke to him directly; they pulled the headphones off their ears and said, "Charlie needs to speak up." A boom mike hovered over him like a target for a leaping orca while a tape measure unrolled from the lens to his nose; a makeup girl scampered around him daubing last-second changes. The director quietly ordered the cameras to roll, repeated by the AD through a bullhorn to begin that chain reaction of bells and screaming PAs from the edge of the set to the lot outside, until a quiet descended that was so deep and pure it felt like time had stalled just a blink before dawn; and then, in a single cylinder of light, Charlie's eyes wide and his face animated, he kicked over a table and ran toward a window, shouting, smashing out the candy glass with a pistol, howling in comic-book rage. Oh, what a bad actor he was. But he was so extravagantly bad that one could not stop watching. Ava was proud of him: proud of all that wild and colorful life he crammed into these scenes as if jump-starting the monotonous days. Over time she grew excited to see him perform each day, and she soon understood his success. He was so accessible, so charismatic, that it somehow didn't matter how dumbly earnest he looked delivering his lines. He was like a child whom everyone rooted for in a school play. No matter how officious and condescending he had been off-camera, when the lights were on him he was washed clean by his indomitable need to be liked. It was a feeling he projected: that if you simply could know this man, he would be your friend for life.

Ava thought nothing of it when her father's personal trainer started coming to the set to watch. Her name was Barbara Hartmann. She had briefly been a model and an actress, but Ava recognized her more from a late-night infomercial in which she peddled protein shakes, workout equipment, and some sort of herbal amphetamine. All day she kept sunglasses perched in her hair, and despite the heat that shimmered off car hoods, she never perspired. Ava was fascinated by the definition around her shoulders—a rise of slender muscle right off the bone—but she was embarrassed to ask what kind of regimen was required for it. The woman was actually more intimidating than attractive. She posed when she walked; she was proud of every step.

Barbara followed Ava around for a few days and tried to make conversation with her. She asked Ava about her "lifetime ambitions" while they waited together outside Charlie's trailer. Before Chris was born, Ava was not particularly insecure about her looks: she was a lanky girl of five feet nine, always athletic but never shapely. She wore baggy T-shirts, sport bras, and ragged shorts that dangled threads over her skinny legs. She had an attractive, angular face, far thinner than any in her family, but still with that trademark dimple in her chin. Her hair was usually dark auburn falling in wavelets over her forehead and down to her green eyes, but after a month in the sun it had bleached to a pumpkin color, sweat-shaped into a trampled bush, and her skin had become a swarm of freckles. Sweat stains broadened beneath her arms. "My lifetime ambitions?"

"Well," said Barbara. "Do you want to go into acting, like your father?"

"My dad was in ads and things before he could crawl. So he didn't really *go* into it. He was born into it."

"I knew that, actually. You didn't have to tell me that."

Barbara continued coming to the set each day until Ava believed she was jockeying for a role in the picture. On the final day of shooting, Ava was in a portable bathroom when over the radio she heard, "Ava, what's your twenty?"

She fumbled for the radio down at her ankles and answered, "Ten one hundred."

"Okay. When you get out, your parental unit would like to speak with you."

Fearing that her father had detected another dairy substance, Ava knocked on his door and prepared to apologize. Charlie told her to come in and have a seat. Barbara was already sitting in the captain's chair, rotated to face into the living quarters. She nervously sipped a Fresca. Charlie was wearing a terry-cloth robe and had green moisturizer smeared beneath his eyes. "Ava. I want to talk to you about something very serious."

"Did I get cheese on something?"

"No. This is even more serious than that."

Ava looked at Barbara, then at her father, both solemn. She said, "This is an intervention, isn't it? You guys think I'm eating too many Ho Ho cakes."

"I'm going to come right out and say it, and I'm hoping that you're going to respect me enough to wait and absorb this. Love is a miraculous thing. There's no rhyme or reason to it. It can come at you from right out of the blue. You're just walking along and *boom!* There it is."

"You fell in love with the boom man?"

"I'm trying to tell you about who I am. I have never felt like this before, and if I have, I don't remember. I want you to understand it."

Barbara leaned forward in her chair and said, "Please listen to him, Ava."

"You guys are scaring me. It's like you joined some kind of cult."

"Barbara and I are head over heels," said Charlie. "The real deal. Crazy, bonkers, out of our heads in love."

Ava nodded and stared at Barbara, who was cradling her drink. "That's great. She seems very nice, Dad, but she's about twelve years old."

"I'm eight years older than you are," said Barbara. "So don't try that. You may not know me very well, but I do have *feelings*."

Ava waited for her to continue her point, but she didn't. Ava shook her head and said, "I'm sorry. I don't know what that means."

"You know what she means," said Charlie. "We're thrilled. We're nuts. We're out of our skulls here. We're bumping into things. That's what she means. We're engaged to be married and we wanted you to know."

"Before you heard it in the press," said Barbara, and slurped.

"I just want to be happy for once in my life," said Charlie. "And I want you to accept that. I think you owe me that much."

Ava smiled broadly. She started to laugh but disguised it as a cough into her fist. "Let me get this straight. She is your—your trainer, right?"

"That's beside the point," said Barbara.

"We've been working together for over a year," said Charlie. "But a few months ago, we just moved to a different kind of relationship."

"You mean you started targeting a new muscle group."

"I didn't expect her to make fun of us," said Barbara.

"It's her mode of defense," said Charlie.

"All right. I'm sorry. Go on. Just let me get over my shock. So, when did you decide?"

"We've known all along. Deep down. Somehow. The age difference isn't the issue here, Ava. The issue is how compatible we are and how passionately we feel toward one another. I proposed this morning. We sat out on the terrace, had breakfast. It was completely natural."

"The breakfast or the proposal?"

"Nothing has ever been forced or awkward between Barbara and I. Is it *Barbara and I* or *Barbara and me*? Anyhow, between *us*. Nothing has ever been forced between us. That's a rare thing in this day and age, Ava. You should be thrilled for me." He pointed back and forth between himself and Ava. "But we're just starting to respect each other as adults, you and I. We're in that awkward transitory phase."

"I hope you mean *transitional*," said Ava.

"And it's my dream, Ava, that all of us could be the best of friends. That you and I can have our time together, and that you and Barbara could go out—you know—and do whatever it is that women do together. Get to know each other as people."

"That's a touching sentiment, Dad."

"He's nervous," said Barbara.

"I'm not nervous. I just want Ava to understand. I want to get this new era off on the right foot."

Ava's radio started a quiet conversation: this was the final setup. The other PAs came onto the radio cheering, so Ava turned it down to only a faint buzz. The three sat in the trailer listening to it. Streaks of light cut through the venetian blinds, floating full of dust. Ava gazed around the customized trailer: its only distinguishing feature was a larger closet and a sit-up platform, now covered with congratulatory fruit baskets.

Charlie said to his fiancée, "Would you like to hang around for the final shot? The martini shot, as we call it around here."

"I would love it," said Barbara.

Ava held the radio up in the air like a flute of champagne. "Then, let's have a toast," she said. "To my new stepmother. And the end of an era."

Barbara held up her Fresca and said, "Thank you, Ava. I think."

Charlie pantomimed a glass in his hand—from the width of his palm it looked like a highball glass—and swilled down his imaginary drink as Barbara sipped her soda, and the voice on the radio said, "I'd like to take this opportunity *not* to thank the *worst* damn crew of PAs I've ever worked with."

After the wrap of the film Ava didn't see her father for months; but she did receive a formal invitation to Barbara's wedding shower. Calligraphy looped like vines around an artist's rendering of Barbara's silhouette.

Ava sat quietly in her father's redecorated living room, on a white sofa chair beside a Steinway. She was amid a circle of warbling, smartly dressed women who squealed over gag gifts—crotchless panties and edible underwear—or swooned for necklaces and silver serving dishes. Ava faintly tapped the highest keys on the piano. They passed earrings around for her to admire, dangling them before her face like a fishing lure.

Ava's gift was in the back of her pickup. It was a piece of furniture from an avant-garde production she'd done: a vanity table composed of fun-house mirrors. When she presented it, Barbara thanked her and the guests seemed uncomfortable around her for the next hour.

Several of Barbara's high school friends attended, and they admitted to not having seen the hostess—former Chino Hills prom queen—in well over a decade. They wandered around the house as if looking at some monument, and when answering Ava's attempts at polite conversation, they were defensive. They seemed to suspect that Ava was some snob or hostile feminist simply because she hadn't spent as much time dressing for the party.

The guests served themselves dinner from a buffet table, then sat in the living room with plates on their knees. They talked between bites. Barbara motioned to the edible underwear and asked, "What do you think they make it out of?"

With her mouth full of salad Ava said, "Lactose."

It was a year before Ava was in that room again: the fastest year of her life, a year she'd tumbled across—from the wedding in her father's terraced backyard beneath circling helicopters, through a Pasadena theater, into and out of love with a lighting technician—to land with a thud on that white sofa chair, staring at her father. She was three months' pregnant and waiting for the right time to tell him.

The room had changed as well. Satin cottage curtains hung around the bay window. Dishes of rose water and potpourri cluttered the glass coffee table, the piano, and the mantel. "Why does this room have to be so deodorized?" asked Ava. "Is there something dead in here?"

"I haven't seen you since the wedding and all you can talk about is how my house smells."

"Well, it's sort of overwhelming. Doesn't Barbara shower after her workouts?"

"I want you two to get over this. Whatever it is between you. You're both making my life miserable."

The skin around his eyes appeared more taut than she remembered. "Obviously not both of us, because you haven't even seen me."

"That's part of the problem, Avie."

She convinced her father to come for a drive with her, hoping for an opportune moment to spring the news; but a mile away from the house his whole demeanor changed and he rambled on about his marital problems. With the warm air blowing through the cab, he said that the potpourri stink was just the tip of the iceberg. He said that certain little things were bothering him inordinately. For one thing, Barbara was his complete political opposite. "I'm not saying politics plays a part in a marriage. But occasionally I just look at her and think, *Good God, Charlie, you married into the gestapo.* I didn't know her politics before we married. And every day she's on that treadmill with the music going and it's abs, pecs, abs, pecs."

Ava said, "The Riefenstahl Workout."

"I'm telling you, it's Orange County. They breed them down there so that they can elect Republican governors. They're cloning little Reagans. You know—they've isolated the gene that determines how you'll feel about the capital gains tax."

"I'll have to get that test done, then," said Ava.

"Oh, you passed it a long time ago. And I'll tell you another thing that drives me crazy."

Apparently Charlie had helped his in-laws buy a Chrysler-Plymouth dealership in La Habra. He had hoped it would be a last sweeping magnanimous gesture, but now he spent every other weekend down at the lot signing visors and T-shirts. He shook hands and posed for snapshots beside Voyagers. "It's like ever since I met Barbara I've been campaigning for some shitty alderman job or something. My life is enough of a fucking campaign without me having to go kiss babies. These fat, fleshy, bug-eyed babies. God! There are some ugly cross-eyed children in this world. I weep for America."

"I have to tell you something, Dad. I've made a really important decision in my life."

"The whole time I'm down there, I'm thinking this is where I'm headed. Two more flops. Two more. If I don't have a hit real soon—then I can retire to Hartmann Plymouth. Fall right off the wagon and into a minivan. That's how I'm going out. Crash right through the showroom and impale myself on a sliding door."

"That's very dramatic," said Ava.

"Blaze of glory."

She didn't tell him. She drove home that night and lay awake, and all the next day it was on her mind. She had discussed it with her mother—who in the end had accepted her decision— but she worried that her father might try to make her choice seem political. When she finally did call him, he said only, "If you just want to give up on everything you ever wanted, then that's fine."

"I'm not giving up on *anything,* Dad. And I never will."

Charlie saw his grandson three times in the first two years, and each time he watched Chris as if he were an alien creature. Ava was a boastful parent. She wanted her father to recognize how early Chris was trying to talk, how keenly he listened, how quickly he absorbed information. But her father was too uncomfortable. Across the floor came the crawling infant in his footsie pajamas, and Charlie's face showed pure terror. It hurt her to see him so awkward. Soon she stopped driving out to the west side, claiming it was because she despised the area—all those houses like opulent leftover sets, the precious little Brentwood and Palisades villages like scraps of Connecticut transplanted to a desert, inhabited only with joggers and nannies by day, jerks with cell phones by night—and Charlie never drove farther east than an overpriced Vietnamese restaurant in West Hollywood. His excuse, which Ava found more reasonable than her own, was that he was uncomfortable loitering around the house of his ex-wife.

By the time Chris was three, it seemed like Ava had lost all connection to her father. Her whole world was condensed around Chris, and in the rare hours that she had to herself, she

worked tirelessly on her sets; but still there were patches of silence into which fell a drop of anxiety that quickly expanded
into guilt. She vowed to call him but never did. For almost a
year her father was only this procrastinated chore growing in
imagined urgency until she was more angry at him than if he
had been right there nagging her.

One day, she saw her father on a talk show. She sat Chris
in her lap and pointed. "That's your grandfather," she said and
suddenly missed him. But Chris still thought of the television as
little more than an appliance. Whatever flickered on its screen
was pure invention, a coloring book set in motion. He squirmed
loose and toddled away to his grandmother, leaving Ava alone
on the floor, watching.

Her father sat before a backdrop of a skyline. He talked about
his movies, his marriage. He was clean-cut, well behaved, and
dull. The audience waited for some of his old theatrics. A
younger Charlie would have pulled an attention-grabbing stunt,
covering Carson with shaving cream or hitting Merv with a pie.

"He should say hello to his grandson," said Ava's mother, Camilla, as she chased after the boy. She had an emery board tucked
behind her ear. Her curled brown hair was streaked with only a
few threads of gray. "He's so rude."

"He's not going to admit to being a grandfather. Besides,
Mother, he probably thinks it would embarrass me."

"You're an emotional masochist," said Camilla, wrangling
Chris back into the room.

Ava grabbed him and hugged him and said, "Grandma uses
big words, doesn't she? Can you say *pop psychology*?"

When Ava answered the phone a month later and heard the
crackle of a cellular breaking up and waited as her father passed
through the tunnel to emerge at the end of his speech, she was
grateful that the fender bender had cut through an awkwardness
between them. If only some small crisis could occur during each
visit, they would never have those agonizing moments in which
they stood and stiffly presented themselves aloud. After the call,
she was relieved, and felt the long, vague grudge might have
finally ended.

Driving home that night she was determined—for the sake of her sleeping marinara-soaked boy—to stop carrying resentments. She was going to clean up her act. No more hang-ups, no more bad memories mulled over late at night. She was going to open up to the world and try her hardest to give everyone a fighting chance.

CHAPTER TWO

In his small town Matt was famous. He had proof. On the wall of his cramped bedroom hung a tabloid article from 1980 that described his birth and the details of the paternity settlement. The adjacent picture showed his father reaching up to shield his face from a camera's lens. In the background palm trees slanted and shop windows glared.

In those days his father was not the type of star to warrant more than a few columns. He was a television actor, a smirking San Diego cop who solved crimes in tight shorts; but he was a burgeoning heart throb. After poring over magazines, Matt knew his father had appeared in a few low-budget films in the seventies, playing a sincere lifeguard, a cheerful camp counselor, a warlock using his powers for good. In an early poster he had thick feathered hair and an unbuttoned shirt. His face, with a vacant smile, emblazoned the sides of lunch boxes. There was even a Charlie West action figure, wearing a tiny motorcycle jumpsuit, a hinge at his waist—almost, as Matt's mother pointed out, anatomically correct.

It was the early morning of Matt's eighteenth birthday, the sun still low beneath the hills. Matt was quietly going over the articles and pictures he'd gathered over the years. Perhaps he was no more an adult than yesterday, but now he believed he was looking at the pictures of his father with a more realistic eye. He was certain he would see that backdrop of eucalyptus groves and Spanish tile roofs for himself. It would be his landscape soon.

He had piles of information on his father, but recently he had begun to underline the stray passages about his sister, the descriptions always in parentheses and progressing from a curt "Ava (age 7)" to the more suggestive "daughter Ava (who is an art student)" to last year's abrupt "Ava (27)." Nevertheless, Matt liked to browse through the pages in the quiet hours before work or school. To rise this early gave him a sense of cheating an extra hour out of the day. He was preparing for something, the same way classmates might pace a hallway outside an exam, repeating answers aloud.

He considered himself a chronicler, a genealogist perhaps. In another box he kept the photos and letters from the family he knew, the Ravendahl family, his Scandinavian pedigree. Long ago Matt fantasized that his last name was West, and he had written it in his childish cursive on the tops of homework and drawings. But after his mother died, his grandmother Grace found the fake signatures and scolded him. She told him that the Ravendahl name was deeply rooted in the northern Cascades, and that his father's name was causing "too much hoopla around this place."

Grace told him, "Now don't grow up feeling like you've been left on a doorstep."

That day Matt inherited a box of her family pictures—the Lundquists—showing a history of sturdy Swedes. Grace sighed and promised him that she was not trying to challenge his masculinity. In fact, she said, her father was an ideal role model. There was a yellowish picture of the man on his wedding day, his glasses catching the glare off the camera's flash. Grace told stories about his vengeful "belt." That belt was everywhere. It made all the tough decisions; it taught her right from wrong. But this great-grandfather was so thin in the picture that Matt couldn't imagine his pants staying up without that belt. He looked like the most timid man on earth, standing in the shadow of his porcine wife, her veil as wide as a mosquito net.

Matt was further disappointed to learn that this sallow ancestor had died of consumption, and that throughout his decline in a bed at St. Anthony's, each of his stout daughters eloped with some member of the hospital's staff. The Ravendahl name came from an aging anesthesiologist whom Grace married, then cared for during a decade of worsening ether abuse. After suffering a stroke that left him aphasic, he spent the last six years of his life bedridden and able to utter only the word "Yahtzee." Grace assured Matt that her husband had been an anomaly in an otherwise heroic family. But no matter how far Matt dug into this history, he could find nothing but meek, expressionless people huddled together in fear of the camera. They were the most rained-on ancestry in America.

The sun was sitting just beneath the hills. The trees were showing in silhouettes now against a whitening sky and Matt could hear his grandmother's radio alarm playing classical music downstairs. He put on his jeans, then stood before the narrow, bowed mirror, flexing a skinny arm. He had a long, lean torso, his ribs showing, his skin as pale as a blank sheet of paper. His shaggy hair was almost white, so that all attention was drawn to his blue eyes and their pale lashes.

"I've come a long way to meet you," he said into the mirror. "Matthew Ravendahl here. The pleasure is all mine." He leaned up close to the glass and observed his face: the light down on his broad cheeks, his chin with that same dimple of his father's, and perhaps the same nose, though his father's was straight and Matt's had been broken, so that there was now a lump at the bridge. He resembled the family he didn't know. What was keeping him in Chelan, Washington? A graduation ceremony in three days, some rinky-dink pomp and circumstance; a humdrum summer job at the lumber mill, where the older employees whistled at him like perverted prisoners while he stacked pallet boards off a conveyor belt. He scanned his room with all of its magazines, and it seemed to him like a waiting room that he had paced for his entire life.

"I'm going to Los Angeles," he told Grace as he ate his breakfast that morning. His mouth was full of cereal, with water instead of milk. Grace continued stirring her mug of tea, then calmly sat down across from him.

"Are you going to wait for your birthday party?"

"I'm beyond rituals like that, Gram. I'm talking about real life here."

She blew on the tea. "I'm too tired to argue with you this morning, Matthew. Please try to think clearly."

"You can't *legally* stop me at this point. I know I've said it before, but this time I'm serious. There's a little voice inside my head, Grandma, and I have to listen to it."

"Just so long as it isn't telling you to kill the president."

Shoveling the cereal into his mouth, flakes falling off his lips, he stared down at the bowl and spoke quickly. "I'm not taking the easy route anymore, Gram. I'm looking the demon in the face. No more counting days. This is my life now. Yeah, I could go to graduation like everybody else. I could wear that stupid conformist costume and try to blend in, just like I could go get a job at Der WienerSchnitzel and wear a uniform and have employee-motivation seminars for the rest of my life. But what I need to do is show some balls. Some courage. You know, for my spiritual well-being."

"Aha," said Grace. "You certainly seem to have your mind made up."

She often responded to him in that gentle, palliative tone, the tone of an unflappable nurse. His grandmother had begun her medical career as the on-site nurse at the mill, where Matt now pictured her administering Band-Aids and stirring medicinal teas for tattooed lumberjacks. But she often described the job as a turning point in her life. Many of the employees were heavy drinkers, and it terrified Grace to see a forklift operator with morning shakes or a man on the green chain swigging from a flask.

The only AA at the time was in a Lutheran church, a squat brick structure with a stained-glass window, a cork bulletin board in the vestibule lined with children's drawings, a mud-stained carpet, and a drip-warped ceiling. The interior could make a person swear that God was just a public administrator.

The loggers and mill workers avoided these meetings. Grace understood why after attending one. In a pinched foldout chair, with the voices reverberating off the wood-paneled walls, Grace felt trapped in front of an unrehearsed school play. A Temperance Society spokeswoman talked about fund-raisers, bake sales, and the will of God. Grace's epiphany that day—Matt had heard the story his whole life—was to take all of her money out of savings and begin the only legitimate treatment facility within a hundred miles.

She bought an abandoned hunting and fishing lodge. Stretched out on one side was the lake, a rippling stretch of silvery water; and on the other side was a steep hill of Douglas firs that blocked the town from view and formed a canopy over the facility. She worked tirelessly in rain that broke into a pine-tinged mist, renovating this main lodge with a wood-burning stove and a banquet table long enough to evoke a medieval castle.

A dozen shacks circled the main lodge like numbers on a clock, each with a dresser, a mirror, and a cot. Rain beat on their tar-paper roofs. They were tethered to the main lodge by a cord of Christmas lights, bouncing in the wind and flashing like beacons through the foggy nights. After a few years of operation, locals nicknamed the facility The Briar Patch, a name that irritated Grace but delighted young Matthew from the first moment he understood it.

The nurses and orderlies lived in a trailer park adjacent to the lodge, upon a muddy clearing that tilted downhill toward the lake. A path of boards, stitched over with weeds and ivy, ran between the shacks. What began as a hacked field of ragweed and alder soon was quickly filled with campers sunk in mud. Deer brush sprang up from underneath the trailers and blackberry bushes tangled into the sunlight between them, so that Matt never saw a nurse without thorn-snagged nylons or a stain of purple juice on her uniform, burrs in her socks, or blades of chickweed dried onto her calves.

Just after dawn each morning, a trail of nurses came out of the fog, pacing along the mossy wooden planks. They whipped open their colored umbrellas and walked single file between ferns and foliage. From his window Matt watched the umbrellas, lit like red and orange lanterns. The nurses broke into their separate routes, the generator started with a growl, and the moans and coughs of the patients began. Breakfast was served downstairs with its clamor of dropped cups and jangling silverware and noses blown into napkins. Classical music was piped in from a turntable. When it caught in a rut of two violin notes, the patients stomped their boots until a tremor knocked the needle back into the flow.

When the mist burned off around noon, the orderlies led the stronger patients out on nature walks. The group was forced to smell pine cones, handle robins' eggs, as if nature were the great gift reserved for the sober. Dinner was subdued; the patients looked worn and defeated. When the record skipped, they ignored it. Past sunset came the testimonials, starting loud and ending in whispers as the drizzle began. The umbrellas would reassemble outside, flashlights illuminating the glistening undergrowth, and the nurses and orderlies would return to their trailers, where they would play cards, or watch the rain, or sit together in one trailer and watch an old movie that would flicker among the trees like a monochrome campfire.

In the early seventies The Briar Patch became popular with Californians. Matt adored those pictures of the place from that time, so many of the patients with sideburns, thick black glasses, and multicolored pants. A group photo showed Grace standing beside all her patients, looking like a gray spot on a psychedelic swirl of colors. Matt would browse through the ledger downstairs. In 1973 a visitor wrote, "Wow. Now I see the forest through the trees. I loved the ducks, the beavers, etc. Loved drying out in this 'Eden.' " This seemed to be the consensus in those early years, and the other entries were full of inside jokes and half-baked philosophies, like the slapdash dedications in Matthew's yearbook.

But the entries improved noticeably in the mid-seventies,

when the clinic unexpectedly became hip with artists. They brought their work along, and Grace needed to hire ex-loggers to work as porters. Down the gravel path came a caravan of easels, guitars, bongo drums. Shacks overflowed with the smells of oil paint and turpentine. Manual typewriters clicked incessantly. "I've had a breakthrough here," wrote one visitor. "I will always be in debt to you."

Grace didn't believe it was possible for her to be more exhausted, until, a few years later, the clinic was discovered by the film industry. "Someone down there described us as *discreet*," Grace explained. "And from then on we were doomed." Hidden away from the press, dozens of actors, actresses, and directors came in the late seventies. The nurses were starstruck. Their trailer interiors were coated with pictures of celebrities slumped over their morning oatmeal. The locals gossiped endlessly in the taverns, the fast-food restaurants, even between the windows of idling cars. Fish stories were replaced by celebrity sightings, many of them fatuous lies. Matt grew up continually pestered by these preposterous stories: "Richard Burton tripped in the mud right here"; "That's where a tree branch crushed David Crosby's shed."

Grace never knew who anyone was, so she couldn't confirm or deny the stories. She once told Matthew, "People up in town, they went so crazy in those days, they were seeing ghosts. Charlie Chaplin waddling down Main Street. They figure a few TV actors come through here and suddenly they're all going to come. But I sure as heck don't remember Norm Crosby being here."

Nevertheless, everyone claimed their own brush with stardom. An old mechanic said he had jump-started Steve McQueen's motorcycle; a notorious drunk spun a yarn about saving Shelley Winters from a bear. Likewise, Matt was often confronted by people who claimed to have been his father's best friend in those days. They had all taken him fishing, canoeing, water-skiing, snorkeling. They rode dune buggies with him; they taught him how to use a chainsaw. Matthew would nod impatiently, tap his foot, look at the sky, and say, "Okay. If I ever meet him I'll tell him you said *hi*."

Matt paddled across the lake after breakfast, and threaded through the forest to the main highway, where across the street lay Stritmatter's place. The old man had built a library from a dairy farm. Books filled up the barn. Magazines and even microfilm carrels sat in the emptied-out creamery vats and in the milking stalls. In winter, the library was so cold that Matt would do his research in mittens; but now, at the onset of summer, there was a wet thawing smell inside. The magazine pages stuck together.

Mr. Stritmatter, the owner, was the sole heir to a long line of robust Swedes who had worked all their lives on that farm. But Stritmatter had been a strange boy, always sneaking away to read in the attic. He stocked his library now with an air of vengeance. Throughout Matt's childhood, the man had been abrupt with him. Matt had always wanted to see back issues of *People* or *TV Guide*. Stritmatter would fish out water-damaged pages from bathtubs and wash basins, handing over magazines that he used to cover the floor while painting. Many were rolled up and covered with smudged insects.

"There you go, boy. Another day, another magazine. This is what universal literacy has come to—*Joanie Loves Chachi*!"

On his last day in town, Matt reeled out stories on microfilm. Searching for an address or number in the fan magazines, Matt instead became captivated by the description of a canceled pilot that his father had done in the mid-seventies. It was a sitcom called *Hay Fever*. He played a hillbilly who, through some vague clerical error, was appointed ambassador to Great Britain. It seemed to Matt that the lost episodes revolved around a prank— say, Charlie spiking the queen's punch with moonshine. When Stritmatter wasn't looking, Matt cut out the article and taped it into his scrapbook. Obscure information gave him a feeling of conquest.

Stritmatter sorted books loudly across the barn. He shouted, "Why don't you read D. H. Lawrence? He's smutty. Or Henry Miller. Or even Burroughs, for Pete's sake. They're full of more sex and debauchery than you'll get in a thousand of those rags. Look at yourself, boy. Playing chicken with the lowest common denominator."

"Don't give yourself a heart attack, Mr. Stritmatter."

"You want to be a rebel, you have to have brains! Nobody ever challenged the system with a celebrity crossword puzzle. You have to embrace the struggle, my boy."

"I'm doing my family tree," said Matt without looking up from the mess of pages in front of him. "Don't distract me."

There was a video monitor set up in a stall, and Matt found a tape of *Hell and Back,* one of West's first starring roles. Stritmatter watched over his shoulder, mumbling, "You bring out the worst in me, kid. You can't escape this. It's like watching a house burn down."

The movie was about a former cop who, after arresting the maniacal head of a biker gang, had retired to the quiet suburbs to become a school bus driver. It was clear that all the children loved him, because the early scenes were filled with rollicking banjo music and madcap driving. But the plot thickened when the biker gang sought revenge on Charlie by kidnapping all the children. While West drove around in the bus formulating his plan, the children squealed from the backs of Harleys and witnessed a lot of bad manners around nightly campfires.

"Why doesn't the fool go get another car?" said Stritmatter. "You're not going to catch those hooligans in a school bus."

Matt stopped the tape and dug back through articles. It was during the filming of *Hell and Back* that his father's drinking problem became notorious. He drank on the set and in his hotel. He drank before guest appearances on game shows, like when he broke into a fit of demonic laughter over *The $20,000 Pyramid* category "Things that expand when wet." He drank during his press junkets, tripping over extension cords and stepping into potted plants. He passed out in makeup chairs and fell out of elevators as they opened. A tabloid reported his arrest for indecent exposure at a nightclub, complete with a picture of two policemen as they escorted him through a parking lot, West with a party hat cupped over his privates.

Matt didn't own a suitcase, so after returning with photocopies and notes, he began to neatly pack his clothes, his books, and his press clippings into a box marked ASPIRIN AND ACE BANDAGES. Grace lingered in the kitchen. She hadn't gone into his room in years, and Matthew was touched that she was still respecting his privacy. When he came tromping down the stairs in his boots, holding the box in his arms, he saw that Grace was preparing a stack of sandwiches for him. She had laid out a long line of bread slices and efficiently slathered them with mustard.

"I'm sure you can borrow a duffel from one of the girls."

"That's okay, Gram. What am I going to do with all of those sandwiches?"

"You're going to eat them, of course."

"There's fifteen sandwiches there. They have food in California."

"They're for the bus ride."

He sat down at the table and watched her. Outside he heard the classical music droning. "I know there's a catch to all this."

"Actually, Matthew, I've been expecting it for quite some time. But if you'll just listen for a minute—I want to make sure you know what you're doing. I called Greyhound and we can afford the ticket. It'll have an open return date."

He looked at the ground, embarrassed by the gust of affection he felt for her.

"I know you have some money saved up. But you don't know very much about the world, Matthew. I don't want you to wander around thinking you're *street smart*. Don't let yourself get hoodwinked down there. Don't go around talking to strangers about your life story."

"I have to talk to *some* strangers."

"You talk to your family and that's it."

"They're strangers. Aren't they?"

"I suppose that's a semantic argument that I don't care to have right now. I want you to call me regularly, and I want you to make sure you take enough underwear."

"I packed underwear."

"Well, go pack some more. I made you all these sandwiches, you can do at least *that* much for me."

Upstairs Matt packed an entire drawer of briefs, his name written on all the waistbands. He felt now that he was simply leaving for camp. He stared out the window at the roofs of the shacks, the lake beyond them, and said to himself, "You're really going." But now that he was leaving, his restlessness vanished. The place no longer seemed a prison, but a landscape he viewed with surprising fondness. He thought of how he would describe this place in stories to his sister, to his father, to his coterie of new friends. He was certain he could find them. He thought of how pleased his mother would have been at his adventure, how she would have fussed over his clothes, licked her palm, and smoothed down his hair.

His mother was conspicuously absent from the stories about The Briar Patch. Sometimes an orderly, sometimes a patient, Sadie was a magnet for catastrophes. She was eighteen years old when Matt was born, and every year she seemed a more frazzled parody of youth. She left the clinic often, traveling around the country and sometimes deep into Mexico. Grace and Matt would tape the postcards she sent to them onto the refrigerator beside his school drawings.

Sometimes they received long letters, written feverishly, always describing a newfound love affair before the backdrop of a natural disaster. She met one man during the Mexico City earthquake. They were in a grocery store when the shaking began, causing an avalanche of grapefruits and peaches. Everyone dove onto the floor. Sadie was trapped when a shelf fell over her. Some of the ceiling collapsed, and when the dust settled, Sadie was pinned between the fallen shelf and the fruit stand.

In the darkness, she moaned in pain. A hand reached through

and touched her head. She heard a man whisper "Shhhh" and sing what sounded like a Spanish lullaby, which calmed her instantly. Sadie "fell in love on the spot." For three hours they lay on their backs, whispering to each other, as they stuffed themselves with fruit and cushioned their heads with bread loaves.

Sometimes Sadie wrote letters addressed only to her son. They were long and passionate about what she was learning in the world, rambling on about how much she would one day teach him. She swore they would live like a normal family. Matt adored his mother more with each colorful postcard. He learned to read *normal* as a place: she'd find it in her travels and send for him. They would float on rafts in pastel-blue waters, bask beneath palm trees. They would dive right into the postcards themselves.

Sadie returned home—claiming it was for good—when Matt was nine. She tried very hard to be a "real" mother, but seemed constantly depressed by her efforts. She was a nervous eater, and after a few sedentary years her cheeks widened and her arms thickened. She complained that Grace was stuffing her with starchy foods.

"Mother is trying to fatten me up so much I won't be able to get out the door," said Sadie. She berated her mother endlessly. Grace treated her like the most hysterical patients, believing that people needed to be sober, calm, and polite simply to be held accountable for what they said. Deep down, Sadie must have perceived this, for with each passing month she became louder and more belligerent, hurling insults at the nurses and patients. She enjoyed being crude and startling people.

"I didn't think I'd get out of Mexico alive. The border officials found some goodies on a friend of mine, and, well . . . let's just say I had to give my share of blow jobs."

Grace put her hand over her mouth to conceal a gasp.

"Look at *Grace*," Sadie continued. "The woman hasn't seen a penis in twenty-five years."

Sadie's last stab at motherhood came at the peak of Charlie West's career. In the eighties he had grown into a bona fide star, an action hero in all kinds of pyrotechnic spectaculars. Sadie took

Matt to his movies and watched attentively beside him, her head cocked to the side, as if listening to a sermon.

Charlie hurdled seats in airports that were about to explode; he whisked women off their feet and ran from skittering bullets. In *Iron Will,* he played a former prizefighter turned steel worker. Shirtless for most of the movie, he had an impressive new physique. Sobriety agreed with him. He punched through wooden fences and karate-kicked scores of corrupt union delegates. Matt was spellbound. He came straight home and head-butted the doorjamb of the main lodge.

When his mother saw the welt on his forehead, she broke into a fit of tears so sudden and intense that Matt was terrified. "I should be stood up and shot," she said. "I am the worst mother on earth. Oh, will you look at him, Grace! He probably has brain damage now."

She avoided Matt for the next several days, staying in her shack with the lights off and the radio murmuring. One day she called him inside and told him to sit at the edge of her bed. The floor was littered with crumpled tissues and her eyes were pink and swollen. She said, "It's not about violence. It's not about who can beat the stuffing out of some poor fool. You have to watch your father's movies with a better eye, Matt. I *remember* him. He's a son of a bitch, sure—but he's also a passionate, intelligent man, and beneath all of that . . ." She waved her arms around to indicate the clutter of violent images while she made explosion noises, spraying spit around her lips. "There's more to it than that stuff. It's about a whole sort of Eastern philosophy of things. I read somewhere that your father converted to Buddhism. Now, Buddhists don't go bashing their heads into things. Do they?"

Uncomfortable with her pleading tone, Matt stared at the open door. She sat up abruptly. "All right, then. You go ahead and get out of here. I'm just a stupid bitch. What do I know?"

The time he spent with her made him appreciate the reserved and logical qualities of his grandmother. When Sadie noticed this, she became fiercely competitive with Grace. She argued with her mother loudly in front of Matt about what was best for him, and she made a great show of setting up activities.

One day Sadie told him that he would never amount to much in this world if he didn't learn to catch a ball or ride a bicycle like other children. "You'll be branded as an outcast," she told him.

She began apprenticing her son to various men who came through the clinic. The patients were happy to pass the time by teaching Matt to dive, to backstroke, to paddle a canoe. From a long procession of men—faces as blurry in his memory as those on a passing train—he learned to bait fishing hooks, shoot an air rifle, paint a landscape, play the guitar. These skills all remained superficial in his lifetime, some of them eroding entirely, but they did leave Matt with the sensation that being a man required proficiency in a great deal of pointless activities.

The recovering patients were kind to him, generally, until the boy began to irritate them with his profound restlessness. "Painting is so *boring*," he said to one of them. The man stroked his brush on the canvas, smiled, and continued speaking about the hazards in life. Everyone warned him about addiction, that abstract bogeyman lingering in his closet. But Matt craved the simplicity of his father's life. He wanted to fight a chain of villains on the wing of an airplane; he wanted to save the world from nuclear destruction.

The painter said, "The most important thing you could learn is concentration."

"I wish I could breathe underwater," said the boy.

"And why is that exactly?"

"In this movie I saw, with my dad, they drove off a cliff in an armored truck, right? With a whole bunch of money in it. And then they swam away with tanks on their backs."

"Your father ran out on you, just like mine," said the painter.

Sadie was sitting on her front step, her bare feet in the pine needles. She was watching the man with sheer admiration. She said, "You listen to him, Matt!"

"What you need to do is learn to meditate on your life a little bit. To start figuring out what *you* want."

"This is so good for him," said Sadie.

"My dad is a kung fu expert. He can punch through a block of ice."

"And is that what you want out of life?" asked the painter.

Matt hated his voice, slow and goading, like a schoolteacher's.

"He knows kung fu, tae kwon do, and Buddhism."

The painter laughed. "But you don't know your father. He might be very different in real life."

Matt looked over at his mother, who was watching intently. He said, "I'm going to know him when I grow up. I don't know him now because I'm illegitimate. There's three bastards at my school." He counted on his fingers. "Me, Bill Sherman, and Thomas. But I'm the only one whose dad is famous. Their dads are in prison."

Sadie stood and said, "Matt, if you're not going to pay attention, just go inside and play in your room."

A few hours later, she crept into his room and stood awkwardly above him. His drawings lay scattered around the floor, and Sadie sorted through them with her bare toes. "Why didn't you do any of these out there with us?"

He shrugged.

She crouched beside him and he watched her. She was impossible to understand, and he loved her so much and feared her disappointment so thoroughly that his heart sank when she approached. She waited and said nothing, and he had the feeling that she was keeping something vital from him, that he would never know what she wanted. She reached over and ran her hand around his hair, twirling the ends of it between her fingers.

"You've got *my* awful hair," she said. "Aren't we lucky? Two peas in a pod. I don't know what we did to get such miserable hair."

The next day, Sadie and the painter were gone.

At twelve years old, Matt had not heard from his mother in well over a year. He lived in his mother's childhood room and covered its walls with pictures of Charlie West. Over his bed,

Matt kept a chart of "genetic information." From a health and fitness magazine, he learned that both he and his father were allergic to shellfish. West was also lactose intolerant. When Matt discovered this tidbit, he went downstairs and drank an entire carton of milk. He was pleased to discover that he felt gaseous as well.

But he didn't begin to organize these piles of magazines until one autumn night that he would always remember. The testimonials were going on downstairs, and Matt could hear murmuring through the floor. The phone rang. He heard his grandmother's slow steps clunking up the wooden staircase. She knocked on his door, then stepped inside with her head down, clearing a path with her foot and ignoring the landfill of papers around her. Because she said nothing about the clutter, Matt knew something serious had happened. It took an act of God to make Grace ignore a mess.

"Matthew? Can you please put down the magazine and look at me for a second?" She had a rehearsed tone that frightened him. Grace normally didn't preface what she said, and a simple change in diction made him feel that all order had been lost. "Can you please just look at me?"

"No," he said.

"Matthew, I'm serious. Look up at me."

"I'm sort of busy."

"I'm sure you are. That's a fine publication. Now, don't make me throw it out the window. Something terrible has happened. Matthew! Put the thing down."

He calmly placed it on the bed beside him. She took off her glasses and they hung from a string around her neck. She never looked like this. Her normal stoic appearance had been overcome by a look of exhaustion. Some trace of exasperation—always upon her—now seemed to have aged into genuine sadness.

"It's Mom," he said. "Isn't it?"

"That was the highway patrol on the phone. All the way from Oregon. I have to go *down* there."

"Was *she* driving?"

"Yes. I'm sorry, Matthew."

"Was she coming home?"

"I don't know that."

Matt picked up the magazine again and pretended to read. Grace stood watching him. He turned the pages when he thought enough time had passed.

Grace said, "Matthew? Do you understand what I'm trying to say?"

"Yeah. She isn't coming back."

Grace shuffled toward the door. Neither looked at the other now. As she faced outward into the hallway she said, "I'll be back tomorrow afternoon. I'll have Paige or Linda see to it that you get to school all right. There'll be a lot to do around here. We can be sure of that. I'm going to need help too. I'm an old lady."

"I'll help," he said quietly.

"It's just us now. Just you and me."

When she left him, she closed the door as quietly as if he'd been sleeping. He said, "It always was." He lay on his back past midnight, not a thought in his head but that family far away, his father in a pool chair, his sister sitting on a diving board with her bare feet skimming the water. At around two he dozed off and awakened quickly with the residue of a sickening dream. He had been crying in his sleep. The world was dark and time had stopped and the only sound was wind through the trees. He took a flashlight and went through the piles of magazines, tearing out pages with trembling hands and stacking them in neat piles. He cleaned everything that night. He made files in his cabinet; he threw away the excess pages; he started a scrapbook; he removed every shred from his walls but the single column that mentioned his birth. He stuffed his clothes into the hamper, made his bed, and dusted his shelves. When he was finished with his room, he brushed his teeth furiously.

Outside it was near dawn. The nurses' flashlights were approaching. The generator started amid the echoes of coughing, like some huge sick creature was waking up at last. Matt sat on his bed and looked over a room so clean it seemed empty.

The town had grown so much since then, now the main strip was encroaching the forest. When Grace drove him to the bus station that early afternoon she complained about all the take-out restaurants and Jiffy Lubes. On windy days, the smell of fast-food grease wafted through the trees. Matt had not driven with her in this truck for almost six years, since the day of the funeral, when she had been blowing at her black veil like it was a swarm of gnats.

Between them sat the box, loaded with sandwiches on top of a layer of underwear, which covered his books and magazines and clothes.

Grace said, "I don't want you to assume you're going to find anything. If it doesn't work out, you come on home. If you get in trouble, anything. You just come back. You've got a long life ahead of you and there's always going to be time to find these people. You say you wrote to everyone?"

"I've written a ton to him, Gram. That doesn't do much. But I've got the address of his accountants, I guess. If it comes to that."

"You've barely got a plan at all. Barely got a brain in that towhead."

"Don't worry. I can take care of myself."

"Nobody could ever stop you from doing what you wanted. You've always been stubborn. Just remember you have someplace to come back to."

When he boarded the bus, refusing to check his box into the compartment beneath, Grace stood beside the truck and waved to him. Matt felt like he was heading off to war. Sitting beside his grandmother, she had always seemed so strong and capable to him; but now, from across the parking lot, she looked old and fragile. As the bus pulled away and her figure receded in the window, it occurred to Matt what a gift she had given to him. He was certain that he would make her proud of him, that he would prove he was strong enough and brave enough to put his life in order. He thought of all the people who sold everything and moved to Los Angeles for a future. Matt almost laughed thinking he was the rarest type—someone headed there in search of a history.

CHAPTER THREE

Ava's mother was asleep on the couch with the television still
blaring a late-night talk show. Applause filled the house as Ava
carried Chris to his bed. She changed him into his pajamas and
tucked him into the sheets. Once beyond the sleepy ritual of
delivering glasses of water, leaving the door open the exact right
amount, and responding to the long volley of good-nights, Ava sat
at the base of the couch. Her mother had dozed with a crossword
puzzle on her chest and a pen still in her fist. Her coils of dark
hair pushed up against the arm of the couch. She had the irritating habit of biting napkins when she was nervous, originally done
to smooth her lipstick but now done even without makeup. Tonight she had moistened the edges of paper towels all over the
house.

"Mmmm. You survived," said her mother, waking slowly.

"Barely." Ava cleaned the trail of papers, then went into the
garage to look over the shipwreck of her leftover sets. Crammed
into every corner around her mother's faded yellow MG were
the posters she had designed, the French doors of scrap wood,
windows of cheesecloth dipped in Earl Grey tea, chandeliers
made from coat hangers, wooden cutouts of trees now bent into
cramped spaces, love seats and Baroque tables turned back into
wilted corrugated cardboard, drip-stained and dusty. There was
a huge balsa-wood rocking chair on its side.

There wasn't enough room to start over. So Ava smoked a joint and sat on the front porch among the crickets creaking like old hinges, and made signs for a garage sale. She wrote, EVERYTHING MUST GO. I'M DROWNING. SURPLUS FURNITURE AND PROPS FROM YEARS OF SET DESIGN. PERFECT FOR HOME OR STAGE OR THE ECCENTRIC COLLECTOR. ODDBALLS WELCOME. On another she wrote, TIRED OF CORDUROYS, MUUMUUS, AND BOZ SCAGGS ALBUMS? COME TO AN EVEN MORE IMPRACTICAL GARAGE SALE! LANDSCAPE YOUR YARD WITH CUTOUT TREES. FURNISH YOUR HOME WITH A TOUCH OF LOUIS XIV. CARDBOARD GOTHIC, FOAM ROCOCO. DISCOUNTS ON ALL TRAGEDIES. HALF OFF EVERYTHING ELIZABETHAN.

Camilla came out onto the porch wearing her pajamas and a robe. She leaned against the railing and said, "Is there something you want to get off your chest, sugar?"

"What makes you say that?"

"It seems an odd time to be planning a clearance sale."

"Mother, please don't just stand there and wait for me to tell you that Dad is an asshole. He was actually rather charming."

"He was probably sedated."

"I'm the one who can't deal with anything. I'm sitting there covered with spaghetti sauce all night like some hillbilly who's never seen a fork before. Chris threw a big tantrum and then my father and Barbara wolfed down their dinners while I was in the *bathroom*. I'm serious. The check was paid by the time I'd gotten the noodles out of my hair. I know it's humiliating for them, sure—but it's not like it was the A-list at this place. It was more like a reception for the Hollywood Squares."

"Chris is too young for a restaurant, Ava. Give him two years and then start slowly. Someplace with singing waiters."

"I could use a singing waiter."

Ava handed the joint to her mother, who took a long drag and handed it back. Ava hadn't achieved the effect she wanted this evening. Instead she had launched herself into an uneasy nostalgia, coupled with a feeling of exhaustion. Her life was now an endless series of chores. Viewed in the abstract there was more purpose to her days. Her son, without a doubt, was the most important person in her life. But some nights the gravity of it all tugged at her and made her long for those years when she was just a lanky, laughing girl out in a world more full of possibilities than of dangers. She had met new people every day. She had dated a man whom she'd met pumping gas across from her at a Chevron. He picked up her unleaded tab and she wrote her number on his receipt, and now—even though the date itself had been an excruciating meal listening to him describe the future of retailing—the opportunity still lingered sweetly. She was younger, maybe not very wise in those days, but she met people everywhere. Plumbers would woo her with their heads beneath her sink, mechanics would flirt while they bashfully discussed her crank shaft, and everyone was a person more than a function. It was only when each room and activity needed to be sanitized for Chris that plumbers simply fixed the pipes, mechanics only tuned the car. Casanovas became stalkers overnight. There was a balance somewhere, a right amount of wariness and openness, and Ava had lost it.

"And how was Chris's conniption fit?" asked her mother.

"You know, Mom, I'm thinking the whole two-parent system was designed so you could at least outnumber the kid. That way you can still have a few hours a day when you're an adult."

"You would need more than two people, Ava. The ideal family unit is about twelve people to every toddler."

"I've started to think like a three-year-old. Where's he going to go? What's he going to grab? How much is he eating? Every day is a campaign for *two more bites*. What can be touched, what can't be touched? This is my job now. Toddler wrangler. Every room I go into I scout out the trouble spots. It's endless. I haven't read a book in two years that didn't have crayon scribbled into it. I can't pick up a spoon anymore without having the urge to make choo-choo noises."

Camilla gestured to the signs and said, "This is the wrong time for you to make decisions about your life."

"Somebody'll come and buy this crap and then I'll have the space to start working again. I've been so tired, and so busy, I sometimes forget how fucking lonely I am. I don't mean to lay all of this on you, Mom, but what the hell am I supposed to do? And here I am tonight trying to befriend my own father. You should hear this speech he gave me this afternoon. We have to *reacquaint ourselves*. He had this huge epiphany that he needed to know me all of a sudden. Then it's like he threw me a surprise party and only invited his own friends. Why does he have to know me at *his* favorite restaurant? And if I show any frustration, then they all kind of give me this *I-told-you-so* tone."

"You have every right," said Camilla, and coughed into her fist. "He played you and you have every right to be upset."

"That's exactly what I didn't want you to say."

Camilla put her hands up and looked around like Ava might be talking to someone else. With the exaggerated mannerisms of a stage actress, she pointed to her own chest and whispered, "Are you talking to me?"

"I didn't want this to turn into the who's-a-better-parent discussion again."

"I thought I had already won that competition, hands down."

"Then, why do you get so much pleasure out of hearing me gripe about him?"

"Well, I enjoy widening my lead."

Ava smiled and shook her head. She went back to coloring in her signs and said, "Go to bed. When you wake up all of this will be gone forever."

Camilla stood and touched her daughter's shoulder, and at the threshold of the door she said, "Don't smoke all of my pot, sugar."

Ava waved and nodded. "Good night, Mom."

Ava went to sleep that night still taking inventory in her head. After a brief dream in which she was haggling over a giant statue of her fifth grade teacher, she was awakened by the phone. Still half asleep, she reached for it. On the other end of the line she heard a tinkle of music and the clanking of dishes. Was it a cellular again? The song sounded like an old sixties tune redone as Muzak. It sounded as if she had been put on hold. Ava repeated,

"Are you there? Hello? Is everyone all right? Is this a survey? I'm happy with my current long-distance plan. But I hate this song. Please make it stop."

A woman called out something and a man responded, "Please."

"What's the matter," said Ava, smacking her lips. She curled down onto the bed with the phone nestled to her ear. She was lapsing back to sleep. The sounds of a distant street were broadcast onto her pillow: a siren rolling across her comforter and an eighteen-wheeler droning over the nightstand. When the traffic passed she could hear breathing. "Who is this?" she said. The bed felt soft and the room faded into darkness. Ava had the spark of a dream in which she hung up the phone; but when she awakened that morning the phone was still on the pillow beside her.

Hours had passed. She listened and heard the din of conversations punctuated with a ringing cash register. She hung up. Moments later it rang again and she put it to her ear without answering.

"Hello?" said her father.

"Jesus. Was that you?"

"Your line was busy for the last half hour. I've been trying to call you since six. I'm on my way to work. I have an early call this morning. This is the last day of this, Ava. My last stupid sequel."

Through the open window she could smell her mother smoking the day's first cigarette on the porch.

"I must have left the phone off the hook."

"I wanted to tell you, first of all, that I had a wonderful time last evening and it was just great to see you again. Second, I wanted to ask you if you'd been by the house."

"By your house? No. Of course not."

"Well, there was a box left on the doorstep. Unmarked. I thought maybe you would know something about it."

"Why would I know anything about it?"

"You know, it was just a strange package. I can live with that. Crazy people out there. Barbara gets a lot of mail from prisoners, you know. They watch her infomercials."

"Dad, are you trying to tell me someone broke into your house last night?"

"Oh, no. No, no. Nothing like that. I was just wondering if you . . . had heard of anything strange. You know. Anyone asking where I lived or anything."

"Stop being so cryptic. What happened?"

"Nothing happened. I was calling to thank you for coming to dinner last night. I know it's hard to come over this far, and I appreciate it."

"Okay, Dad. Thank you for waking me up even before *Chris* gets up. A family full of early birds."

"Work, work, work," he said. "Okay, well. I'll call you again and see what you're doing. I'm insanely busy this week. Running around like a chicken with my head cut off."

"Well, good luck."

"Thanks. I have to go—there's road construction up ahead."

Once Ava had dragged most of her belongings into the front yard, she began organizing them according to theme. There was a scattering of birthday presents, appliances, and leftover sets. She unrolled her backdrops—a blue sky, a forest, the town of Mycenae, the battle of Agincourt—and stretched them out on a clothesline. She laid the props out chronologically, beginning with *Electra* beside the driveway, stepping right across the gnarled papier-mâché trees of *Lear,* around the rocking chairs and stern interiors of Strindburg and Ibsen, blending into the snow-covered facade of a Russian inn (which was *Vera,* or *The Nihilists*), and into a mishmash of contemporary works, warped picket fences, and hollowed-out televisions from the worst of the avant-garde, to end amid the chaotic pile of things from Ava's own life.

The sun was just edging above the San Gabriel Mountains when she began to arrange these everyday items. Barbara gave her weight equipment every year, and Ava placed it all beside the baby carriages and strollers, jumpers and mobiles, so that there appeared to be graduated levels of apparatus from birth until that final NordicTrack. Bathtub squeaky toys filled a trash can from

Endgame. On a cardboard table she stacked a pyramid of Barbara's weight-loss powder. Festoons of old clothes hung from plywood palm trees, and all along the arc of a peeling rainbow the linens were draped.

She brought out her T-shirts, Chris's baby clothes, clothes left by her old boyfriends and by Chris's father. Camilla even reluctantly surrendered a few pairs of old shoes. She was annoyed when Ava shoved a pair of red pumps under the facade of the inn and sang, "Ding-dong the witch is dead, the wicked witch is dead."

Camilla sat in a lawn chair, soaking her feet in an inflatable pool. She tried to read the newspaper without smudging her freshly done nails. "Don't ask me for any favors, then." Her voice was hoarse.

"You're not doing anything anyway, Mother."

"My sciatica."

"Poor baby," said Ava.

"You wouldn't make a nickel without my help. You'd *give* everything away."

For some reason Chris sat down in his old car seat on the front lawn and tried to strap himself in place. Camilla rose, groaning, took the seat, and dragged it across the lawn. "*Beep beep,*" she said, and made engine noises until she coughed. "That's enough driving for me, Chris. Grandma feels pretty rotten this morning."

The sun was evaporating the last dew off the lawns and easing over the roofs when the first browsers began to arrive. Visitors sorted, knocked on wooden surfaces, modeled shirts for themselves in a cracked mirror. Ava cut her price in half for three consecutive sales, so Camilla refused to let her haggle anymore. Ava wandered into the garage to salvage the last bit of her history—a warped pool table her father had given her on her thirteenth birthday.

As Ava was struggling to drag it out onto the driveway, she heard her mother say to a customer. "Oh, sugar, you know you can pay a bit more than *that*. You're not a burglar, are you? Your own peace of mind is worth an extra dollar."

The surface of the pool table was as undulating as a putting green, and the felt was discolored to a cabbage tint. Ava cleared mounds of deflated kiddie pools and rafts from the top of it, then grabbed a rail and yanked. But the table was heavy and only tilted, spilling the faded billiard balls down the slope of the driveway and into the gutter below.

"Don't let those get away," said Ava. "We need those."

With each pull, more of the debris in the garage collapsed behind the table. Camilla walked to the driveway and peered in at her daughter, who was now standing in the wreckage of fallen props from a ship's facade, old hammocks strung out like cobwebs, and the flotsam of forgotten suitcases. "Sweetie, that table is holding up everything. Just let it go for now."

"Mother, why did you just leave this in the garage all those years?"

"Okay, Ava. Make me a list of everything I'm supposed to do differently."

"I'm not fighting with you. It's just a practical question."

Trying to clear a path for the pool table, Ava hauled out a tattered sofa with the cushions lost, two armchairs, a frayed rug, a nightstand with names carved into it; and when she had arranged them on the lawn, she realized that she had unintentionally re-created the exact layout of her childhood living room. She half-expected to find Tom Sloan in the garage beneath a croquet set or a Slip 'N Slide.

Her memory sharpened now by these moldering relics, Ava sat on the old couch and daydreamed. She was five when Camilla had thrown yet another party—one of those parties during which Ava tried to sleep but all the laughter and voices seemed amplified through the crease in her door—and the next morning Tom Sloan was on the couch. He stayed practically in the same spot for half a decade.

In the year before he'd passed out and overslept into their lives, he had fought in Vietnam despite severe myopia. He had left home with ten extra pairs of glasses and came back with one pair held together with surgical tape and wire. Camilla used to say that everything about Sloan was held together with tape. He watched television for nearly twelve hours a day, and after several months of it, he got into the habit of shouting at the screen. At night he would climb onto the roof and drink beer, sometimes falling asleep as he leaned back against the slope.

When Ava was ten, Sloan began to pull out of his stupor. He watched Ava with an anthropological interest. Anything that interested her he considered the wave of the future. He used all of his savings to buy a collection of video arcade games. Ava rode with him in a pickup truck dragging a horse trailer full of *Space Invaders* and *Lunar Landers*. They set them out like traps in Laundromats and grocery stores; and every few weeks they would make the rounds to collect the quarters. Sloan was always disappointed with the returns, and he would become so morose that he refused to count them. He complained that it was impossible to count enough quarters to be rich. It was like having to earn every coin twice. He also feared having to confront an actual number, preferring to look at the piles that accumulated in the pantry. They covered every surface and slowly grew into stacks on the end tables and nightstands.

Camilla never took them to the bank either, possibly because she enjoyed referring to Sloan as "a man who couldn't turn four quarters into a dollar." Whenever she and Ava needed something, they would scoop up a handful. Long lines formed behind them at department stores. Ava was always mortified, but Camilla would only chuckle to herself. Holding her daughter's hand, she would turn to the crowd of impatient customers, the fretting saleswomen, and the harried managers, and say, "Does anyone need *change?*"

The entire house had a metallic smell, and the sun came through dusty air onto the luster of forgotten piles. Ants threaded through the house, attracted to the coins, because—Sloan theorized—the quarters still carried the residue of soda pop from the sticky fingers of children. Over the years, they came to rely solely on this money. Camilla had not had much acting work.

Before Ava was born, Camilla had shown a few years of promise, appearing mostly in horror films. She was sixteen when she witnessed a robbery in a Monrovia grocery store. She screamed.

The thief was never caught. But a talent scout was hunkered down in the frozen-foods section. While Camilla was trembling and distraught, he handed her his card and said, "Kid, you've got the face of an angel and the lungs of an opera singer."

She eventually became one of the city's most reliable screamers. She screamed at giant mice, swarms of insects, and a mass of run-of-the-mill psychopaths. She also spent long afternoons dubbing over the halfhearted screams of other actresses. Sometimes every scream in a movie was hers: the taken-by-surprise screams, the worst-fears-confirmed screams, and even the screams of terrified disbelief. Every year she lost a bit of her voice until she was permanently hoarse.

Ava's father managed to get Camilla into a few of his own movies as his status began to grow. Camilla screamed into the faces of thugs and hoodlums, swooned in West's arms, and rode around on the back of his motorcycle.

After the divorce, she was able to find work as bimbos and temptresses. She was a bit player in a spy film, carrying a martini on a tray and later trying to kill the hero with two switchblades that sprung automatically from her bra. She played a gangster moll twice, and three times a strutting nurse, but as she grew older, crow's feet deepening, she resembled an aged showgirl more than an actress. She played a sex-starved schoolteacher and a tragically awkward stripper, then the roles became more scarce.

Sloan said the word *career* like it was a disease. He hated the work Camilla did. The two of them had loud fights at night that sometimes ended with spare change being thrown across the room, shattering light fixtures and pictures on the wall. She tried to return to the horror genre, but Camilla's shouting at home had weakened her voice to a whisper until she could scarcely find a voice-over job.

Even now, when Ava watched cheap horror flicks, she could distinguish her mother's younger screams from the older ones. The youthful ones seemed almost giddy; the older ones, exasperated. One late night when Ava was a freshman in college, *They Are Among Us* was replaying, a movie originally released in the early eighties. In it was Camilla's last scream—placed into the mouth of a villainously cute teenager. Ava rose up in her bunk bed. The scream had been done a few nights after Sloan had left them, dragging a knapsack full of quarters that left a ditch in the front yard. When the scream came, during a scene in which the heroine was confronted at last by the alien identity of her heretofore dashing lover, it was full of depth and longing. It was not a scream so much as a wail, a deep gospel bellow that carried until the voice cracked with it. For Ava to see it in that little girl's face gave her a pang of desperation, and she stood up in her dorm room and screamed along with it.

Throughout Ava's childhood her father had never once set foot in her house, but he was a presence nonetheless.

Ava visited him for one week a year, and each time he was more successful. During the first visits they went to movies, ate junk food, watched television at his small house, and spent blistering long days at the beach (after which she called her mother crying about her sunburns). Often Charlie had different girlfriends, women who were cordial but awkward around Ava. Women who said things like "You'd be such a pretty girl if you combed that hair out. I would kill for that hair." On a later visit, he took her skiing in Sun Valley, Idaho, where he had rented an enormous cabin and hired a team of ski instructors, nannies, and cooks.

She received progressively more lavish gifts for each birthday. One year it was a quadraphonic stereo system built into its own dresser and vanity chest. Camilla looked upset and said, "You know, if I was a millionaire I'd buy you *two* of those things."

Camilla was chronically unemployed by then, still dressing like a Bond extra (she was frozen in hairstyle, lingo, and fashion at the most promising moment of her career). She worked nights as a waitress and took acting workshops during the day. Charlie West became Ava's bargaining chip. When Ava and Camilla had a fight—like the time Ava tried to dye her hair black—Ava would mention her father as if he understood all her deepest secrets. "I'm going to live with my dad. My dad would understand. My dad doesn't give a shit what color my hair is because he has a life."

After hearing the man praised for years, Camilla finally broke. She said, "Ava, your father would sooner die than have you live with him. He has more *teenage* girls in his life than he can handle. So there. You're stuck with your pathetic mother."

When Ava called him, Charlie said, "Oh, Jesus, Avie. You know how much I love you, but I'm starting a picture next month. Next week I have to go to Europe to promote this thing. I just don't think you'd be happy living that kind of lifestyle. It's really exhausting."

"I understand," said Ava. "Thank you."

"No. Thank *you*," said Charlie.

Ava skipped her annual visit.

Because of the expensive stereos and all the clothes Charlie sent to Ava, most of which she then gave to her mother, the two women never believed entirely in their own poverty. Eleven months out of the year they lived on a waitress's salary. Their power was intermittently shut off, so that candles stuck into bottles would reflect off a big-screen television (birthday number fourteen). They crawled on their hands and knees hunting for lost quarters, finding them like a trail Sloan left, wedged behind their ratty couch and in the holes of chairs that bled stuffing. They rationed SpaghettiOs, filling the bowl with oyster crackers that Camilla stole from work. When they went dead broke, they would stay up late at night discussing what to sell. Ava lobbied to keep her stereo; Camilla fought for every pair of shoes. In the end, they compromised by holding enormous garage sales in which they sold all of their *own* garbage. Every year the house was more empty, until they lived almost exclusively surrounded by Charlie's gifts. It was like winning a small lottery each year, except that the bigger Charlie got, the more impractical the gifts became. One year Ava sold her bed and dresser to keep this pool table that was now warped and stained and up for sale on the lawn.

In Portland, Matt left the bus in order to do a bit more prelimi-
nary research in the public library. After finding a parenthetical
mention of his sister that suggested she worked in the theater,
he spent hours scanning microfilm of the *Los Angeles Times, The
Valley News, The Sentinel,* and any other paper he could find that
might carry blurbs or reviews. At last, his mind a jumble of spinning headlines like those pivotal montages in old movies, he
found a review for a play called *Make It Happen* in which a vitri-
olic reviewer described the production as "aggressively unpleas-
ant" and mentioned his sister in passing. "The sets, designed by
none other than daughter of action star and possible Antichrist
Charlie West, are adequate." Matt highlighted the line and made
a note: *The Next Step Theater.* He was even proud of his sister.
Achieving a rank of adequate when compared with such a play,
not to mention the Antichrist, was quite an accomplishment
indeed.

So, with a new batch of copies from the racks of magazines,
Matt boarded a southbound bus. His folder and his scrapbook
rested on top of his box full of supplies. The bus had the stuffy
air of an infirmary, and as he scanned the seats he saw dozens of
transients sagging down, looking forlorn and carsick. Just outside
the city, speeding past the dairy farms and rolling hills, Matt un-
packed his sandwiches and began walking along the aisles and

handing them out to the bewildered passengers. Pleased with his own generosity, he sat back down and spread his notes before him on the tray table.

This spell, however, was abruptly broken when a passenger walked back, sat across the aisle from him, and complained that his sandwich was soggy.

"It's not soggy," said Matt. "It's a perfectly good sandwich."

"Well, I don't want it. I'm not even hungry," said the man. He had caved-in cheeks and a hollow look in his eyes. He looked like he hadn't eaten in days, and Matt was furious that he would reject a perfectly good sandwich.

"My grandmother took hours making those. Just eat it, you ingrate."

The man said that he didn't even like turkey, and that the thing was loaded with mayonnaise. That alone made him nauseous. He told Matt to eat it himself, and within a few minutes all but two of the transients had returned their sandwiches with a similar complaint. Matt was so livid he couldn't concentrate on his notes.

He shouted, "You people think you're too good for a boxed lunch. It's all filet mignons for you jet-setters."

By the time his flash temper subsided—a temper that had always muddled his head—he realized that he had just insulted a bus full of angry junkies, and that it was very likely he was now in danger. So he packed up his belongings and sat down just behind the driver's partition, beside a pious-looking old woman to whom he whispered, "You can't even try to share anything with people anymore. Everybody just hates everybody."

She nodded and went back to staring out the window.

Matt began cutting out an interview from a 1994 issue of *Real Scoop*, which dealt primarily with Charlie's longtime struggle with allergies to lactose and bee stings. The piece was entitled "Nauseous in the Land of Milk and Honey." The front page showed his father's backyard, with palm trees around a pool, a Spanish-style bungalow. His father stood beside the pool in khaki pants, and the caption snaking beneath his oxfords read, "How did this bad boy get so good?" Matt Scotch-taped a portion into his book:

> The role of "family man" is not altogether new to West. He has a daughter, Ava, from his stormy first marriage to actress Camilla Snow (*Creature Comforts, Teacher's Pet*). West admits to having at times neglected this first family. "I had Ava when I was so young," he says, stirring his patented fat-free carbonara sauce. "It was too much for me to handle at that point in my life. I wasn't a man yet. I didn't understand what it meant to be a man. But she and I are pals now. We laugh about it. She's really my friend more than my daughter, and in a business like this, that's important."
>
> Does daughter Ava—*yes, she is named for actress Ava Gardner*— want to follow in her father's footsteps?
>
> "You mean act?" says West. He tastes his sauce. Perfect! "I'm not sure what she wants to do with her life. She's sort of all over the place. She has a lot of natural, God-given talent, but she doesn't quite know what to apply it to. I know she was taking some courses at one of those colleges out by Pasadena. In Glendale or someplace. But I think she's finished with all that business.

Matt circled a passage of comments about his marriage. Apparently he and his wife were coauthoring a fat-free cookbook. Matt tapped the woman beside him and showed her a picture of his father in an apron. "He's writing a cookbook for whipped husbands," he said. He continued onward.

> "Barbara had helped me to be more grounded," says West. "And it wasn't until I was truly grounded that I could begin to grow as an actor and as a person. But here I am. Grounded."

Matt jotted down some notes about his sister. He believed that she would understand his journey—or perhaps he should call it his *quest*—more than Charlie West, who was embroiled in this new world. In tiny handwriting, he wrote, "A touch of a philosophical nature; a love for theater—reaction to or against father? twenty-seven years old now—unsure of choices. Seems from snippets to be brilliant and deeply spiritual, but not sure. Don't overanalyze. God-given talent parlayed into 'adequate sets.' Must want more. Mother is actress, showbiz in blood."

They were passing through northern California at sunset, lights squiggling by in the windows, when he asked the woman beside him, "Do you believe that people's personalities are determined genetically?"

"I hope not," she said, staring at him like he was insane.

"Well, I think so. I think people inherit certain aptitudes. I've always felt like I've had certain abilities and I didn't know where they came from. Like, for instance, my maternal side of the family was very clumsy. And I'm rather agile. It's not that I have a great deal of talents, I'm not saying that. In fact, I took one of those career aptitude tests for my school, and it said I was going to be a *shepherd*. I didn't even know there were shepherds anymore. It must have been an old test or something. But you see, I have these relatives down in Los Angeles, and they're all obviously extremely gifted people. My father is a movie star. Granted he's one of those big shoot-'em-up stars, and even though I know that doesn't *seem* to require a lot of talent, I think there's a kind of savvy there. A *knack*. I think it's an underappreciated skill—like being a circus performer."

"So, you're running away to join the circus?"

"In a sense, ma'am."

He did not sleep that night, but watched the countryside pass by through the windows, and sat awake amid all the rhythms of sleeping breath. It was dawn as the bus came into Los Angeles County, passing over dry hills on widening freeways that seemed to fill up with cars from nowhere. In an hour they were still driving on the same coiling freeways, winding together and splitting again, until at last, with the sun already high and hot, Matt got off the bus at a station in Hollywood and walked along Vine Street.

His aesthetic disappointment came first. Walking north with his box in his arms and the sun bleaching out the sky, he passed rows of squat minimalls and open two-story motels of peeling granular yellow, like buildings composed of hardening mustard. He found the Walk of Fame after a half hour, and he followed it westward, staring at his feet as he passed cluttered souvenir shops blasting their competing radios, and squeezed through flocks of tourists who stood videotaping the ground. Several people were offering seats for free screenings or television shows, shouting side-by-side with vagrants demanding handouts, and in the clutter Matt could barely distinguish between them. Graffiti covered some store awnings, blending in with the logos and phrases on T-shirts that hung in the open storefronts. By the time Matt had reached the end of the strip, passing the Chinese Theatre and wandering onward, hot and delirious, he had a feeling that he had just stumbled through the dangerous section of Disneyland.

He walked farther along a residential strip of squat apartment buildings, the boulevard narrowing and becoming gradually cleaner, until at last he found a pretty young Hispanic girl, no older than ten, selling star maps as she leaned against the trunk of a palm tree.

Matt said, "How can I be sure those maps are accurate?"

She promised as she fanned herself with a handful of them.

"What is the source of your information?" he asked.

"I don't know," said the little girl. "Just people who know."

Matt argued that he wasn't going to buy anything unless he had some assurance that it was thorough and accurate. The little girl rolled her eyes and told him that she had the best maps in the city.

"You're too young for this kind of work," he said, putting the box down and fishing the money from his pocket. "You need a lemonade stand."

"Lemonade is nasty."

The map he bought was cryptic:

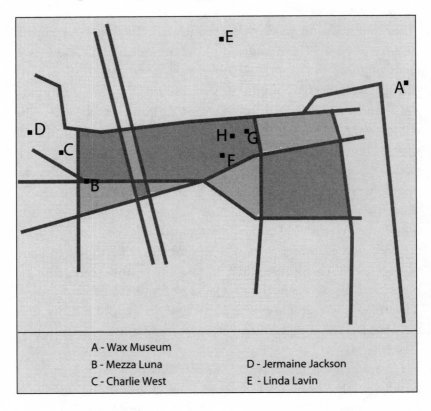

A - Wax Museum
B - Mezza Luna
C - Charlie West
D - Jermaine Jackson
E - Linda Lavin

He spent all afternoon trying to decipher his location in relation to various stripes and squares. He rode a public bus down Sunset, and then wandered around the palatial pink houses of Beverly Hills, where he asked another truant child selling maps to help him interpret the one he already had. The kid asked for a consultant's fee, and Matt reluctantly paid him. Then the young cartographer told him to head toward Brentwood, where someone else would help him.

"Who says you kids don't know geography," Matt told him.

Along his winding bus ride, Matt had intermittent bursts of anxiety about what he would do or say if he actually found his father's home. For all he knew, there were armed guards pacing in front of the gates, reinforced on the inside by a pack of Doberman pinschers, and deep in the house's inner sanctum his father would be eating grapes on a divan and watching footage from

security cameras. Matt tried to calm himself with relaxation exercises. There was no reason to assume his father lived like the
head of a cartel. But Matt believed a less confrontational route
would be to find his half-sister.

His momentum led him onward, though, if only to see this
house and confirm that his adventure was truly happening. He
stepped off the bus in a grove of sycamores, and doled out another few dollars to buy the exact address from a teenager, this
one selling his wares from a lawn chair with a parasol fastened to
the edge.

With legs aching from the miles he had walked and elbows
stiff from carrying his box, Matt limped down the final street, a
shady tributary off Sunset where New England–style homes
were partitioned by neatly groomed hedges. Oak and olive trees
formed a colonnade. Even the sound of the boulevard receded,
and after a few hundred yards it was lost amid the chatter of
sprinklers. The only traffic on this street was an occasional pickup
truck carrying pool-cleaning equipment or garden tools and severed branches.

The droning sound of some industrial lawn mower increased
as he approached. He followed a gutter rushing with sprinkler
runoff, past a Yorkshire terrier tethered to a pole and yipping at
him, all the way to a cul-de-sac that branched off the main street.
It was crammed full of trucks, and the droning sound was now
as loud as a passing squadron of planes.

To one side of him was a sealed garage with a Spanish tile
roof, and to the other an ivy-covered wall with a monogrammed
plaque that read CW. It was a formidable wall, evoking images of
boiling oil being poured off the top. He had seen angles of this
house in pictures—*Free Style* had done an entire feature—but
now it came to life and Matt was light-headed with excitement.
Through a tall wooden door hanging open, Matt could see a
courtyard with bushy gingko trees. He recognized it from a pho-
tograph in which Charlie was planting herbs and proudly brandishing a soiled garden spade.

A cloud of dust puffed up in the courtyard, billowing over the
top of the wall to mar the broad windows of the second story,

which were catching the late sunlight. When the droning stopped, a legion of gardeners emerged out the wooden door with leaf blowers strapped to their backs. They unharnessed these jet packs and began loading the trucks.

Matt stood holding his box in his arms. One of the gardeners looked up at him, and just as Matt was about to run, the man smiled and gestured to the box with a flip of his chin. "That a package?" he asked.

Matt nodded.

"The lady isn't here. Put it on the doorstep inside."

So Matt stepped into the courtyard lined with burbling fountains and walked to a beveled-glass front door. Upon the steps sat two other boxes, a stuffed manila envelope, two fruit baskets wrapped in cellophane, and a vase of tulips. Behind the door stretched a wall full of framed photographs showing disheveled families stooped outside trailers and abandoned cars. Portraits of extreme poverty. Matt was thrilled to think that these people might be Charlie's relatives. Perhaps the child actor was actually the culmination of his parents' Horatio Alger story. But then Matt saw a Dorathea Lange in the group, and scratched his theory altogether.

In the cul-de-sac outside, the gardeners continued loading the truck and hollering at one another. Matt felt surrounded. He couldn't nonchalantly walk past them again carrying the same box, so he left it beside the largest fruit basket and trotted back outside. One of the men closed the door behind him, and they rumbled off into the dusk in their trucks full of hacked leaves. Matt assessed the high wall and his chances of retrieving the box. There was a flattened soccer ball in front of the next house. Matt tossed it over into his father's courtyard so that if he was caught, he reasoned, he could pretend to be some doltish adolescent retrieving his ball.

He tried to get a foothold on the ornate latch of the door. When he pressed, the door swung open. "Jesus," he said. He was angry that the gardeners would forget to lock up in a city like this. What kind of people left a house wide open? He stepped inside and eased the door back so it was only slightly ajar. Curiosity got the best of him.

Beside the house there was an alley full of garbage cans, and Matt sneaked through it to peek into the backyard—the very yard of the magazine picture, with the turquoise pool and the guest bungalow. He trudged through the ivy to a small pool shed, where he squatted down and surveyed the landscape. He was on a terrace that overlooked hills carpeted with transplanted trees, chimneys poking up between them.

Just as he was looking up at the main house and a bay window with gauzy curtains, he saw a light come on. He scrambled across the ivy and crouched down behind the shed, which was scarcely larger than a chicken coop. It vibrated as a heater activated. Lights flashed on beneath the pool's surface—a bright blue that made the water appear like a tub of Easter egg dye—while a Roman bath that sat above it ignited to red and turned into a fountain that spilled into the pool beneath. A door opened in the house, and a woman dragged out a mat along with some type of sadistic exercise equipment composed of large rubber bands. She was coming his way, and Matt slid open the door to the pool shed and crammed himself inside next to the heating equipment, burning his back until he managed to shield himself with a deflated raft. He pulled the door closed while the woman continued setting up, and in the dimness it took him a few moments to place the strange smell. Among the chlorine bottles there sat what appeared to be a Scotch sampler, a dozen tiny bottles from the Isle of Islay to the Isle of Skye. Sitting upon the heater were other emptied bottles, and as Matt squirmed to adjust himself, they toppled. He found a crack in the boards and peered through: the woman hadn't heard him. He lay still, sweating. His heart felt synchronized to the thumping of the heater. He wasn't sure how long he could stand it, his legs were already cramping, but his grandmother had always told him that bad judgment required some degree of punishment. So here he was in a hot box, waiting.

Squinting as if through a scope, he watched the woman step in and out of a last patch of sunlight in her checkered bathing suit. She lay down, and through the sliver he could see only a single leg rising and falling. Then, with her back to him, she stretched, legs skewed out of his range of vision.

She clicked on a boom box and a song began with a piano riff. Matt recognized it as the kind of milquetoast jazz that played throughout romantic comedies. The woman was doing crunches, breathing in tempo. Soon her legs were kicking frantically. Matt peeked through the sliver as if into a smutty nickelodeon. The woman exercised with such an absurd mixture of anger, determination, and even an occasional groan of pleasure that Matt was becoming aroused, which only worsened his predicament in this tiny space. So he closed his eyes and focused on his worries, the bus ride, the ugly buildings, the terror of his situation; but no, each song on her tape sounded progressively more like a stripper's soundtrack, and she moaned and talked to herself like her own body was a stubborn pony: "Come on now. Get going. Come on."

Was this the woman who was so grounded? The woman who had changed his father's life?

"Don't you quit on me," she said.

A quick peek revealed that she had moved onto a bench, where she was doing crablike arm exercises, breathing slowly now. With each phase of her workout, she became gradually more frustrated, until at one point she kicked the bench over and sat down on a lounge chair, crying. Matt's problem subsided. He was afraid she would find him and beat the living hell out of him. In a hysterical voice she said, "Don't *do* this. I can't deal with this right now. You stand up and you go on. You shut up with this. I won't have it. You shut up now, Barbara."

The workout lasted until past sunset, her movements triggering a motion-sensitive light, and every few minutes she stopped and kicked something. Matt curled into the fetal position beside a bend in the pipes. When the tape ran out, he could hear splashing: hard swimming, the chopping of the crawl so violent it splashed water over the edges.

From the door of the main house, a man's voice began approaching. Matt was so upset with himself for this stupid move, so devastated to hear his father's voice while he, like a troll, was stooped down hiding, that he let his mind roll across a sweep of absurd images. He momentarily believed that he had stuffed himself into his own cardboard box and mailed it to this address.

"I told Ava we'd meet her at eight," said his father. "We have to start getting ready."

His father sounded less authoritative in person, a bit more nasal.

"Remind me to fire the pool man," said his wife. "He put so much chlorine in here, my hair is going to turn green."

"Somebody crashed into me," said Charlie. "But I don't imagine you care."

"Where?" she said, her voice trembling off the pool water that still purled against the edges.

"Just past Sepulveda."

"No, I mean where on the *car?*"

"My neck is bothering me, you know. I might have whiplash."

"You don't have whiplash, Charlie. You have some sort of mental illness. You're a hypochondriac."

"Just because I'm a hypochondriac doesn't mean I can't have a hurt neck. Hypochondriacs are just as injury-prone as everyone else. And paranoid people get followed just as often."

"I'm sure you have a severely hurt neck. I'm just going to finish my laps."

"There's no way you could know from there—just by looking at me. For all you know I'm bleeding internally."

"Then as soon as I get out I'll drive you to the hospital!"

"You can't. We're having dinner with my daughter."

"She can visit you in the emergency room."

"Maybe it's just tension," he said. "I just have these knots in my back. I literally don't know how to relax anymore."

From the sound of his hard-soled shoes, he paced along the edge of the pool as his wife swam. Matt heard the sliding-glass door of the bungalow pull open, and muffled from inside the room West's voice called out, "Did a fax come from PMK?"

The splashing stopped. "What?"

"Did a fax come?"

"Charlie. Let me finish, please. I only have six more to do. Then we can talk all about your horrendous day."

"You don't have to say that so sarcastically. Go. Swim. Don't think twice about it." The splashing resumed and he called out, "Two more laps and I'll throw you a mackerel."

He was mumbling to himself until his wife stepped out of the pool with the sound of dripping water and bare feet on the ground. Through the sliver, Matt watched her towel herself. They returned to the main house.

Matt opened the shed door and gasped at the cool air. An ashen halo of light still hovered over the mountains. From an open balcony door in the main house, Matt could hear them both. As she came close, she was saying, "Because you're driving me crazy, Charlie. You act like this is some lavish dinner engagement—she's just your daughter. Yes, I'm wearing this. She's probably going to be wearing sweatpants. Charles, you're not annoyed at me, you're annoyed at *her*. If this is so difficult, then I say *why go?* All right, all right. Have it your way. I won't say another word, then." Next came the whirring of a blow-dryer.

Before long the house was quiet and the lights went off upstairs and in the hall and in a row of windows downstairs. Matt waited to be sure. A dog barked far away, perhaps the same Yorkshire terrier. A trace of barbecue smoke floated on the air. *Dear Gram,* he thought, *It's my first day and already I'm a burglar and a Peeping Tom.*

While he massaged the cramps from his legs, he heard an electronic ringing coming from inside the bungalow, and he noticed that West had left the sliding-glass door open. He crept slowly toward the opening. The pool was lit, so that wavy shadows were projected onto the walls and the bottoms of trees, making the backyard shimmer like an undersea kingdom.

The ringing continued. Matt peeked into the room and saw a paper unrolling from a fax machine. As his eyes adjusted to the darkness, he could see the walls emblazoned with pictures, and toward a small alcove bathroom there was a shelf of golden trinkets. Matt waved his hand and the motion-detecting light spotlighted the room. The shelf was a collection of awards. A table was cluttered with mail. Several fax pages unrolled and dropped onto the carpet.

When he stepped inside, details came at him in a rush. First he felt like he had entered Charlie's secret vault, but it soon appeared more likely that this bungalow was used to store many of the artifacts that were too embarrassing for the main house. Over the desk there was a picture of Charlie arm in arm with Michael Dukakis. On the wall hung a gift from the Tanzanian government: an elephant tusk mounted on a plaque that read, FOUND, NOT POACHED. A sequined jumpsuit was framed and mounted. The walls were crammed with stills from movies: explosions caught at their widest and reddest; Charlie greased and sweating; Charlie with a machine gun casting off blurred shells. On the shelves, amid a jumble of little golden cameras mounted on stands, there was a row of oblong glass monstrosities called People's Choice Awards.

Matt knew what he wanted. He found the Rolodex on the desk and flipped through it frantically. But unable to find the right address in his growing panic, he took the entire thing and dashed back out into the backyard, through the alley of garbage cans, and went after his box of clothes in the front. The front steps were empty. He couldn't sleep in that pool shed, hoping for another chance. He'd lost all his clothes, his scrapbook, most of his money, and a heap of rapidly deteriorating sandwiches. With nothing but the money in his pocket and a stolen Rolodex, Matt unlocked the door in the front wall and trotted away down a dark, quiet street.

In a gas station bathroom he washed his face and looked at himself in the mirror. His ragged blond hair was long enough in front to reach the tip of his nose, but he wetted it down and combed it back. The light beard beginning on his face was so pale it looked like foam coming through his pores. He faced himself, held an imaginary phone to his ear, and said, "This call may seem completely out of the blue, but I'm your brother."

He grimaced. "I just broke into your father's house and watched a woman do aerobics for two hours. How about having a cup of coffee with me? Oh—and, can I sleep on your couch? Yeah, that'll work. Great plan."

Outside he made a collect call to his grandmother. Without saying hello, she asked if he was in trouble. Matt swallowed and said, "Not really. But I was wondering if you could wire me some money, Grandma. I swear I'll pay it back. I just made sort of an error of judgment."

"Oh, good God, Matthew. You didn't pick up a prostitute, did you?"

"Jesus, Gram. What are you talking about?"

"Tell me you didn't do something foolish like that."

"Right, Grandma. And please send me more money for *crack.*"

"Where are you?"

"I'm in front of a gas station. I am not in trouble, I swear. I just misplaced my things. I made a stupid blunder that could happen to anybody. There's a Western Union right over in this grocery store here."

"You got robbed, didn't you? Some con artist. I'll send you the money on one condition—that you use it to come straight home."

"Straight home? *Grandma.* I've been here about twelve hours. What do you think I'm doing? I'm on a quest here. This is, like, an epic journey. I'm finding my roots. I'm finding my *center.* You know what I'm talking about—I'm dealing with serious *issues* here. You can't rush these things. You don't just find yourself in twelve hours. It takes at least a week."

Grace agreed; but the money couldn't be sent until the following morning. Matt had eighteen dollars on him. He wandered along the streets of San Vicente and Wilshire that night, biding his time in coffee shops. The lack of sleep was taking its toll, but with the surge of caffeine and adrenaline, he had a second wind past midnight and felt like he would never need sleep again. In a diner, sitting safely nestled in a vinyl booth, Matt went through the Rolodex. He had lost track of how many cups he'd drunk—beginning with *lattes* and moving on to chalky black coffee—but his hands were shaking and he had a delirious charge of confidence.

He found Ava West's card. On the diner's phone, sitting beside a fake flagstone wall and a plastic plant, Matt dialed her number with his teeth numb from caffeine, his eyeballs tingling. Right above him, a speaker was blaring a Muzak version of "In-A-Gadda-Da-Vida."

She answered in a sleepy voice. "Are you there? Hello? Is everyone all right? Is this a survey? I'm happy with my current long-distance plan. But I hate this song. Please make it stop." She was hoarse.

He fed quarters into the slot. He was overcome. Her voice was so languid and peaceful.

He listened to her fall back to sleep and he rolled in quarter after quarter. For more than an hour he sat there between rest room doors. He listened to her slow breathing, a soft rhythm, the hint of a snore sometimes and then a smack of lips, and for a while—gloriously—she was exhaling right through her nose into the phone like a breeze. Matt listened and wanted to know who she was and what she was like; and while the waitress refilled his cup and eyed him suspiciously, Matt stayed there stooped down, like a puppy with his ear to a clock.

He had her address. Beside it on the card was written, "+ C and son," making her sound like a repair shop. The waitress asked him, "Are you going to want another refill, sir?"

He put his finger to his lips and whispered, "Shhh. Please."

"What's the matter," said Ava, smacking her lips. "Who is this?" She faded back to sleep, and Matt listened until the breakfast crowd began to fill up the diner.

At eight A.M., Matt picked up the money, and then took the first of several buses east toward Pasadena. The daylight was an affront. He had been up for so long, it seemed like time itself now moved differently, a slow change of light from hour to hour, speeding up at sunrise and sunset. He could barely remember being home in his bed. It felt like years ago, a whole separate life. He dozed on the bus, and when he awakened the driver was shouting at him over the intercom. The day was several shades brighter. He looked out at someplace else he'd never seen before, feeling dreamy and carsick. He asked directions to Altadena, and the driver handed him a handful of bus schedules and shooed him away.

He found a drugstore, and there the last vestiges of a forgotten dream were washed from his head by fluorescent lights. He bought soap, razors, deodorant, a Lakers T-shirt, a bag of tube socks, and a bottle of cologne.

CHAPTER FIVE

While sitting in the makeup chair having a painted latex wound put on his cheek, Charlie could no longer keep his worries to himself. Something about the attention focused on his face made him feel safe, and he believed that any man was more prone to confess something to a barber or a makeup lady than to a therapist or a priest.

Yesterday his personal assistant had found an unmarked box. She had told Charlie about it, laughing, claiming that the box was filled with sandwiches on the top, and that beneath a protective layer of garbage bags lay underwear, pants, T-shirts, and tube socks.

"Someone sent me a troubling care package," Charlie said.

"And what was in this *care* package," said the makeup lady. She was an elderly British woman who exaggerated the gentility of her accent in order to please Americans.

Long after his assistant had gone home last night, Charlie crept out to the pool-house office and went through the box. There was a scrapbook filled with tabloid clippings about Charlie's career, with frantic notes in the margins. On the waistband of each pair of underwear—clean white Jockeys—was written the name *M. Ravendahl.*

"Someone's underwear," he said.

"Well, a man in your position ought to expect a few packages like that. Did she send a picture as well?"

"No, it wasn't like that. They were boys' underwear."

"Oh, I see. Charlie, listen, don't worry unduly about it. It's as natural as anything else and it means nothing as far as you're concerned. I, for one, think you're *very* masculine."

"No, no, no. The point is, I know the person who sent this. Except there was no address on it, so I have this terrible feeling that this guy came to my house."

"Another day, another stalker. You're all finished, Charlie. You've got a fabulous gaping wound on your cheek."

"Do you think it's too much?"

"No, I think you're as handsome as ever."

Today was going to be unusually difficult for Charlie, and he tried to put last night's shock out of his mind. He had another talk-show appearance scheduled for that afternoon, so he wouldn't make the wrap party. This meant that he'd have to endure all the good-byes and hugging and brownnosing while he was still on the set. They came at him from all sides: sweaty ADs whose names he couldn't remember; hairdressers turning sentimental while brandishing an aerosol can. Charlie assumed they would ridicule him behind his back at the party, so he couldn't enjoy being everyone's best friend for these last hours.

His driver was the worst of all. Charlie first hired Sloan on a picture called *Without Remorse* as a way to ensure that his daughter didn't starve. Surprisingly, Camilla was gun-shy about directly asking for money, despite the fact that the three of them lived in a tiny house on virtually no income. Charlie pictured it in medieval squalor: a crooked old cottage where they danced at night around a fire and shared leaden cups of moonshine and spit-roasted whatever pigeon they could slingshot from a tree. No one in his family knew how to survive. He hated to think where they would be without him: out combing the beach with metal detectors, living in abandoned lifeguard stations, and foraging through kelp at low tide. He was the last line of defense for these people, but he was never rewarded with a simple *thank-you*. Instead he received endless toadying.

Today, as Charlie was stepping out of the makeup trailer, Sloan threw him a surprise party. Charlie had a ring of paper around his neck to keep the base off his collar. The crew was gathered beside a giant wrapped box. When Sloan got them all to sing "For He's a Jolly Good Fellow," Charlie wanted to hide under his trailer.

"You're the man, Chuck. You're man. I'm just honored to be around you." Sloan put his arm over Charlie, and with that nervous, acidic breath, he said, "I can't tell you how much you mean to me. I prize your friendship, Chuck. They could stop paying me and I'd still love this job. Let's hear it. Is this guy the best or what?"

The crew clapped lethargically.

"We just wanted you to know, Chuck, that it is—as always, man—a total thrill to work with you."

"That's kind of you."

Sloan urged Charlie to open the package. Charlie stepped forward, worried that some jittery stripper-gram was about to burst out of it. He opened it to find a pile of bubble wrap. He gave the sheets to the crew, who divvied it up and popped it incessantly. At the bottom of the box lay oxygen tanks and coils of tubing.

"Wow," said Charlie. "Some kind of life-support system."

"This is the complete state-of-the-art diving setup, Chuck. SCUBA. Self-Contained Underwater Breathing Apparatus. This is what the best in the world use."

"Imagine what I'll be able to do with it, then."

Sloan led another round of applause and then the crew dispersed, calling to Charlie, "Catch a big fish," and, "Go find a pretty little mermaid."

Sloan put his arm over Charlie's shoulders and walked him back toward the trailer.

"Listen, Chuck. I need to talk to you about something. I've been really nervous about this, so bear with me. This is more of a ceremonial gift than a practical one."

"All right. Then thank you for the ceremony."

"Right. But it did run me pretty much all of my salary. Which is fine, I'm not expecting you to fully reimburse me. God knows, I already appreciate everything you've done for me over the years, Chuck. I mean that. The reason you and I work so well together is that there's this genuine respect between the two of us. Now I'm on to something here, and I don't want you to turn up your nose. Don't just pooh-pooh my idea. Hear me out. All right?"

"I don't just pooh-pooh everything. Not anymore."

"I've gotten together with some investors. Some very respected, successful, one-hundred-percent-legitimate investors."

"You must have found the only ones."

"These men are willing to put up a large portion of the backing I need. In fact, they're willing to match whatever I bring to the table. Now, don't stop me. Like I said, the gift is ceremonial. It's symbolism, Chuck. Because I know you're an idea man, like myself."

"Sloan, I got to get ready for the next shot. My head is all over the place. I had a sort of crisis last night. Everything is happening at once."

"The Azores, Chuck. The Azores."

Charlie waited for him to explain. He hated it when people expected him to know all about obscure things.

"Do you know what that is, Chuck?"

"When the moon hits your eye like a big pizza pie. Right?"

"No, no. That's *amore*. I'm talking about an island chain. A great Portuguese stronghold. It's a repository of wealth beyond your wildest imagination. Even by Hollywood standards. Years of sunken galleons carrying everything from precious coins to nutmeg. Riches from all over the world. Historical treasures. And it's right there. Everybody knows where it is, but nobody has the finances to just go and get it."

"So *I* have to get it?"

"Like I said, the scuba gear was ceremonial. But I know people who have the diving experience. We could get it off the ground. I'm talking about hundreds of millions of dollars—and a rare historical find to boot—just for a few-hundred-thousand-dollar investment."

"You're really crazy, aren't you? You need a hundred thousand dollars to go snorkeling?"

"It's sophisticated stuff. You need sonar, you need salvage equipment. You don't just dive down there with a shovel and scoop it up."

"I could really use a shovel for this story." Charlie leaned against his trailer and sighed. "Listen. Today is a big day for me. It's impossible for me to . . ." He covered his face and shook his head.

"Assimilate all the information?"

"My head is a big jumble. I'm so tense right now I could snap."

"Right. This is a big decision. I understand that."

"So, why don't you . . ."

"Give you a little time to relax and consider all of the various details."

"Yes, that. Thank you, Sloan. Thank you for everything. I'm going into my trailer now."

Sloan opened the door for him. He said, "I'll have the grips store the equipment in the trailer closet. For now. By the way, did you enjoy that kiwi?"

"Yes, yes. Fabulous," said Charlie. "Just fabulous."

Safely in his trailer, Charlie reflected on all of Sloan's schemes over the years. He was a pure huckster who in another era would have stood on a stage and peddled health tonics to gawking spectators. Years ago he had borrowed six grand from Charlie to start a shelter for fad pets that had gone out of fashion. He filled his house with iguanas, descented skunks, ferrets, and potbellied pigs. He believed the venture would be like buying a promising stock at its low point: eventually the ferret craze would begin again and he'd sell his vermin for profit. But even if this had been the case, Sloan grew so attached to the little beasts that he no longer considered selling them. Instead, he devised a heroic plan to reintroduce each to its natural habitat—a quest that ended tragically when Sloan was detained in an Ecuadorian airport with two sea iguanas, both confiscated by men who "didn't know the first thing about animals."

By the time the grips trundled in the scuba tank and dropped it into his closet, Charlie had a throbbing headache. After all this, today he deserved a drink. *Anyone* would. He found a PA and bribed the kid to run out for a bottle of Baker's bourbon, but when the boy said that he was only twenty, Charlie grew exasperated and said, "What do we pay you little shits for, anyway?" He ordered the boy to find him some potent cold medicine, and that afternoon, waiting in his hot trailer before the final setup and his ride to Burbank, Charlie luxuriated on a cocktail of Alka-Seltzer PM spiked with the last of his hidden vodka.

Traffic was at a standstill coming into the valley, so Charlie gave his preinterview over the phone in the limousine. He spoke to an obsequious young woman who kept repeating "Excellent, excellent," until she abruptly lapsed into the tone of a therapist. She asked, "What was your childhood like, Charlie? With former child actors like yourself, he usually likes to talk about your first kiss. You know. Was it on-screen or was it real?"

The bar in the limousine was stocked, and Charlie poured himself a shallow glass of Maker's Mark. He said, "What makes you think kisses on-screen aren't real?"

She apologized for the wording, and in an almost querulous tone asked for the stories of his long-forgotten first career.

His debut role was as an infant model in a series of pictorial ads for a formula company that eventually went bankrupt. "I grew up with a whole heap of allergies, and I blame every one of them on that company," he said. "They say that when a child isn't breast-fed, he's prone to allergies."

Perhaps because he was sniffling constantly, the majority of Charlie's parts had revolved around his sickliness. He was at his cutest with a thermometer in his mouth, and in countless ads he was doped up with different cold medicines, swigging spoonfuls of syrup, living in an oil slick of cherry-flavored cough suppressants, chewing through mounds of aspirin shaped like barnyard animals. He was a listless, fey child who was oddly beautiful in his pallor.

At seven, Charlie had full-time work on a soap opera in which he played a mute child stricken with several illnesses that changed from season to season. His on-set tutor, he recalled, was a lovely woman in her twenties with a childlike quality, and Charlie used to imagine that the trailer compartment in which they studied was a secret hideout. She had puffy blond hair and wore clouds of perfume and Charlie loved her. He loved how she stared down over his shoulder and breathed upon his neck as he transcribed cursive letters into a workbook. She took his hand and guided it over the dips of *M*'s and the loops of *O*'s.

"And she was your first kiss?"

"No, no. God, no. You see, it's all connected, though. I never had any education whatsoever. I'm a complete autocrat. Everything I know I learned with my own two hands." After work on the soap, Charlie tested at kindergarten level. He couldn't read, could barely copy those giant letters, had no arithmetic skills, and stubbornly refused to listen. His parents couldn't bear the thought of their ten-year-old languishing in a nursery school, waiting for nap time while he sat Indian-legged on a carpet, so they placed him for six months in a school for children with developmental problems. The room was full of children with thick glasses, patches over their eyes, imitating animals instead of speaking. A pigeon-toed girl chased Charlie every morning and licked his face. "I suppose you could say *she* was my first kiss." There was a row of boys who couldn't control their bladders, and each day one would spontaneously break out crying while the others scooted away from him. There was a boy who took off his clothes and banged on the window with such hysteria that Charlie feared the world was coming to an end.

"This is all very interesting, Mr. West. But I don't know if it really works in our format."

A few years later he was the unbearably cute wisecracker on a sitcom called *The Mouths of Babes*. There was an immediate shift in his life. Charlie had associated the school with the helplessness of childhood, so he flung himself at the new job with a determination to become an adult. The show was about a classic nuclear family who sang popular songs. It was a musical version of *The Donna Reed Show,* and at the end of each episode, the moral of the story was happily sung by a bunch of adorable kids who danced around like the Von Trapps. Off-camera, Charlie flirted with the teenage actresses, the show's mother, the script supervisor, and the wardrobe ladies. He was a miniature lounge lizard, snapping his fingers and winking at grown women, calling everyone "honey pie" and "baby doll." He pinched asses. He said, "Hubba, hubba." Everyone laughed and mussed his hair. It amused them to see these repulsive characteristics mimicked by a small child. "I used to sneak behind the set and make out with my sister. The actress who *played* my sister, you understand. Eventually one of the grips found us and we were both given chaperones for the rest of the season."

The show had a decent run, and Charlie's school-free ride— this time with a male tutor who often fell asleep with a cigarette burning in his mouth—might have gone on longer had Charlie not hit an early and miserably awkward puberty at thirteen. Up until then he had been supporting both parents. His father had once been able to make a living as a stuntman, but after one head injury too many, he had retired in his early forties. He and his wife hired a series of nannies to look after Charlie while they lived in an ever-expanding cocktail hour. They entertained an onslaught of fringe celebrities, set designers, and writers. They would sit around a small kidney-shaped pool, penned in by dying willows. They described, again and again, their few films. Both of Charlie's parents were such merciless name droppers that it became their own language. Celebrities simply replaced nouns, verbs, and adjectives. His mother's stories, always punctuated with a laugh that turned into a smoker's cough, rolled over the pool and echoed in the backyard as dusk fell.

These cocktail parties took on a different tone as Charlie went a few years without work. While at an experimental school for troubled teens, he was unable to land a single role. *Of course Charlie would still be working right now if he hadn't gone Mickey Rooney on us all of a sudden.* The parties began to seem like a gathering of stubborn colonials having a last drink before the coup. They sat around the pool later into the night, soaking their swollen feet, the sky streaked red all around them, and then, in darkness, they would sit quietly, waiting.

Somewhere in his memory, Charlie attached those evenings to his father's death. That look on the man's face—what now? what next?—haunted him all his life. When Charlie was sixteen, his father died of throat cancer. "It was the worst year of my life."

"We're not going to have time to get into all of this, Mr. West."

His mother sold the house and they lived a painful year in a furnished apartment full of stagnant air and wall-to-wall carpeting. She would go weeks without speaking. She aged decades in that year. She broke her hip falling down the entry stairs, and afterward she started taking painkillers each day with a Long Island iced tea. She slurred her criticisms of TV shows and fell asleep at four P.M. After a year of trying to fight his way through high school and receiving Ds and Fs, Charlie began loading his mother into the car and taking her along on auditions. When he landed a role as a young auto mechanic at seventeen—a lifesaving role—he needed his mother to sign the consent forms. Her hand shook. She couldn't hold the pen. She started to cry again, and Charlie picked up her hand and placed it beside the X and guided her pen in broad cursive strokes.

"Well, Mr. West, we don't necessarily *have* to talk about your early career. You could talk about your marriage. You must have some funny observations about that."

Backstage at the show, all the publicists and producers were scurrying around, promising that Charlie was in for a big surprise. Charlie hated surprises. His paranoia returned, and however illogical it was, he imagined the host bringing out his lost son. The boy would wave to the crowd, perhaps wearing those glaring white briefs, and he would then beat Charlie senseless while the applause sign flashed out of control, prompting a standing ovation from the crowd. He knew he was being absurd, but that ragged feeling was back. He was one slip away from being the scorn of America.

Once out in the hot lights, in front of an eager crowd, the interview went smoothly. The cackling host did the majority of the talking. The surprise turned out to be a clip from an embarrassing Disney movie Charlie had done in the mid-seventies. Everyone laughed at his long hair and his goofy mannerisms, while Charlie clapped like it was the funniest prank ever conceived.

"You're a great sport," the host told him during the break. He escorted Charlie to the curtain. Charlie was then surrounded by a team of handlers, who led him out to his waiting limousine. A tangle of arms waved good-bye; the voices blended together into a cacophony of compliments, until he slammed the door and sealed himself into the dark car. It was only a few minutes before the silence was equally unbearable.

He called his assistant back at home. "What about this box?" he asked. "Any news?"

She told him that there were muddy footprints around the pool, and that several items were missing from the office. She had done some research. According to Westec Security, a party on Anita Street had gotten out of hand. A local gang called the PLB—one of those upper-class gangs hoping to make a name for themselves—had smashed car windows, slashed tires, and stolen mailboxes.

"That's wonderful," said Charlie. "I'm sure that's what it is. We just got one of their lunch boxes. Or survival kits. Nevertheless, we better not tell Barbara anything. Okay? Not a word about the box. Scout's honor."

He told his assistant to go home, and that evening he headed toward the bungalow, avoiding his wife, who was in the kitchen lecturing the new cook. God help him if Barbara ever smelled a trace of booze. Alcohol, she always said, was murder on the fat metabolism. The box was in the office, sitting amid the piles of his mail. His assistant apparently ran out of tasks during the day, so she had taken to organizing the fan letters by the personality defects she believed they exhibited; but this box remained, as of yet, uncategorized. He took it and sneaked it out to the small pool shed, where he hid it alongside all his tiny bottles. Just as he was closing the door, he noticed that most of the bottles had been tipped onto their sides.

Across the pool and the low branches of a maple, Barbara was now pacing behind the windows with a cordless phone. She was wearing her leotard and had her ponytail strung through the back of a Hartmann Plymouth ball cap. Charlie was not sure if she'd discovered his hiding place—really more a collection of souvenirs than a bar—or if his worst fears had just been confirmed. Wedged between his two lives, he watched his pretty wife in the lit rooms of the house and vowed that he would tell her everything. His entire life previous to her had been reduced to a brief biographical note, a list of vices, a difference in body fat and measurements; but now it was swelling up again to overtake him.

He would explain everything, if only he could remember, and Barbara would feel even more strongly that she'd rescued him.

They were meeting friends that evening at an Italian restaurant on San Vicente, and Charlie tried to confess to his wife. "I've made some very poor decisions in my life, Barbara. Not *decisions*—because they weren't decisions. I was just going with a sort of flow, but it was a very, very bad flow."

"Charlie, if you're going to start bemoaning your career again, then I've heard this routine. Everything you do is aimed at the teenage libido, and your target audience is a focus group for Clearasil. Blah, blah, blah. I'm not listening, and I don't agree. You've done fine work, Charlie, and you'll continue to do fine work. Now, try to cheer up before they get here." She held out a breadstick like a cigar, twiddling it in her fingers.

The waiter came and Barbara sent him away, then looked back at Charlie with a concerned look. Outside the broad windows, their dinner guests were approaching across the grassy median.

"I've done some things that are hard to explain, Barbara. But

I think they're coming back to haunt me. I think my old life is coming back to bite me in the ass."

"Well, please try to keep quiet about it. I don't like arguing in front of company. You can think about your life and the terrible things you seem to believe you've done, but tonight you're going to be your charming self."

"I've stepped on people. I've abandoned people and I've acted like nothing else was important but me and my career, and I've hidden from everything. I'm a weak person, Barbara. I'm sick about it, but I just had to tell you. I'm a liar and a cheat. And this is payback."

"Somebody's blood sugar is falling fast."

"I think someone was in our yard last night, Barbara. I think someone was watching us."

Smiling and speaking through her teeth, she said, "They're coming. Now cut it out."

Their dinner companions stopped to greet friends at another table. Barbara made sure they weren't looking, then squeezed Charlie's hand and said, "Will you *please* have a good time? I'm sure whoever broke in is a film critic who's already seen *Born Ready* and hates it, and I'm sure your whole life is falling apart and everybody is coming to get you. Are you happy now? Because from where I'm sitting I see a wonderful, handsome man, who's open and caring and generous to every freeloader in town. I see a world that adores him. I see a great life and one heck of a career. So, from my vantage point here, *honey,* it starts to sound a wee bit spoiled to hear you talk on and on about how dismal it all is—just because there's some random idiots here and there who don't worship you. Everything is just fine and I wish you would accept that."

The companions had greeted their friends and now were heading toward Charlie and Barbara. Barbara looked up and said, "Well, hello there, strangers."

"You're going to find out a few things about me," said Charlie.

"We haven't ordered yet. Sit down, sit down. Oh, Charlie, please stop pouting like that."

"I wish you knew what I was talking about, Barbara."

"Oh, don't listen to him. He's carrying the weight of the world over there. He's just finished shooting one film today and he's already running around promoting another one. We're so rarely on time, you know. Ten minutes and his blood sugar is already plummeting. Try to relax, Charlie. Everybody loves you. *Don't we, folks?*"

By late afternoon Ava had sold only some weathered camping gear. She was bringing sunblock out to Chris and her mother when she saw a young man carrying pool balls bunched into his Lakers shirt. He was placing them one by one onto the lawn, as delicately as if they were eggs, until Camilla thanked him and told him to just leave them anywhere. Something about his mannerisms immediately drew Ava's attention. With a sunburned face and almost white hair he couldn't have been more than eighteen or nineteen, but he scrutinized everything in the yard with the intensity of a detective. He read the labels on Barbara's diet powder, checked the sizes on all the men's shirts, and stood in front of the painted backdrops like they were great works of art. Strangest of all, he thumbed through her college textbooks and appeared to be reading the margin notes.

"That kid over there is giving me the creeps, Mother. Get rid of him."

"You have no idea how to run a business, Ava."

Ava continued cleaning the garage and tried to ignore him, but every time she peeked out into the sunlight, he was still there, looking more sunburned and more enthralled with some magazine or videotape. She overheard him say to Camilla, "You have an awful lot of *workout* tapes. I think I know this woman on the cover."

"Oh—she's just one of those fanatics. You have to talk to my daughter about it. She's the local authority."

After he had snooped around for nearly an hour and a half, Ava became irritated. She knew garage sales were beacons for the maladjusted: middle-aged Trekkies waddling around in search of William Shatner novels; doddering old men in floppy tennis hats, desperately in need of hood ornaments or Boy Scout paraphernalia. But this kid didn't seem old enough to have developed such hardened eccentricities. His fascination with her things was troubling.

She returned to the pool table and began pulling at it again, scooting it a few inches with loud scrapes. The young man came over to her and said, "Can I help you with that?"

The scent of cologne on him was suffocating.

"Oh, no. No, thank you. I'm just fine."

She heaved and scooted it a few inches more. He was staring at her. He had a square, handsome face, with large blue eyes that seemed nervous and bewildered. His hair had been recently wetted and combed but was already rising into a cowlick, and his Lakers T-shirt still had the price tag poking out of its collar.

"Is there something I could help *you* with?" she asked.

"It's heavy because it's so waterlogged."

"Aha," said Ava. "That's probably true. Are you looking for anything specifically over there, or just browsing?"

"I don't mean to get in the way," he said. He shifted his weight constantly when he spoke. "It's just that this whole *garage sale*—it's really a stroke of luck for me. A godsend. Right? Because I'm new here, and I got rolled yesterday. Ripped off. *Poof*—everything I own. *Sayonara*." He saluted at the sky above, then continued, "My clothes, my books, my whole life. I'm a man without a country."

"That's terrible."

"Major tragedy. So I saw that you were having a sale, and I just thought: *jackpot*."

"Well, I'm not as much of a pushover as you might think."

"No, no. I didn't mean that. Oh! And I was really impressed by all of the *art*. That's yours, right? That's incredible. Really elaborate. I was just staring at it and I was transported. I mean that. To a whole different time.''

"Mom! You think you might want to help me bring out some of these old board games?''

"Oh, *I'll* do that,'' he said.

"No, really. I appreciate your enthusiasm, but we've got all this under control here. Thank you.'' He stood there, smiling awkwardly, and Ava felt a pang of guilt. Perhaps he was just some lost rube, wandered astray from a theme park and desperate for company. "I really *am* sorry you got ripped off. I suppose you're going to hang around and wait for our prices to fall.''

"They're falling?''

"We're slashing prices on everything,'' she said, and lifted an edge of the pool table. He stumbled around the clutter and lifted the other edge. He began walking so quickly that Ava had to take rapid baby steps to keep up with him. "Okay, okay. Put it down here.'' She stopped and wiped the hair from her face, then said, "Well, I'll tell you what. Because I'm going for worst sales-man of the year, why don't you just go over and pick out some clothes. On the house.''

"Whose are they?''

"Listen to this guy. What do you want—the written history?'' She paced over to the table and started sorting through shirts and jeans. "Let's see. Boyfriend, boyfriend.'' She threw aside a horizontal-striped T-shirt and a series of progressively more retro button-ups. "Boyfriend, my *mother's* boyfriend, boyfriend.''

"Man. How many boyfriends have you had?''

"Only a few. But they each come with several outfits.''

For another half hour he tried on shirts in front of a mirror as the sun began to sink down past the houses. Dusk came and he was modeling for Camilla and Chris, who would applaud certain choices. He mimicked a model on a ramp, then a J. Crew ad with sweaters slung over his shoulder. Camilla and Chris laughed at some of his costumes, especially when he tied a sweater around his neck and posed with a broken tennis racquet. Chris became so excited at the new game of dress-up that he began to stumble around in oversized shirts, a game that didn't satisfy his gust of enthusiasm until he began hitting the young man's leg with a rubber snake. This eternal browser—this guest who wouldn't leave even as darkness was falling, gnats were swarming around the furniture, and sprinklers were hissing to life on the adjacent lawns—acted as if they might never get rid of him. Ava paced in her garage, now lit with a fresh fluorescent bulb, wringing her hands and trying to figure out what on earth this stranger was doing. Was her son so starved for entertainment that he would cling to any goofball off the street? Under the auspices of cleaning up, she began making trips back out to the lawn. Chris had grabbed onto his leg. He sat on his foot and rode it as the young man made huge robotic footsteps.

"Mother, could you take Chris inside and give him his bath? I'll take care of everything out here." Camilla groaned, climbed out of her chair, and tried to pry Chris off the visitor's leg. She patted the young man's shoulder and said, "I hope you find your things. Chris, thank this person for hauling you around."

He had settled upon a weathered tan corduroy jacket, a professorial one that smelled of mothballs and may have belonged to Sloan once upon a time. A tattered pair of jeans were slung over his shoulder. He'd tied the pant legs, and the jeans were loaded like a satchel full of items: Barbara's diet powder, some of Ava's old books. "Listen," he said. "I know this is all really out of the blue. But I would love the chance to talk. If you and I could just sit someplace for a few minutes, I promise you—it'll be worth it. You see, we have something really important in common. You might not know it. Anyplace would be fine. I could buy you a cup of coffee or something."

Ava smiled and shook her head. She began refolding all the clothes on the table. "Aren't you a bit young to be doing this?"

"It isn't like that, Ava. I really have some important things to say, and this isn't the place."

"Is this what happens when you give someone a pair of pants?"

"Look, I'm not the world's greatest communicator. But even *I* know there are certain things that have to be done with some tact. You don't just go to somebody's door like you're Publisher's Clearing House and say, 'Surprise!' There are some really *significant* moments in life. You don't want to be having one right when the sprinklers come on. That didn't sound right at all."

"Did I win the sweepstakes?"

"Let me try this a different way. I'm not some weirdo off the street. Well, technically I did come off the street, yes, and I am sort of a weirdo. I accept that. But you see, I have a connection to you."

"A cosmic one. Right?"

"My name is Matthew Ravendahl. Maybe you've already heard of me?"

"Of course," said Ava. "I'm your biggest fan. Now—I have to go and take care of my son. Okay? So as much as I'm flattered by this strange little presentation, you're going to have to move along. Besides, I certainly don't think you need a cup of coffee. It's been great meeting you, and I wish you luck with your . . . acting career."

He covered his face. "I'm not an actor. I just think it would be very rewarding for both of us if we just sat at a table and talked for a minute."

Ava sighed. She felt a twinge of curiosity about him, another of those droves of people drawn here by the tragic gravity of this town. He was actually trembling. She was no longer irritated, but rather fascinated by the energy and nervousness that was pouring off him.

"Okay," she said, and she began dragging one of the tables back toward the garage. The two of them arranged chairs around it. Ava told him to sit down. She said, "I warn you, though. My mother can scream louder than anyone in America."

"It won't be necessary. I'm a total gentleman."

"We may have to cut this tea party a bit short. My son is being a little difficult about his bath this evening."

She had brought the visitor a cup of tea while she cradled a mug full of Merlot. He sat at the rickety card table, which wobbled as he rested his elbows upon it. She wedged a rain-warped picture book beneath one of the legs. All around the garage lay the debris of the unsuccessful sale, and Ava began sweeping up the pieces of a spilled jigsaw puzzle. "Okay," she said. "Let's hear this remarkable story of yours."

"I've been rehearsing this in my head for a long time," he said. "So forgive me if it sounds a little like a speech."

"Go for it. Give me the whole infomercial."

"My name is Matthew Ravendahl and I'm from a small town just outside of Leavenworth, Washington. There's a chance you've heard of me."

"Nope," she said, fixated on her sweeping. "Doesn't ring a bell."

"So you haven't heard of me. That's all right." He took a deep breath, and something about his nervousness made Ava look up at him. He began speaking quickly. "I grew up alone with my grandmother most of the time, and I didn't know the other half of my family. I can see that you're a skeptical person by nature, and I did have more scientific proof, except that all of my stuff was stolen. Not actually stolen so much as misplaced. But I can tell you that a paternity case was settled out of court, and my family got child-support checks with an address in Century City. One of the reasons it was settled so easily out of court—even though my mother *did* have her share of admirers—was because, you see, even for a standard ABO blood test it was pretty straightforward. My father and I both have AB negative blood, which is rare to begin with, and there's a good chance you've got it too. But maybe I don't know you well enough yet to talk about your blood type, so the long and the short of what I'm saying is that I'm on a serious quest here. Right? This is the most important thing in the world for me, and I wanted to find *you*. I tried to find my father but it didn't work. The place was like . . . a training center for landscapers or something."

She looked away from him for a moment, counted the steps between her and the door to the kitchen. Through her mind went a rush of stalker stories. There was once a man who dressed in a cape, then broke into homes, spray-painting her father's name onto every wall and reorganizing the rooms in demented ways: he put the frozen peas in the medicine bottles and stacked chairs in the bathtub. When he was finally arrested, he claimed to be Charlie West. But a thread of hope ran through her as well, and she scrutinized this young man's expressions, glancing back at his blue eyes and feeling an inexplicable hope that the world could truly be this full of surprises.

"You called me last night, didn't you?"

"Yeah," he said. "Sorry. I would have called you a long time ago, but you have an unlisted phone number."

"And you're trying to say that . . . *we're* that family you're looking for."

"I'm saying that I'm your brother. But I understand if that upsets you, or if you don't want to believe me right away."

She pulled up a chair and sat down across from him. It was a baffling experience—a person who moments ago was a complete stranger, a passerby, a bit of irritating background at this sale, was now telling her something that could potentially change her life. She had the dizzy feeling of too sudden a change, and she tried to orient herself with details. She looked closely at his features: his broad cheeks, his light eyebrows and eyes almost as pale blue as a husky's, and opaque blond hair split and drifting upward at the rough edges. All these isolated features, abstractly familiar, didn't make him any less a stranger. Nor could she so quickly sort out the good from the bad in this sweep of emotions. If this were true, she would be furious at her mother and father for hiding it from her. But she was likewise amazed at how emphatically she hoped it were true: a little brother, in all his awkward splendor, as if fashioned from the mess of a garage sale.

"I'm not saying I don't believe you. *Matthew.* In fact, something about it actually seems to make sense to me. Maybe because it's the fantasy of the only child. But I can't believe that my family would keep a secret like that from me for . . . how old are you?"

"Eighteen."

She squinted at him. She was almost angry at him for even the possibility that he might be a fraud, but she calmed herself and promised to wait. "And you're traveling around all by your-self? You're insane. And you went to my father's house?"

"It was a dumb maneuver. But back home I'd called the place on the checks, you know, and they weren't very helpful. They were on a street called Avenue of the Stars."

"Yeah. Avenue of the Stars' Accountants."

In the kitchen Chris was wailing again, scampering around naked and wet, having escaped from his bath. Ava said, "Mom! Do I have to come in there again?"

"It's under control," said Camilla.

"One night a week I don't give him his bath, and all hell breaks loose. He's really a very sweet-natured kid."

"You seem like a good mother."

With a flourish she finished the wine in her mug. "No won-der you're such a fidgety little guy. I thought you were casing the house. Just saying hypothetically that I believed you—you must be angry. You must just want to *kill* him. You know, my father can honestly be one hell of a jerk."

"I guess," said Matt. "I just have a feeling like I have to meet him. I've read about him and seen his movies and whatever else, but at a certain point I just knew I had to see who he *really* was."

"Let me know what you find."

"My grandmother always says it's useless to hate a person's weaknesses."

"So she's now the patron saint of what? Bad actors?"

Matt had a laugh that was like a suppressed sneeze.

"Okay. And you said all this about blood types—well, would you believe I'm one of those people who doesn't remember my blood type? So you don't have to get this technical with me. You're not a clone, right? So we can dispense with all the DNA jargon. I'll believe you if you tell me the story. Just talk." She was fixated on all of his flustered mannerisms, watching the way he furrowed his brow, bit his lower lip, and nodded continu-ously. She was not accustomed to watching a person so closely. "I *want* to believe you actually. I mean, you're a little jittery, but you don't froth at the mouth. If you're a stalker, I suppose you get some credit for having such an elaborate story. Just explain some things to me. You're from Butterworth, Washington, or wherever, the middle of nowhere—no offense—and how exactly does my father *impregnate* your mother. Oops, there's an unfortunate choice of words. How does a romantic moment occur between these two people? How would they even meet? My father never meets anybody that isn't in the industry."

"I know the stories I've heard. It's sort of a legend by now."

"Then fire when ready."

Matt leaned forward and composed himself, and from the expression on his face, Ava already figured out the first clue. He was about to present what looked like a testimonial, and Ava nodded. Of course, he was conceived in that mysterious year when her father had vanished to take care of all those "grown-up" problems. Before he finished the first sentence, she noticed that awful legacy: a tiny indentation in his chin.

PART TWO

KING FIVE

AND THE

CHRISTIAN

RADIO

FRONTIER

Charlie West arrived at The Briar Patch on an autumn day in 1979. A driver opened the back door of a sedan and out of it wafted a juniper smell so strong that it drew patients out of their shacks. The driver helped West to his feet from the backseat.

"Get him into the lodge," said Grace. "He's got to sign in."

West walked with a jerk, as if his leg froze with every third step. He stopped at the brook trickling down the hillside, calmly removed his tan corduroy jacket, then knelt and vomited into the stream.

Sadie Ravendahl was working that autumn as a porter with a few of her classmates. The first evening Grace asked them to search the actor's bags. "This fellow here is going to try to smuggle in his own distillery."

Sadie recorded in her diary a list of what West brought: "A golf bag—like *we* have a golf course!!!? A whole bunch of bikini underwear—ha ha ha—what a homo! The script for some movie about a stuntman that Jess and I read out loud and it really was *not* good AT ALL! I tried to tell him that there was no golf course, but he was puking like crazy, so I go, 'Thanks a lot for the tip,' because I figure caddies are supposed to get tips. Right? And he goes, 'Whatever kid.' "

Word of his presence spread rapidly through town, and at school, Sadie's teachers wanted to know about his condition.

"I'm afraid that's confidential," she said.

"Good Lord," said her history teacher. "It's not like he's J. Edgar Hoover. He's only an actor."

Throughout her day, the other seniors wanted to know what West was like—if he was handsome in person, if he was shorter than she had expected, or if he had any exceptionally foul habits. They were impressed that she had seen him vomit and had handled his underwear, but they wanted to know more.

Sadie tired of repeating the same stories to everyone, so she walked home alone one day. She took a shortcut down the embankment and through the trees to emerge from the forest onto the soggy back lawn of the clinic. West was sitting on the porch, cradling a glass. When he saw her, he was startled and spilled his drink onto his pants. Sadie would later write in her diary, "He looked at me as if I was some kind of beautiful wood nymph."

"It's only water," he said.

"I don't care what it is." Before stepping onto the lawn, she removed her purple shoes. She tiptoed across to the steps, where she then fussily picked the wet grass blades off her feet. Her toenails were painted bright red, chipped around the edges.

"You're not some spy, are you?" said the actor.

"You're supposed to be supervised."

"Tell me you're not some kind of ashram spy—hired to follow me around. Make sure I'm not comfortable. Maybe you're some sort of candy striper."

"I live here," she said. "I carried your stupid golf clubs yesterday."

"Of course. That changes everything. Sorry. I'm so wound up, I don't know who to trust around here."

With her feet now clean, Sadie knocked her shoes against the steps to get the pine needles off the bottoms.

"Are those new shoes or something?"

"I hate getting crap all over them."

"They're very nice. Very *you*."

Sadie scooted over and smelled his drink. "How did you get that in here, you scum?"

"You're not a spy, right? You got to promise this is our secret. I'm supposed to be in that little tool shed as it is. Swear you won't tell. The magic golf bag. A golf bag has got a lot of pockets, kid. Unknown, mysterious pockets."

"That's why you brought that! It was a minibar."

"I have a whole bunch of those little tiny airplane bottles," he said. "You know? Those little tiny ones for degenerate elves. You know what I'm talking about? You ever been on a plane?"

"*Yes,* I've been on a plane."

"You have? When?"

She stared off at the forest and grimaced.

"That's the reason I came up here in the first place," said West. "I'm not a drunk, you know—I just had to come up here to satisfy this director. See, I'm going to be doing a real movie, I mean, a decent film, for once, and the director and the studio—everybody—they told me I had to get into rehab before rehearsals start. Well, I don't have to tell you, this place is famous for being easy. I mean, there are some places that are like goddamn sanitariums. Mattresses on the walls."

"You know you're an alky, you liar."

He put up two fingers like a Boy Scout.

Sadie lay down on her side. "I can never get anything past my mother. She has X-ray eyes when it comes to me."

Even with her loose blouse, the position showed the sharp cut of her small waist curving up into the sloped denim over her hip. She bent her elbow against the porch boards and supported her head in her cupped hand. Hair spilled over one cheek; her collarbone slanted across two open buttons. West said, "I wish I had X-ray eyes."

She sat up and slapped his knee. "You're so terrible. Don't try to flirt with me."

"I wouldn't think of it."

"So, how many bottles did you steal from this big, amazing airplane?"

"All of them," he said, smirking.

"The stewardesses didn't notice, I guess."

"She was the one that offered. She was my accomplice. My partner in crime. People just offer me things wherever I go. It's a curse."

"*I'm* not offering you anything."

"That's because you're a person of great moral strength," he said.

She made a blowing sound and rolled her eyes. "Yeah, right!"

"Really. I could tell the moment I saw you. I said, 'Holy smokes, check out the morals on that girl.' "

"You're so terrible," she said. "I *hate* you."

"Of course you hate me. Every good girl hates me. I offend them."

She cleared a handful of hair from her face and combed it back theatrically. "That's probably because you throw up in their yards."

He toasted his glass. "Of course. That must be it."

The rain increased. It tapped on the tar flaps over their heads and rattled on a tin can somewhere on the lawn. Sadie tied her hair into a ponytail, watching the actor as he looked out over the gray and green scenery. The fog was sinking lower and now covered the treetops. She found a blade of grass and tickled it through the hairs on her forearm.

"So, what do you do for fun around here?" he asked.

"I don't know. Most people just cruise around at night."

"Are you *most* people?"

"No." She held out her hand. "I'm Sadie."

He put his glass on the railing and took her hand in both of his, turning to her in the chair and leaning down to face her with exaggerated sincerity. "Well, what does the lovely *Sadie* do for fun around here?"

"Beats me."

"Now, that I consider a tragedy. With all these activities around—these nature walks or whatever they are—we should be able to come up with something. I can't bear to think of anyone being bored."

"Even me, huh?"

"*Especially* you," said West.

She wrote in her diary, "The kids at school are all talking about, 'he's so hot because of this and that and the dumb movies he's in.' But he's really not like he is in those movies. He really understands people. He just sensed something in me almost instantly. It was like he knew how much I have to get away from this place. How boring it is and how much more there is in the world for a person like me. He can see it. He's very passionate, I think. He's much more passionate and intelligent than anyone would ever think."

She sat with Charlie on the porch each day after school when he would sneak away from his shack. They would share complaints. Sadie ridiculed her "narrow-minded Podunk town." Charlie bemoaned the idiocy of the film industry.

With that slight sneer—which Grace had said made her look like a snotty little princess—Sadie told stories about her hormonally maladjusted friends. They stole bowling balls and rolled them down hills. They shot firecrackers at tombstones. They spent whole summer vacations dragged on inner tubes behind speed boats and bumming beer outside liquor stores. She described all these things like the quirks of a recently dumped boyfriend.

Charlie West listened with a clinical interest. He believed she was the most normal—or, better yet—the most representative teenager he'd ever met. He was tickled by her annoyances, but also sympathetic to the restlessness she felt. He wondered if she dreamed of being an actress.

She was anxious to show West that she was not innocent. She told him about her disappointing sexual experiences: once during a rainy night out in the woods; another time on a Naugahyde couch that turned sticky and made flatulent noises with each wiggle until Sadie busted out laughing and offended the boy.

"You're still young," said West. "I wouldn't push all this too hard."

"Really? How hard would you push?"

"Jesus, kid. You've got a one-track mind."

After a week of trudging through the forest with the orderlies, giving his testimonials, doing listless calisthenics, and receiving vitamin shots in the mornings, Charlie was frazzled. He began to confess to Sadie about what infuriated him most.

She listened with her determined eyes held so steadily on his that she couldn't hear him. Trying too hard to look understanding, she distracted herself. She nodded at every pause in his speeches, and put her hand on his knee whenever she saw emotion in his face.

"You have to be grateful to your audience, I guess," said Charlie. "And I wouldn't mind if I was in movies that were for the rowdy kids. But this stuff is for all the squares. Paste-eaters. I'm on a lunch box now, for God's sake, and I just cringe thinking of the wet sandwiches probably carried around in there. I saw the people that lined up for my last couple of movies, Sadie, and you could get a better gene pool at the DMV. These are some rotten little parts. And the pilots I've done—Christ. I'd rather be doing big, dumb action movies. Anything. I may look like a nice guy to you, kid, but I swear: I got some serious pain in here. Some real Ingmar Bergman kind of gloom. And here I am taking directions like, 'Chuck, step back, you're blocking the mule.' My whole life is a knock-knock joke, and I'm not laughing."

He waited for her to respond. She was afraid. She worried that if she reassured him about his silly films and TV shows, he would think she too was a member of that audience he hated. She affected a serious face, furrowing her brow, bending down her lips. She said, "You have to follow your heart. You have to do, like, *dramatic* movies. Passionate movies. Almost like those foreign films. 'Cause that's what you are. You're not a lunch box. No way. You're much, much more."

From far across the lot, Grace was calling to Sadie.

Charlie said, "I wish there were a few more kids like you out there."

"I'm not a kid. I'm out of this place in June."

"Too old to own a lunch box."

"Never had one."

"Then I love you," he said. "Let's go steal a bowling ball."

In those days Sadie lived in an upstairs room in the main lodge, a room her son would later inherit. With its slanted ceiling and single dim window it had a stuffy feel. She kept her door open in the evening so she could hear the testimonials around the banquet table. When Charlie spoke to the group, she crawled up to the banister on her stomach and listened.

He spoke stiffly, almost defensively—and she knew he was a better speaker than that. He talked about his parents, both of them alcoholics, and he said all the requisite things. But somehow on those damp October evenings, each day the sun falling sooner past the mist, the days condensing and gathering speed, the air smelling of wood smoke, Sadie knew that he saved his real confessions for *her*. Only she knew about his hunger. She would hear more. The rest—abusive parents, uncontrollable drinking, the depths of depression—she had heard it all before. Everyone who came through the clinic could blame their troubles on something or someone. But *Charlie,* he could blame them on the world. The public didn't understand or respect him, and what a wonderful conspiratorial feeling it gave Sadie to hear it from him, to grab his sleeve and tell him that the whole world was wrong.

Sadie awakened that night and saw a flashlight moving across the path beneath her window. She leaned over the sill and watched the light move in circles around the yard. It was too early for the orderlies or nurses. When it came closer, she could see the bottom of Charlie's face illuminated. He walked in the stream up to his ankles and rooted around in the bushes. He found something beneath a rock. He shut off the light and traipsed through the darkness back to his shack.

The next day, she refused all rides from her friends and again walked home along the highway. Horns blared as the cars gusted past her, arms hanging from open windows. She followed the stream. Behind every few rocks she found an airline bottle of booze, smeared with muck. She washed them in the water until they showed their polished colors, like smooth stones. She was happier with each one she found.

Around midnight, she tied her sheets to the bedpost and used them to climb out of her window. She had a flashlight. She hid in a thicket of blackberry bushes beside the stream, and when she saw his shadow stumbling along the wet banks, she clamped down on her cheeks to keep from laughing.

Charlie threw rocks and cursed quietly. He stopped and shook the blood back into his hands. He splashed through the water, whispering, "Fucking hell. What the fuck?"

When Sadie shined the light on him, he stopped and crouched in the stream. He put his hands in the air and squinted at the light. It showed the stubble on his face.

"Who is that?" he said. "You caught me. All right? You happy? Are you going to strap me to my bed now? Because that's what I need. I'm a sick man. I'm weak. I have no willpower. Zero. I came here for help and look at me. I'm in a stream. Is that my fault or yours? Because I don't think you can expect much from me, Nurse Ratched, or whoever the fuck that is back there. Who is that anyway?"

"Stewardess patrol," said Sadie. "We're investigating some stolen goods."

Charlie dropped his hands and covered his face. He sat on the damp bank, leaned his head back, and laughed up at the sky so loud that the sound broke out of the forest and trembled off the lake in the distance. "You scared the shit out of me, kid!"

"Shhhh. You'll wake up the whole town."

He tromped back through the stream and sat beside the thicket. A net of thorn bushes hung between them in the light. When she shut it off, her eyes took a moment to adjust, then she could see the blue of the lake peeking through between the dark tree trunks and shacks. His shadow was perched on the sloped ground beside her. He smelled muddy.

"So, you caught me," he said. "What's the penalty for smuggling in an airline cart?"

"You have to earn them back." She tried to make it sound full of implications.

West didn't understand, and he replied, "What do I have to do, your chores or something? Carry people's bags?"

She scooted forward into the bush, wincing as she snagged her arm on a thorn.

"Careful. That's a sticker bush." His jaw chattered while he spoke.

Sadie leaned forward toward him and her hair caught in the thicket.

"Ow, fuck!"

West slid over and tried to untangle her from a clump of thorns. He couldn't do it, so instead he broke off part of the bush and left it dangling in her hair.

"I'm feeling a little queasy," he said. "This is all cute, Sadie, but I'll see you tomorrow."

"I've got it all still. I'll give you a bottle." Her voice cracked with nerves, embarrassing her further. "But you have to give me one kiss."

"Come on," he said. "You're a wonderful girl, but you don't want to play around with a guy like me."

She was sniffling mostly from the cold, but he seemed to think that she was overcome with emotion, and he put his arm over her shoulders. He gave her a long speech—most of which she didn't listen to—about how the right guy was out there for her, waiting, probably hanging around a liquor store or shoplifting inside it, and how he didn't want to come between them. He was too old and too fucked up for her, though he was still a young man, of course, and flattered that she had such a crush on him. . . .

She leaned in and kissed him while he was talking. Two mouths fell together. His lips stiffened and hers were wide open, part movie kiss and part CPR. He started laughing, but she pressed so hard against him that he couldn't exhale and the laughter came like hiccups. She reached her hands between his legs and drove him backward into the soggy ground.

Almost as if fighting her off him, he kissed her back with jerks in his neck until she rolled off to his side.

"Oh, God," she said. "You must think I'm a total slut."

"It's okay. It's okay. Just try to calm down a little. Don't hurry so much."

They kissed again. This time he ran his hand through her hair and stung himself on the thorn.

"That's it," he said. "Smooth and calm. Don't rush. I'm not going anywhere. Except hell."

The next night, just before nine, Sadie waited outside a liquor store called The Duck Blind. She studied the faces of the men going inside. When a pickup truck rumbled up on monster tires carrying two boys in their twenties—probably not much younger than Charlie but seeming like children to Sadie now— she leaned up against a tire and said, "Hey. What's going on? Can I ask you a *huge* favor?"

"Sweetheart, you can ask me anything."

"If I gave you the cash, would you buy me some stuff in there? I have a list of things I need."

The list read: 1 bottle of Stolichnaya, 1 bottle of Single Malt Scotch (preferably Laphroaig), 1 bottle of Courvoisier (for dessert).

"Shit," said the man. He had long, stringy hair over his eyes. "You are an alco-fucking-holic, baby. What is all this shit?"

"It's some kind of classy Scotch," she said.

The man leaned against his huge tire and, in a terrible imitation of a blue-blooded accent, said, "Well, la-di-da. Oh-nly the figh-nest quah-lity Scotch."

"I have a hundred dollars," she said. "There should be a lot of change, but you could have some as payment."

The two men paced away from her and whispered to each other. They were cackling and the driver called out, "Are you fucking shitting me, you motherfucker? You got to be fucking shitting me."

To Sadie he said, "What's a pretty little thing like you want with all this shit? You don't want any of this, baby. You want some Red Bull. You want some fucking malt liquor, baby. That's the good shit."

"I have to have what's on that list."

They argued a while and then consented. They took her hundred, went into the store, and came out with a full grocery bag. They handed it to Sadie and walked quickly to the truck. She looked inside and saw four plastic bottles of something called Big Time bourbon. She ran at the truck and said, "Hey! Hey! What the hell!" The boys screeched away on their huge tires, and one of them leaned out the window waving a wad of cash. He shouted, "Don't drink it all at once!"

Sadie was on the verge of tears when she knocked on Charlie's door that night. He ushered her inside and closed the door behind her. She put the bag onto his bed. He was trembling all over. "I've been going nuts in here," he said. "This place is the *worst*. I'm just about chewing on the fucking window caulking."

He opened the bag and stood there, silent. "Hmmm," he said.

Sadie sat down on the edge of his bed and covered her face. "I am so sorry," she said. "I tried and I just . . ."

Charlie took one of the bottles out of the sack and turned it around in the light. "What a unique color this has."

Sadie started to cry. "It's so awful. I tried. I had the list and everything. I just fucked up."

Charlie unscrewed the cap and smelled it. He bent his mouth down at the edges and nodded. "Did you pick up any astringent while you were out? Some witch hazel or, I don't know, lighter fluid?"

"I'll take it back if you don't like it."

"Oh, sure. A teenage girl with eight dollars of store credit. Maybe you can trade them in for a magazine. This is just amazing stuff here, Sadie. What is this sediment on the bottom?" He took a sip and swallowed it with his teeth flared. "Oh, boy. That is some first-rate firewater, kid. Good enough."

"I wanted to get you what you liked."

"Sadie, two more days in this place and I'm going to like airplane glue. You did just fine. What am I going to do? I've corrupted you enough already."

She rolled her eyes and sighed loudly. Already this was becoming a tactic he used, treating her like a child sometimes, other times like a woman, depending on what suited his moods. As Charlie sat on the floor taking progressively bigger sips, squinting his eyes and shaking his head after each, Sadie leaned back on his cot and watched him.

"You're not corrupting me, okay. I'm, like . . . my own person. I was already corrupted before you came along. Wait. That's not right. I mean, I can corrupt myself just fine without *you* doing it."

"Well said, my dear."

"Why don't you ever say that I'm corrupting *you*? You're the one who's being corrupted."

"And I already said thank you."

"Yeah, well, maybe you didn't say it nicely enough."

He took a hard gulp and swallowed with a grimace.

"Can I have a sip?" she asked.

"This stuff would put you in the hospital."

"Yeah, right. How do you know?"

He handed her the bottle and said, "They're making up a nice room for me in hell."

"Why do you keep saying that all the time?"

"Because I hate myself when I'm sober."

"That's why I deserve some appreciation around here. Scum. I got you this and you should be my slave for the night."

"I'm even cheaper than I thought."

Sadie put the bottle up to her nose and pulled it away, jerking her head back as if it were smelling salts. She rose and slid his dressing stand in front of the door. Charlie said, "What are you doing to me?"

She sat down on the cot, took off her shoes, and poured a stream of bourbon onto her toes.

"They're going to smell this in another state," he said.

She rubbed traces of it on her feet and legs, then took two fingers and dabbed it on the insides of her thighs beneath her skirt.

"You're just full of games, aren't you?"

"And you know you love it." She wiggled her toes in front of him.

Charlie took her delicate foot and regarded it for a long time. "You have good feet. They deserve to be soaked in better booze." He ran his tongue between her toes and kissed along her feet and up her calves. "This isn't your flavor at all."

"What is?"

"Something a little lighter. Maybe a wine cooler."

"No, thank you. How about the finest English Scotch?"

"Sure," said Charlie. "Or some of that really good Russian vodka."

He kissed a trail up her leg, around her knee, along the insides of her thighs, the warm smell of her finally competing with the bourbon. She placed her hands on the back of his head and whispered, "Take off my panties."

"You're such a bossy young lady."

He reached under her skirt and she helped him roll them down her legs.

"Oh, now I'm bossy, huh? Poor Charlie. Nobody has a gun to your head, you know."

"Not yet."

She stared out the fogged windows hardening with frost: it was the coldest night of the season so far, the air still clear and the moonlight shining in the windows and upon the stream.

Lying back in his cot, Charlie told her that this couldn't happen again. He said, "You're one fantastic young lady. I mean that. If the world was different, if I was eighteen or nineteen myself, I'd fall head over heels for you." He talked on about his ex-wife and his daughter and his career; he apologized for perhaps misleading her. All she heard was that he *might* have loved her had the world been different, and she wondered how she could change the world before he left.

He said, "I'm really not a good person. I may seem like a nice guy, but if you knew me, you wouldn't want anything to do with me. My ex-wife, she called me the worst son of a bitch she ever knew."

Sadie said, "Then, she's an idiot."

Charlie talked about how painful his divorce had been, and Sadie didn't listen to a word. She laid her head down on his chest and thought, *This is honesty. This is the way real lovers talk.* What he said was so full of depth and loneliness, so beautifully painful, that she ached for him and wanted to make love to him again.

"I can't, Sadie."

"I can wait until you're ready."

"No, I mean, *we* can't. You're not listening to anything I'm saying. I've done enough harm already. I promise you that when I first saw you, I said to myself that is a very beautiful young woman. Pure heartbreaker. And I think you are going to have a *great* life out there. You're going to fall in love and I envy the guy. Some lucky bastard. But not me, Sadie. I'm nobody. I'm a bad catch. It can't happen. I'm a bad seed, a dog. The longer this goes on, the harder it's going to be. You know that. We both know that. I've been listening in at these meetings, and I'm failing here. I've got to start growing up, taking control of myself."

"You can't listen to these people here."

"I got to stop acting like the whole world is against me."

"But it is."

"So many things are going to start happening for you. I remember being your age. Actually, it was pretty awful for me. But I see good things in store for Sadie Ravendahl."

Sadie sat up on the cot. She stared out the window. The moon had reached high enough to fill in shadows and paint the hills and trees with silver light. He stroked her back and she wanted to turn and bite his hand. She had a nauseous, sinking feeling. "Yeah, thanks," she said. "I guess you're *recovering*."

"Don't hate me."

She shrugged. "I don't hate anybody. Go back to your audience. Your retarded fans probably miss you."

"Okay. I'm sure they do."

She rose in the darkness, covering her breasts with her crossed arms. She found her clothes strewn about the room, and as she dressed, she could feel him watching her. She said, "Getting a last look, huh? Pervert."

"Don't be angry at me, Sadie."

"Why would I be angry? You're the one who's an idiot. Why would you think I even give a shit about you? Try to get over yourself, okay. You fucking egomaniac. Like I'm some virgin loser who's going to follow you. Yeah, right!"

"Okay. There's a sock over there in that corner."

Sadie crept back to her room through the main lodge and looked out at the cold night and the darkened shacks. She wrote in her diary, "You are one stupid bitch."

Over the years Sadie would reread that single entry often and write comments in the margins around it: "and proud of it"; "cheer up"; "not as stupid as the rest of this place." As she grew older her thinking changed about that moment, until she remembered more clearly the nights that came before it, the wonderful daze of being in love. She recalled the smell of bourbon left in her shoes and socks, and how it had still given her a conspiratorial thrill. She took pride in the fact that she had loved him so much and so recklessly, and she knew that it was his weakness and that oppressive place that destroyed it. Her faith in romance—tested in the years that followed—still managed to grow. Sadie thought the world was simply frightened of people who loved each other violently and desperately. The world wanted routine marriages full of domestic chores, couples partitioned by a morning newspaper, old scowling pairs who never really felt the way she could. That was what she thought each time she read the entry from that night. She loved the girl who wrote it, and she dedicated her life to that memory, staying wild and alive and never forcing herself into the life of some pinched little housewife, some tight-lipped prude hanging her husband's gargantuan jeans from a clothesline. With Charlie she had consummated a reckless life, sometimes fantastic, sometimes terrifying, but whatever it was, it was far removed from that flock of timid nurses and her mother, shriveled and sexless, pummeled silent by passing years.

This was the woman Matt remembered and described. At five or six years old, he was beginning to perceive the differences between his life and the lives of other children. He would sit at the foot of her bed at night while she was propped up on pillows browsing through radio stations, ravenously eating some snack and giving her son a speech about the nature of *real* passion. She told him that she had frightened his father with her straightforwardness, and that the town could never accept her because she refused to be cowed. It didn't matter, she said, that she rarely left her room nowadays, for certain battles were primarily abstract. "It takes courage to be who you are in this world," she said. "And you're going to do the same."

She spoke of Charlie in reverential terms. He was not above blame; it was simply that Sadie believed herself superior enough to forgive a man for his profound weakness. She told her son often, "He just wasn't as strong as I was. But he's a brilliant and very emotional man, and I know what I did for him. Everything you see from him is a little bit of a tribute to us, Matt. Just you remember it. There's a touch of coward in him, but he can't help that. Sometimes an artist has to draw on the strength of other people."

Perhaps even as a young boy Matt knew that this man was not quite an artist. But it was vital to his mother's health that he be treated as one. He had disappeared, after all, for the sake of his work, and thus it was only during his movies that Matt ever saw his mother cry. In the flickering lights she would cover her face and gasp, and to this day he wondered if she hadn't perhaps cried because she felt the pang of abandonment more strongly when confronted with the pointless spectacle of his worst films. "Look at him go," she would squeak to her son. Matt would concentrate on the screen, searching for clues. "He's one tough *hombre,*" she would say, sniffling. "That's your daddy up there."

When Charlie left that soggy morning in 1979, Sadie ran to the ledger to see what he had written. He had signed his name and scribbled the single word *Cured.* She flipped through the pages. There was nothing else.

Grace came back into the lodge and watched her daughter.

"Is this all he wrote?"

Grace nodded, her arms crossed over her chest.

"Did he leave me a note?"

"Not that I'm aware of."

"Don't you dare fucking hide something from me. If he left me a note, then you better give it to me. Right now."

Grace kept her eyes locked on her daughter. Sadie was impatient with the silence. It took her mother too long to think. "What did you do with it?"

"There was no note," said Grace. "Sadie. Listen to me. I know when you're a young woman you're anxious for your whole life to change, and you get ideas in your head, but he is a *grown* man and he has his problems."

"Oh, Jesus," said Sadie. "Spare me. You don't know anything about me. You don't know the first thing."

"You'd be surprised," said Grace. "I'll be on the lookout, then. For a lost note. Sadie, it's all right to like somebody, but that man is not who you think he is. He's a very sad, very weak man."

"You'd never be able to comprehend it, *Grace*. Not in a million years."

Over the next two months, winter reached into the hills. That steady rain condensed into the first ashen-colored snow, wafting down through the trees and spotting the ground.

Sadie lay awake and watched the first snowstorm, like a swirling ghost outside her window. She had been crying, writing and rewriting a letter to him all night. She was certain now, and she didn't know how to tell anyone.

Ice patches grew into crystals on the glass. Even the stream was now frozen into a slick ribbon that reflected the Christmas lights.

Near dawn, Sadie climbed down from her window and walked to a storage shed. Her breath steamed. She shivered in jolts, jerking as she tied on her skates, and in gusts her face would squeeze up and she would feel like crying. To stifle it she breathed deeply through her cold nose and mouth.

The lake had frozen unevenly over the past weeks. The ground around the shore was white and snow-dusted, and inward toward the center, the ice was wet and translucent, thin as parchment paper. Roots and rocks poked up along the edges.

With a trace of light in the skies, Sadie began skating on the thicker ice around the shore. Clumps of crusty snow shook her skates, but she pushed on harder and ignored the wobbling. She stepped over rocks and pebbles and debris. In some sections the ice sank palpably, with a hollow crunching sound. Sadie wiped her face and skated over it, gliding farther out, seeing the rifts and indentations behind her, the trace of moisture washing and crystallizing over her path.

Minutes before dawn—the sky changing slowly white to blend in around the treetops and the ground so that Sadie felt alone in a cloud—neighbors stepped out of their bright-lit homes and called to her. They stood on the shore in their longjohns, with curlers in their hair and steaming mugs, shouting and waving. As she turned for another lap, she saw more spectators. In every clearing, between hemlocks with their fingers of roots, men and women stood hunched beneath blankets, jogging in place, their tissues of breath all drifting and dissembling. They walked out onto their iced-in docks and hollered to her as she passed, lap upon lap, "Get off of there, Sadie. Get off of there!"

Stoves were lit, so that smoke piped from chimneys. The windows flickered orange and the air filled with the smell of cedar kindling. Sadie rounded a corner, skidded through a fishing cove, and when she turned, all the Christmas lights were blinking at the clinic. The morning music had come on: a classical accompaniment. Sadie lifted her back leg and glided over the wet ice, which clefted and came apart like a jigsaw puzzle behind her. She saw the patients along the shore, huddled together, and the nurses bursting out of the foliage, white as the sky; and her mother, at last, walking in careful footsteps out onto the ice.

Sadie started to spin. She did a pirouette with her arms at her sides, slowly, and increased her speed as she raised them into the air. When she broke from it, she skated backward, trying to hear the distant music and stay in sync with it. She splashed through a puddle and stumbled. The sky was turning glaring white, and she could hear the panic onshore. Sadie stopped in the middle of the lake, winded and sweating. She stomped her feet.

Across the lake a family had dragged their rowboat onto the ice. Its hull made a scraping sound. One man sat inside and another pulled, and the rowboat broke through in sections. They tried to row across the chipping ice, the boat like a clumsy turtle with its flapping oars.

From the other end Grace was walking toward her, sidestepping the puddles.

Everything around them, from the new trace of falling snow to the dense white sky, made it seem like a way station high in the air. Grace stopped a hundred yards away. Something she saw in the ice frightened her. She stood there, pacing, then turned around. The rowboat was scraping toward Sadie. In it she could see Stritmatter and an old lumberjack, once a patient. They were calling to her, "You just stay right there, honey. Right there and we've got you," and something about them in their vests and flannel made it seem like a routine fishing trip. Sadie laughed so hard the cold seeped into her teeth, and she skated circles around the rowboat as it came. Water spilled into the grooves around her. She would fall any minute, and she wanted to time it right, so she spun a last pirouette as a chunk of scissored ice broke free and tilted with her upon it, like a music box, she thought, until with a last violent plunge the wind was ripped from her. She shot downward and the water was so frigid all her muscles locked in place. As if by some inertia she still spun a few more times as she sank, a scarf unraveling in the water above her.

In her disorientation, she must have imagined it was Charlie. For when she felt arms around her, lifting, and when she once again punctured the surface to hear cheering in the distance and the agonized breath of a man, she said, "I love you so much."

"Just hang on," said Stritmatter. "You're not going anywhere, Sadie. We've got you. We've got you right here."

CHAPTER EIGHT

In the daylight, Ava had seemed tremendously self-assured: the way she held eye contact and spoke quickly and with assertiveness. Matt had thought, *This is someone who has had everything she wanted in the world.* She was perhaps like those rare tomboys in his high school, so sexy with scuffed knees and in soccer cleats, always on their way home to tutor their neckless boyfriends—the girls who shrugged off straight As, scolded quarterbacks like they were grubby little boys, and came to the prom in a perfume of grass stains, too cocky to care; girls who had a dozen platonic male friends, each of whom heard her life story and gave her hugs and commiserated with her about anything, then went home and wanted her so desperately that their bones ached. But that night, as he told his family story, his impression changed.

The bleached fluorescent light seemed to display her with new clarity. With her oversized flannel shirt that hung past her cutoff jeans, she no longer seemed like she was dressed coquettishly in a boyfriend's clothes, but like she had indifferently fished things out of the hamper. She nervously picked at her hair, coiling a strand around her finger. In his town, he never saw the mannerisms of a wallflower acted out by an attractive woman, but his sister seemed almost to have cultivated an awkwardness.

Matt didn't have the full story, but he was shocked at how much he could assemble from bits he'd heard over the years in gossip and cautionary tales. When he finished, Ava was quiet for a long time. Finally she rose and walked to the door of the house, where she leaned inside and said, "Mother! Can you come out here please?"

Ava's mother came out adjusting a scarf she had tied over her head. Beside her the little boy was wearing Spiderman pajamas and carrying a decapitated G.I. Joe. Ava said, "This guy here, Mother, is from a little town in Washington."

Camilla cleared her throat. She projected her voice across the garage, "Please don't harass my daughter all night, young man." She delivered her speech as if toward a larger audience than just Matt. "I've taken the liberty of calling my ex–live-in boyfriend, who just so happens to be a Vietnam veteran and prone to flashbacks."

"Just listen, Mother. This has to do with Dad."

"Oh, good Lord. You people never quit."

"Ms. Snow," said Matt. "I grew up in Chelan, Washington, in a clinic that my grandmother ran. My name is Matthew Ravendahl, and my mother's name was Sadie."

"Don't try to sell us some Third World cause," said Camilla. "If you want a donation from Charlie, you have to go through his business managers just like the rest of us."

"Just listen to him, Mother."

"I don't know what I have to do to convince all of you. If you guys know a decent amount of genetics—like I said, the blood tests were conclusive. They eliminated all the rest of my mother's lovers. And I also share some basic traits I researched over the years. For instance, Charlie and I are both left-handed. That's the southpaw gene. We're both extremely allergic to shellfish, and we both don't digest dairy products very easily. I know that's a bit of a tangent. But if you believe talent is an inherited trait, then I'm sorry—I'm one lousy actor."

"That would actually make sense," said Ava.

"I don't necessarily think that *bad* acting is in the genes." Camilla considered this and said, "Although you could make a case with a few of those Baldwin brothers." She tapped her foot while she thought. "So, you're the boy? You must think we're terribly inhospitable. Oh, isn't it a shame how suspicious everyone is these days? I wish I would have known. We could have spared you this song and dance. Oh, your *father*. Don't get me started. Of course, I always knew he was completely guilty of whatever happened up there. It's just so wonderful of you to come and see us. Wow. How courageous. And you look great. Fit. Tall. Why don't we go inside where it's more comfortable?"

"Mom, did you know about all this? I'm going to go ballistic here if you *knew* about this."

Chris started to fret.

"Oh, stop scaring him." Camilla pointed to Matt and said, "Come over here, sugar."

Matt stepped up to her and Camilla put her lacquered nails onto his cheeks. She gasped.

"Will you look at that? He's got Charlie's bone structure. Well, that settles it. I once did makeovers for a living, and I tell you, I'm more reliable than any *blood* test." Still reaching up and patting his cheeks, she turned to Ava and said, "He looks just like Charlie."

"Crossed with an albino, maybe."

"I come from a long line of pasty Scandinavians," said Matt.

"That settles it, then," said Camilla. "We're going inside. We'll fix this boy a smorgasbord and we'll talk this through."

Sitting in the breakfast nook, Ava tried to comfort her bewildered son. She said, "I'm just mad, honey. I'm just a little mad at Grandma. That's all. Because she never told me any of this and she knows that's a pretty lousy thing to do."

The inside of the house was far more disorganized than the sale had been. Toys, clothes, and coloring books were strewn across a narrow hallway. The sink was filled with dishes, and a trail of ants ran along the wainscoting. On one burner, Ava was boiling a bag filled with an unidentifiable white substance. After fishing out the bag, she poured the boiling water into three cups and made tea. "Three teas and a bag of cream chipped beef for the little one."

"What a wonderful cook you are, dear," said her mother. Camilla slurped her tea, then bit a napkin to wipe away the traces of it. Napkins all around her had lipstick mouth prints on them. She said, "For one thing, Matthew, your father won't have anything to do with a person if he thinks they don't simply adore him. He's surrounded himself with yes-men, even though he doesn't believe a word they say."

"Mom, stick to the point. No one wants to hear your invective all night."

"Well, at certain times in his life, Charlie has come to me for some honest-to-goodness advice. He doesn't listen to it, of course, but he's occasionally treated me like a kind of translator between him and the outside world. It happened more before he remarried. He'd call and ask if I thought he was a terrible human being. Basically, he wanted me to say, 'Yes, you're a terrible person, but such an *important* one.' I could never quite give him what he wanted. I'd say, 'Oh, sure, you're a jerk, but who isn't?' He hated that.

"There was one time he called me high on something. This was the early eighties, so what was it? Some kind of barbiturates or something. How old are you, Matt?"

"Eighteen."

"Oh, you're just a baby. Look at him, Ava. He's so cute. He looks so much like him, it's spooky."

"I don't see it," said Ava.

"Anyway—eighteen, eighteen. So it was around 1980. Right. Disco's fading, Reagan's rising—exactly. Charlie is talking like a madman. He tells me the story of this girl—*your* mother. She was very young, I take it. I would assume jail bait, but apparently she had a birthday sometime during foreplay. He tells me part of this story and asks if it's the worst thing he could possibly have done. Mind you, he asks this with a sort of funny tone—like if it *isn't* the worst thing, he's going to be just as upset as if it is. Well, I was so angry at him I could have strangled him. I knew nothing about the situation, but I assumed it was real—and here we were using it to have some sort of *moment* between us. We'd had a couple of brief flings since our divorce, and he had this way of wrapping up all his worst emotions and presenting them to me like a love poem. Like the way a cat leaves a dead mouse on your doorstep. You appreciate it, but you need a paper towel to pick it up.

"But the more I listened, the more worried I got. Charlie had this obsession back then about discovering new feelings. New sides of himself. The whole world was a rehearsal. But the real tragedy of it was that the more obsessed he became, the worse an actor he was. Instead of dragging a touch of his real life onto the screen with him, he dragged all of his stiffness and posturing into his own life. Pretty soon, he couldn't say two natural words. Now here he was, giving me this heartfelt confession about this girl—your mother—and a boy that he said was his son—that would be you—and he's screwed out of his gourd on these pills and still just listening to himself talk, and I just thought, *Now you've done it, Charlie*. It had really gone too far.

"So I started yelling at him. I don't like to do that, you see. I've always been sort of embarrassed about getting angry. My mother used to tell me that it made my face look unattractive. But there I was, just livid and shouting at him, and he broke down sobbing like a child. He promised me that he was going to support this girl—your mother. He said he was going to make sure that she was comfortable, and that his son had a good life. He was in pretty heavy debt those years, with a house he couldn't afford and obviously a fairly expensive drug habit, but he swore to me that he was going to take care of things. That was it. I told him I loved him. It was like he and I reconciled something, and when I hung up the phone, I realized that I had said to him all the things I'd always wanted to about Ava and myself. He was paying us a tiny amount for child support and alimony because he'd barely had a job when we split up. Every day of my life I was frustrated, thinking of him pouring all of his money into his liver. I never said a word. I wanted to prove that I could have a *career* just as well as he could. Then I heard about this girl that I'd never met—who was no more real to me than Madame friggin' Bovary—and I wouldn't let it rest until I was sure she'd be taken care of. I wish I'd asked for more help myself. I had to give up so much."

"I didn't make you give up your career, Mother."

"Of course not, sugar. You were out earning a living almost immediately. That's all I can tell you, Matt. I guess it doesn't really cut the mustard."

"Why didn't anybody tell *me*?" asked Ava. "This is what I want to hear. You knew all this time that I had a brother and you didn't say a word."

Camilla bit a napkin. She said, "Okay, Matt. Notice how this is all going to become *my* fault."

"You could have said something."

"Good morning, Ava. Time for school. By the way, you have an illegitimate brother in Washington."

"It's a start."

"I haven't had a cigarette in five days," said Camilla, taking one out of her purse. "You see what she does to me?"

"You had one this morning."

"Did I?"

"I'm not here to condemn the guy," said Matt. "I'm just here to figure out what kind of person he is. I feel like it'll totally resolve . . ."

They both waited for him to continue. Camilla held her cigarette aloft and Ava waved the smoke away from Chris's head, whispering, "Pew. Stinky."

Matt said, "I don't care about things like money or child support."

"Of course not, sugar."

"I just looked at my life one day, and I'd always felt like there was something wrong. This nagging feeling. Like I only had half the story."

"Tell me about it!" said Ava.

Camilla held her mug in the air and said, "All right. Here. To the other half of the story. Whatever it is."

A lack of sleep had left Matt with short breath and a raw feeling, and when the cups clinked together—like a pact being sealed—he had a tremor in his throat. He closed his eyes and his nose began to run. He grabbed one of the napkins, wiped his face, and rocked a few times trying not to become emotional.

"Gesundheit," said Ava.

When Matt recovered himself, both women dipped napkins into his tea and started wiping his face. "Hold still, Matt. You've got lipstick all over you."

That night Ava drove Matt to a motel on Lake Boulevard. She explained that because she had been so taken by surprise, she wasn't prepared to "roll out the red carpet yet."

When they reached the parking lot of the Thousand Palms motel, she told him that she would pay for his room from her garage-sale proceeds. "There's absolutely no way I'm going to let you pay. You just let me get everything cleaned up and settled at home. This is a temporary arrangement until I can get my act together. You understand, this is a real jolt for me. It's not your fault, of course. But I just can't imagine how angry you must be at my father. *Our* father."

"I definitely have a shitload of issues."

"Okay," said Ava. "And what issues are those?"

"You know. The whole collection. Abandonment, isolation, rage. I'm sure you can relate."

"I think I only have issues with the word *issue*. Unless you're talking about the *National Geographic*."

He stared at her, bewildered, frowning like a child deep in concentration.

"What do you say we get you a room?"

The motel was a stucco rectangle built around an atrium with a neglected garden. Maidenhair ferns drooped over an algae-filled birdbath. They entered a front office, a hot, wood-paneled room with brown carpet. Behind the desk, a small room was blocked off by a bead curtain, and through the strands they could see a television flickering. Ava rang the bell, and while they waited, Matt went through brochures on the desk. "See. I'll be fine here. 'Where country charm meets big-city glamour.'"

"Right. The glamour of Pasadena."

At the door to his room, Ava said good-bye, and they stood staring at one another. Ava stalled her departure by asking him if the room was adequate, and she hung on the doorjamb while Matt paced around the brown carpet. "Looks fine," he said.

He came back to the doorway and hugged her abruptly, catching her arms off guard so that they were pinned against her sides. He squeezed tight and said, "I'm ecstatic that I found you."

"Okay," said Ava. "Me too. You *better* be my brother."

He broke the hug and put his hand on her shoulder and shook it while he said, "I can't tell you enough."

"Yes, you can. Just get a good night's sleep and I'll be back here tomorrow morning. We'll make plans from there."

After a volley of good-byes, Ava closing the door slowly and peeking back in continually to wave and say good night as if he were a child who needed the door left open a crease, she was gone. Matt sprang up and began leaping on his bed.

"Yes, yes, yes!" he said. He bounced himself so high that he needed to duck his head and protect it with his hands, grating his knuckles against the coarse plaster roof. He trampolined himself across the room and thudded into the wall.

As he brushed his teeth with the toothbrush Ava had lent him, he sang with a frothy mouth and said into the mirror: "I'll tell you my basic philosophy of the world. Really? That's *fascinating*. I'm amazed at how brilliant you all are." He held the toothbrush to his lips like a microphone, spit the froth into the sink, and said, "Yes, it was an arduous journey. But I believe that people have to take that leap of faith sometimes, in order to truly discover . . . Shut up, you geek!" He spit toothpaste onto the mirror. He rolled up his sleeves, slicked back his hair, and said, "You want me to kick his ass, sis? I'll kick his *fucking* ass."

He was still deliriously happy when he called his grandmother. He said, "No, I haven't met my father. But my sister and her mom—they're *beautiful* people, Gram. Totally centered. Actually, maybe not, but they have, like, these amazing attitudes about the world."

"Matthew. It's time for you to be as reasonable as possible. You get excited and you don't think clearly."

"I gave my sister a hug and I was like: this is real. You know? Not like an image in my head anymore. Holy shit. I'm totally growing as a fucking person here, Gram. I'm confronting all of that shit that I was talking about."

"Matthew, watch your language. And settle down. You've been there two days. You still don't know these people, and I want you to be careful. Get a good night's sleep and call me tomorrow."

"I am so on top of this, Gram. If you saw how smooth I was, you would flip. I am the king."

"Time for bed, Matthew."

"I'm huge, Grandma. Huge."

"All right, Matthew. You're very large. Now go to bed."

He lay on his back in the dark for hours. At last he dozed off and had a quick series of violent dreams. His bed was opposite the laundry room. At dawn he was awakened by what he thought was an earthquake but was merely an unbalanced spin cycle. The room was partially underground so that his window showed the shins of passing pedestrians. A garbage truck was emptying the bins with a loud crashing, fading away into the scared twittering of sparrows in the atrium. Two maids shouted to each other between rooms. Toilets flushed as loud as torpedoes in the pipes. Just past eight the sun reflected off the sidewalk beside his window and turned the room into a sweltering flurry of dust particles churning slowly as if scored by the rhythmic clanking of traffic passing over a loose manhole cover.

He watched television until Ava came to his door at ten with a bag of BLT sandwiches. She wore her same cutoff jeans and a delivery boy's T-shirt from a pizza restaurant. Her coppery hair was bundled in a ponytail. Her posture and expressions had changed, as if a night's rest had eliminated her last remaining doubts. She suddenly seemed anxious to impress him.

She waited outside by the birdbath while he dressed, then took him on a tour of Los Angeles, a mixture of tourist traps, her childhood homes, and her jobs as a teenager. "That's Universal City right there. I lived in Studio City right over there with my mom for a while. And I worked at this place called Du-

Pars. I've had so many wretched jobs, Matt. If I could just tell you. One summer when my mom lived in Fullerton, I was Bashful at Disneyland. You know, the dwarf. Three months of Disney brainwashing, sweating, frat boys squeezing my ass, kids kicking my shins. I've just started to get over it."

As she drove, she talked nonstop. Matt was thrilled to see that she was experiencing the same adrenaline rush that he was, but it was difficult for him to harness himself long enough to stay quiet. He kept repeating to himself what Grace always said: "It takes more imagination to be a good listener than a good talker."

Soon Ava began explaining her game plan. Charlie was unfortunately at the busiest part of his promotion, so she suggested that Matt stay with her for a while, get used to the area, and let Charlie do his job. "Then, when you're settled a bit, we'll arrange a meeting."

They drove beneath a chalky sky, along sun-baked hills. Ava said, "I've thought about it all night, and I understand what you're doing. I just wanted you to know that. I really used to feel the same way that you do." The wind off the freeway was hot and loud, and Ava needed to shout over it. When a loose strand of hair flapped over her eyes, she finally rolled up the window. "I know that floating feeling. You want to be attached to something, to some kind of history. You feel like the wind could pick you up and blow you right off the planet. I know. Believe me. So you go out looking for something and you don't really have a plan. But I'm here now, and we're going to work this out."

Traffic slowed until they were stopped beneath hills crowned with elaborate homes, the highest ones obscured by a milky haze.

"You've come a long way to meet Dad and I know you must be pretty worked up about it, but I have to warn you: he's not going to come through the way you think. He's not like that. Whatever you've imagined—say, going out back and throwing the ball around or something—you're going to have to get over it."

"I suck at baseball anyway," said Matt.

"He's a very guarded person. Literally and figuratively. He has a hard time confronting anything or showing affection. I don't hold that against him: I just figure it's one of his traits. Like being left-handed."

Matt watched her profile. She had a frustrated look on her face, and he couldn't tell if it corresponded to her speech or the traffic in front of her.

"It's gotten much worse since he married Barbara. She's impossible to know. There may be a person there, but she's just wrapped in such bullshit. Steroid Barbie. But I don't even really know her. I shouldn't talk."

At a burger stand they shared a mound of ketchup-drenched fries, grabbing at the clean edges like it was a game of pick-up-sticks. Ava began telling Matt about their genealogy, and he listened with rapt attention, as if she were filling in the gaps of his extensive research. "His original name was Westman, which was an Ellis Island name changed from something completely unpronounceable. I'll look it up if you want. My grandfather was a set designer—so there's your genetic theory. Guess it skips a generation. He married a dizzy midwestern lady who was under contract at Paramount during the war. Sort of a lifelong extra. I'm basically a dash of everything. Dutch, Irish, Russian Jew, and some mystery chromosome."

"I always felt different at home. You think it's in my blood?"

"No. I think people probably treated you differently."

Matt told her that he would have been different regardless, for he had lived in a town where adults were still stunted by their years of teenage conformity. He described his childhood and his series of rushed apprenticeships. "I can do a whole lot of things halfway," he said. "And nothing really well." He remembered this chain of mentors more for the artifacts they left behind: an easel had taught him basic watercolors; a guitar had shown him two dozen chords. Throughout his childhood he had weekly obsessions, from the bongo drums to lanyards to an unfortunate bout with improvisational dance.

"The problem was, I was really a lousy actor."

They returned to the car and he continued his story on a slow-moving freeway.

Everyone in his town knew that Charlie West was his father, and they watched Matt over the years like he was an experiment. They wanted to see what sort of abilities he displayed, what he would look like. He was assigned the lead in every school play, whether he wanted it or not, and the town would gather to listen to him sing off-key. They would discuss whether or not talent skipped a generation.

"Everyone had a strange attitude about it. They thought my mother was a slut, and they thought I was sort of low-class—but they were all starstruck at the same time. They would talk about my dad as if I knew him. As if they knew him."

In fourth grade, Matt was forced by his teacher to go from class to class and explain who his father was. She was new at the school, both giddy and condescending. Matt faced rows of children, their eyes going slowly from sleepy indifference to curiosity, as if they were being taught the art of star worship. Matt prepared to give a show-and-tell about an invisible father. He could easily have coasted, done what he was supposed to do, but something came over him, some feeling of hostility toward that perfumed teacher and her officious tone. He took a deep breath and said as rapidly as he could, "My father is Charlie West, the actor. He impregnated my mother when she was underage, then he countersued her to try and prove I was somebody else's. But my mother won the case because of my blood tests and because of the fact that she'd only slept with two other guys around that time and one of them was Asian."

"Okay, Matthew. That's enough. Back to class now."

He ignored her and went on, pacing the aisles of the class. "I've never met the man. So I'm basically just the product of his semen."

"Matthew!" shouted the teacher.

"But I do sometimes think about sending him Christmas cards to thank him for his zygote. And he does send checks, you know, paying for the sperm that got away."

"Let's go, Mr. Ravendahl. Right now. Right to the principal's office."

She came after him and he dashed around the aisles, avoiding her. She finally caught him and pulled him by the ear, all the way across the glossed halls and to the office of a tired, meek principal. His teacher then left the two of them alone, facing one another. The principal offered Matt some caramels. While they both chewed loudly, he said, "You know, you shouldn't be so crude. I know your mother. She's a very troubled young lady, but she deserves respect."

With his mouth stuffed full, Matt said, "I don't know anything about my dad."

"Well, maybe that could be a project for you. Maybe you could find out. There's an awful lot of material about him. I'll talk to Mrs. Danner. Maybe you could receive extra credit. How do you like those caramels? Good, huh? I think you should begin a project, Matthew. A bit of research. I know your mother would be pleased."

So he became the local authority, and a relationship developed with a man he'd never met. He grew up and began to defend the reputation of his mother. He had fantasies that one day his father would find him and would tell everyone that he had loved her, and whoever questioned it would get a stiff pop in the mouth. Some days he loved and worshiped his father; some days he hated the man. There was a kind of confusion about seeing him on-screen and on television so often, like knowing a doppelgänger instead of the man; and thus Matt certainly was more a fan than a son. Charlie West the celebrity usurped Charlie West the vanished father.

When he finished talking, Ava was exiting the freeway. She dropped him off at his room and promised to return later that evening. He lay on his bed in the heat, watching a Western with the sound blaring. The air conditioner produced only a lukewarm trickle of dust. He worried that he had scared Ava with his rant that afternoon. But a few hours later, he heard Camilla's voice.

"Knock-knock," she said as she rapped on the door. He opened it and saw all three of them, Chris fidgeting in Ava's arms and Camilla holding a grocery bag.

"Surprise," said Ava. "Dinner is served."

They arranged a picnic on his carpet while Chris toddled around the room and played with complimentary soap bars and washcloths. Ava scurried after him. She changed the channel to a program with singing Winnie the Pooh characters and dumped a bag of toys onto the floor: bits of slime, jumbo Legos, dolls with their arms ripped loose. Chris put a bedraggled group of plastic animals into the toilet and Ava sighed and fished them out, saying as she washed them in the sink, "That's not a very good watering hole, Chris. Animals don't like that lake. It's stinky."

"They want to go fimming," said Chris. He had trouble with the *sw* construction.

"They can go fimming here in the sink," said Ava. She pulled up a chair for him to kneel on while Camilla sat Indian-legged on the floor, listing everything they'd brought: ". . . smoked oysters; this is Caesar salad; this is some form of potato salad; this, oh, *what* is this?" She handed Matt a bottle of wine and a cork-screw. "Do the honors."

He shredded the cork.

Chris splashed water all over the mirrors and the bathroom counter.

"So, Matt. We've come up with a plan of attack this evening," said Camilla, pouring wine into a paper cup and picking out the bits of cork. Both she and Ava took off their shoes and threw them at the far wall.

"You stick with us," said Ava.

"We have hatched a plan. You were wise to come to us first, Matt. We're both flattered."

"Mother, this potato salad is a study in mayonnaise."

Matt said, "Look, I don't want to cause a family crisis."

"Well, what fun are you, then?"

"They're sarks!" said Chris.

"I know, Chris. Big sharks. Don't let them nibble your fingers."

As Ava started to explain her plan, Chris kept shouting out

"Sarks" and humming atonally. Ava said, "First of all, you are going to move out of this fleabag motel and stay with us. I'm sorry that I was initially a little suspicious."

"She's not always sure *I'm* her mother."

"That's because you look too young to be my mother."

"Oh, aren't you sweet. You liar."

That night as they shared the bottle of wine—with Camilla acting far more tipsy than Matt thought possible from the small amount—Ava systematically went through her plan. Matt could move into her living room tomorrow if he promised to clean up after himself. She said that he was "a funny bird," but that they trusted him. She would talk to her father, hopefully before the big premiere. She could catch him in a lull, arrange a meeting. "Hopefully without Barbara."

Before this plan seemed anywhere near settled to Matt, the two women seemed satisfied that all was well. They took off their socks and lounged back against the wall. With a trace of wine in them, they giggled at jokes and nudged each other with knees and elbows. Ava lay Chris down on the bed, and by nine he was fast asleep with his mouth open. The feeling in the room changed. Matt saw all at once that these were two very energetic women, both laughing hard and flirting with him, as if some dormant part of them awakened the moment the little boy fell asleep. They slapped at Matt's legs and feet and interrupted each other saying, "Wait a minute, wait a minute. Let *me* tell him this story."

Ava grabbed his arm when she began talking, as if worried he might leave. She became more animated and more physical with her mother watching.

She said, "So I took these stupid Lamaze classes with Chris's dad. Right? He's a good guy—don't say anything, Mother. And so, later, when it's getting close, I've got his beeper number in case I go into labor. Right? Like this guy's going to show up with his tool belt and scrub down and come in and be my coach. It isn't that far-fetched, really. Except that he's out of town when I go into labor. So who's there?"

"Mommy," said Camilla.

"Yeah, and Mommy has that little MG that no normal pregnant woman could fit into. But it's an ego thing, you know. Nobody will ever admit that there's something impractical about their *car* in this town. So she gets me in with a shoe horn and there we are: zooming along in this little convertible, and I am *not* feeling good about this. She's swerving around all over the place—passing people in the emergency lane, pretty much driving under big trucks, and I'm going. 'Mom, just slow down. We're not in this big a hurry.' She was ten times as stressed out as my original coach."

"What does he know? He's an electrician."

"And the whole time, yelling over the wind and the horns, she's going, 'I sure hope you can deliver this kid. You have very narrow hips.' *Narrow* hips. I'm timing my contractions, doing my special little breathing exercises, and Jane Russell here is criticizing my figure."

"I didn't mean for it to be traumatic."

"So I just go off the deep end. I say, 'Okay, Mom, if that's the way you want it,' and I bet her that I'd have a shorter labor than she did."

"Worst bet I ever made."

"Well, turns out, Ms. Birthing Hips here didn't have too easy a time."

"It was a different era. I was unconscious for most of it."

"So four short hours later I have a beautiful son."

"Oh, bravo, sugar."

Matt leaned forward and asked, "What was the bet?"

The women looked at each other and shrugged. "We never decided," said Ava.

Staring at Chris on the bed, Camilla said, "But I have a sneaky suspicion it's working itself out anyway."

"You know you love being useful, Mother."

"I do indeed."

Ava then told her mother about Matt's life as if it were her discovery. He felt uncomfortable listening to Ava summarize the story he'd told her that afternoon.

"And when did you decide to come and find your crazy sister?" asked Camilla.

"I guess when I read an article. Your dad was talking about how you didn't really know where you were going in life. And I just figured we'd get along."

The bottle was empty. Camilla noticed that her daughter was upset and she suggested that someone go and buy more wine. Ava said, "I guess I can't go. I'm such a drifter I wouldn't know how to get there. I'd just wind up in an alley somewhere."

"Oh, stop it. You're so sensitive."

"What else did he say?"

"Don't tell her, Matt. She'll blow it all out of proportion."

"He just said you didn't know what you were going to do."

"I know what I'm going to do. I'm going to kill him."

Camilla went outside to smoke a cigarette, and her daughter went with her. Matt took the opportunity to take a short walk along the street, a wide, empty boulevard, bathed in yellow streetlights.

When he returned, both women had gone to sleep on his bed. Chris lay between them, nuzzled up to his mother's back, and Camilla lay facing the ceiling, her fingers laced together primly over her stomach.

Matt stole a pillow and lay on the floor. He listened to them breathing steadily above him, and after a few rapidly forgotten dreams, a trace of light came through the windows, the cars once again were clanking over the manhole cover, and he heard Chris awaken with smacking lips and say, "Mom, we forgot to go *home*."

"I know, baby. We're all here. It's just a change of scenery."

In a strip of connected suites, Charlie began his press junket for the electronic media. He sat in a velvet armchair before a black curtain. A ficus tree drooped beside him.

He noticed a different mood. The studio publicist was curt with him and many of the journalists were distracted before the interviews began, fastening microphones to their lapels and neglecting to greet him. Three years ago they acted like there was no suite on earth more exciting, but today they yawned and checked their watches. All of these factors—combined with an insultingly slapdash display of cold cuts and crudités on a foldout table—added to Charlie's growing paranoia. The grosses of his last films had been down, true, several of them way down, but that couldn't have drained all the enthusiasm from the room. His upcoming film was not testing well either. Reporters who once shamelessly sucked up to him were now vaguely condescending.

"How does it feel not to be named to *In Crowd* magazine's 'Sexiest People over Forty' list? It's the first time you've been snubbed." The young man asked his question with the same tone talk-show hosts used for their final guests—precocious children or old ladies who carved presidential busts out of potatoes.

"Obviously, honors such as those . . . they're temporary by nature. You can't get wound up in the specifics of who's hot this week and who's hot next week. Who might be hot tomorrow. These are very *effeminate* things. They're here today and gone tomorrow. What's important is the wholeness and the solidness of the work."

"You've settled down a lot in recent years, Charlie. And your movies have settled down also. Does this have anything to do with a healthy marriage to Barbara Hartmann?"

"I think it has everything to do with her in one respect, but in other respects, really nothing at all. Personal discipline has to come from the person within. And I have to be that person. Nobody else is going to do it for me."

"So you've seen the light?"

"I've seen a whole lot of lights in my time. A whole city full of them."

Charlie was handed a bottle of water. The studio publicist told him that he was doing wonderfully, then stepped away to take a call. The last reporter left without thanking him. The next one plopped into the chair. The chain was growing longer. It sounded like they were conspiring in the adjacent suite. Charlie's publicist winked to him across the crowd and gave him a thumbs-up sign.

The interviews passed, wave upon wave, as Charlie slid farther down in his fat armchair. His bottle of bubbly water went flat. He perspired through his pancake makeup. Between interviews, he imagined terrorist scenarios in order to keep up his energy. Armed mercenaries were lining up in the hallway; but in his fantasies he couldn't decide if they were coming to save him or to gun him down. He wanted a drink.

Interview #11: *Talk Nation*

TALK: First off, Charlie, you're looking wonderfully fit. How do you manage to keep in shape with your busy schedule?

WEST: Fitness is a state of mind, really. And I've been in this state for a while now.

TALK: Marriage, family life, recently remodeled home, and a career that's still kicking after all these years—what's next?

WEST: In this business, if you stop, you die. So I have to keep challenging myself at every level. I have an enormous pendant for always trying to go further, an inclination to push, and push, and really . . . *push*. I feel that if I don't achieve the, um, *penultimate* level of—not so much stardom—but *achievement*, then I really haven't done my job.

TALK: You're very driven to achieve. Aren't you?

WEST: I always have been. It's the quality that's really spurned my career. Onward and upward. I'm going to be here for a very long time.

Interview #19: *Glitz!*

GLITZ: A lot of people have criticized your movies for their excessive violence, their basic disregard for human life, their misogyny, their condoning of smoking, drinking, promiscuity, and heavy artillery, as well as criticizing you for the excesses of your private life. Do you see a parallel there?

WEST: I know that the people who *know* me, and know my values, my heart—so to speak—they know what I stand for. I stand for a whole lot of good things. Like my work with animal rights, or my . . . dedication to improving . . . lives. Look, movies are entertainment. Their job is to distract people from their troubles. If they can provide a personal and a poignant, um, ideal, or a politically potent message—then hey! All the more reason to buy a ticket.

GLITZ: In many of your movies you've played a sort of dashing ladies' man. In *Born Ready,* you're a family guy. How much of an adjustment was that for you?

WEST: Well, I don't want to give away the story, but basically I'm an actor and I can be married. I can be single. I could be widowed. I'm not limited to one thing.

Interview #29: *Bizzy Bodies*

BIZ: How is your work going with animal rights?

WEST: Oh, it's so rewarding. You see, I've always been inordinately fond of animals. From the smallest microcosm to the largest carnivore. Animals aren't like you or me. You and *I*, excuse me. They don't make judgments, they don't . . . fight wars. They don't pollute the environment. They just are what they are. So I don't believe they should have products tested on them. It just enrages me to think that some poor rabbit has to go bald so my wife can have a better hair remover.

Charlie paced around the suites to stretch his legs. He moved into the entryway between the closet and the bathroom. He opened the minibar and seized a handful of miniature bottles. In his rush he inadvertently grabbed a bottle of Bacardi and a small bell-shaped bottle of Kahlúa. Luckily there was also a Courvoisier. In the bathroom he hid the other two bottles inside tubes of toilet paper. He sat on the closed toilet lid and savored his cognac, drinking it in sips that he held luxuriantly on his tongue, inhaling and letting the warmth bloom through his nose and down his insides. He relaxed slowly. Afterward, he splashed water on his face and gargled with the hotel mouthwash, coughing in the midst of it so that he swallowed some. He emerged back into the open suites.

Interview #44: *The Gossip Gal*

GG: So what's the scoop? Barbara and Charlie sittin' in a tree. K-I-S-S-I-N-G. Are you in heaven or what?

WEST: Died and gone to heaven.

GG: I've never seen you so in love, so happy, so *complete*.

WEST: The whole enchilada.

GG: Do you cook? Does she cook? What's life like in the bedroom?

WEST: I cook. She cooks. We also *have* a cook. And amazing.
Fireworks. *Boom!*

The publicists were concerned that Charlie was losing his
focus. He went to the bathroom again and polished off the Kahlúa while holding his nose. When he returned, he began fidgeting in his chair, shaking his knees, and rolling his ankles from
side to side. His publicist whispered, "Calm down, Charlie. You
look like Tom Arnold."

Interview #60, *The Christian Radio Frontier*

CHRISTIAN: Many of your movies, Charlie, have been about pre-
serving the American way of life at a heavy price. In *No
Guns No Glory* you made a profound statement about the
importance of the Second Amendment. But here, Charlie,
you appear to have focused more on traditional family values. I wanted to commend you for that.

WEST: Yes. Family is the key element to essentially everything.
And I wanted to *stress* that.

CHRISTIAN: Do you think "family" is in the equation as far as your
personal life is concerned?

WEST: I think it's not only in the *equation,* I think it's in my plans
as well. Barbara and I would very much love to have a child.
I have always been fond of children. You see, children don't
judge you. They are who they are. They're beautiful and
they're . . . free. They don't, um, pollute the environment.
(*Charlie stares idly at the ground, nodding and rocking in his
chair.*) That's why we shouldn't test products on them. I'm
working to change that.

CHRISTIAN: Charlie? When it's all said and done, and you're standing at the Pearly Gates with Saint Peter—what would you
like him to say to you?

WEST: (*as if startled awake*) Oh, God. You mean I'm *dead* now?

KING 5: Terrorism. The movie deals with terrorism. It obviously touches all of our lives in some way. How has it touched yours?

WEST: Oh, terrorism, yes, yes. Yes! This is the *plague* of the . . . twentieth century. *Terrorism*. It's a scary *word* even.

KING 5: Yes, it is. How do you think it's affected your life?

WEST: I'll tell you a story. Just recently, I was confronted with the *terror* . . . of having a certain person—let's let them remain anonymous—wander into my yard. Sort of *domestic* terrorism. Now, this may not sound like much. But the feeling of *violation,* whether a large violation or just a small misdemeanor, it makes you think. You begin to live in fear, and that fear can control you. Unless you dig down deep and use it in your performance.

KING 5: Are you serious?

WEST: Oh, very. I've always been very serious. It's really the element that's permutated my career.

KING 5: Is it do or die for you this time, Charlie?

WEST: (*laughing nervously*) Of course not. You people act like I've never acted before. I've done everything. I've done Shakespeare, pal. What a piece of work is man. How noble in spirit, how infinite his faculty. When apprehended, how like a god. The beauty of the world, the paradigm of animals, the whole *nine* yards.

The studio publicist was pacing the suites, swilling a bottle of Pellegrino. A femme fatale, Charlie thought, in her cherry-red sport coat. She began dialing a number on her cell phone, so furious that she punched it out of her own hand. Charlie focused on the extension cords tangled across the floor, and briefly fantasized about coiling them around his neck. He could take a running leap off the balcony. *Action hero dies in tragic press junket.* His dying request: a decent opening weekend. And at the Pearly Gates St. Peter is sitting in a director's chair with *Variety* on his lap. "The numbers aren't in yet," he'll say. "Have a seat."

x: Who do you think would win in a street fight, you or
    Mickey Rourke?

WEST: Don't ask me that.

x: Come on, Charlie boy.

WEST: I'd kick his pretty little ass.

x: The old Chuck West. He's back. He's badder than ever. Back
    from the dead. When are you going to go back and do your
    kung fu flicks?

WEST: Beats me. I've made my share of turkeys.

x: Which turkeys are you talking about?

WEST: I'm not a clown. I'm an actor. And I'm a sick man.

Slumped back in the limousine, Charlie stared out the window at a circle of handlers. The studio publicist was livid, shouting and pointing, as the others nodded and calmed her. They
stood beside an elaborate fountain constructed of clam shells.
The water dribbled from the highest shell down to a pool of
turquoise tile that made the rippling runoff look like aquavit.

Sloan sat in the driver's seat, his beard flowing over the lapels
of his coat. He said, "Hey, Chuck? You get a chance to think
about that proposal of mine?"

"Fuck you, Sloan."

"I'll give you more time."

Charlie's publicist came toward him, heels clicking on the
marble steps. She knocked on the window, then sat down across
from Charlie. She assured him that what she was about to say
was not *criticism,* but merely a series of concerns that the studio
had expressed. She was relaying them as a friend. "Remember,
I'm on your side, Charlie." She reminded him that his movies
did not have the same built-in audience they once had. "We
need your help. You need to bust your butt a little bit. A few
years back, sure. Maybe then nobody would have a problem
with this sort of shenanigans. It might even have seemed charming. Trash a hotel room, do a little smack—ah, youth! But it's
no good now, Charlie. Now it's just sad." She agreed that press

junkets required tremendous stamina, and she promised him that today was not the end of the world. There was still work ahead and Charlie needed to remain focused. "This is what they pay you the big bucks for, Charlie. And we want to stay on top of it. Keep control. Stay on the straight and narrow, at least until after the film's release in Europe—but, of course, that's Europe and *c'est la vie*. Now, I know you don't want me to talk to Barbara about this little episode. So let's just keep this discussion between you and me. I'm your friend, Charlie. I want what's best for you."

Charlie put his hands over his face. "The tone in there. My God. It just sucked the life out of me."

She left him with a tap on the shoulder and a wink. "Stay clean, Charlie," she whispered. "Or you're going to be toasting the end of your career."

While stopped in traffic on the ride home, Sloan craned his head around and said, "I guess the wheels came off the proverbial wagon."

"I got to get out of this town, Sloan. I'm a sick man. I lost my ability to speak in there. It was a fucking train wreck. I'm not good on my feet like that, Sloan—especially with all these distractions."

"Are you talking about Ava's troubles over there?"

Charlie shook his head. "What are you rambling on about now?"

"You didn't hear? Ava had some runaway following her around like a puppy. I don't know all the details. I just know that when I called Millie the other night with a business proposal, she said they had a houseguest. She was particularly hush-hush on the whole deal, which obviously caught my attention. Especially with a girl who's as in your face as good old Mills."

"It *is* him," said Charlie.

"I want you to know, Chuck, that I'm here for you. Come what may. If you've got nobody to talk to, then you have a friend in me."

"He thinks he's got everybody fooled. This kid is trying to play us all." Charlie spoke with a dramatic flair, and the sound of his own voice reminded him of one of his favorite films. He squinted and looked out through the tinted windows at the cars flickering past, and he imagined looking out across the sands of North Africa, ghosts stirred out of dust, and somewhere on the darkening horizon was his nemesis. "You sly fox," he said. "I know you're out there."

"You're mumbling, Chuck."

"I was just thinking out loud."

"Then, no wonder I couldn't hear you."

Charlie was not feeling drunk anymore, despite the fact that he'd sweated through his clothes and his skin had turned clammy. He was sobered by this new development and panicked by the thought of seeing Barbara. At this hour of the evening she would still be stomping around the house commanding the staff as they clipped, vacuumed, watered plants, caulked tile, tuned a piano that was never used. The domestic crew had grown so large that Charlie felt like a guest on a manic cruise ship, eternally moored.

And he knew the exact moment when he had lost control of that ship.

Years ago, Barbara had convinced Charlie to have surgery. The skin around his eyes had begun to sag and he briefly looked his age. There were roles in which he played opposite young women—younger than Ava—and the press commented that Charlie looked as if he needed a stuntman for the love scenes. Barbara was resolute. This was part of his job. Whatever masculine prejudice he had against plastic surgery, she didn't want to hear it. That summer Charlie had a touch-up. It was a simple procedure, but Charlie turned out to be allergic to the anti-inflammatory pills. He suffered from a minor infection and needed to spend weeks wearing a blindfold of gauze and an ice pack.

The press reported that Charlie was on a bender. He'd come out of the hospital and gone straight into seclusion. While he lay in bed the paparazzi gathered in the cul-de-sac to catch a glimpse of him soused. He believed the rumors were better than the actual truth, but on the second day Barbara held a press conference in front of the garage. She said that Charlie would never see a drink as long as he was married to her, and informed the entire world that her once two-fisted husband was now bedridden after a massive face-lift.

She commandeered his life. Suddenly he noticed how even the smell of his house had changed. Her perfume entered a room before she did. The carpet was so deodorized and the curtains so drenched in scent that he began to imagine himself blindfolded in a department store.

During his recovery, everything Barbara said sounded like it had a demented edge beneath the sweetness. Sometimes he imagined she was speaking to him with a crazed sock-puppet on her hand. It was as if only the sight of her pretty face could deactivate the unnerving effect of her voice. Soon his mental image of her was transformed entirely as she belted out "How is my little man doing today? Would you like me to tell you what's on your plate right now? I had June cook you a great big breakfast!" Charlie tried to convince himself that he was merely irritable because of his condition, but her shrill enthusiasm kept further changing his image of her until he imagined her jacked up on amphetamines, lipstick smeared all over her chin, her hair in uneven pigtails, and her body crammed into a cheerleader's uniform two sizes too small. "Well, hooray, Charlie! It's a beautiful morning today and we're going to get those yucky bandages off any day now!"

His image of himself grew more pathetic as well. He was a drooling patient in some condemned hospital. Some days he was surrounded by the children from the school of his youth: the bed wetters bawling, the little pigeon-toed girl lurking in the darkness, waiting to lick his only patch of exposed chin.

Some days Charlie refused to get out of bed. "No. Leave me here to die."

If it were only the blindfold, he could place a cigarette in his mouth and spend the rest of his imprisonment pretending to stoically await his execution. "I'm going to meet my Maker," he'd say. But instead he met only his plastic surgeon, a pinched little man who boasted about all his celebrity chin tucks. He expressed concern that Charlie was not healing as quickly as other stars, and he said it in a way that made Charlie feel competitive.

Each night Barbara placed over his eyes a blue ice pack shaped like the Lone Ranger's mask—a mask for the Lone Ranger in a retirement home, his bed adjacent to that of a doped-up Tonto smoking a peace pipe full of Darvocet. Nurses and doctors would humor him: *There, there, Mr. Ranger. I'm sure Silver misses you too. Medicine time. Open wide. Hi-ho and away.*

By the end of one week, Charlie wanted to die from a combination of boredom and humiliation. Barbara asked, "What has gotten into you, Charlie. You're so gloomy."

"I'm tired of just sitting here in bed and listening to *Dobie Gillis.*"

"Charlie, don't take your frustration out on me. I'm the good guy here."

"I'm so fucking bored I'm going to throw myself off the balcony just to see what happens."

So Barbara, as well intentioned as she was in that first year, began hiring entertainment.

First, a violin trio gathered in his bedroom and played Brahms sonatas. Charlie was propped up on pillows, listening and wondering if Barbara was dangerous. He wanted to know what this "Requiem for a Wrinkle" was costing him. When he didn't seem to enjoy it—God knows, Barbara must have been standing there monitoring changes in the expression on his mouth—she went and got a dreadful child prodigy who tinkered on the piano downstairs. He was followed a day later by an accordion player honking out Bavarian folk songs.

"I just haven't found the right thing yet," she said. "You need something more male."

Charlie thought he couldn't take another act in this terrible play staged just outside his mummy wrap; but one day he was sitting on the bed, hearing the sound of car engines in the distance and a single hyperactive bird crooning outside, when he was touched on the arm by a clammy hand. He shook it. He heard a gruff voice.

"Charlie. It's Norman Mailer here. I'm going to be reading to you from my new novel, *Harlot's Ghost*."

Sloan idled in the cul-de-sac out front, and Charlie—suddenly more nervous than he had been at the junket—gargled with a soft drink, then stepped outside and spit into the ivy. He thanked Sloan. "Of course, of course," he told him. "I'll consider every investment. Good-bye." When Charlie stumbled upstairs he found Barbara getting a massage in the bedroom. An earnest-looking cabana boy was rubbing her shoulders. Towels were draped over her and the room smelled of oil.

"Charlie," she said, her face pressed down into the massage table. "Go look at my dresses. Oh, that's good."

Charlie continued into the walk-in closet, where he saw a row of elaborate gowns hung along the walls.

"Which one?" she yelled from the other room. The masseur shushed her. "For the premiere."

Charlie spun around his shoe rack and pulled a pint-sized bottle of Jim Beam out of a cowboy boot. He took two huge gulps, baring his teeth as he swallowed, then stuffed it back down into the boot. It was the mixing of drinks that was foolish. But what sort of person kept *Kahlúa* in a boot? He regarded her dresses hanging amid all the others, like shed skins from all the other premieres and ceremonies. No dress could be worn twice. He took a bottle of her perfume and misted the closet with it, then sprayed a cloud into his mouth.

"Charlie? Are you there?"

"I love them all!" he shouted, reemerging into the bedroom. He had nearly blinded himself squirting the perfume into his eyes.

"I got a call from your publicist," said Barbara. "She's very worried about you. She was suspicious that you were . . . well, I won't say it. But she was suspicious about you. I assured her that you're just extremely tense these days."

The masseur started to karate-chop sections of her back. Barbara continued to speak as the strikes vibrated into her voice.

"I—*uh uh uh*—know when you start to doubt yourself—*uh uh uh*—you get into trouble. You lose your—*uh uh uh*—ambition. But this is the break of your ca—*uh uh uh*—reer, Charlie. You can't blow this by just letting your mind wander off into—*that's enough, Kevin*—off into who-knows-where."

"Yeah, that's true. I got to get my head on straight. What do you think, Kevin?"

"I agree," said the masseur.

"As soon as we finish up here," said Barbara, "I need to try on a few of those for you. We have to *decide*. The premiere is next week, Charlie. God, your head is in the clouds."

Charlie walked past her and looked out from the balcony. Beneath him the pool was lit blue in the dusk. In the distance the lights of Westwood were twinkling, spotlights circling around the clouds to advertise a premiere, or an opening, or a jail break.

Barbara said something he couldn't hear. He heard her shout his daughter's name.

"What about Ava?"

"You're not listening to me. Ava called and I think she's finally *met* someone."

"What are you talking about?"

"I mean, she sounded serious for once in her life. She said that there was someone she was going to bring over. Someone who she wanted you to meet. She went on and on about—oh, that's *wonderful*, Kevin. She said she needed to talk to you when you had time to really sit down and listen. And well—*mmm, yes, right there*—I said that could be years from now. This girl seems to think that everything revolves around her little life. What does she do, anyway? I wish somebody would explain to her that the rest of us don't have a single free moment. Kevin, you're an absolute *genius*."

"You're right. I'm too busy right now."

"So I told her she could bring her friend to the premiere."

"You said *what*?"

"They don't have to sit right there with us. You barely have to say two words to them. You let her come to the premiere of *The Last Stand Two*. I don't see what the problem is. Really, I don't understand you, Charlie. You go on and on about how you want to be closer to your daughter, and then the second I suggest a reasonable way to *involve* her in your life—*ouch*. Boy, that's a real knot there. I thought she could impress her friend." The masseur was kneading the tops of her hamstrings beneath the towels. The masseur whispered something. Barbara said, "See, Charlie, you've gotten me all tense again. Why are you so worried about everything? Maybe Ava will get married to this person. Maybe he has a decent job."

"She's not marrying this guy, Barbara. Unless we've really gone Appalachian around here."

"I get the strangest pains in my right hip. I stretch and stretch, but it's right there, Kevin. Right where the ligament comes off the bone."

Charlie walked down the stairs and Barbara called after him, "Don't take it out on me, Charlie. I'm the good guy here. Argue with Ava about it. She's coming over sometime this week. She says you bought a chair from her. You know, I hope it isn't another one of those awful sculptures. The Goodwill won't even take those things. How did she manage to have so little talent, Charlie? You must have dropped her on her head as an infant. Charlie? Where did you run off to? Charlie, I can't relax when you make me yell after you."

Down below, passing out the glass back doors, Charlie could still hear her through the open balcony door. He removed his sport coat and his shoes, and then, in the rest of his clothes, he plunged into the pool and floated on his back, the water overtaking his senses. When he began a slow backstroke, he could see Barbara in a robe on the balcony, the darkening sky beyond her.

"Have you gone completely insane?"

"Just exercising," he said, and spit a mouthful of water into the air.

CHAPTER TEN

When Matt moved into the house, he so diligently set about repairing the porch, killing the trails of ants across the kitchen, and fixing the leaking faucets that Camilla called him "our little farmhand." He mended the fence using old stage trees, so that a two-dimensional jungle surrounded the house. He strung Christmas lights around the kumquat trees. He built a small baseball backstop out of leftover plywood. Ava complained that he was turning the house into a miniature golf course, but she still enjoyed sitting on the back steps to watch him work. She'd pour herself a glass of wine and lounge amid the smell of oleanders, yellow grass cooked in sunlight, and the rusty scent of hose water in the air as he trudged through ivy to spray the parched corners of the yard. Beyond the tangle of branches and phone wires, finches darted between all the gardens strung together beneath a scrubby mountain that lurked in the haze.

Ava helped him from time to time. She explained. "You just get so used to looking at something broken, you know. You don't remember it ever worked."

Matt found quarters trapped under appliances and stuck in creases of the wainscoting. He dropped them into coffee tins so that all day the house sounded like a slot machine trickling out its humble winnings. The following day, he climbed up the house on a ladder, and beside the pigeons cooing in the attic crawl space he dislodged crumpled Schlitz cans from the rain gutters. Ava urged him not to do anymore, but when Matt persisted, Camilla made out lists of chores. She said, "Maybe we could paint the trim. It's looking extremely ratty these days."

At first he tried a bit too hard to be tidy and unobtrusive. Tiptoeing is louder than stomping, and Matt's awkward courtesy continually reminded Ava that he was a stranger. He refused to dirty the glasses, so he cleaned out a Smuckers jam jar to drink from, and he circled around the yard each morning with it full of cranberry juice diluted with water. On a pad stuck to the refrigerator he kept a running tally of everything he borrowed— one jar of orange juice, six spoons of peanut butter, soap, banana—promising to reimburse Ava and Camilla with labor.

"What exactly is a banana's worth of labor?" asked Ava.

He estimated the exact amount of shampoo he used by "headfuls," until they assured him that the shampoo was on the house. All of his clothes, borrowed from the failed garage sale, were folded neatly into a stereo box that Camilla had given him, and Ava said to her, "Gee, aren't you thoughtful, Mom? Maybe you can build him a fire outside in an oil drum."

"He seemed to like it, sugar."

He frequently drank Barbara's diet powder, using it simply to flavor water. He didn't appear to like it, but he drank with a quiet politeness, as if it were his duty to consume it all.

"You have to stop thanking us so often, sugar. We want you to make yourself at home. Act like you did at your own house."

"I am," said Matt.

"Then, act even more relaxed than that."

After several days, however, Matt's demeanor changed. It began during the night, just past Chris's bedtime. He often wanted to engage in long theoretical conversations. He was, by all means, a bright eighteen-year-old, but Ava had forgotten how intelligence at his age was often laced with a youthful conceitedness. Those with the least experiences were always the most righteous; thus, Matthew, flicking his hair out of his eyes and speaking in an adamant tone incommensurate with his rather obvious statements, would often speak about the nation's decaying morality.

"It's totally like this: no real moral system has replaced religion. But science is our religion now, for most of us, and it doesn't have any—you know—code of ethics."

"That's very perceptive," Camilla told him while she scrubbed a pan in the sink.

Matt's rants were different from those of Ava's half-forgotten roommates, or Camilla's long procession of drug-philosopher boyfriends. Many of those had had an aggressively political slant, quickly degenerating into hyperbole about police states and the corporate brainwashing, whereas Matt's ideas tended more toward the pseudoscientific. Every leaping assertion he made was "mathematically verifiable," and every human shortcoming could be directly attributed to some chemical deficiency in the brain.

"You see, we all have addictive personalities here, especially you and me, Ava. Because we've inherited that gene from our father. It has something to do with a lack of serotonin in the brain, I think—but I might be getting the wrong neurotransmitter. The thing is, I grew up just with my grandmother, you know. And studies show that it keeps a child from forming the same amount of neural connections."

"Growing up with your grandmother is bad for the brain," said Ava. "That's what you're telling me?"

"Not exactly like that. But you see—nobody is very physical in my family. There was no real ongoing stimulus for me as an infant. A toddler like Chris, he's got, like, a billion neural connections. His brain scan is like one of those population-density maps of China, you know. But us—we're like Greenland, man. A couple of settlements along the coast. So, if you want all those people to stay and build highways and cities in your kid's brain, then you have to be in his *face*, like, all the time. Puppets and puzzles and all that shit. See, I'm here to learn about my life and my family. But it can't really change my personality very much, because all that is totally set by about the age of four."

"That's a very fatalistic view you have, Matt."

"It's science."

Matt created an atmosphere that could be compared only to a dorm room in the opening week of a particularly lax boarding school. Camilla had refused to reveal her marijuana stash (believing that he was just a young man and should discover such things on his own), but he scarcely needed it.

His tone became more forceful as he became more unsure of himself. Ava didn't hold it against the boy. But she did wonder what it was about her that inspired men to talk this way. Every man in her life acted as if she had just been enrolled in his class. She did her best to nod at Matt and encourage him, to keep eye contact, to be appreciative of his energy; but at one point it occurred to her that she was being lectured on the human mind by a teenage hillbilly.

Just as she was willing to believe that her newfound brother was hopelessly irritating, she was surprised by something: he had a sense of humor about himself. Ava and Camilla soon stopped trying to respond like eager students. They began to say things like "Dear, would you like another glass of serotonin?"

Matt would chuckle, blush, and say, "I know. I'm a geek."

He was almost grateful for a gentle remonstration. In fact, he seemed to be more comfortable when he knew that no one was taking him entirely seriously. He wanted to talk about the existence of God, possibilities for further evolution of mankind ("the pinkie and the little toe will go, but cranial space will increase"), futuristic viruses, and movies.

How, then, could they have become so relaxed with his company? Late nights they lounged around to the sound of the radio instead of the television, and listened to Matt, and responded when they felt like it; maybe they played Rummy 500, drinking their Cape Codders, while Matt paced around the table. "Do you believe in extraterrestrials?" he once asked.

"Oh, honey, we just don't *care,*" said Camilla.

Ava and her mother would laugh and tell him he was of course welcome to expound any hypothesis about how little frog men had constructed the pyramids. He was more amused than they were, but never lost any of his enthusiasm. In just over a week, both women came to enjoy his rants, viewing him like some rambunctious boy who was revving the engine of his new car while staying put in the garage.

"I'll tell you what's wrong with *society,*" he said. "I've got a bone to pick with capitalism."

"Matt, don't form a militia tonight, okay, sweetie?"

"We're feudal here, Matt. You're preaching to the converted."

But during the days he scarcely uttered a polysyllabic word. He played stick-'em-up games with Chris around the house, drawing up all sorts of scenarios. "Okay, we're on a spaceship, right? And everything outside is deep space, so if you go out there it makes you move in *really* slow motion." They played a wrestling game in which Matt repeatedly flung Chris against the couch. Ava thought it looked rather dangerous, but when she tried to stop them, Chris shouted at her and said, "No, Mom! No!"

"All right. You certainly have your mind made up. Matt, don't hurt his neural connections."

They ran around like village idiots in the sprinklers; they squirted each other with the hose; they made a fort out of dirt and wood and pummeled one another with Styrofoam swords. Chris made rabid screeching noises that Ava had never heard before, but each time she came out to voice concern, he seemed more thrilled at the whole enterprise. Once upon a time, his bath had been more about a bedtime routine than actual cleanliness. Now it was a strenuous job that turned the bath water coffee-colored with mud and left rings of grass blades around the tub. His laundry was now streaked with Popsicle drool, garden mulch, and unidentifiable stains; he brought recently killed bugs into the house; he smeared dirt around his face; and he shouted things to his new playmate, like "I'm coming to kill you!"

"Is this healthy?" she asked her mother.

"As far as I know it's completely normal. I think this is proba-bly just what he needed."

"You're saying he needed me to throw him in the mud occasionally."

"Well, some variation perhaps. I think it's perfectly healthy, sugar. Think of it as camp."

Ava stared out the kitchen window at the backyard. Matt was lying sprawled on the lawn and Chris was repeatedly heaving a waterlogged lounge cushion onto him. "He can barely lift that thing. I think maybe we should encourage more structured activity." Chris hoisted the pillow onto his shoulder and fell down from the weight of it. "What an odd kid," Ava continued.

"Which one?"

"The big one," she said. "The thing is—I always used to imagine that I had a brother. Always. But he wasn't like this kid. He was older than me, of course. Tremendously insightful. Full of advice. Always looking out for me. Confident, composed. Had a girlfriend I couldn't stand. He was going to grow up and marry and have kids. He'd have me over to dinner all the time, and he'd know a whole lot about wine. And he'd be a hell of a good cook too."

"What happened to him?"

Ava stared out the window. Matt stood up and flexed his skinny arms. He made roaring noises at Chris, then posed in the same absurd manner for Ava. "I think this kid ate him."

One evening Ava sat Matt down and told him that she'd been unable to get in touch with her father. "But I talked to my stepmother and she invited us to his premiere. It's a huge pain in the ass. But who knows, maybe you'd enjoy it. I'm not sure if she knows who you are or not, but I figured you should at least meet everybody first. I'm tired of chasing Dad around, and I think maybe we should just quit the nonsense. Introduce you. Let him work out his own problems." She told Matt that she was going to deliver a chair to her father. She asked if he wanted to come with her.

"Should I get dressed up?"

"No, Matt. Not to deliver a chair."

They tied the giant balsa wood rocking chair into the bed of her pickup truck. Ava explained that it had been for a Children's Theater production of *Alice in Wonderland,* and that her father had paid her in advance for an unspecified piece of stage furniture. "You can't exactly sit in this, but it's symbolic." As they wrapped the ropes over it, she said, "You'll meet Dad, but it will all be very casual. I know it will be a shock to him, but, you see, you kind of have to shock Dad in order to get him to do anything."

"He probably knows I'm here," said Matt.

"How would he know that?"

Matt smiled shyly and said, "Just a hunch."

When they reached the west side of the city, Matt was trembling. Ava asked him if he was all right, and he said, "I feel like I'm going to puke."

"Carsick?"

"Nervous. I'm insanely nervous."

"Don't be nervous. I'm here to take care of you *and* the situation. You should have no expectations right now. Just say hello and let him think about it. You have to be patient with Dad. He's not going to invite you out back to play horseshoes. But you give him time, let him mull it over like he does everything, and *voilà.* You'll get an unexpected phone call and he'll invite you to a pretentious restaurant."

"Don't even talk about food, Ava. I'm going to throw up on my biological father."

"Think about something else. Tell me some more about Roswell."

"I can't. It reminds me of him."

"The alien storage depot reminds you of our father?"

"Because he did that movie *The Invasion* where that space virus got loose and killed everybody on that tropical island."

"You're an encyclopedia, my boy."

When they reached the house, Matt climbed out and untied the legs of the chair, working with feverish concentration. Ava pushed a button on the stone wall and through an intercom came her father's voice. "Who is it?" he said.

"Dad, it's me. I've got a present for you." She looked up at Matt and said, "Should I tell him that his rightful heir has returned?"

"Please don't."

The chair was so light that even with its size, Matt was able to lift it over his head. Just as he was hoisting it up, Charlie swung open the front door. His hair was matted down with sweat and he squinted at the sunlight as if he had been underground for days. Ava could smell a trace of booze on him, like an acidic cologne. He put his hand on the doorjamb to steady himself.

Matt appeared to forget the chair held aloft, despite the fact that he was doing a two-step to balance it as it wobbled overhead. He swayed and dipped and Charlie followed the chair with his eyes. Matt eased it to the ground.

Charlie fixated on the chair with an expression of fear and reverence that looked absurd to Ava. He shuffled out and paced around it.

"Ava, you've outdone yourself. Oh, it's just fabulous. An absolute throne. Fit for a king, Ava. I swear it."

"It'll break if you sit in it."

"Fit for a very *light* king. I can't tell you how amazing it is. Thank you so much." He looked up at Matt and said, as stiffly as in his worst films, "And thank you. Thank you for putting it down."

"No problem. Your daughter is insanely gifted."

"Dad, this is Matthew. He's been staying with me for the last week or so."

Charlie's expressions had been slowed and animated by a few drinks. Ava could see it in the way he scanned Matt up and down, staring at his crossed arms and then at the blond hairs that stood out brightly on his sunburned legs. "Wonderful," he said. "That's great news. Good for both of you."

Matt unfolded his arms and began slapping his hands against his thighs, a loud nervous tic that seemed to frighten Charlie.

Charlie was such a bad actor. Ava saw him make a decision: he was going to treat this young man like a random stranger. But he wasn't remotely convincing. He glanced over at Matt every other second, with startled eyes and blushing cheeks. Matt drummed harder on his legs, biting his lower lip, and then almost stalking a circle around his father. He looked predatorial, and Charlie hunched up as if he expected an attack. Ava realized the serious error she'd made. She felt a lump in her throat, she was so worried she had betrayed her father. Whenever she wanted to be her most breezy and spontaneous, she came off the most calculating.

"Tall guy," said Charlie. "He's a tall guy, isn't he?"

"Six-two," said Matt. "That's pretty normal."

"Pretty *tall,* I'd say. Well, good for you. I think that's just great. It's good to be tall."

"You have an amazing house."

"Oh, no. No, we're thinking of moving. It's too . . . sterile. I mean, too impersonal. And there's, well, there's security problems."

"Can I shake your hand?"

"Oh, of course."

The two men shook hands beside the truck, Charlie looking seasick, Matt looking as if he were hyperventilating. Ava was prepared to leap between them.

"I've seen all your movies," said Matt.

"Oh, God. I'm sorry for you."

They broke hands and stood facing one another until Barbara came to the front door in her robe, a towel bundled around her neck. She said, "Ava! It's just stunning. Simply your best yet." She wore slippers and shuffled into the cul-de-sac. When she noticed Matt, she walked flirtatiously up to him. She put her hand on his arm and said, "Here's the mystery man! I'm Barbara. And you must be . . ."

"Matt."

"That's right. Well, it is so *sweet* of you to help Ava carry that great big thing. She'll put you to work. Be careful of that girl. It must have weighed a thousand pounds. Thank you so much. I mean that. I don't know what Charlie has been telling you, but don't listen to him. Ava is a very nice person."

"I enjoy your diet shakes," said Matt.

"Well, aren't you a sweetheart."

Charlie rushed back toward the house with his head down. Both Ava and Matt watched him go, turning away from Barbara as she said, "I'd be interested in hearing any suggestions. I've had such wonderful responses from people over the years; you'd simply be amazed at how many people there are out there struggling to control their weight. Men also. Of course, you don't appear to have a *thing* to worry about."

"Where's he going?" asked Ava.

"Oh, don't mind him. He's been a complete basket case these past few days. I've had to keep my eye on him like a hawk. It's the film. He's always so anxious right before it all happens, and then there's nothing to worry about in the end. Thank you so much for coming by with this, but . . . I don't think Charlie is in the best state for company right now."

"How much has he had to drink?" asked Ava.

"No, no, no," said Barbara. "He hasn't had a drink since he's been with me, Ava. Not a sip. He just gets frantic. All this running around. He's like a chicken with his head cut off. Basically, he needs to learn to rest when he has the chance. Part of being in good shape is knowing when you can be lazy, and Charlie has never learned that. But I'm sure *you* understand, Ava. It was so nice of you to bring this over. You are coming to the premiere, aren't you? I know Charlie would be devastated if you missed it."

Matt climbed into the bed of the truck and looped together the ropes. He sat down and stared at the house with the pouting expression of a child.

Ava said, "Yeah, the premiere. Okay. If you say so. Can I just go in and ask him?"

Barbara shrugged and said, "I'm not sure if now is the time."

"Matt, wait here. I'll be right back."

Ava dashed across the courtyard and all the way through the house to the backyard, where she found her father sitting in the bungalow beside a desk covered with mail. He was tearing open the envelopes and dumping out the contents. Ava paused beside the sliding-glass door. She opened it a space and leaned her head through, but her father ignored her.

"Dad?"

"What?"

"I tried to call you a hundred times."

"Right. I got a hundred messages."

"Why didn't you call me back? I would've talked to you about this. He's a good kid, Dad. He's a brave, smart kid who just wants to know us. He just wants to meet you and talk to you."

He stared at the pile until Ava began fidgeting against the door.

"You're just going to sit there like that? You're not even going to look at me?"

He said, "What exactly do you want me to do, Ava? Huh? Tell me. Gee, thanks for bringing your *friend* over. Does he want to move in? Do I make up the couch for him? What am I supposed to do? I've got a million things going on in my life—what *now*? What is it that you, in your infinite wisdom, think I should do *now*? Because I'd love to know."

"All right, Dad. Have it your way."

"My way. What way is that, exactly?"

"You made your point."

"I'm not making a point at all! I'm asking a fucking question. There's a difference between a question and a point. Or are you too fucking stupid to know that?"

Ava took a deep breath and calmed her face and with her eyes closed said, "I'm not stupid."

"Of course not. You're a genius. You're all fucking geniuses. It's just my luck, I'm surrounded by geniuses. I ought to get an honorary Ph.D., I'm supporting so many fucking geniuses around here."

"Your generosity is just overwhelming."

"Ava, my life is much more complicated than you could possibly imagine."

"Why is that, Dad? Don't you even want to talk to your *son*? This is it? You just want to hide in this big ugly house."

"I just want everyone to leave me alone! That's what I want."

"Well, that's just superb. I hope your movie is a big fucking hit, Dad. How is it testing with your illegitimate children?"

"They're the target audience."

"Good one," she said. She leaped up the back steps into the house, ran through the living room, knocking the potpourri dishes to the floor, and continued back to the cul-de-sac, where Barbara was giving Matt a lecture on nutrition.

"We're going," said Ava.

"Okay," said Barbara. "It was *so* wonderful to meet you, Matt. I can't tell you. You *are* coming to the premiere, I hope."

"Definitely," said Matt.

Ava jumped into the driver's seat and stared forward, gripping the wheel. Barbara waved and asked Matt if she was all right.

"She's fine. We'll see you Wednesday. I'll remember that about niacin. Thanks."

Ava backed out and accelerated rapidly down the narrow street. She drove to Sunset and turned in the wrong direction. She raced around tight corners.

"I don't need this shit," she said. She spit the words out, scrunching her eyes and face. "I have my own fucking life and my own fucking problems without that asshole."

"Pull over. Pull over, Ava. You can't drive if you're upset."

She sniffed loudly and said, "If I didn't know how to drive upset, I'd never get anyplace in this fucking town. Where the hell do you think you are, Ravendahl? My whole life takes place in this truck. Just stay with me."

"Where would I go?"

With a laugh that sounded almost like she was about to cry, she said, "I know your type. You think you can dive out of a moving car."

"You'd have to slow down a little."

"Well, I'm not going to."

She stopped at a pay phone to call Chris and her mother. From a distance Matt heard her comforting her son. Perhaps he had been troubled by the distress he detected in her voice. Afterward, she drove out to the bluffs that overlooked the ocean. Now the sun was setting, casting glinting streaks across the ruffled water, and beyond the slopes of scrub brush a highway was dotted with passing lights. The sandy beaches were the same gray color as the twilight. The swells were covered with the last surfers in their red and turquoise wet suits. The capes reached out, showing the queen's necklace of lights. Palos Verdes and Malibu were like the edges of a pincer claw snapping up its share of ocean. With the windows rolled up, the windshield began to mist as if a mass of fog were rising off the water.

"I really messed everything up." She slipped off her tennis shoes. "I thought we could just waltz in there, keep it brief, keep it casual. What an idiot I am."

"Don't apologize," said Matt. "What else are you supposed to do?"

"If you're hell-bent on going to this premiere, then I'll find you a date. But I sure can't go. Barbara just wants to show off. Get everybody together at a big schmoozer festival. She's trying to turn me into some kind of groupie for my own father. *'And how much did you love the movie, Ava?'* I don't know how it happened, but somewhere along the line everything got mixed up. He thinks I'm the one that doesn't love him. I don't love him if I don't fawn all over him. I'm like the Cordelia in his sick little play."

The fog inside the windshield thickened, so that the lights outside had halos around them.

"Obviously you love him."

"Yeah," said Ava. "I'm just not a big enough fan."

"Of course you are."

"No, Matt. I'm really *not*. My point is that I love him, but I'm not a fan of his work."

"Not even the stuff from, say, the early eighties?"

"Look. I hate every vile, misogynist piece of shit he's ever been in."

"You don't mean that. You're projecting your anger onto his movies."

"Let me ask you something, Matt. Forget all these little catch-phrases for a minute. Why do I have to like his movies? I'm serious. Why does that have to be the starting point for every-thing? If he was a dentist, I wouldn't have to *love* his bridgework. If he was a plumber, my whole relationship wouldn't be based upon his . . . what would that be?"

"Pipe fittings."

"Exactly. So he was a huge star once. That's great. He fit right in with Desert Storm. But they're the same damn movies, Matt, and the explosions are starting to get a little hollow. I'm sorry this didn't work out well today. I really screwed up."

"I'm not discouraged, Ava. Don't apologize. But I am totally pumped about this movie. I *have* to go."

"Thata boy. Into the belly of the monster."

While she waited in silence for him to respond, she watched his profile: broad in the cheeks, his nose widened at the base as if broken repeatedly, his ledge of blond hair that hung over his forehead and into his eyes; but the closer she looked, the more he did resemble her father. What made Matt attractive was the very thing that made him seem so different from Charlie: a crease between his eyebrows that made him seem to be always concentrating.

"You know what's the strangest part about seeing him in per-son?" he said. "I mean, aside from how short he was. It's that I suddenly miss my mother. I haven't missed her in years. That's the only part that feels real. And that's the only part that upsets me, Ava. I just look at this guy and think, he never gave a damn about my mother up there. And you know, she thought about *him* all the time. I guess it's just that the closer I get, the more he seems like a real person who blew us off."

"Your mother ran out on you?"

"No, she died when I was a kid."

"I'm sorry."

"I just looked at this short, sweaty little guy and thought: fuck-ing-A, man. This is the guy? I guess I just thought he was going to be more of something. Something that would make up for everything."

"He's just as troubled by that as you are, Matt. Believe me. His whole life is some sort of competition with whoever he is on-screen. That's why he can't lose it. It's consumed everything else. You might have lost out a little bit, but he's the one who's really missed out. He should have known you, and maybe he should have known your mother. His life might have been better. At least broader. He should know me, he should know his fantastic little grandson. But he can't stand being anything less than a giant. He'll spend his life in hiding rather than admit he's just a normal, fucked-up guy. Oh, of course he'll have his troubles—but they have to be breaking news. He can't just be like you and me, sitting in a damn pickup. A couple of kids trying to sort it out."

"He doesn't pay any attention to Chris, huh?"

"He's just a grandfather. He doesn't need to."

"Well, you're a good mother. Chris has got a good family."

She put her head on the steering wheel and sighed. "God, you must think we're all crazy. You must want to run for the hills."

"I've been in the hills."

"Of course."

"Besides, we got craziness in the genes, you and me."

"The nutcase gene," she said and poked his side.

Matt placed his hand on her shoulder and shook it. They turned and with both hands jostled each other until Ava said, "What are you doing?"

"I'm shaking some sense into you."

He shoved her playfully and she pushed him back. "There's eighteen years of pillow fighting to catch up on."

"Eighteen? You'd hit me in my crib? You witch."

He pulled at her hair and she squirmed and rotated on the seat to kick at him. He seized her foot and tickled it.

"I'm not ticklish, you bully."

It was hot now in the cab, so Ava rolled down the window. They watched the steam slowly evaporate from the windshield like it was a picture reemerging. The sky had darkened and now the flow of taillights thickened beneath them. The ocean looked like a wide, empty space from which there came a wind that gathered strength, rustling the eucalyptus trees and stirring up dust from the hill. Ava started the engine.

"Truce," she said. "Try to grow up a little before we get home."

Ava had refused to go to the premiere, but Camilla badgered her for the next two days. Her nagging culminated in an argument on Wednesday afternoon. Charlie was on television giving an interview, and Matt watched with Chris as the two women stomped between rooms and the short hallway, slamming doors on one another.

"Do they always fight like this?" asked Matt.

Chris nodded. He grabbed his shirt and said, "Mommy's sirts are too big."

"Her shirts or skirts? You should practice that sound. She sells seashells. Say that."

He made a raspberry sound and Matt said that it was good enough.

Eventually Ava said she would go if she had a dress, and Camilla shouted at her for selling all her clothes at the garage sale. "It's self-destructive, Ava. I'd offer you one of mine, but you wouldn't fill it."

"Then I'll stuff my bra with Matt's tube socks."

"My, my. You two have gotten awfully chummy."

Matt and Chris fixated on the television. Matt told Chris that the man broadcast onto the screen was his grandfather.

Charlie appeared distracted on-screen. His head lolled to the side and he grimaced and said, "I don't know. Jeez. Ask me something else."

"Steubenville, Ohio!"

A caller, voice full of static, said, "Charlie, I've loved all your action movies. When are you going to do another sequel to *The Last Stand*?"

Charlie was sitting hunched over, staring blankly at the camera. He adjusted his earpiece.

"A sequel to *The Last Stand Two*," reiterated the host. "Which would make it *The Last Stand Three*. That's a lot of stands, Charlie."

Charlie swatted at something in his ear. He spoke to someone off-screen, complaining that the earpiece was vibrating and tickling him. A hand thrust out and readjusted the clip-on mike at his collar, and then Charlie's head sprung up and he said, "I think I already have. Which film?"

"Are you difficult to work with, Charlie?"

"Oh, I don't think so. I think I just demand a hundred percent from everyone. Including myself."

"So, you're a perfectionist, then?"

"No, in this picture I play a man fighting against terrorists. He's just an everyday man like you and me, but he really rises to the challenge."

"Wear this one, Ava!"

"How is the movie testing?"

"Mother. I'm not wearing *that*. Who am I, Stevie Nicks?"

"Numbers, numbers. Who knows anything about numbers? I don't."

"Okay, sugar. Let's not get into an argument about taste. Miss Longjohns-under-a-skirt."

"It isn't testing well, then?"

"Well, they hated it in Reseda. Who cares?"

"Oh, I get it. My awkward phase was worse than your awkward phase."

"That doesn't concern you, Charlie. You're an old pro, right?"

"They hate everything in Reseda, Larry. It's the Valley, for God's sake. It's not like it's the Nobel committee we're talking about here."

The host's shoulders bounced a few times as if he were going to laugh, then he turned serious, pointed, and said, "But this is an action picture. It's not an art film, Charlie."

"It's just a fucking movie anyway, Mother. I can wear jeans and a T-shirt."

"It's an artistic action picture. That's all I'm going to say about it."

"Then you better accessorize up the wazoo, sugar."

"How do you prepare for an artistic action picture? As you call it."

"Well, Larry, you can never be a hundred percent prepared."

"I'm not doing anything up the wazoo."

"But I have had years of . . ."

"You're going to get all upset if somebody takes your picture and you're wearing a dirty T-shirt."

"Years of . . . forcing myself . . ."

"Why don't you ask Matt what he thinks?"

". . . to grow and ultimately to flourish as an actor."

"Because Matt has his own set of aesthetic problems and we haven't even begun to get into that."

"Terrorism is an issue that plagues humanity currently, and I think this film deals with it in a responsible and artistic manner."

"Hazleton, Pennsylvania! You're on with Charlie West, star of the soon-to-be-blockbuster-movie—even though they hated it in Reseda—*Born Ready*."

"Charlie, I've been a big fan of yours ever since you were that kid in that series—what was the name of it? Hmmm. It's on the tip of my tongue."

"Do you have a question, sir?"

"Oh, you *do* still have that dress. Oh, that's nice. See. That's perfect."

"I'm getting ready now, Mother. Get out of my face."

"Yeah, I wanted to ask Charlie . . ."

"All right. If you need me, I'll be in the living room with fashion crisis number two."

"I'll call you if I need you to zip something."

". . . because I am also a recovering alcoholic, I wanted to know now that you've, um . . . worked through the process of recovering and healing . . . how has your life changed?"

"Whoa," said Charlie. "A big one. A whopper."

"Your private time. What's different?" said the host. "Hobbies, errands, loves, dreams. The whole shebang."

Camilla came into the living room and said, "Oh, what are these old turkeys going on about now?"

"Everything is different. I've basically fallen in love with living. With life itself. I'm having a love affair with life. Um, with exercise, and literature, and all of the good things. But most of all, family. Family. This movie is about a family—partially—and at *heart,* I'm really a family man."

Camilla said, "He must have just had a heart transplant. Oh, dear, I hope his body doesn't reject it."

From the other room, Ava called out, "Did I hear that right?"

Camilla got down onto her knees and slapped her hand against the side of the television. "There must be something wrong with the reception." She pounded on it again and again, mumbling, "Snap out of it, Charlie. Snap out of it." She looked up finally and said, "Ava. Your dear father is drinking again."

"I know," Ava called back.

Gently Camilla touched Matt's arm and whispered, "Don't let him embarrass himself tonight. I'm serious."

Matt nodded.

"Good boy," she whispered.

Camilla turned her scrutiny to Matt, and for the next hour she dressed him in a mishmash of clothes left by various boyfriends over the years. Ava peeked out of the bathroom and giggled. He wore a baggy pair of slacks once owned by Sloan, a dress shirt that belonged to Chris's father, a tie from some awful one-night stand Ava had back when she worked as a temp secretary, and a pair of Charlie's shoes that Ava wore in her gothic phase. Somehow Camilla, by letting out alterations here and there, managed to bring it all together in a way that made Matt look indifferently stylish—a young man at ease in hand-me-downs. He'd fit in well with all the kitsch-hounds who liked Charlie's movies. But the shoes were too tight and he gimped around in them like his ankles were sprained.

Ava came out of the bathroom fully dressed and said, "I'm taking my little brother to the prom."

"Ava! You look so beautiful. I have to get my camera."

She wore a thin black dress that hung to her knees, and with high heels her height made her appear more statuesque. Her hair was in a chignon with tendrils spilling onto her forehead. With it held back, Matt could see how fragile and pale her neck was, how thin her features were. Yet something about the scattering of freckles on her shoulders and cheeks made her still appear to be a tomboy playing dress-up for the night. It was disconcerting now to see that she walked with wide, boyish strides. "Please don't take my picture, Mother."

Camilla snapped a series of her anyway as she said good-bye to Chris, who looked up at her with shock and began crying. Ava told Matt to go wait in the truck. She coaxed Chris to stop, saying that she was still Mommy.

Once in the cab of the pickup, she said, "He has this instinct about fancy clothes. I think he associates them with tragedy. You know, funerals and weddings. Maybe an occasional movie premiere."

She pulled out onto the boulevard. Wind blew through the cab, loosening more strands of her hair.

"I'm glad you decided to come with me," said Matt. "I might have gotten arrested if I went alone."

"He would have stopped us if he didn't want us to come. He's more comfortable in this setting than at home." She crossed her fingers and said, "God, please don't let this movie be awful."

"It's going to be a blast, Ava. Relax."

"And he's already fallen off the wagon. Barbara can tell when he needs more fucking zinc in his diet, but she can't tell when he's shitfaced."

She looked elegant. Matt wondered if she'd always had such a foul mouth. He didn't notice as much when she was dressed casually.

He said, "Maybe he's spiking her diet powder."

"Yum. Dexatrim daiquiris."

As they drove into Hollywood over the hills, the last traces of a sunset hung on the sky and blended with an approaching marine layer. A stripe of haze and smog hung around the mountains like the aftermath of a strafing. The sirens were increasing in number with each increment of darkness.

Ava parked two blocks away, explaining that she had a principle against valet parking at movie theaters. As they crossed the street and approached the lights of the premiere, the wind was increasing and blowing paper bags, newspapers, and fliers out of the gutter. Spotlights circled on the haze overhead. Up ahead was a red carpet lined with cameras and boom mikes, the wind scattering boxes and papers across it. Barbara was standing in a cylinder of bright light, trying to hold her gown in place, giving an interview into the thicket of microphones. She was covered with ribbons. Behind her Charlie stood on the carpet before an embankment of shotgun mikes, looking dizzy and lost.

Beyond the thin layer of press, the sidewalks were quiet. A few tourists in turquoise shorts and T-shirts were inserting their own feet into the celebrity imprints around the theater, and closer to the street, a handful of fans were screaming for various celebrities. But there was only a small group of such diehards, and they seemed like escaped bedlamites causing trouble. Hare Krishnas had gathered on the corner and were making more noise than the genuine fans. Across from them, a pathetic band of protesters—about a half dozen in all—held signs declaiming against Charlie's GLAMOROUS DEPICTION OF VIOLENCE until a gust of wind yanked the signs loose and sent them tumbling down the street.

A section of the boulevard had been blocked off to make room for a bleacher, now half full of winos cheering facetiously and heckling two exhausted-looking traffic cops who were directing limousines into the parking lot.

Ava and Matt bypassed the carpet and the ticket pagoda, gave their names to a team of bewildered-looking security guards, and were led into the theater. A few reporters were milling around so that the lobby seemed like a backstage: coils of wire laid on the floor beside men reloading cameras, and gossip reporters having their makeup retouched as they leaned against the concession stand. Matt saw a woman he recognized from a news-magazine show. She was adjusting her skirt in front of a camera and barking at someone behind it. "How about here?" she asked. "Here? Well, tell me where to *stand,* for God's sake."

A member of the event staff led Ava and Matt straight into the theater, where they sat down in a section cordoned off for "Guests of West." No one had taken their seats yet, so Ava felt absurd being roped off from the rest of an empty theater. "I have a bad feeling about this."

"There were a ton of people milling around out there. This'll be packed in no time."

"Yeah, with Hare Krishnas, maybe."

The theater filled up slowly with a strange mixture of people. There were tourists who had been recruited from attractions all over the city, many of them still wearing their Universal Studios T-shirts or their Venice novelty items: sunglasses shaped like lips, sweatshirts that depicted Mickey Mouse giving the finger. There was a designated section for them, and it filled up first, like a human repository of souvenirs. They sat with cameras in their laps, slurping huge canisters of soda, and swatted at yammering children.

Soon the celebrities began to arrive. Most of their faces were only vaguely recognizable, like distant memories. They entered to a twinkling of camera flashes; they shook hands like politicians; then they sat sullenly in their chairs, waiting for the darkness to hide them.

A section in the front was reserved for the crew of the film, and the grips and electricians straggled in late with their wives, whistling to one another and hugging over spilled popcorn and drinks.

With fifteen minutes to go, the theater was only half full. It seemed a matter of pride that the star couldn't sit down before there was a packed house. Soon the press was filling seats along the back as other people were herded in off the sidewalk, many looking unsure of where they were.

In the row ahead of Ava, two teenagers were making fart noises on their arms. It somehow created the impression that there was no real enthusiasm with even the target audience.

At last Charlie entered to a flurry of pictures. He couldn't find his seat, and he wandered around the aisles, flinching as several belligerent fans shouted at him. Barbara scampered after him and pulled him to his reserved chair on the other side of the Guests of West area. Ava waved to him, but he didn't notice her until Barbara nudged him. He stood up and saluted Ava sarcastically.

"Is he wasted?" she asked. "What kind of hello was that?"

The lights went down; the theater was dark; the mechanical curtain was opening. "You might have to hold my hand," Ava said to her brother. "I get emotional at movies."

CHAPTER ELEVEN

FADE IN.

INT. ARCHITECT'S STUDIO (DAY)

To the score of jaunty piano music, on-screen Charlie is scrutinizing the model of a tall office building. He paces around it, nodding his head. He likes what he sees. He is a handsome man, and one infers from his athletic physique that he knows how to take care of himself in a bind. Yet his expression is kind and gentle. His portable phone rings.

CHARLIE

Phil Glass here. Oh, hi, honey. No, not yet. Doesn't look like this deal is going to be closed until later. I know. This is the last time. Let me talk to her, then. (*Continuing in baby talk*) Hi, sweetheart. Did you have fun at school today? You did? Well, Daddy wants to see your drawing the second he gets home. Okay. Put Mommy back on. (*Resuming in the architect tone*) Yeah, looks like I'm going to have to catch the red-eye home.

CUT TO:

THE RED-EYE HOME

Our hero is on a plane full of sleeping passengers. Camera pans across the aisle to show three suspicious, ethnically indeterminate Europeans dressed in foreboding black.

STEWARDESS
Enjoying your flight, sir?

HEAD EUROPEAN
(*with a vaguely eastern European accent and a clearly lewd
tone*)
I'm just beginning to, my dear. *Just* beginning to.

Ava whispered, "That stewardess is his personal assistant."

Next came an extravagant rising-crane shot of the Glass household, the camera passing through an open bedroom window, cottage curtains rustling in the breeze, to show the lovely Everydaughter in her country pajamas, dozing to the lullaby of the same piano theme now slowed down, credits striping her angelic face. The camera glided, silently as a ghost, downstairs to show her beautiful mother sitting in an opulent living room. It occurred to Ava that whenever a character in a movie was unjustifiably wealthy, he was always an architect.

The theater was echoing with sniffles and stifled coughs. The more quiet the scene, the more it sounded like an infirmary, except that bubble gum was cackling and drinks were slurped, and after a few more dull scenes, whispers rose through the aisles along with snorts of repressed laughter.

Matt tapped Ava and said, "Maybe we can all have a cup of coffee after the movie."

"We might need some."

INT. AIRPORT (NIGHT)
*On-screen Charlie picks up a suitcase. The swarthy Europeans are joking
in a loud, uncouth manner beside the baggage claim. They pick out a
bag identical to our hero's.*

Titters of laughter passed through the crowd. Charlie sank down in his seat. Barbara stared ahead with a wide smile, but the rest of the audience seemed distracted already. Charlie had initially liked all the sensitive buildup with the family, but now, with the dainty music, he wasn't sure. Maybe attention spans had become too short for any dialogue at all. He tried to watch objectively. Was he bored or just overly sedated? He had already taken two Valiums at home, and after sneaking a small drink in the men's room, he was feeling seasick from the movement on-screen.

INT. BEDROOM (NIGHT)

On-screen Charlie is home now. He puts his suitcase on the bed as he loosens his tie; and the camera pans to the suitcase, staying on it long enough to satisfy the slowest members of the audience and the good people from Samsonite. He kisses his gorgeous thirty-something wife (in a manner that indicates the spark is still there), *and then he moves to his daughter's bedroom.*

ANGELIC DAUGHTER
Daddy, I had a scary dream. These men were chasing me.

CHARLIE
Well, don't you worry. I won't ever let anyone get you, pumpkin. Daddy is home now.

Ava winced.

ANGELIC DAUGHTER
You promise?

CHARLIE
Cross my heart.

ANGELIC DAUGHTER
And hope to die?

CHARLIE
And hope to die.

The whispers were increasing behind Charlie. He thought he heard his daughter say something in the crowd, and he turned to see rows of solemn faces. Ava was lodged down in her chair, covering her face and watching through spread fingers. His son was beside her, watching the flickering lights with a crazed look, as if it were an oncoming train. Charlie was so disoriented that he imagined he might be in this theater for the rest of his life, with an angry son staring over his shoulder, his entire history condensed into twenty square feet of cushioned seats.

"How did Lincoln die?" he asked Barbara. "Did he get shot from right behind?"

"Watch the movie, Charlie."

Charlie stood, squeezed out into the aisle past Barbara, and rushed to the men's room. A few pictures were snapped of him in the lobby. He felt like throwing up, but at the bathroom sink he splashed water onto his face and calmed himself. He had a half-pint of bourbon in his coat pocket and he swigged from it. He faced his reflection and said, "You're all right. You're doing just fine. They don't know a thing, these people. You're doing just fine. You can handle *anything*." A turkey on-screen, a family in shambles, a press core that hated him: he clenched his teeth and swore he could take it.

When he entered the theater again, his character was back at work the following day, noticing a few cars with tinted windows that surrounded his office building. Despite a vague feeling of uneasiness, his character carried on with his job, displaying great charm and courtesy to his underlings. Charlie was sure this scene would endear him to the crowd.

CHARLIE

Glenda, can you get me LAX on the phone? Last night I picked up a suitcase and I don't think it's mine. I couldn't get the lock to open.

The Lost and Found Department is indifferent to Charlie's worries—putting him on hold. He waits a few moments. But when Charlie sees a deployment of Armani-clad, slightly swarthy men outside his building, he has a funny feeling. He ducks out the back.

INT. HOUSING PROJECT (DAY)

Charlie is touring one of his ambitious designs. The housing project teems with delightful children.

CHARLIE

It's so gratifying to be able to take time out to design affordable housing for the underprivileged.

OBSEQUIOUS YOUNGER ARCHITECT

Taking time out of *your* busy schedule? Wow. You're an inspiration, Mr. Glass.

Neither notices the three mysterious men. Charlie and the Obsequious Younger Architect step into an elevator with them. They begin their ascent. Eastern European #1 reaches out and presses the emergency button, stopping the elevator.

EUROPEAN #1

It's a pleasure to finally make your acquaintance. You are, I presume, the famous Mr. Glass. Family man. Upstanding citizen. Contributor to numerous charities. Designer of the famous Shutaki building in Tokyo. It's a thrill to meet you.

CHARLIE

Do I know you?

EUROPEAN #1

We are not people to be trifled with, Mr. Glass. I believe you have something of ours. It would be wise of you to return it.

To prove the point, European #3 pulls out a gun and shoots the Obsequious Younger Architect. Charlie kicks the gun out of his hand. While the others fire shots at him, missing despite the close range, Charlie climbs out of the elevator through the access panel. The elevator begins its ascent toward a grating at the top floor that will crush Charlie. Charlie leaps and grabs the adjacent elevator cable, and slides downward to land upon the roof of another car.

Matt perked up during the gunplay, but, like the rest of the audience, he was disappointed with the slow pace and piano score that followed. Charlie discovered that the mystery suitcase contained cocaine, after which Ava nudged Matt and said, "This movie is way behind the times. It's all smack and cell phones these days."

In the half hour that followed, Charlie learned that the police, customs officials, airport security, and perhaps a few co-workers at his architectural firm were also involved. This accidental switch had, in fact, been *no* accident.

It was clear by this point that everyone in the movie-family loved each other so devoutly that eventually someone would be taken hostage. The crowd was turning mutinous after another scene with Charlie and his daughter, a girl so increasingly adorable with each scene that Ava wished she would come down with a raging case of measles. Each plot twist was explained two or three times, and the apologies began early for the upcoming violence. Charlie wound up a music box for the girl and told her about the wrongness of killing. They watched a porcelain ballerina dance to the tinny music.

CHARLIE
Sometimes good people have to do bad things.

In the scene that followed, Charlie lured his enemies into a construction site. He proceeded to kill three foot soldiers with a nail gun, leaving the crowd to assume this was one of those "bad things."

It was the first sustained action scene in the film, but by now the crowd appeared too lethargic to notice. During a shoot-out in an abandoned warehouse, a recently wounded drug runner explained the convoluted plot while bleeding to death. Years ago Charlie had accepted a contract to rebuild structures in Kuwait shortly after Desert Storm. During a brief visit, Charlie had come across a buried Iraqi biological weapons depot funded with money from an eastern European drug cartel in conjunction with the World Bank and the CIA. Unfortunately, our helpful terrorist died before he could make his conspiracy theory very convincing.

Next came the requisite skewering and gouging, throwing vaguely developed villains down stairwells, discovering that bland supporting good guys were actually bland supporting bad guys, and Charlie—armed with only wits, his social conscience, and a generous supply of power tools—managed to rally together tenants from his buildings to help catch the last remaining drug lords. The extreme brutality was even more disturbing because it was all so routine. Charlie's earlier moral quandary was resolved with a few smug one-liners. The audience groaned at severed limbs and graphic decapitations. With the help of sledgehammers, posthole diggers, and some rather bold Foley artists, Charlie began eliminating his foes, each time shouting "I want my life back!" and each time prompting the audience to duck lower in their chairs.

Someone in the audience shouted, "Yeah, give him his life back!"

All of the heads in the crowd turned. Attention left the movie, and now the clutter of on-screen violence looked more like passing scenery. The heckler shouted, "Give him his life back and let's get the hell out of this disaster."

The crowd was more stunned than if this had been any heckler, because while the voice was hoarse and angry, more shallow than the voices cast out through the speakers, it was still a version of the on-screen voice. At first, Matt thought there was a speaker in the center of the theater. But, along with the rest of the crowd, he soon realized that it was Charlie West. The actor cupped his hands over his mouth and shouted, "Boo! Boo! You talentless loser! You idiot. Boo!"

The crowd seemed terrified. While the heroic Charlie stalked a drug dealer across darkened scaffolding, the other Charlie, a fidgeting shadow in front of him, appeared far more dangerous. Barbara grabbed him and tried to silence him. He fought to his feet and his silhouette poked through the chin of his own close-up. He flung his arms and shouted like an indignant sports fan, "You make me sick! You are the *worst*! You are a rotten actor, in a miserable movie. You are the world's worst, pal. You are the all-time low!"

Ava gripped down tightly on Matt's arm. She said, "He's out of his mind. Matt, listen to me. Go get him. Get him out of here."

"Go get him? What the hell am I going to do?"

"Just get him out of here, Matt. Discreetly."

"What about all those cameras out front?"

"Then take him out the back. Just do it before they haul him out of here in a straitjacket."

"Does he think people don't know it's him yelling?"

"He's not thinking. Please. Carry him if you have to."

Charlie fought past bent knees toward the aisle. He began wavering up the slope, muttering, "This is a fucking horror show, a fucking insult to humanity. You fucking people don't know a goddamn thing about anything. You people are a bunch of fucking sheep. *Baaa. Baaa.*"

Matt caught up to him and put his arm around him. Charlie was still bleating. He wiggled to get away, but Matt clamped down and held him in place. He spun him around and walked him toward a side exit between two ornamented pillars. The crowd watched. "We're just going to walk this one off, Mr. West. It's a nice night outside. Outside is *good*. We like it there."

The smell of booze was so heavy that Matt's eyes watered. Charlie had a hitch in his step, and each time it came Matt lifted him and carried him a few paces.

CHARLIE

Now it's my turn to call the shots, pal. Say hello to my new friends.

They limped down the aisle toward the climactic shoot-out. Bullets clanged off steel girders.

Ava moved to intercept Barbara. From where she was, Charlie and Matt looked like a single creature with four legs tangling together. A few people in the crowd called to Charlie as he was dragged past, a mixture of cheers and heckling, as if the lead character of the film had simply been yanked off the screen.

Matt threw Charlie through the exit and into the parking lot outside. Charlie teetered backward and balanced himself against the chassis of an Explorer. He looked poisoned. He was so saturated that his face had swelled. He squinted at the streetlights. "I should've known," he said and swallowed, "that you were planning a stunt like this. That girl has been plotting against me since the day she was born."

His legs weakened, and he slid downward with his back against the truck until he plopped onto the ground beside the tire. Pedestrians were filing past on the sidewalk a few yards away. One of the parking attendants noticed Charlie, and was watching from his booth.

Matt said, "Nobody's against you. You just lost your shit in there."

"My life has been about the challenges of . . . of new," Charlie slurred, then lost his thought and stared at a helicopter passing low over rooftops, crossing the roaming spotlights cast from the theater. "This place is under siege."

"I should get you out of here. You think you could walk with me across the street? It looks like there's a coffee shop over there."

"I could walk a thousand miles. *You.*" He pointed at Matt and held up his finger until he had formulated his words. "You are that tall young man again. You are a goddamned *trooper.*"

"Come on. See if you can stand up."

"And I am the flop to end all flops."

"That's good. Let's get off the ground."

Charlie rocked his head and sighed. He said, "Don't toy with me, mister. I know exactly what's happening here. I know the rules of this game—I *invented* this game."

"Ava wanted me to get you out of there, and I did. Now let's go."

"Ava. Sure. She said, 'You hold the pillow over his head, and I'll shoot him.' "

"This is perfect. I finally meet you and you're too far gone for me to ask you anything."

"Questions!" Charlie shouted so loud that Matt glanced over his shoulder to see if anyone had noticed. "I can answer a whole load of questions! How did I research this role? How does my marriage last? Who's hot and who's in and who's on first and who the *fuck* are you? Blah, blah, blah. My life in a nutshell."

"That's fascinating." Matt could feel the blood rushing to his face, and he bit his lip for a moment and breathed deeply, calming himself. "That's all you've got to say to me, huh?"

"That's all I've got to say to *anybody,* kid. I'm a fucking quote machine."

"Well, then, listen, you souse. You're going to stand up, and you're going to walk with me over to that coffee shop, and you're going to drink caffeine until you make sense. Then we're going to find your daughter, and we'll all start working these problems out. Understand?"

Charlie closed his eyes and tilted his head to the side, then he spun a single finger in the air and said, "Hooray."

Matt grabbed his collar. "Listen to me. I'm now the voice of motherfucking reason here. You are way out of line. I came a long way, and I expect to go home with something more than your puke on my shoes." He lifted his father and pounded him a few times against the truck. Charlie's eyes opened wide with fear and surprise, and Matt kept talking right into his face. "Now, let's avoid those cameras and go stop this bullshit. You big crybaby. So your movie sucks. So you have to go home to your mansion now and not everybody on the planet loves you. Boo-fucking-hoo! Let's just get your fat, rationalizing ass up off this pavement."

"Rationalizing? Oh, no. You're one of them."

Matt lifted him by the collar and slammed him one last time into the truck, setting off a car alarm. Charlie ran out of the parking lot—a dizzy, weaving run as if he were on the deck of a ship. When Matt caught up to him, he seized his arm and guided him through the traffic to the Hamburger Hamlet across the street, where he pushed him into a booth beside the window. Charlie lay down in the fetal position on the Naugahyde.

"Don't hurt me," said Charlie. "Please."

"Yeah, okay," said Matt. "Take a nap down there."

"You hate me so much."

"You just stay down. The movie is letting out."

Across the street, the flashbulbs of cameras flickered like distant heat lightning. A crowd had now condensed around the entrance area, which was full of cement handprints and footprints. Matt looked for Barbara or Ava, moving his head to look around the fogged patches he left on the glass. A waitress came to the table and asked if they would be having dinner.

"He needs coffee." Matt pulled out a few crumpled-up bills, his remaining three dollars.

"We might have to go in a hurry, though, so just bring us as much as this buys."

"He wants to kill me," said Charlie, his face pressed against the booth and his voice muffled.

The waitress glanced up at the enormous poster of Charlie across the street, in which he was holding a machine gun and wearing a shredded business suit.

"Yeah, that's him," said Matt. "It's a long story."

Charlie mumbled, "Get me out of this place. Get me out of this *town*."

The waitress filled two cups and hurried away.

"Just camp out down there, buddy. We'll figure it out."

"My life is in danger. You don't understand, kid." He climbed up in the booth and looked around, his hair mussed into a cowlick, his face pink from having stuck to the seat. He slurped his coffee. "I'm dead. You don't know me from Adam, but you've got to listen to me. I'm finished. I *have* to get out of this city. If you want to kill me, give me at least that last request."

Matt nodded, glancing between his father and the window. "We'll just find your wife and Ava. Nobody's killing anybody. Try to calm down."

A crowd began to gather just outside the window. When Matt

looked away from them, he noticed a heavyset man in sandals who was videotaping them from beside the coat rack.

"What I'm trying to say is: we *can't* find my wife and Ava. They're the bad guys."

"Try to get hold of yourself. That asshole over there is filming us."

"I'm telling you. They're everywhere. They won't let you breathe. This is the chance you wanted, kid. This is destiny. I know who you are. I know all about you. We can escape all of this. We go and get my driver—and we head for Mexico. We go on his scuba trip to fucking Antwerp or wherever it was. We don't ever look back. You don't know me, I don't know you. So what? But if you're really so damn hot to come in here and save my life—"

"I never said that."

"—then you get me out of here. We'll head south. We'll be in Baja by sunrise—easy. Then we forget about all this, this, this . . . *coffee*. This horror show. Father and son, man to man, *mano a mano*."

"That means *hand to hand*."

"We've got a lifetime of catching up to do—right? Well, it has to be done in Mexico. It cannot be done in this present . . . environment. This situation. No! It has to be done far, far away from here." He pointed at the man with the camcorder. "That is very rude, sir!"

Matt stared out the window at the growing crowd. They were entirely unashamed, with bored, captive expressions as if they were peering into an aquarium. Matt said, "I can't just leave Ava in there. She's done everything for me."

"Don't make me laugh."

"She's been lied to more than I have."

"One word: *Mexico*."

"Did you ever wonder about me? Did you ever think about me at all?"

"Of course I did. Every day of my life. But it isn't safe here. We can't talk. This place is crawling with informants. Those prep cooks over there are really the foreign press. Look—I'll give you my wallet." He dug into his pocket and threw an alligator-skin wallet onto the table, then rummaged through each pocket of his coat until he found his cell phone. "Get a cab. Then I'll tell you whatever you want to hear. Right now I have to go get sick."

As Charlie weaved to the bathroom, the man with the camcorder followed him.

In the taxi Charlie's rush of adrenaline subsided, and once again he was listless and incoherent. Matt couldn't figure out if he had managed to sneak another drink or if he was simply fading from exhaustion, but Charlie passed out with his head propped against the window. The cabbie had a heavy Russian accent, and he peered back and asked, "He is movie actor, no?"

"Right. He says we have to go to an address in Sherman Oaks."

Matt dialed Ava's number on the cell phone. He felt ridiculous using the tiny handheld device. Charlie was making a low moaning sound. Matt left a message: "He's here with me, Ava, but I have no idea what the hell we're doing. I'm just telling you that he's not dead—and we're both all right. I hope you check this message soon so you don't drive around looking for us. I'll call you back."

The taxi dropped them off at the address Charlie had given in his delirium, and Matt was certain that it was the wrong place. A small house, looking warped and earthquake-damaged, stood amid a forest of overgrown bamboo. On a dried-out lawn lay dozens of overturned gnome statues, rusted car parts, trash cans stinking of brine and filled with shells, and kennels stacked beside a sagging fence. The one lit window was blocked out by a paisley tapestry.

Charlie paid the driver, then wandered up the yard, kicking aside beer cans. "Sloan!" he shouted. "Wake up, you freeloader! You lazy son of a bitch, wake up!"

Charlie wobbled along a paved path that led to an overgrown garden in the backyard. In the dim light from the house next door, Matt could see a giant trailer covered by a tarp. "Sloan! Wake up, you idiot. I'm here with an investor! We want to fund a fucking scuba trip."

The light on the back porch came on and a screen door swung open. The man came out walking gingerly on bare feet, wearing nothing but a pair of baggy boxer shorts. He had a long beard held in place with a rubber band, and he was so pale that he had a ghostlike appearance in the dark.

"There he is," said Charlie. "We want to dig up a buried treasure, Sloan. Yo-ho-ho and a bottle of rum. Guess who this is? Look. Look at his face."

"I'm no good with faces," said the man.

The setting had become so absurd to Matt that he felt as if he were onstage, and the darkness all around him was an auditorium full of watching parents, and the dull moonlight was that ambient glow when the lights were down. Here he was, with his father, in a shabby lot talking to a man in his underwear who was entirely nonplussed.

Sloan said, "What can I do for you, gentlemen?"

"Guess who he is, Sloan. Look at him. That's my *son*. My real live son. Look how big he is. And he hasn't killed me yet. What a guy, huh? Can you believe that? So listen here, Sloan. We want the key to the mobile home. The key to salvation."

Matt wrapped his knuckles on the Winnebago beneath the tarp, and he asked, "You own this?"

"I own everything," said Charlie. "I own the whole fucking world, and it's Sloan's job to keep the birds from shitting on it."

"It's nice to meet you," said Sloan. "I obviously don't know all the particulars of your situation, but as far as I can say, your father is a first-rate human being."

"What a kiss-ass. I love this brownnosing son of a bitch. Even though he's always got his hands in my pocket."

"Ah, Chuck. That's not true."

"Give us the key, Sloan. We have to drive off into the sunset here. Or the sunrise. Get with the program."

"I don't think you're in any state to drive a recreational vehicle, Chuck."

Charlie shook his head over and over, an animated shaking that became strong enough to sway his shoulders from side to side. "Nope. My boy here is driving. He's sixteen now, and he's driving me. I think he might even be *older* than sixteen. So he is officially replacing *you,* Sloan. But never fear—all of your scuba dreams will come true. Now give me the key to *my* mobile home."

Sloan returned to the house, and while he was inside, Charlie and Matt paced around the Winnebago, trying to pull off the tarp. Charlie nearly lost his balance several times, but he appeared to be recharged with energy. A dog was barking at them in the next yard. When all the lights had gone out in the house, they were left in darkness beneath a starless sky, among the faint screech of crickets. Charlie headed toward the house. "I don't think he's getting the keys."

Charlie stumbled through the dark rooms, shouting, and Matt followed him, picking up the overturned chairs and plants knocked out of their pots. Sloan sat on his couch, watching television and ignoring Charlie's theatrics. Eventually Matt joined him, while Charlie crawled on his hands and knees to search through drawers and under tables, calling, "*Please.* I'm a sick man, Sloan. I have to get away."

Frustrated at the lack of attention, Charlie snatched a bottle of malt liquor from the refrigerator and locked himself in the bathroom. By the time Sloan had managed to pick the lock, Charlie was passed out in the tub using a loofah as a pillow.

Sloan said, "I'll open up the trailer, then, and the two of you can crash in there for the night."

As they maneuvered around Charlie to hoist him out of the tub, Sloan said, "It must be exciting to meet him after all this time."

"It's not exactly the way I pictured it."

They groaned as they lifted him, and they shuffled their feet as they carried him out of the house. "Watch your hands," said Sloan as they passed through the back door. "But just think— when he wakes up tomorrow, you can meet him for the first time all over again."

Matt looked at the sky and estimated the time: it was at least past one. His father lay on a foldout bed in the back, snoring. The inside of the Winnebago was stuffy and smelled heavily of disinfectant, so Matt sat in the passenger seat and rolled down the window. He called on the cell phone again.

He didn't recognize the voice that answered Ava's phone. She simply dropped the receiver and said, "It's him. Your friend. Your . . . whoever."

Ava came on and said, "Jesus, Matt. Thank God. I've been out of my mind. What took you so long?"

"I've still got him with me. He's out cold, I think."

"I guess I figured you would meet me at the car."

"Who answered the phone? Who was that?"

"It's a long story. Just get him home now, okay. Matt. I'm sorry this had to happen."

She covered the receiver and said something back into the room. Matt could hear Chris calling and he pictured Ava holding him. It added to his sense of urgency. "I have to go, Matt. Talk to my mom for a second."

Camilla came on and said, cheerful as ever, "Hello, Matt."

"What's happening there?"

"You know, crisis headquarters. We've got you on our NORAD screen."

"Can you tell Ava something for me? Please. Tell her I have it under control. Sort of. Tell her that I'm not altogether sure what we're going to do, but she should trust me."

"Of course. We both trust you."

"I can take care of this. But I want Ava, and you and Chris— I want all of you to know that I'm glad I know you. I've got my own plan now, but getting to know the three of you—that was the best thing that ever could've happened to me."

"You can tell her that yourself, Matt."

"Just tell her how happy I was with all of you. That's all."

"This is very cryptic. You two don't have some kind of suicide pact, do you?"

In the back, Charlie was groaning and holding the keys in the air. He was mumbling that he had stolen a pair from Sloan's house, and he slurred something about fleeing to Mexico.

"Just tell her I'm not going to Mexico," said Matt. "Tell her I'll be home soon."

PART THREE

WH●'S

WHO

Once Matt had pushed Charlie out of the theater, the audience started to talk and the din blocked out the sound of the movie. Ava rushed to her father's empty seat and was surprised that Barbara was the only person still focused on the movie. Ava waited a few minutes for the voices to quiet.

"I'm sorry, Barbara. You must feel like . . . ." She stopped, about to say "*killing someone,*" but too many grisly murders were occurring on-screen for it to sound tactful.

"What must I feel like?"

Ava didn't answer. They watched the rest of the movie: bullets skittering, explosions, the family reunited in their pajamas. Barbara was looking up at the screen with stunned eyes that reflected glints of color from the screen.

When the credits rolled, the crowd rose and pushed into the aisles.

Ava said, "Looks like an evacuation is under way."

"Are you coming to the reception?" asked Barbara.

"You're kidding."

"What else would I do? We can't all have a nervous breakdown."

"Don't torture yourself, Barbara."

"Of course not."

"It's not your job to cover for him. Everybody in here saw him stumble out of here, throwing a fit."

The lights were still down and shadows of the audience filed past in long, exhausted lines. Barbara took out a compact with a crescent of light around the rims, and in the shell-shaped mirror her mouth was illuminated. She ran a pencil around her lips. Ava couldn't see her eyes in it, only the floating mouth.

"It's a party, Ava." She snapped the compact shut. The audience was pushing past her. "I deserve it as much as he does."

"Don't be so defensive. I know what you're going through."

"What am I going through, Ava? Please. Enlighten me. If you think I'm just going to go away, go home, and sit with my hands in my lap because he can't handle a little pressure . . . well, then you don't know me. This is my premiere too, Ava. I've put more into this than you could possibly imagine."

"He just got *dragged* out of here."

Barbara stood and joined the passing crowd. Ava waited a few breaths, watching the last credits, and when fake gaslights brightened around the walls, Ava hopped up and walked to the lobby. Cameras were blocking the exits. Bright lights fired. Ava passed a series of shouted interviews. A TV actor said, "Wow. I'm really impressed. I don't have any idea what happened in there. But a great flick. I got to go." In the clamor of voices Ava heard an undercurrent of her father's name. She couldn't piece together the sentences, but could hear his name overlapping itself with urgency. Ava was knocked in front of a camera as an actress was being interviewed. Ava apologized and said, "I love your dress," and continued through the fray toward the flashing lights and the red cordon outside.

A drizzle had begun and much of the press was camped out under a tarp, looking like a Chinese dragon in a parade, shotgun mikes reaching out like feelers. Everyone in the jostling crowd looked so serious and aggressive that Ava started laughing in the midst of it. Barbara stood in a glare of lights, mikes aimed at her from every angle. A scream came from somewhere in back and Ava worried they'd trampled some poor usher. To clear a wider circle for Barbara, the mob pressed outward and Ava was caught amid the shoving. She kept her eyes on her stepmother, who was wildly animated, a glinting smile and a sweetness in her eyes like a lunatic beauty contestant. Her head bobbed with sincerity as she spoke. Ava wrestled closer. She heard Barbara say, "He just gets so *nervous*. He's such a little boy sometimes. It's adorable, really. He doesn't like to see himself on-screen. He wants people to like it so much, and I just know they do. Don't we, folks? He'll show up at the reception once he has a chance to think. Don't worry for a second."

The reporters thanked Barbara. Everyone was so saccharine that Ava panicked. They all sounded like stewardesses on a plane that was crashing. *I'm going to have to ask you to put up your tray table, honey. Seems we're going to be plunging into the Pacific now.*

But farther back in the crowd the reporters were more vicious—pushing so hard that Barbara was almost knocked off her thin heels. Ava caught up to her as she was getting into the limousine. Barbara waved over the tops of reporters and cameras. "Ava? Ava?" she said. "Excuse me, can you let that young lady through?"

Ava stopped before the door. Barbara, with the same ferocious smile, said, "Do you need a ride someplace?"

The offer was so unexpected that Ava leaped forward. She stepped down into the car and closed the door, sealing off the tangle of arms and torsos.

Barbara's expression sank all at once. She took a few deep breaths, patted her chest, and said, "So. Since you're the expert, Ava, where did our dates run off to?"

"That's not my date, Barbara. Just so you know."

Barbara said to the driver, "Mr. West has apparently found himself a dive bar. So could you please just drive around for a while until we get our bearings here?"

They drove past the spotlights still rotating circles on the undersides of clouds, out of the clutter surrounding the theater, the temporary bleacher now empty, the shedding decorations on the streetlights, and east down Hollywood Boulevard, where the stores were locked shut with aluminum cages.

"This is not good at all," said Barbara. "People were asking me the strangest questions. We have to find him and get him to that reception. I'm not much for bar-hopping, though. You know this side of him better than I do. Which rock should we turn over first? Or would you like to split up and look separately?"

"I'm parked over by that Scientology building on La Brea."

"Why don't you ever use the valet?"

"It makes me uncomfortable."

"If I live forever, Ava, I'll never understand the way you think."

"Thank you."

"Just ride with me for a while," said Barbara. "I don't like being alone. Did you think at least the movie turned out well? You see what I've been saying all this time. It's a change of direction for him."

"Sort of an apologetic action film. Without much action," said Ava, scanning the windows as they passed locked souvenir stands. "I like the concept."

"I don't think of his movies as action pictures, Ava. That's a phenomenally simplistic view. No offense. Charlie has always had people doing that to him. I believe that these are essentially *morality* plays. Like Westerns. Charlie has this down-to-earth quality, and that's what has extended his career this long. But this is the era of political correctness, and goodness knows, we can't have a hero like Charlie anymore."

"This isn't the time for this, Barbara."

"You don't agree? He's an old-fashioned, *moral* hero, and people are trying very hard to act like they don't want that anymore."

"What's moral about going on a bender at your own premiere?"

"I'm talking about the film, Ava."

"Oh, right. The film where he executed everybody with power tools."

"My God, Ava. Has it gone so far that we can't shoot the bad guys anymore? What kind of movie would it be if they all just got a *fair* trial and that was the end? You people are the ACLU. This is exactly what I'm talking about. Everyone around here identifies more with the villains than they do with Charlie."

Ava said, "It's funny how whenever a white guy isn't doing

as well these days it has to do with political correctness. And these are the same people who say minorities blame too much on racism."

"I never know whose side you're on."

"I have to be honest with you, Barbara. I'm a bit troubled by your attitude. You're more worried about how he looked on-screen. He just poisoned himself and ran screaming out of the theater."

"I'm dealing with this the way I know how, Ava. Thank you very much."

"Matt's not going to take him to a bar. They might be in a diner someplace. I'm trying to figure out what this kid would do."

"Charlie is defending certain American ideals, and people have no right to criticize that. This is why he's so panicked. Because it's coming from all sides."

"I think maybe Matt can handle this—but it's definitely not the reunion he was hoping for."

"If Charlie would just *listen* to me. If he just presented himself with more force. Out in the world, I mean. This is a twenty-four-hour-a-day job and sometimes he's just such an infant."

While the car waited at a stoplight, a man in a truck idling beside them mugged for his own reflection in the tinted glass. He pulled his mouth open and stuck his tongue out.

Barbara watched him. She said, "So, where do I go, then, Ava? If I don't go to this reception. Charlie should be there."

"He's not in any shape for it. Just pray to God that Matt's still with him. I suppose sobering him up could be a sort of bonding moment too."

"I certainly don't feel like combing the streets all night."

"Okay. You and I will go someplace and figure this out. But I do have to use your phone to see how Chris is doing."

The man in the truck made moose horns with his hands and twiddled them on his head.

"I don't know if I feel *welcome* with you, Ava."

"Oh, stop. You're perfectly welcome. Do you mind if I use it?" She picked up the phone and began dialing.

Barbara noticed the man still making faces outside and she said, "Oh, who are these people? What's happening to this town?" She looked at Ava, who was crouched down with her ear to the phone.

Ava asked her mother, "Is he asleep? Did you have a hard time getting him down? I know. It's because of this excitement in the air. Well, you'll hear the whole story, Mother. Not now. Yeah, I'd say it's *that* bad." She got all the details of Chris's bed-time procedure, then timidly asked if Matt had called. "A what? A taxi dispatcher? Well, maybe he used Dad's cell phone and there was some sort of interference. I hope they haven't been arrested."

When she hung up, Barbara said, "You know, you don't give me the credit I deserve. You act like I'm just along for the ride. Well, let me tell you something: Charlie has never done a thing on his own. Some men succeed in the world because they know how to surround themselves with the right people. Well, I'm the right person."

"And you've got him surrounded."

"I'm not the enemy here, Ava. I'm just the one who has to keep this ship from sinking. I didn't ask for the job, it was just given to me."

"How long has he been hitting the sauce?"

"We don't have any liquor in the house. So I don't know."

"Cough syrup?"

"He's never done this with me. I don't know. He leads a very structured life."

"Has he taken up any new hobbies? Maybe model airplanes?"

"No, no. He's working too hard for that."

"There was a little phase in the eighties when he fiddled around with some kind of pet tranquilizer."

"Well, we don't have any pets. He's allergic to them."

"Why don't you come back with me, Barbara. There's not a lot of traffic at this hour. I'll give you a ride. We'll sit up, we'll figure this out. He's with Matt right now, and I'm sure they'll call my house."

"I don't know much about this friend of yours. Should we be worried?"

Ava sighed. "You and Dad don't talk very much, do you?"

"We never *stop* talking."

"He's going to call my house," said Ava. "You're welcome to come."

"You mean your *mother's* house."

"Whatever," said Ava. "Come back with me if you want to. My truck is parked right back there. You're invited, but there's no obligation." She thought for a moment, then said, "Take it or leave it."

Ava was surprised when she accepted.

The limousine dropped them off at the corner, and Barbara sat stiffly in the cab of Ava's pickup. She looked afraid to touch anything. The wind poured through Ava's open window and unraveled her hair and flapped it against the headrest beside Barbara. Passing Griffith Park, Barbara thanked Ava and said that she hoped she wasn't an imposition. She then asked if Ava could please roll up her window; and when Glendale came and went, the foothills ahead, she said, "What a long drive. How inconvenient for you."

When Camilla opened the front door and saw Barbara, she said with delight, "A crisis at last."

"I'm sure you two need no introduction," said Ava.

Barbara said, "*She* talked me into this."

"Oh, nonsense, sugar. Come in, come in. Everybody inside this instant. I want to know every sordid detail."

In the kitchen, lit only by light from the television, Ava and her mother shared a joint and a carton of ice cream while Barbara watched them with a horrified expression. To Ava she looked like a Jesuit among the heathens. Once Ava had smoked the joint to a short roach, the ice cream itself began to taste smoky and resinous. She whispered with her mouth full, "Everybody's on a binge today."

Camilla said loudly to Barbara, "Can I get you anything, honey?" Ava shushed her and pointed at Chris's room.

"It's not that we don't want to wake him," said Ava. "It's that the kid can't keep a secret."

They both swallowed and laughed.

Camilla whispered, "Barbara, you have to go easy on yourself. Charlie will run you ragged. At a certain point I just refused to play these sorts of games anymore. Pamper yourself."

"I don't need pampering, thank you."

"Mother, you *enabler*."

"The thing about Charlie, see, is that he's very hung up on the idea he led an artificial life," Camilla said, then paused to scoop out another bite from the carton. "He's terrified at the idea that's he's sheltered. So every now and then, he'll do this. He used to do it much more. He thinks he's being wild and spontaneous, instead of just a buffoon. But you see, Charlie is not blessed with a great deal of self-awareness. That's why he hires so many people to be aware of him."

Barbara said, "You're talking about a different person as far as I'm concerned. How can you smoke like that when there's a child in the house?"

Camilla inhaled, and with her voice small and swallowed she said, "I know, honey. He's going to grow up and turn us in someday. Let me just tell you one more thing. In the seventies, Charlie did most of his drinking at a strip club down there."

"You are the biggest liar, mother."

"Ava. As God is my witness, I do *know* a few things."

"How would you know that?"

"I just do. I have a certain clairvoyance."

"Were you working there?"

"My, my. The gloves are off now, aren't they? All right, so maybe I went with him a few times. It was a more permissive era. What do you care?"

"I'm just trying to get a real picture of this. There you are with Dad, sloshed, in a strip club."

"I was doing research for a role."

"Oh, of course. Your field work."

"I'm trying to console your stepmother, dear."

"Don't listen to her, Barbara. She was just as crazy as he was."

"Ava. That's the nicest thing you've ever said to me."

"You like that?"

"Yes. I do, in fact. I suppose I did give that dog a run for his money. Luckily you came along. Forced me to clean up my act."

"You'd be in a straitjacket otherwise."

"Save something for my old age. Padded walls and osteoporosis."

Barbara said, "Don't worry. You're getting your calcium." She tapped the carton.

"Exactly." With her face scrunched, Camilla leaned close to Ava, nudged her shoulder, and said, "I like your new friend here. I approve." Both of them laughed and shushed each other.

Ava and Camilla dozed off sometime past midnight, stretched out on an area rug with throw pillows and neckrolls beneath their faces. They had offered Barbara the couch, but she just sat on it, watching them. She returned to the kitchen and Ava awakened to see her sitting in the pale light from the television.

"I'm sorry. Do you need a ride back?" said Ava.

"I'm waiting for the phone call. Then I'm calling a cab."

When the phone finally rang it awakened Ava from the spark of a dream. She could hear Chris rustling and fretting in the other room. Barbara answered the phone and whispered, "It's him. It's your friend—your . . . whoever."

Ava got on the phone with Matt, but she was distracted and said that she needed to go get Chris—so she handed the phone off to Camilla.

Chris was frightened of something, and Ava walked into his room, leaned down to him, and said, "Shhh. That's just your uncle and your soused grandfather. One big happy family."

She stroked his hair while he lay still, watching her. He said, "I'm scared, Mom."

"Don't be. Just go back to sleep. We're all just being silly in there. Don't worry. We're still in charge. You don't have anything to worry about."

He closed his eyes and started to breathe more peacefully.

"I know. When I was little, I used to watch my mom come

home, and everybody was stoned and giggling, and I stayed up just like you, worrying what would happen if there was a fire or a flood or whatever. Couple years older than you, Chris, and I was walking around the house making sure the stove was off. Stubbing out cigarettes. I was scared every night, because I thought nobody was sailing the ship. Nobody came into my room like this and explained things to me. But you see, you don't have anything to worry about because I'm too good at worrying. I do *all* the worrying around here. Okay? That's my job: I'm the official worrier."

"Where's Matt?"

"He's not here, sweetie. You'll be just fine without him. *I'm* here." It must have seemed to Chris that Matt had lived there a very long time. Children could perceive permanent changes in a single moment. "Do you want Matt to be here?"

"Uh-huh."

"Why?"

"He's big."

"Yeah, he is kind of big. That's true. Do you think that's a requirement for every household? A big person?"

"No-o."

"Because we could get Kareem Abdul-Jabbar to come and baby-sit."

"No, Mom."

"Or maybe I could just put on some more weight. How big would I have to be?"

He said, "Two," followed by a nonsensical word punctuated with a raspberry.

"Well, that's awfully large, Chris. I may not have the frame for that kind of weight."

Slowly he fell back to sleep. The house was silent except for a chorus of breathing in the rooms. The air was so still that the freeway sounded as if it were moving beneath the floor, a hollow washing sound like the tide. Ava sat back against the wall of Chris's room, watching the windows fill with moonlight, and she felt a loneliness so deep it ached. She whispered to Chris while his eyelids were twitching with dreams, "Everybody's

going to be just fine. Everything will be all right." She was crying silently when she stroked his hair. She said, "Shhhh. Just
sleep. Stay asleep. Good boy. I'm fine."

Barbara had fallen asleep on the couch while waiting for a taxi.
The next morning she was furious at Ava and Camilla for not
having awakened her when it arrived, assuming that it had idled
outside and waited for her. She was too angry to speak to either
Ava or Camilla, and she refused all offers of breakfast, the
shower, or spare clean clothes. She said she was going to call her
limousine service, but after a prolonged argument Ava convinced
her to accept a ride. She drove her home with Chris in the car.
His car seat was nestled between them in the front cab of the
truck. He whipped a rubber snake around while Barbara pressed
herself closer to the window. Traffic was worse than usual, and
Barbara appeared so annoyed that Ava worried she might step
out of the car and walk along the breakdown lane.

When they reached Charlie's house, the cul-de-sac was filled
with minivans. At first Ava thought Barbara's family was visiting,
but she saw cords tangled in the ivy and cameras sitting on car
hoods. In front of the entrance a few men were kicking around
a flattened soccer ball. They watched Ava park the truck, and
when they saw Barbara, they dashed to their van and came at
her with tape recorders. Video cameras were mounted onto
shoulders, and with wobbling steps they hurried toward her.

"What the hell is this?" said Ava.

Before they even reached her, they were calling out questions.
What was most jarring to Ava was the way she had awakened a
bored atmosphere: the men and women had been lounging
around as if they were uninvited guests at a barbecue. There was
a dozen of them—no more—but they squeezed together around
Barbara to simulate a mob scene for the cameras. *They'd get into
a circle to stone someone,* Ava thought. Ava picked up Chris and
carried him close to her chest, watching as the group moved
along with Barbara toward the front door, two dozen feet shuf-
fling in sync. From the logos on microphones and vans, Ava

could tell that these were all the basic tabloid shows, with a smattering of more obscure magazines.

They all shouted questions about Charlie. One man tripped over a garbage bag as he was backpedaling with a microphone. In the mix, Ava could hear questions covering everything from binge drinking to an attempted suicide to a possible abduction. They all seemed to be performing for one another like competitive extras in some hysterical play. Before Barbara could unlock the door in the stone wall, she had to deny a few of the more ridiculous theories from the group.

"No, no, no," she said. "He's very much alive. As far as I know, he's alive and well." She answered another question: "No, I don't think he's home. But I'm sure he'll appreciate you waiting up for him."

Before opening the door, Barbara looked out at the cul-de-sac, as if expecting something more. No one asked Ava a single question—perhaps, she thought, because she looked too unkempt to be anyone of importance.

For the next few hours, Barbara and Ava watched the press from the tall bedroom windows overhead. They seemed momentarily like friends now that the house was surrounded. Chris scribbled in coloring books on the bed, fortified with pillows all around him. The group below didn't appear to be getting any larger. They were impatient. They tired of passing the flat ball, and instead began kicking it off the garage door. Another man played solitaire on the hood of his car.

"Charlie would be upset that there weren't more people," said Barbara, holding back the drape. "There was a lot more attention than this at our wedding."

Ava asked if she could search through Charlie's things. Barbara said, "If you think that's necessary."

In his closet, beneath a black and white security monitor that showed the reporters milling around as if in the lobby of a theater, Ava searched her father's clothes and found several miniature bottles: J&B, Stolichnaya, Tanqueray. She piled them all on the carpet while Barbara watched.

"He's awfully eclectic," said Barbara. "So many empty calories."

Ava looked through the pockets of his shirts, the history of a slave to fashion, stretching from his pastel sport coats of the mid-eighties all the way back to his Nehru jackets. She piled all the bottles into a Hawaiian shirt and tied it up like a knapsack.

"Why are you keeping them in that shirt?" asked Barbara.

"For the big luau."

Outside there came the loud siren of an ambulance. In the monitor, the group had gathered around a fallen reporter. Barbara went downstairs and returned with news that someone had tried to scale the wall and slipped. "You don't think they could sue for something like that, do you?"

A half hour passed, with another two dozen uncovered bottles. Barbara's masseur arrived, causing a commotion as he trundled his folding table across the cul-de-sac. The reporters barred his entrance until he answered a few questions. Ava said, "They'll probably make up some story—say he's your lover or something."

Barbara gave her a contemptuous look. "Well, that is just *too* preposterous. Really. Why would you even suggest something like that?"

"I wasn't. I was talking about the reporters out there."

Upstairs, Chris was napping on top of the covers. Barbara sent her masseur home, telling him she was too tense for a massage right now, and Ava called her mother.

"Well, I have some fascinating news from crisis headquarters," said Camilla. "Just about an hour ago I got a very urgent call from a certain Mr. Tom Sloan. He was all in a tizzy."

"What does he want now?"

"He told me that last night Charlie came over and passed out in his trailer. Sloan woke up this morning and it was gone. Now, I didn't even know that Charlie owned his own trailer—but you know, he likes to own everything around him. So he can be feudal lord, I suppose."

Left to herself for a while, Barbara was now railing against the attitude of the press. She paced around the house wringing her hands. She begged Ava not to leave because she couldn't stand being alone in "a house under attack"—but it seemed more likely that she was worried Ava would say something inappropriate to the reporters as she left. By the look of it, they were about to get bored and go home anyway. Such a slight could push Barbara over the edge.

Ava asked Barbara for the number to the phone in the trailer.

Barbara said that the Rolodex had been misplaced by Charlie's assistant, "that little idiot," and that the only people who had the number memorized were Charlie, Charlie's publicist, Charlie's agent, and "that awful hairy man who takes care of the damn thing."

"You mean Sloan?"

"I don't know him by name," said Barbara.

Ava called her mother for Sloan's number. When she called Sloan, there was grief in his voice. Ava tried to sound cheerful, but he was inconsolable.

"I feel like I lost my best friend."

"Sloan, Dad will be fine. I promise. We just have to get in touch with them."

After a pause full of breathing so labored that she imagined him in his scuba gear, he said, "I just wish he had asked *me,* Ava. I mean, I *am* his driver. If he wanted to go someplace, I really wish he just would have asked me. I'll drive anywhere."

"I know that. You are a wonderful driver."

With her forehead resting in her hand, her sweaty hair stuck on her face and neck, Ava tried to sound calm. She convinced Sloan that he was still the most important person when it came to the Winnebago. She told him that he had been a vital part of both her life and her father's life, that her love for him was boundless and low-maintenance, but that now she needed his help. "This isn't the time to mope around, Sloan. This isn't a job you got screwed out of. There are no unions involved. I don't mean to sound preachy, but you're not listening. We have to try to think like a team. I have to get that number and figure out where they are, and then maybe somebody has to go get them."

"I'd appreciate it if you'd let me be a part of any search-and-rescue activity."

"Just give me the number, Sloan. Then you can be the designated driver from here to kingdom come."

He gave her the number, but not without first threatening to come to the house so he could "become familiarized with the nature of the salvage mission."

"Sloan. Don't take this the wrong way, but you're watching *way* too many police shows."

Ava called the mobile home. The phone rang a fourth, fifth, sixth time far out in the darkness, the ringing like a slow pulse, and she waited, her son now throwing grapes onto the floor, her stepmother flipping through television channels to search for coverage of her own life. The phone rang and rang. "Come on, Matt," she said. "You're there. Don't go crazy on me now."

Out in the rolling desert north of Los Angeles, Matt sat in a lawn chair beside the trailer. The late morning sun was glaring off the dried riverbeds, which snaked through an expanse of scrub. He rested in the warm creosote wind, a stinging trace of sand upon it, and he ate a carton of stale Fig Newtons. The trailer rocked each time Charlie climbed to his feet and struggled to the bath-room. It was hot and stuffy in there, polluted with the smell of that blue disinfectant water; but outside the sky was clean and streaked full of high clouds, and the earth warmed like a rock in the sun.

Last night at two A.M. with the keys and what appeared to be a tacit acceptance from Sloan, Matt had driven out of the city, watching the dawn out the passenger window and feeling as if he had hijacked a room from Charlie's house. He was delirious with the thrill of decisive action. But the daylight brought a more sober light, transforming him from a crusader into a chauffeur for a vomiting prima donna. Now Charlie had forgotten where he was. He shouted questions from his bathroom cove. The air conditioner was broken, and the RV heated up like a kiln. Matt needed to calm himself, meditate on his purpose.

He paced around the trailer in his tight shoes, blisters stinging. Along a ridge, he removed his shoes and tiptoed on the hot gravel. When he returned, the phone was ringing. He rushed inside but missed it.

"How long was it ringing?" he asked Charlie, who was now lying on his back in the bedroom. When he didn't respond, Matt said, "Eat some breakfast. Eat one of these fruit baskets before they all rot."

Charlie raised his head and squinted at him. The skin around his eyes had turned to a bruised color and his face was beaded with sweat.

"Why didn't you get the phone?" asked Matt.

"Hello?" he said up into the air. "Nobody's home right now."

"How much do you remember from last night?"

He lay on his back and stared at the ceiling, his stomach bobbing with each labored breath. After swallowing a few times, he said, "I was doing something in Mexico. Everybody was there. Ava and Barbara and . . . *you*."

"You were at your premiere. Do you still know who I am?"

Charlie groaned and covered his face.

"I'll take that as a yes. I'm just going to keep driving. Do you want a bowl in case you have to throw up again?"

"God, you really hate me. Where are you taking me anyway? Are we in Mexico?"

Matt settled himself into the captain's chair, adjusted the side mirror, fastened his seat belt. "Your whole family is worried about you. You should think about that the next time the phone rings."

"My family is an insolent bunch of . . . is it *insolent* or *indolent*?"

"Probably both."

"Well, whatever they are, they don't give two shits about me." He spoke slowly, breathing between words, sprawled on his back like a wounded animal. "Nobody understands respect. It's all ass kissers and back stabbers."

Matt started the engine and revved it a few times. With a crunching of gravel beneath the tires, he drove along the dirt road back onto the highway again. After a few miles, Charlie crawled into the bathroom and stayed there for nearly fifty miles. He emerged on his feet, walking and supporting himself along the walls.

The heat in the trailer was stifling. Charlie moved to the passenger seat and hung his head out the window like a dog. He was still in the rumpled suit from the night before, stained on the lapels, and when he brought his head back into the trailer, the mixture of wind and old hair spray had formed a ratty pompadour. He watched Matt drive, and he said, "It's astonishing. You're like a younger version of me. You even *look* like me."

"Thank you."

Charlie rocked in his seat, mumbling to himself. There was a fresh vigor to his mannerisms. He pointed and whispered, as if rehearsing something, and then he faced Matt with a strained, serious expression. He said, "Listen. I've been doing a lot of thinking."

"In the bathroom?"

"Obviously there's a lot of unsettled business between you and I."

"You and *me*," said Matt, glancing at him. Charlie was leaning forward in his chair with a dramatic pose, his eyes wide open and eager. Matt was certain he had found a drink somewhere.

"Whatever. The two of us. I want *you* to know, though, despite whatever has or hasn't happened between us, whatever time we have or haven't spent together, you're my son. And I love you."

Matt smiled despite pushing his lips shut. He swallowed a laugh. It trembled in his shoulders and chest and slipped out through his nose in a snort.

"You find that amusing?"

"In a really sad way."

"I'm not a genius with words, okay. What I'm feeling is very complex, and it maybe can't be put into language."

"Or shouldn't be."

"I'm particularly uncomfortable expressing affection to other men."

Matt began laughing out loud. The harder he tried to stop himself, the louder he laughed. "Come on, man," he said. "Last night you hugged that guy Sloan in his underwear."

"Why are you laughing at me?"

"Because I've never *heard* anything so full of shit. I'm sorry. But I'm tired and I'm just overwhelmed by the bullshit in this camper right now."

"Well, you have much more of an attitude than I expected."

Charlie folded his arms over his chest and pouted for a while. Matt drove in silence, smiling still despite the numbness of disappointment that had come over him. They watched the passing landscape, the fences flickering past, the green plots of alfalfa farms. They passed into wine country. Charlie talked about how he loved Mexico, and didn't seem to notice that all the signs were in English.

"Have you ever heard of Strasberg?" he asked his son.

Matt shook his head.

"Well, I studied with him. The quintessential class we're talking about. I'm really one of the few truly *method* action stars. Strasberg used to say that I was more full of shit than anyone he'd ever known."

"And what did you do to him?"

"I was upset. I went and tried harder. What do you think I did? Club him over the head? Anyway, I don't know if this is any consolation, but I'm going to tell you a story. Did you ever see a movie called *True Vengeance*?"

"Of course."

"So I'm playing a former POW who has to go back and save his Vietnamese girlfriend."

"From Soviet arms dealers."

"Exactly. Then you remember when I found out that she'd had my child, and that he had also been kidnapped and was being held hostage. I had to play the surprise and the thrill of realizing that I was a father and—at the same time—knowing that I had to take serious action. I had to draw something from my own experience there. And I thought of you constantly. I imagined that I was saving *you*. Up in Oregon."

"Washington."

"Whatever. That isn't the point. The point is that I've always cared about you, but our lives are just very different."

"Damn," said Matt. "You can just stop now. You're starting to depress me."

"Why would that depress you? I'm trying to share something with you here. That's more than you're doing."

"I'm supposed to be flattered that I was an acting exercise? Wow, thanks."

"Oh," said Charlie. He looked thunderstruck. "I guess I didn't mean it like that. I just mean, I've thought about you. That's all. What kind of father does that to his only son? It's despicable."

"I don't need you to apologize like that either."

"What the hell do you want, then, kid? Give me a clue here."

"Ava warned me about this."

"I'm not good at this sort of thing. Just talk to me here. Tell me what you pictured when you thought about me. What did you hope I would be?"

"All right," said Matt, thumping his fingers on the wheel as he thought. "I'll give you an example. But you're not going to like it. I'm going to use a movie, since you did."

"One of mine?"

"No. This is extremely stupid, but when I was a little kid, my grandma took me to see *Bambi*. That was the first movie I ever saw—before my mother started taking me to all your movies. Now, I was just a little kid back then, so I didn't know much. But I pictured you being sort of like the dad. That fucking deer was long gone for the whole movie, and nobody cared. He had things to do. Right? He had a forest to look after. He was probably a selfish, womanizing son of a bitch, you know—out carousing with the other bucks. Maybe he had all sorts of deer issues to work out with *his* father. But the second there was a fire—presto—there he was. 'Get up, Bambi.' I cried all night over that one scene. Because he was watching the whole time. And when they finally met, there was no apologizing, no hang-ups, nothing. They just ran around and saved all the other little critters."

Charlie slapped his hands over his face. He seemed to become abruptly more hungover. "I don't know if I can live up to Bambi's dad."

"It's just an analogy. I was seven."

"What are we supposed to do? Go scurry around in the woods for a while?"

"It's better than all your talk about acting classes."

"*Bambi* is a cartoon."

"Yeah. So are you."

Charlie got up and stomped to the bedroom. For a few miles, Matt craned his head around repeatedly to see him sitting there with his arms crossed like a sullen child. Charlie called across the RV, "We're not even in Mexico, are we?"

"Bravo."

"I can't believe how much you hate me."

He walked forward again, bracing himself against the table and the walls. With a sigh he slouched back into the passenger seat and seemed to assume its shape. "You look more like your mother than me," he said. "She was a knockout, though. I do remember that."

"I'm sorry about the cartoon crack. My grandmother always said I had a lot of bottled-up hostility. But I don't hate you. In fact, for a while I was your biggest fan."

Matt was approaching a slow-moving oil rig, their rounded reflection growing in its convex tail. Matt clicked the turn signal and leaned down to study his side mirror.

"I would have hated me," Charlie said, "if I were in your shoes."

"Well, you're not," said Matt. "I'm in yours."

By evening Matt was exhausted. He pulled into a parking lot and lay down on the couch. He told Charlie to watch television, and he closed his eyes, intending to rest for only a moment. But the lack of sleep caught up with him, and when he awakened it was dark and the television was broadcasting the late news. Charlie was gone.

The phone was ringing. He answered it, licking his chapped lips.

"Everybody here has completely lost grip," said Ava on the phone. "Please tell me you have him and you're okay."

"It's all fine."

"So you two are off, doing what? Playing catch in a cornfield? Because everybody here is really freaking out. Well, actually Barbara is just sort of confused; and Sloan is more concerned about the state of the RV; and my mother is almost amused by the whole thing. But *I'm* worried."

"I know. Just trust me. He was begging me to get him out of there."

"You should turn around, Matt. Just turn around and come back here. Whatever it is going on between you two, you can work it out in the backyard."

"No, Ava. I don't know if I can right this second. But he'll come back to that town looking like his old self again."

He heard a loud breath into the receiver. "Matt, you don't know what his *old self* was like."

"I think I have a pretty fair idea."

"No, you don't. You've just seen a lot of movies."

"You're going to have to trust me."

"Matt, listen carefully. I believe you *think* you know what you're doing. I believe you have all the best intentions. But you have to understand what's happening here. He's missing all sorts of engagements and interviews and God knows what else."

"He wouldn't be able to do them anyway."

"You're not doing this in a vacuum."

"Did your mother tell you what I said?"

"I know. You're honored to have known me. How sweet. Turn around."

"Whatever happens, I just want you to know that. I was happy living there with you and your family."

There was a long pause on the line. "Okay, Matt. Go rob your bank. Go have your shoot-out, or whatever. I'll be here comforting the grieving wife on her treadmill."

"I'll call you when we get to where we're going."

"But time's awasting. I reckon winter's coming early this year, and if that Winnebago gets stuck at the pass, well, then you'll have to eat each other. So go on now, cowboy. Hurry."

When Matt hung up the phone, Ava's sarcasm stayed with him and upset him, even as he went looking for his father.

A half mile south, beside a tow yard of weeds and rusted car bodies, there was a saloon—a long wooden shack with shuttered windows, burned-out beer signs, and a neon boot flickering over its corrugated tin roof. The boot tilted back and forth like the tapping foot of some impatient god. Matt pulled into the dirt parking lot. His feet were now too swollen to cram back into the wing tips, so he entered the bar in socks.

From the outside, he imagined he was stepping into the Old West. But instead, the place had the decor of a sports bar. Electronic dart boards made blips and belches; televisions blared from their perches in every corner. An unsteady cowboy was feeding quarters into an automated crane, trying to fish out a toy.

Charlie was the loudest person at the bar. He was slumped forward over the rails, shouting out to a bartender, who was paying very little attention. Matt was beginning to notice the particulars of Charlie's speech pattern when drunk. He didn't slur, but rather he spoke slowly and overarticulated each syllable, emphasizing everyday words as if they were so extravagant and precise, they would need time to linger. "The Hollywood *industry* . . . is not the day-care *industry.* You *cannot* expect Hollywood to take care of . . . to *raise* people's . . . *children.*"

Another man at the bar was nodding along while staring at a napkin Charlie had autographed. "I couldn't agree more," he said. "I raise my own children. Five of them. I think."

Charlie toasted the man with his glass of bourbon. Out of the corner of his eye he saw Matt, and turned, toasting him as well. "Aha!" he said. "Look what the cat . . ."

"Right. Look what the cat dragged in," said Matt. "Me."

"I was just telling some of these fine *gentlemen,* that the *media* has put too much . . . something . . . onto the shoulders . . . of *artists* like myself."

Matt sat down on a barstool beside his father.

The bartender saw him and walked over, drying off a glass. He asked to see ID from Matt, and Charlie turned to him indignantly. It was an outrage so exaggerated by booze that Matt thought he was kidding. "This is my son, for God's sake! This is my boy here. Are you going to look me in the face . . . mister bar-*person* . . . and tell me that my *son,* my—"

The bartender interrupted and assured Charlie that—while he had always enjoyed his movies—rules were rules. He was cordial and gracious and seemed to frustrate Charlie even further with his easy demeanor.

Charlie leaned forward across the bar and gestured for him to lean closer. He whispered to the bartender, "I ran out on him. I was not a good father. I was a *very* sad excuse for a father. Let me just make it up to him with a drink. I have to prove that I'm . . . you know . . . that I'm *here* for him."

The bartender glanced at Matt and said, "Why don't you take your old man out of here now, son."

"You mean he's *your* son now. Holy mother of God! Well, that makes everything easier."

"Come on, pal. The kid is going to take you home now. Sleep it off."

At first Charlie resisted. But when the cowboy limped over from the crane, and the bartender came around with a towel over his shoulder, Charlie stood and said, "All right. I can walk as well as the next guy."

Matt helped him out the front door. Charlie whispered to him, "I'm terribly, terribly, terribly . . ."

"Okay," said Matt. "Just keep walking. We're going to your trailer."

"To my trailer! *Lonely,* I was going to say." Then he sang, "Terribly, terribly, terribly, terribly . . . life is but a dream."

"I'm listening. Come on. Walk. Move your feet."

"I would trade *all* of my money . . . well, *a lot* of it . . . for some friends in this world."

Charlie stepped down hard on Matt's shoeless foot. When Matt broke loose to hop off the pain, Charlie sat down in front of the RV's front tire.

"What are those, steel-toed shoes?"

"We could be friends," Charlie said, leaning his head back. "You know what a son of a bitch I am. And you don't care. Right? Get up, Bambi. The forest is on fire."

"All right. I'm sorry I said that."

"*No*. It was beautiful. *Exactly*. I'm going to save your life someday. Just . . . swoop in and save the day."

"Thank you. That's a very nice thought. Can you stand up?"

"You know, I would give my life for some people. For instance, I would take a bullet for Ava."

"I know you would."

"I'd take a bullet for *anybody*."

Matt leaned down and lifted his father around the torso, then dragged him along the dirt toward the RV's door. He opened it, and watched his father sit on the bottom stair, murmuring a list of all the things he'd do to save his children. He would rappel into an erupting volcano to plug up the vent; he would smother a live grenade; he would leap before a speeding train. "I would belly-flop into shark-infested waters."

"Okay," said Matt. "Right now you just have to crawl up that last step."

Matt drove north another hour that night, stopping finally near midnight at a campground dug into the base of a pine-covered hill. It was packed full of campers, with only a single orange tent draped among them and glowing like a pumpkin. The recreation vehicles crowded into every corner as if preparing for a low-budget invasion.

Matt showered in the public rest room. He smelled the chlorine in the water mixing with the charcoal smoke from outside. Laughter was coming from at least three dozen televisions. He had no towel, so he put on his cutoffs and walked back soaking wet. Pine needles stuck in clumps to his feet. Behind each window he passed, either Letterman or Leno strutted through his monologue. They seemed to be gesturing to each other across the campsites.

Matt sat at the entrance to the Winnebago and scraped the needles off his feet. Charlie was slouched in the glow of his small television. Letterman was going through the Top Ten Least Popular Olympic Events. Number 6: Robert Downey, Jr., and Charlie West's Synchronized Sobriety Test.

"I didn't catch whether or not Leno made a joke about me." A short nap seemed to have revived him, but he was now listless.

Mosquitoes nipped at Matt's ears. Far across the clutter of applause and commercial jingles, a scared owl was hooting, sounding like a lone heckler in a studio audience.

"We got to keep this screen door shut," said Matt. "I've never seen so many mosquitoes. All these bilge tanks must drain into standing water."

"They said that my movie is doing so badly that now I'm drinking myself to death."

"The showers are okay. You might want to take one."

"But I was drinking myself to death long before this piece of garbage. I just wasn't as focused."

"Maybe you shouldn't watch TV. Go take a shower."

"I can't go out there," said Charlie. "This place is full of old ladies. I'll get mauled. It'd be like walking into a Kmart." He peeked out the window like a surrounded outlaw. His face already showed a bristly growth. He had lost his sport coat in the bar, so that now he wore only beer-soaked slacks and a black T-shirt. His shoes caked in dust, leaves stuck under his belt loops. He appeared a bit like a lounge singer who had been roughed up outside his piano bar.

"You can go out there," said Matt. "You look like such shit, nobody'd recognize you."

"You don't know anything. I'm trapped here. I haven't eaten in days."

Matt opened the cabinet and threw the rest of the Fig Newtons to him.

"A real dinner. Come on, kid. Who do you think you're dealing with here?"

"Eat," said Matt. "You're going to throw up anyway."

"I'm glad you never worked for me."

"And while you're at it, eat the rest of this disgusting fruit before we have to pass an agricultural station. We probably have Medflies."

"You're going to just let me starve."

"There's a vending machine next to the bathroom."

"Please get something for me, Matt. Please. Any one of those old ladies see me and it's going to be like a memorabilia show out there. There'll be two thousand old bags who claim they went to high school with my mother. Please."

"You're pathetic."

"I know. I know I am. I have to work on that. Please."

Simply tired of the argument, Matt tried to find a patch of trees where he could sit alone and visualize nature. He watched the televisions cast flickering light across the pine needles. From the vending machine, he bought three packages of corn chips, then watched his father chew on them.

Charlie said, "Nice of you to get me some packaging."

"They were out of the pâté."

"Ha," said Charlie. "I've never been able to eat anything like that. You should see what I eat. Especially when I'm training— I live on fucking kidney beans and lentils and bran. I live on thin air. All I do is lift weights and fart all day."

He stayed in the trailer all through the night, watching television that reflected off his waxen face. Matt leaned back in the captain's chair and tried to sleep with his feet on the console. He was captivated by the windshield, wide as a movie screen, with all the campers filled with the sounds of coughs, the sky thickening with mist, and in the silence near dawn, the sound of a creek—just a starved trickle—cutting across the landscape. Charlie was sick again in the bathroom, then he lay down on the carpet.

Matt dozed for a few moments. When he awakened the sky was a deep lavender. A halo of light over the trees and peaks made it appear that the sun was hovering just behind the mountains. Charlie was sitting in the passenger seat now. "Are you awake?" he asked.

"Yeah."

A lone bird chirped.

"I was wondering if your mother ever talked about me. What did she tell you?"

"Not very much. She said that she'd been crazy about you."

"She must have just wanted me to drop dead. I can imagine. But she was a tough cookie, your mother."

"What does that mean?"

"Just what it sounds like. She was strong."

"She was not even remotely strong," said Matt.

"Well, she was a wonderful woman."

"You didn't know her. I loved her so much as a kid that it hurt. But I don't think you should even pretend to know anything about her."

"I suppose I deserve that. But listen, Matt. I came from one of those heralded nuclear families and it was a nightmare also. Everyone has to do their best with what they've got."

Matt looked over at the profile of his face. His skin was a ghostly color, the stubble of his beard mottled with gray patches, rings sunken under his eyes. His face looked bloated, as if trying to settle into a different shape but still pinned high on his cheeks. It looked to Matt as if his true age were just beneath his skin and beginning to seep through his pores.

The sky was brightening.

"I don't even know where we are. Where are we going?"

"We're just taking a trip," said Matt. "I know you say you had a tough time with your family growing up, but you have a great family *now*. I think your daughter, your ex-wife, and your grandson are really good people."

"That's not quite a family, Matt. It's more of a club. It always seemed more like that was Camilla's side of things."

"Yeah, but an ex-wife is still family. Right?"

"They all conspire against me."

"No, they don't. They just don't hold anything back. Ava and I got so close so fast. I couldn't quite sort it out. Some nights over there I felt like my head was spinning, like I was falling in love. I'd just settle myself down and say that I was confused. I figure it takes time to learn the different kinds of love. Every-body's still a stranger. And blood maybe isn't as thick as I used to think. I figured instincts would just help everything fall into place. But here I am. I got a schoolboy crush on my sister, and I won a fan-of-the-year vacation with a movie star. At this point I'd take a nuclear family any day."

"You are my son, Matt. And you're Ava's brother. It just takes time."

Matt wasn't sure why they were easier with one another now, far away and in an hour when no one else was awake. He was ashamed that he had, without knowing it at the time, used his father to escape an increasingly complicated situation down there. "I'm not going to have much time if I don't learn some patience," said Matt.

"You will. I was eighteen once, you know. I thought I wouldn't live another ten years. Of course, I woke up a few days later and I was fifty."

The smell of grease and gasoline wafted through the air that morning. Matt reclined in his seat while Charlie talked to his wife on the phone.

"Uh-huh. I know. Sorry. Sorry."

The way Charlie bowed his head, it seemed like his apologies were a mantra, each sending him further into a trance.

"I can't, Barb. I'm sorry. Sorry. Okay, sorry. Just don't give me an ultimatum. There's too much happening in my life right now. Yeah, camping. Right. Have Ava explain it. Who? Just tell them anything you want. Well, how many people is it exactly? That's all? Christ. No, don't tell me that. All right, tell me. What were the grosses the first two nights? Oh. No, I'm fine. You didn't upset me. What about the reviews? Okay. Well, she hates everything I do. Uh-huh. Thumbs down. Well, the bald one has always hated me. Oh, that sounds good. From who? The Movie Nut Website. That's something, I guess. No, Barbara, I'm not going to kill myself. I hope so too. I can't talk anymore. Somebody's listening. You don't know him. Right, him. Oh, God, Barb, are you serious? All right." He handed the phone to Matt. "She wants to talk to you about my diet."

Matt said, "Hello, Mrs. West."

"Hartmann-West. I hyphenate." Barbara explained that Charlie had a specific and important diet, and that if it was broken, they were going to lose all the work that they had so carefully done. She went on to say that while alcohol was not technically a part of that diet, she was interested in cutting her losses. She wanted Matt to promise that Charlie wasn't going to indulge in a lot of fatty foods, and she made him swear that Charlie would continue his maintenance ab work no matter how far off the wagon he was.

Matt tried to explain that Charlie was a genuinely sick man.

"He's sick because he's off his routine. I need you to pay attention now. He has a strong negative reaction to any kind of lactose. It's his irritable colon syndrome. Now, I don't know how much he's drinking, but I do know that any dairy product is going to exacerbate his problems. I don't know his preferences in this particular area, but basically, the worst things would be Kahlúa and milk or Baileys Irish Cream."

"For anyone," said Matt.

"Also, he's prone to lower back pains. If he doesn't do his stretching exercises every night, he knots up and then he'll complain for weeks. Basically, it's a very simple exercise. He just lies on his back and raises his legs into the air and rolls on his spine."

"He seems to be doing that one."

"And last but not least, usually when he has a movie out, I try to protect him a little. You know, from TV and the papers. Particularly now, he can't see any newspapers and he shouldn't watch any television except maybe PBS or the Discovery Channel. He can watch ESPN, but you have to change it when there's a commercial for the film. This film doesn't look like it's going to open well, so we have to be careful.

"It's okay that he's out of town. Sometimes he and I would go to a dude ranch and just wait for the commotion to die down.

In this case, the commotion is more about his disappearance. But I don't want him worrying about that either."

"Keep him away from news about his disappearance. Check."

"All right. And you can call me Barbara in any future . . . negotiations. Ava says this isn't a kidnapping or anything, so maybe that isn't the correct term. She says Charlie knows you and that you're not psychotic. You don't hear voices or anything."

"Just yours," said Matt.

"Well, that's okay, then. Hopefully you two will come to your senses and—gosh, I guess I don't know what I want. You understand. I'm a little hurt by all of this."

"Yes, ma'am. If it makes you feel any better, it sounded like he was moaning your name last night."

"Well, that's something. Thank you."

They said their mutual good-byes. Matt started up the engine and bounced upward across the rutted road out to the highway again, where he continued north through a redwood forest. He was nearing the Oregon border. When he crossed it, he inadvertently began counting the mile markers, waiting for the one he'd memorized. As he passed the spot—which he had always imagined as a perilous stretch of winding road—it was only a slight bend north of Klamath Falls. It flickered past in the side mirror, receding into the distance.

CHAPTER FOURTEEN

Chris discovered a canister of Barbara's diet powder sitting open in the pantry. Within minutes he converted the entire area into a chocolate sandbox, throwing handfuls in all directions. Ava was embarrassed and assured Barbara that Chris never acted this way at home. "It's like he senses something. The kid is a conduit. Whenever there's tension he just tosses everything onto the ground." She gave him a bath upstairs, and he turned the water into cocoa while she scrubbed patches of the substance off his stringy hair.

"We have a Slim-Fast swamp here," said Ava. Chocolate-tainted shampoo was lathered on her arms.

"Everybody is mad now."

"Not mad, Chris. Just crazed and narcissistic."

"Narcizzizzizz . . ." he said and lost the word in nonsensical buzzing. "There's big sarks in the bafftub."

"I hope there aren't any sharks in the bathtub."

Through the branches and vines outside the window, she could see the press below in the cul-de-sac. She felt hidden away in the tower of a castle. Lights began firing down there, flash photography sparkling in all corners. Someone was delivering a press conference.

"Hold on, Chris. Don't splash." She opened the bathroom window and heard the jumble of shouted questions. A silence followed in which she heard a single voice, a mixture of a salesman's trochaic inflections—*step* right *up,* folks—and the muddled rhythms of legalese. There was a strange tone of insincerity that was audible even from fifty feet. It was Sloan.

"Come on, Chris. You're clean. You little cocoa puff. Let's dry you off."

Sloan was standing in a bright spotlight at the front door. Ava eavesdropped beside the window.

"Charlie is a bold man," he said. "A dramatic man who lives a life of symbolism. I am his principle confidant, but because of my enduring respect for the man, I lamentably cannot divulge any information about his recent family crisis."

"Oh, no," said Ava. "You idiot."

More questions were shouted.

Sloan answered, "It's important to emphasize that Charlie's reliance on a wide array of intoxicants is the Achilles' heel of an otherwise first-rate human being."

Questions.

"I cannot enumerate all of the illicit substances to which my good friend is currently engaged—not without a lawyer present—but I can say that they are of a quality worthy of a man of his stature. I cannot confirm or deny any of the reports of abduction, but I can say that Charlie's mobile home—of which I am, in fact, the sole custodian—was taken by Charlie and an associate last night at approximately"—he checked his watch and continued—"oh two hundred hours. The young man in whose care the vehicle is currently entrusted is, I believe, a close personal relation of Charlie's. There's no more I can divulge at this particular moment in time. What I can do is express to you our deep concern over Charlie's safety, emphasize our love and fond affection for him—if he's watching—and assure you that we are doing everything within our power—myself particularly—to control this very important situation. I'll answer one or two more questions."

Shouts.

Ava walked over to the intercom beside her father's bed. She held down a button and broadcast her voice into the speaker in the front wall. "What a surprise, Sloan. Are you delivering a package?"

After a pause, during which she assumed he was digging for the intercom in the ivy, Sloan responded, "Hello? Let me in, Ava."

"I don't know if I'm able at this particular moment in time. I'm currently engaged in vital domestic activities. What's the password?"

When Sloan pressed his end of the intercom, she could hear the reporters still hollering behind him. He leaned up close so that a hot whisper of air blew into the speaker. "Please. Pretty please. Pretty please with sugar and marshmallows on top."

She buzzed him in just as Barbara called from the stairwell, "Who is this person harassing us on the intercom?"

"He's related to the trailer."

Once inside, Sloan immediately made himself at home. After he rummaged through the macrobiotic section of the refrigerator and made himself an improvised falafel, he lurked in the kitchen for an hour, talking on the phone with his mouth full to more friends than Ava believed he could possibly have. He referred to Charlie as his "partner." With his duplicitous tone, he repeated that his scuba venture was now a lock.

The phone rang between his calls and Ava lunged for it. It was Camilla. When Ava described the scene, complete with Sloan now spooning up the last of Barbara's tabbouleh, Camilla said, "I'm not going to just sit here and let him invade that poor woman's home. I'm coming right over."

Before she arrived, Sloan trailed Barbara around the house peddling his products. He had numerous businesses on the side. For one thing, her cutting boards in the kitchen were all wrong. He could offer her a new line of salmonella-proof material. He also had his own line of carbonating tablets, so that one could convert purified water into Perrier without having to pay Perrier prices.

"I certainly respect an entrepreneur," said Barbara. "I have quite a few products myself. But *please,* Mr. Sloan, not now."

To avoid the reporters out front, Camilla parked her backfiring MG behind the house. The terraced yard was separated from its eastern neighbor by a high, ivy-covered wall. Camilla climbed it, holding the straps of her high-heeled shoes in her teeth. She shimmied up an adjacent eucalyptus, then used it to hoist herself over the top, finally wiggling down into Charlie's rose garden with leaves stuck into the scarf upon her head. Ava watched from the top terrace. It was a spectacular athletic feat for a woman who had scarcely moved in more than ten years. Ava applauded. "Look at Olga Korbut down there!"

Camilla put her shoes on, dusted herself off, and trotted up the stone steps to join them beside the pool. "If there's a crisis, then I'm capable of anything."

Barbara sat beside a glass coffee table. She said, "I feel like I'm being inducted into some awful club."

"Honey, you were already in it." Camilla panted. She turned to Sloan, patting her palm upon her chest to stifle a cough. "*You,* my friend, are the world's biggest opportunist."

With everyone seated on the deck chairs beneath a parasol covered with acorns, the energy of this family event quickly degenerated into the pace of a disastrous cocktail party. The adults were so uncomfortable with one another that, after a few attempts at small talk, each began competing to entertain Chris. Ava held him on her lap, dandling him to the rhythm of "Pony boy," while Sloan showed him tricks with a quarter, Camilla spoke of his bone structure, Barbara flattered him with elaborate baby talk, and Ava boasted about his knowledge of the sea. Chris was bewildered by this sudden onslaught of attention and covered his face. It was as if four adults had crammed themselves into a sandbox with him, hoping that by regressing far enough they might find that they had something in common.

Eventually the boy squirmed loose from his mother, found himself a spot on the ground, and began playing quietly with three packets of saccharine, pretending they were boats and whispering noises to himself.

"He's very independent," said Ava.

The silence between them was excruciating.

Barbara asked, "So, what is it you people *do* anyway? Camilla?"

"Most recently I was a paleomanicurist."

Ava clarified, "She did old ladies' nails."

"It's amazing the intensity of a child's playing," said Sloan. "If I could concentrate like that . . . the sky's the limit."

"Why don't you go sell him some of those subliminal learning tapes, sweetie?"

"Barbara here understands. We entrepreneurs have to stick together."

"Please," said Barbara. "Don't include me in your little schemes."

A breeze came across the pool, momentarily billowing the parasol so that the acorns rained onto the patio. When it died, everyone stared up for a while, lost again in the doldrums. At last Ava couldn't take it anymore, and she brought up the only earthly reason why Barbara and Sloan would ever sit at the same table.

"So, let's talk about Dad, okay? Now that we're all such good friends. What do we do?"

Everyone slid forward in their chairs.

Barbara said, "Ava. Forgive me for saying this, but this really has nothing whatsoever to do with you. With any of you. If you came over here because you think you're being supportive, that's irritating enough. But if you think you're going to draw up some plan and save my marriage, well, that's between Charlie and me."

Ava raised her eyebrows and looked at her mother. "Okay. But we could at least *find* him. Right?"

"And how exactly would you do that?"

Sloan leaned forward and said, "How do you know I don't have a tracking beacon in the mobile home?"

"Oh, please."

Camilla lit a cigarette. She leaned back and exhaled away from the table. "I think it's important that Barbara gets the entire story here."

"I'm about fed up with you people prying into my personal life. I'll give you the story. Charlie is a weakling. He is a weak, impressionable man, and for years now I've been the only source of discipline, motivation, or purpose in his life. Then he says he misses his family. All of you people. I suppose he just filled in the *dependents* box on his taxes, and he got a pang of nostalgia. So the moment he gets in touch with you again, everything falls to pieces. That's the story."

"That's catchy," said Camilla, blowing out a stream of smoke. "But you must be at least curious about our boy Matthew. He isn't just a henchman, you know."

"He is as far as I'm concerned."

Ava rested her elbows on the table and faced Barbara. She said, "Matthew is his son. Okay? He came here to meet Dad, and Dad knew all about it. So we're not just here spreading evil this time, Barbara—although thank you for the thought. In fact, if Dad wants to throw a temper tantrum in front of thousands of people, he can go right ahead. You'll have him back here strapped to a sit-up bench in no time. But I *am* worried about my little brother, who is a decent, extremely naïve kid."

Barbara was incredulous. She gave an exaggerated laugh and said, "I don't believe a word you just said."

Ava began to explain the story, speaking very quickly, detailing what she knew about blood tests, about Sadie, the clinic, the paternity case. She found herself inadvertently giving a spin to Matt's story: "His mother was basically just a very sensual, very aggressive woman, but she lived in such a backward town that she was hated for it." She said, "He grew up with his grandmother and a whole bunch of nurses and doctors, and so he speaks a couple different jargons. Some sort of pidgin psychobabble mixed with his teenage patois." She explained that Charlie had admitted to her face that Matt was his son; and though their builds were different, their faces were similar. They shared a handful of allergies. When she was nearly out of breath, Sloan interrupted.

"I actually met him the other night. That kid is a tall drink of water. I didn't remember at the time, but Chuck told me about that particular incident when it happened."

When Sloan and Charlie had first become friends in the early eighties, Charlie had confessed everything. "He had his place in the hills back then. He was in and out of AA, never really able to stick with it for very long." When Sloan found him one day, Charlie had been holed up for a week with sheets and blankets taped over the windows. The entire house was covered with bottles, "like a ringtoss on the floor." His sinks were full of ashes, his shower curtain partially burned. Every mirror and flat surface in the house had a film of powder on it, and Charlie looked as if he'd been awake for days. Sloan stayed with him. He picked up bottles and scooped up ashes, feeling like the world was coming to an end, like the blankets had been thrown over the sun. Sloan tucked him into bed and stayed with him. Three days later they sat together in a clean house with sun filling windows, the days realigned and the hours intact, and Charlie was listless. His new sobriety was like an unconquerable boredom.

"And then he told me he had a baby boy out there. He said the kid would be better off if they never met. He called himself a liar and a cheat, said that all he'd ever do for a son would be to screw his head up. Permanently. He was telling me stories about his father, and how the man was just this stiff, angry presence in the house, like a squeaky piece of furniture. Chuck wanted the kid to grow up fantasizing that his father was some great courageous figure. A hero. He didn't want him to know the truth about him. Not so much that he was a drunk, but that he wasn't perfect. I love that man. But he's terrified of his own shadow."

Camilla reached over and patted Sloan's clasped hands. She said, "Told with the flair of a country-western singer, my dear."

Chris climbed back into his mother's lap and dozed against her. Darkness had spread out overhead, still diluted along the western horizon. A helicopter circled the hills, and Barbara glanced up at it—with a trace of hope—to see if it was coming to film her yard. It wasn't.

"I don't care if this person *is* his son." She now spoke through her teeth. "I don't care one bit about a thing like that. You act like that entitles this person to something."

"It sort of does, Barbara."

"I don't want to get into a philosophical argument with you, Ava. A couple of allergies, a little puddle of DNA, that does not wipe out everything that a person has chosen in his life. Family has to do with *time invested*. Not just some ridiculous blood test."

She rose up and stormed into the house, slamming the door behind her so violently that the windows rattled.

Ava kissed her son's hair, then glanced between her mother and Sloan. "She's afraid she's losing her investment."

Ava moved inside and sat down on the couch, letting her son sleep against her. In the past hour the air outside had become cool and damp. She lay Chris on the white cushions beside the coffee table covered with potpourri, then she searched around the house for a blanket. Barbara was stomping up and down the stairs.

"I want all of you people out of my house."

"Shhhh," said Ava, pointing to her son.

Barbara whispered, "I don't care. I want you all to go back to your tree house and leave me alone. I don't know anything about your little world and I don't want to."

She ran upstairs and returned dragging a suitcase on wheels. It thudded down each step. Ava whispered, "Where are you going?"

"I'm not going anywhere. Did it ever occur to anyone that Charlie might need a change of *clothes*? I don't think so. You're all too busy lining up to take advantage of him." Her voice broke from whispering and she began talking normally again. "Of his generosity and his ambition. I think you have absolutely no understanding of what kind of man he is. There's press outside, and I'm the only one who knows how to handle them. I'm his wife, and I'm the one that knows how to protect Charlie's career."

"I'm not thinking only of his career right now," said Ava.

"Obviously not. And these people you're telling me about— like this lunatic son, as if this is all some remedial biology class— well, I don't want to hear about it. And if any of this were true, these drugs and all this ugliness, then Charlie would have told me. Charlie isn't smart enough to keep a secret. He's honest to a fault."

"You're telling me that *lying* is a sign of intelligence?"

"What makes me so upset though, Ava, is the way you people seem to delight in that man's troubles. You gather around here like vultures, and all you want to do is just revel in his downfall." The veins in her neck swelled, and her voice cracked. "And he has done nothing but kind things for you people. Nothing. He's given you jobs, gifts, money when you needed it. He's paid for all your little mistakes, Ava. And some of the great big ones too." She pointed at Chris on the couch.

Ava took a deep breath. She leaned down to her son and whispered, "Chris, I'm sorry, kiddo. You have to get up. We're being evicted from this lovely couch."

"Yes, thank you," said Barbara.

Ava lifted Chris as he rubbed his eyes with his fists. She carried him into the kitchen, where she handed him to Camilla, who was sitting by the counter talking to Sloan. Quietly Ava said, "I need you to help me out here, Mother. I need you to take Chris out to my truck and wait for me. I'll be out in about five minutes."

Startled by the forceful tone, Camilla said, "What's happening?"

"Just help me out. Chris, Grandma's going to take you out to the truck and I'm coming along right after you. You're a good kid. You've been so good these last few days, and I appreciate it. And Sloan, why don't you go with them. There might be a few stragglers out there and he gets scared of the cameras."

She waited until they had taken Chris through the courtyard, then she walked upstairs to the closet where Barbara was packing. Barbara folded shirts and jeans and placed them into a black valise. It smelled like a perfume bottle had been spilled. "I thought I told you to get out of here," said Barbara.

"I'm on my way."

"You must be lost. The front door is that big rectangular thing with a handle on it."

"I want to know what you're planning to do before I go."

"Whatever I do, it isn't any concern of yours." She wedged Charlie's dress shoes along the sides of the valise. She had a garment bag full of suits that lay on a full suitcase.

"I want you to know, Barbara, that if you ever say anything like that again in front of my son, I'm going to kill you. I mean it. I'm going to take one of those designer belts right there, and I'm going to wrap it around your neck. Do you understand?"

"Don't threaten me, Ava. It's so vulgar."

"And don't ever accuse me of trying to hurt my father, because I happen to love him. Maybe when we all get together we don't talk like you're used to, but don't be fooled. Those two people downstairs may even ridicule him, but they'd also die for him. We're the ones that have seen all these little tantrums, and we're the ones who still care about him. And believe it or not, he needs us."

"Oh, please. Why don't you go tell it to the reporters outside. Maybe they'll believe you."

"There's something you don't seem to be getting, Barb. The *reporters,* they're not going to hang around for very long. There are younger, hipper boys out there doing much trendier drugs, so don't act like you're at the heart of some media frenzy. Forget about them."

Barbara took a belt off the rack and threw it at Ava. "Go ahead," she said. "Strangle me."

"Are you even listening?"

"Oh, I'm listening. I just so happen to be the one who has to *deal* with all of this. I don't know where all of you people get the right to judge my life. Just because I happen to know how much Charlie's career means to his whole existence." She yanked at a cowboy boot and a bottle of whiskey fell out onto the carpet. She picked it up nonchalantly and shoved it back into the boot.

Ava said, "So that's how you're going to find him, right? You're figuring he left a trail of bottles."

"He's probably headed for one of our vacation spots."

"Of course," said Ava. "I'm sure he's throwing a dinner party as we speak."

"I don't hear you anymore, Ava. You're now officially invisible around here."

Ava watched Barbara clean out Charlie's drawers for a while, fascinated by the woman's ability to tune her out. "I guess I don't mind being invisible," said Ava. "Just so long as the right people still see me. Good-bye, Barbara. Good luck with the press."

Outside the last two reporters played cards on a car hood beside a floodlight. They were older, tired-looking men. Ava walked past them carrying her bag of baby gear. One snapped a picture of her for good measure, and it blinded her so that she had trouble finding her mother and Sloan in the dark. Sloan put his arm around her and guided her. "The good news, Ava, is that these boys don't have any idea who Chuck is with or why. And as far as I'm concerned, they're not *going* to know."

"That woman makes me so angry," said Ava. "She was basically just rearranging her closet space."

Sloan replied, "Listen, Ava. I've thought this out, and I'm going to go after them. Millie says that you know where they're headed. I want you to brief me on the whole deal. I know Chuck in these situations and I've been there for him in the past. Not to mention the fact that the trailer is my responsibility. Let's go home, Ava. We're going to mobilize."

Ava stared at the house, its highest windows lit above the walls strung with ivy. She thought for a while, then said, "You've been giving Dad whatever he asks for. Haven't you, Sloan? You've been his supplier all these years."

He was quiet for a moment. "I've made some errors, Ava. Yes. But I'd like to redeem myself now."

Camilla put an arm around each of them and said, "Or at least we can redeem all those bottles."

Back at the house, Ava put Chris to bed. He'd gotten tired of his picture books, and was now interested in a fishing encyclopedia that Ava had bought years ago for a camping trip. She flipped through, showing him pictures of an amberjack, an alewife, a shad. He was most interested in sharks, and she lingered until he fell asleep on the Shortfin Mako as she read the caption, ". . . is probably the fastest-swimming shark, capable of speed bursts up to forty-six miles per hour."

Sloan and Camilla talked quietly in the other room. When Ava joined them, they had already mapped out a plan, with all the enthusiasm of one of Sloan's reconnaissance missions. Camilla showered and returned with a towel wrapped around her head Nefertiti-style. Sloan had bought himself a six-pack, and there was a residue of foam in his beard.

Ava said, "Matt is going to get nervous and he's going to stick to what he knows. And he did say he was going *home*. So this place, let's see." She pulled an atlas out of a small bookshelf nestled into the corner. Each state was scribbled on with a crayon or a marker. Ava found the state of Washington, then looked through frantic purple crayon streaks to find Matt's hometown.

"I guess it's a few hours from Seattle. That is, if we take this magic purple highway."

"We can fly up, rent a car," said Sloan. "Have an extra ticket back for Charlie."

"Maybe two extra tickets back," said Ava. "I can't do this, though. I don't like how much I've been hauling Chris around as it is."

"Good God, Ava. I took you on planes all the time when you were three. You couldn't get enough of it."

"When?"

"Whenever I went anywhere."

Ava looked back at the map, shaking her head.

"Besides, he should learn about the places he's defaced."

Ava turned the page. Chris had colored Wyoming brown, staying carefully within the borders. Everyone agreed that he had done quite a nice job. They admired the tornado twists of green in Nebraska, the orange fault lines across California.

Ava said, "But this would cost us a fortune, Mom. We don't have the money to just pick up at a moment's notice—"

"I'll cover it," said Sloan. "I'm also going after the trailer, so maybe I can write it off as a business trip."

Camilla said, "My heroes have always been accountants."

The next day, they rushed to finish packing, frantically searching through the house. They lined up for the bathroom. In all the frenzy, Ava felt somehow comfortable. Sloan had slept on the couch, and though Camilla was by no means affectionate toward him, there was a camaraderie between them. When she came out of the bathroom in her robe, Sloan goosed her. She threw her hairbrush at him.

They drove in a caravan to the airport, in the pickup and the MG. In her rearview mirror, Ava saw the scarf on her mother's head flapping alongside Sloan's disheveled ponytail. She explained to Chris that his ears would pop on the plane, and that the air was dry, so that he would need to load up with ginger ale; and she explained that he would go so high in the air that the state would look like the map he had scribbled on. She talked incessantly, but Chris was disinterested, choosing to study his new favorite book, *The Fishing Encyclopedia*. While Ava briefed him for his traveling experience, he responded with "Blue sark," or "This is a mako sark. Wow."

"I feel the same way," said Ava. "I can't get enough of those fish."

The last time Ava had been in an airport, she was a ragged kid herself, with nothing but a backpack full of socks and underwear, ten minutes early, headphones on no matter what she did; and somehow, between then and now, she had become one of those mothers toting a mountain of pillows and blankets, bags full of diversions, Igloo coolers, and Ziplocks stuffed full of sliced vegetables: she felt like a stooped camel hauling the contents of a day-care center across LAX.

It took her minutes just to unload everything onto a conveyor belt so that Chris's stuffed animals and fruit juice boxes could be X-rayed, the insides of a Barney sliding past. Sloan was stopped at the security checkpoint in order to unload roll after roll of quarters into the tin.

Once flying above the desert, a few green squares of farmland stitched beneath them on a lumpy brown landscape, Chris looked through his window at the unraveling dried riverbeds and told his mother that he had drawn all of them. A row behind them, Camilla and Sloan were reminiscing foundly about all their worst memories as a couple. Ava recognized the fragment of a camping trip. Sloan had forgotten to waterproof the tent, and it rained all night while the three of them shivered and clung together for warmth. Sloan went out in the dark to try to find the car, but he impaled himself on a branch, then came back whining that his ribs were broken, and they shivered all night under wet goose down, waiting for dawn to get him to a hospital. They talked about it now like it had been a pleasant experience.

Chris didn't cry until the plane began to descend. Ava taught him to pop his ears. She made him yawn with her, and when it didn't seem to help the pressure building up in his head, she showed him how to hold his nose. "Pretend you're jumping into a pool. Okay, now very lightly, try to blow your nose." He let go and blew his nose all over himself, and as he started to cry again, Ava wiped him off with a cocktail napkin.

The plane landed with a screeching of wheels and the trauma was over, but, exhausted from it, Chris fell asleep in the airport waiting for the luggage, and Ava had to lug him around while pushing a cart with a jammed wheel. Every few steps she had to hoist Chris higher into her arms, then lunge out and kick the cart until it faced the right direction.

Finally, in the backseat of a pristine white rental car, Ava said, "Why don't we all just pull over and take a nap."

"You go ahead. I'm driving, your mother's navigating," Sloan said.

"I feel like getting smashed," said Ava. "We *are* going to a detox clinic. Why don't we all get lit so we have something to do when we get there."

"Just take your little nap, honey. Good night. We'll wake you up when we're there."

While Ava's eyes were closed, following the bumps and turns of the road in her mind, Sloan got lost somewhere east of Seattle and drove them into a frightening imitation of a Bavarian village. The stores were painted in bright colors, and the store owners all waddled around in lederhosen. A huge sign, painted to look like gingerbread, spelled out WILLKOMMEN TO LEAVENWORTH. Everyone in the car was silent, as if frightened by this spectacle.

Camilla walked into a wurst restaurant for directions, and

when she returned, she urged everyone to come inside. A huge buffet of bratwurst and sauerkraut stretched out the length of the restaurant. Camilla led them across the dining room to a wall in back that was covered with pictures of German celebrities: mostly shots of Werner Klemperer. Prominently displayed upon the wall—Ava lifted Chris to see—was a placemat shaped like a German cottage. On it was Charlie's autograph. It read, "How the hell did I wind up in Germany? Charlie West."

"The waitress told me that he was in here just this morning," said Camilla. "Said he spent most of the time with his head down on the table." Camilla gestured to the waitress. "Excuse me. *Fräulein.* Can you just help us for a second?"

The waitress came over.

"Was he sick?"

"I didn't recognize him at first," said the waitress. "He looks much older in person. He was pretty out of it too. He kept trying to speak some funny language."

"Maybe German," said Ava.

"He was with this kid. A tall kid. Real nervous. Kept telling him to sit up straight and stop acting like a baby. Telling him he wasn't in Germany."

She gave them directions to Chelan, but warned them that it was a dreary place. "Kind of like here, before we went Bavarian." She drew them a map on the back of a children's menu, which folded into a hat.

They followed the map through miles of dense pine and fir trees, the branches tightening and reaching out over the road, and came to a clearing, where, glittering in a valley below, lay a silvery lake catching a glare of late-afternoon sunlight. Winding down a mountainside, they emerged into a town cramped around a few narrow streets. On Ava's side there was a cemetery. The statues around it had been painted with graffiti. Bunched together along the strip were fast-food restaurants with the signs burned out. A Dairy Queen bulletin board raised high over the street read, CO--R--LATIONS -LASS OF 19--. The clouds were blowing overhead swiftly, casting moving shadows along the street.

Sloan promised to stop and ask directions, but before he could think of it, they passed the final stoplight and were driving out of town on a weathered road. Mount Baker stood in the distance. They drove for another ten minutes until they found a driveway in which to turn around. Before them was a plain of green grass, a few weathered barns, and a sagging fence.

Ava pointed to an old man walking between barns with a stack of papers in his hand. She waved out the window to him and he approached. He was an old man with skin the color of his gravel driveway. He had a hooked nose and a swoop of heavy gray hair down over his eyes. When he neared, Ava saw that he was holding a pile of gossip and fan-club magazines.

"Excuse me," she said, leaning out the window. "We're looking for *The Briar Patch* treatment center. Have you heard of it?"

"Have I heard of it? I'll say. Just the other day I saw that relief pitcher from the New York Yankees. Had to haul his car out of a ditch. Oh, it's a big attraction. You should come in and see my library sometime. I don't get many visitors these days, but I've got all sorts of information."

"Thank you," said Ava. "But we just have to find this place right now."

He drew her a map in the gravel with a stick. Sloan got out of the car to study it. When they all thanked the man, he leaned up close to the window and said, "I don't read these magazines, mind you. Smutty stuff. Personally, I never was interested. But you never know what somebody might like. So . . . these aren't mine, in case you're wondering."

"That's fine, sir," said Ava.

"I cater to all kinds here," he said. "So if you prefer science or history . . . well, I can accommodate a wide range of interests."

"Thank you," said Camilla.

As they drove away, everyone in the car agreed that they had now met the oldest and loneliest man in the world.

CHAPTER FIFTEEN

When Matt drove past Stritmatter's farm, he recalled the piles of information he'd collected on his father, and for a moment he felt as if he'd pasted them all together into the man now snoring on the couch. He turned onto the gravel access road, the RV rocking over the bumps and grooves. Along the ridge above the clinic a nurse was walking in her uniform, looking like a single bleached spot on a vast green landscape. The drizzle passed quickly, and the sun rolled out from behind the clouds, lighting the trees and changing their shades to a dusty color. He drove down the winding road toward the cabin, where a thread of wood smoke slanted upward and broke apart in the wind.

Charlie was jolted awake. A button from one of the couch's throw pillows had pressed a circular indentation into his forehead. Matt drove toward the ragged lot behind the clinic, where he saw the orderlies' trailers catching the sunlight, a glare coming off a new satellite dish. He steered around the main cabin and looked for a spot in back.

Matt didn't notice a clothesline strung across the lot like a trip wire, and he drove right through it, ripping loose the damp uniforms, several of which slapped onto the windshield and blinded him. He turned on the wipers to clear them, leaving only a sock and a brassiere. Then he drove the Winnebago over the crown of the lot until it rested on a slope facing downhill toward the lake. The water sparkled and glinted between the alder saplings. He wedged down the parking brake and tossed the keys beneath the seat.

"I'm not going out there," said Charlie. "I didn't know this was a fucking intervention."

"First of all, this is where I live."

Charlie peered out the front window, then ducked down behind the driver's chair. His fretful tone was exaggerated by a slight tremor in his hands. "This place is my worst recurring nightmare. I don't know what kind of idea you had, but it stops right here. I'm not stepping one foot outside."

The shadows of clouds slipped across blackberry bushes and clusters of sunflowers. Charlie tromped to the bedroom and pulled a sheet over his head.

Matt said, "It's not like they're going to shoot you with a tranquilizer dart. Everybody is perfectly civilized. And I need my things. I need some clothes that *fit* me, for God's sake."

"You're a manipulative little bastard."

"This is my home. It isn't just your *recurrent* nightmare."

Matt stared a while at the shivering lump under the sheet. Charlie looked like an overgrown trick-or-treater. Outside Matt gathered up most of the clothes he had run over, folded them, and stacked them on the hood of an old Nova sunken in dirt near the entrance. Two new orderlies stood on the pathway gaping at him. He squeezed past them, noticing that the undergrowth had reclaimed sections of the path since he had gone. "Hi there. I'm not a patient, don't worry. Good to meet you."

Standing at the end of the path beneath the hanging cord of Christmas lights—most of the bulbs now burned out—was Grace. She had on a flannel shirt covered with ink stains. She had tried to slide a pen behind her ear, but had missed and shoved it into the tight bundle of gray hair. She said, "Good Lord, he gave you a camper."

"No, no, Gram. He's in there. It's a long story. He said he needed to get away."

She put on her glasses and squinted at the Winnebago. "Get away from what? The police?"

"It's all perfectly legal. Maybe you heard something on the news. He made kind of an ass out of himself at his premiere."

"And that's newsworthy?"

"Just let me go inside. I'm all greasy and I smell like an animal. He's been sick the whole trip."

"You look worn to a frazzle."

She took him by the sleeve and led him into the main cabin. Matt plopped onto a dusty old couch in the banquet room, beneath the rafters now netted with cobwebs. The floor in the kitchen had been hastily mopped and was drying unevenly. Grace closed the door and sealed them into the dim, wood-scented room.

"You went down there and got yourself sick," she said. "Look at you."

"He's been drinking and taking painkillers, and he hasn't eaten much in days."

"I might be too old to deal with him, Matthew. The first time he was practically the end of me."

"He needs to dry out here, Gram. I'm not talking about a couple of spritzers here and there. This guy gets torqued."

"We'll do what we have to. I don't have to be happy about it though, Matthew." She asked for some of the specifics. Matt guessed at the length of the binge, the time since his last drink. Grace seemed eager to have Charlie shaped once again into a simple patient by these details.

She said, "We have to be careful he doesn't go into DTs, then. There's always a chance. I'll have Paige look at him. Maybe have a shot of diazepam ready." She sighed and looked at the ceiling, her energy renewed. "I'll fix you a cup of tea. I want to know how on earth you ended up carting that poor fool around. It's my worst fears realized." She filled a kettle with water, the pipes rattling faintly, and lit the burner.

She dragged a chair over and sat down facing the couch. Behind her, Matt could see the indentation where as a child he had butted his head into the wall. He was surprised by how low to the ground it was.

"I was worried you were going to come back brainwashed by

all the hoopla. The fame and fortune. It's like a cult almost. Your mother just lost her common sense, pure and simple. I'd never seen a girl so starstruck in all my life, and he wasn't even so much of a star back then. I have never understood it, Matthew."

"This place has gone to hell just since I've been gone."

"Oh, we managed all right. But it's like pulling teeth trying to get anyone to do anything around here. You rest, though. Don't worry about that just yet. I don't know how I'll deal with that man out there. I can barely stand to look at him."

"You said I could come back if I was in trouble, Grandma."

"I suppose I didn't mean if *he* was in trouble. But it's too late for that."

"I got up north and I started to get nervous. I really didn't know what to do. I guess I was worried he might die like some rock star in his little lavatory."

"Do rock stars all die in lavatories these days?"

"Well, you know. They choke on vomit. That sort of thing."

"So you rushed off with him, thinking you could fix everything. It's difficult, isn't it? You know, Matthew, you don't have to solve these folks' problems just to be a part of the family. You're impatient, and I understand that—you're young. But you're trying to cram a lifetime into a few good deeds. And that's even assuming this *is* a good deed. It may be the worst decision you ever made."

"Well, I'm riding it out now. Start to finish." He cupped his hands over his face and lay there, smelling the mildew in the couch. "I just wanted one lucid moment with the guy. I just wanted him to clear his head for thirty seconds so he could look at me. So he could be straight with me."

"If you want your father to know you, that doesn't mean you have to jump off a cliff with him." The kettle began to whistle and she rose to get it. With his hands still over his eyes, he listened to her pour water into a mug, heard the spoon clanging as she stirred.

When she gave it to him, he took it outside and went for a walk around the clinic. The clouds were soaring overhead and the shadows slid along the ground. He found a spot in the woods beside the creek, and there he sat down and looked at the lake below, sipping his drink. The sound of wind through the trees blended with the trickling water. As he blew on his tea, he felt a lump in his throat, so he clenched his teeth and breathed deeply, and repeated to himself that he had done nothing wrong. It was not sadness but a panic that he felt: the fear of a boy separated from his family at an amusement park. The fact that it came over him here, beside the cabin with its chimney hiccuping smoke, did not lessen it, but rather intensified the feeling. It was not simply that he was lost, it was that he palpably felt how lost everyone else was also. The order of the universe was coming unraveled. The moment of his conception had lost its passionate inevitability and become a whim on a rainy night; his father the movie star had become any random scoundrel; and the last vestiges of his mother's fantasies—her rebellion against the world, her death in a blaze of glory—now appeared tragically arbitrary.

He didn't want to think this way.

So that afternoon he cleared the cobwebs from the rafters, washed the wood floors and the windows, and trimmed the vines back from the walkways. He took a hose and washed the RV. As he was spraying the bugs out of the grille, Matt saw his father watching him through the windshield. Matt stared back at him, and—as if the glass were protecting them—they observed each other like pictures. Matt smiled. He put his thumb over the nozzle and sprayed right at his father.

At four o'clock the patients returned from a hike in the woods, and they gathered in the banquet room to watch an hour of television. They idly discussed ways to flush the actor out of the Winnebago, one of them cackling as he suggested feeding carbon monoxide into it through a hose. There was an arrogant friendship among them that Matt had never noticed with previous groups. As one patient was flipping through channels, Matt caught a glimpse of Barbara. "Stop," he said. "Go back to that."

It was a tawdry news-magazine show, promising stories about an actress leaving her husband, a country-western singer charged with domestic violence, and a Chupacabra sighting in Puerto Rico. But first, there was a quick interview with Barbara.

A woman in a pink business suit leaned forward and asked, "Where do you go from here, Barbara? How do you get through this?"

"I have to carry on. We can't all have the luxury of such behavior. I have my *revolutionary* new dietary powder, and I have a whole new series of videos out in the spring. I can't give up who I am, because of who he is. I have to help myself get through this by helping millions more discover the easy Hart 'n' Soul way to reach their fitness goals."

"You're a courageous woman," said the interviewer.

"I have to be."

Matt was restringing the clothesline when he heard the car. Up the hill in the distance, dust rose off the access road and approached like a stampede. Gravel crunched. Matt walked out to the edge of the lot to see who was coming. A Toyota Celica streaked with dirt rounded the trees and came into sight. In the front seat were Sloan and Camilla. Against the back window he saw red hair piled against the glass.

The car stopped, the doors swung open, and Ava awakened in the backseat. They stepped out, stretching and groaning. Camilla said, "It is just paradise, Matthew. Paradise on earth." She tiptoed over to him and grabbed his face. "Hello there, *you*."

Ava carried Chris as she smelled the air and looked up at the treetops. Her eyes were puffy from sleeping and a tuft of hair stood up where she had leaned against the window.

Matt had a thrilling and terrifying feeling that this newfound family had accepted him entirely. For better or worse, they would follow him to the ends of the earth. His heart raced when Ava approached. She leaned against Matt and hugged him with Chris stuck between them. She kissed his cheek beside the ear and whispered, "You're not getting away this easily." The sleeping scent of her was hovering around him. "Big sister is watching."

Sloan circled the trailer. Camilla was following behind him and smelling a pine cone. Ava put Chris down and he ran to Camilla and took the cone from her.

"I don't know how you found us so easily."

"You're not dealing with chimps here," said Ava. "You know, Chris really missed you. He's just a kid and he doesn't understand any of this."

"I don't either," said Matt.

From inside the trailer, Charlie heard the muffled voices of his family. He had drank the last of his secret stash that afternoon, sneezing from an allergy to something outside, flipping idly through TV channels, hanging towels over the blinds, and now he was disoriented. He needed to concentrate to remember where he was.

In the late afternoon he had been captivated by the tabloid shows. But to Charlie's horror, he was not mentioned until late in these programs, losing out to buxom actresses having babies, younger actors punching cameramen, and even a soap star who admitted to having an eating disorder. When Charlie was finally mentioned, the programs focused almost exclusively on Barbara. She had sacrificed her career in workout videos in order to help Charlie stay clean. Now he had betrayed her. There were shots of her walking very rapidly beside microphones. There was a clip of her stepping out of the Range Rover outside one of her favorite restaurants. She paused and adjusted her blouse in front of the camera. "I've never been so humiliated. I think it's terrible for all of you to prey on human suffering like this. You can safely say that I never really knew my husband, and that I've been hurt and disturbed by recent events. My life is a public spectacle now, and you can print that."

Charlie drank until his vision blurred. Had his publicists managed to control the negative publicity? Or was he really less important than a Laker girl who had just cut a salsa album? If his marriage was in such trouble, he couldn't stand the idea that it would fizzle out like this. He wanted something passionate, screaming brawls that ended with both of them sweating and sobbing and devastated, like when he and Camilla were divorced.

The light now filtered in through the orange towels and the earthen colors of the upholstery. Charlie crawled into the bathroom alcove to escape the sound of Sloan outside. He watched the last light slide off the ceiling and fade in the transom. He imagined being entombed in this mobile home. It could be wrapped in cellophane like a giant fruit basket and lowered into the ground.

Outside Ava knocked on the door and said, "Dad? I'm here to take your dinner order. Dad. They're ready for you on the set. Boy, nothing is fooling him today."

Matt said, "He's worse than you think."

"Dad, your co-dependents are here. Open up. It's your support network. I hear the TV on, so I know you're in there."

Camilla walked over and began knocking as well. "Olly olly oxen free. Charlie? No one cares what you look like, sweetie. We've all seen worse. Come on, honey. It's a gorgeous evening and everybody's here for you and Matthew. Ava and Sloan and all of these nurses in their darling little outfits. Come on, sugar. Baby steps to the door."

"It's like negotiating a hostage situation," said Ava. "Does somebody have a bullhorn?"

"I hear *Barbara,*" said Camilla. "Did she stow away in there?"

"I think it's the TV," said Matt. Then he invited everyone inside. Ava said she was simply worried that he would hurt himself in there, but after some deliberation, Matt led them into the main cabin, where dinner was about to be served.

Charlie watched them leave along the wooden path. From the darkening sky, he knew it was nearing prime time. The most lurid of the gossip shows began. Charlie's story was more prominent on these fake news magazines with the more hostile air to them. A still shot of Barbara came onto the screen. Beneath it the caption read, "Fed up?" Next came an interview she had given at Hartmann Plymouth. Minivans glimmered in the sunset. With her mother and father each placing a supportive hand on the shoulders of her padded jacket, her blond siblings in a phalanx behind her—looking like an angry Dockers ad—and a row of microphones before her, Barbara said, "I have no comment at this time. Because I realize that chemical addiction is a disease, I can forgive him for it. But I cannot forgive him for willfully sabotaging our marriage, our love, his career. If you're out there listening, Charlie—and I'm sure you're not—I kept up my end of things. I was *here* for you." She wiped a tear from her eye and comforting hands squeezed in unison. "I was *here* for you. I kept up my end of the bargain, Charlie." She leaned her face down into her fist and her ribs shook as the sporty siblings embraced her one by one.

In his delirium Charlie lost track of what she had been talking about, and her exaggerated facial expressions made him think that she had just won some kind of beauty contest. Miss Voyager 1998. She composed herself and answered a few questions from the crowd.

"A career and a relationship take work," she said. "Hard work. And people have to be willing to do that work. To go the extra mile. To swim that last lap. To really bear down and make a difference. In life and in love. There is no such thing as a free ride. That's all I have to say on the matter."

The family nodded vigorously.

"Oh, screw you people," said Charlie. "Those are *my* minivans."

Finally a "Hollywood insider" came onto the show. Charlie had never seen him before and figured he was nothing more than some pompous clown who colored in the trades with a Day-Glo marker. He said, "It looks like West has really burned his last bridge. The studio invested a tremendous amount in marketing this picture, and Charlie is certainly *persona non grata* with them."

"Gee, thank you," said Charlie. "And they *pay* you for that?"

Amid the shivering flames of gas lamps, the patients stooped over their meals at the banquet table. The generator had gone out and wouldn't restart despite Matt's efforts, so everyone had their own flashlight illuminating a patch of table beside them. In one row sat Camilla, Sloan, Ava with Chris on her lap, and Matt. Grace lurked at the darkened head of the table, occasionally flashing her light onto someone. The meal was a gristly stew of leftovers.

Matt whispered to Ava, "I used to call this Heimlich stew."

Chewing devotedly on a single piece of meat, Ava said, "Tell me this is at least *beef*."

"It's the patients who don't make it," said Matt.

"It's the taste of sobriety," said an old man across from them. To show them who he was, he shined his light on his chin, making the loose skin on his neck look ghoulish.

"Here, here," said Sloan.

Grace knocked on the table. "I'm still here, you know. I'm not deaf."

"Sorry, Grandma. They're just not used to it."

"You people are spoiled rotten."

"I'm sorry, Mrs. Ravendahl. I was just kidding around. I really appreciate your hospitality," said Ava.

At the dim edges of the lantern's reach, Camilla was seated beside Grace. She put her hand on Grace's arm. Grace looked at the hand like it was a gesture she'd never seen. "She's just a smart aleck, sugar. We love her just the same."

Ava was captivated by the sight of these two women staring at one another: the matriarchs of two distinct lines now meeting at the corner of a table in slanted shadows, one woman gray and hunched over with the wiggle of lights upon her glasses; the other, just a decade younger, freshly made up and biting lipstick prints onto her napkin. Camilla's hand was placed out gently to say that whatever suffering was implicit in Grace's bad mood, by all means she understood.

"You can all go back and have dinner with Wolfman Puck."

"Oh, dear," said Camilla. "He doesn't hold a candle to you, Grace. Although I enjoyed his radio program."

Ava leaned forward and waved her flashlight. "She's right, Mrs. Ravendahl. You've been very kind. It's beautiful here."

"Seventh heaven," said Camilla. "And believe me, I know. I have seen some pretty miserable spots to dry out—but you come here, and you smell the air, and you look at those big *trees* all over the place, and you're halfway home. I haven't smoked a cigarette since I got off the plane."

"Well, whoop-de-doo," said Grace. She tapped her knife on the table and said to Matt, "You should bring a bowl out to that camper."

Matt's cheeks were bulging full of invincible chunks of meat.

"That's kind of you, ma'am," said Sloan, "but Charlie won't eat it. He's making a point out there. If I know Charlie, this is his—how do you say it?" He waved his arm. The candle flames swayed around the room. "What's the phrase I'm looking for, Millie? It's a French expression."

"Il ne mange pas le fromage."

"No, no. A common phrase."

The man with the flashlight shining under his chin said, *"Où est l'hôtel?"*

"It's on the tip of my tongue."

A man at the far end of the table cleared his throat. Sloan shined a light on him. He wore a plaid hat with earflaps. He said, *"Voulez-vous coucher avec moi ce soir?"*

"Never mind," said Sloan.

Grace stood. "Well, we better clear the table for you Parisians. You sure brought in a sophisticated bunch, Matthew." She walked into the kitchen and came back with a towel and a sponge. She tossed them to Matt and said, "There you go, *garçon.*"

While Matt cleaned the table and washed the dishes, Ava brought a bowl of salad—dressing on the side—to her father. Pickup trucks began to drive up and park beside the lodge. As Ava was traipsing through the weeds and along the warped boards, she heard Matthew laboring with the generator. It would sputter a few times and die. He called to some of the men in the trucks, telling them there couldn't be a meeting tonight without any electricity. Someone was talking about a six-month chip, and he said, "Well, I'll have to get it in the dark, then." As Ava walked into the lot full of trailers, darkened now, she found her father's easily—it was the only one with its own generator humming. Its lights glowed through the orange and brown curtains, so that the trailer looked like a jack-o'-lantern against the night sky.

"Dad? I brought you something to eat. Can I come in for a minute?"

He opened the door and Ava was struck first by a gust of pungent air. She smelled the booze, sweat, bathroom disinfectant, and the odd, overripe smell of something decaying. Her father was wearing the remains of his clothes from the premiere, looking shipwrecked, the collar of his shirt torn, his pants rolled up around his bare feet.

"Oh, my God," said Ava. "Dad, come on out of there. You look horrible."

Behind him she could hear the cheerful theme song of an entertainment-news show. He kneeled down in the doorway, put his hands out, and said, "Ava. *Please.* Please, baby."

"Please what, Dad?"

"Please get me out of here. Please. I'm so sorry for what I've done. I'm sorry. I'll say it a thousand times, just please get me out of here."

"I think you should come inside, Dad. I think you should have something to eat. Have a shower. Lie down."

"No. No, sweetheart. Ava. It's *me.* It's your father. Tell her I'm sorry. She'll never forgive me. You have to tell her. You have to tell her for me."

"Tell who, Dad?"

"Her," he shouted. "The girl. Tell her I failed. At everything."

She stood paralyzed, holding the salad. He crumpled up on the carpet beside the door.

"Are you talking about Barbara, Dad?"

He responded with an exasperated sigh. Ava put the salad on the ground, then leaned through the doorway and tried to lift him. She said, "Come on. We're going inside."

He roiled loose from her so violently that she leaped backward. He kicked the door shut and locked it. "Just leave me, then," he said from behind it.

With a growl, the generator started in the main cabin. A burst of applause echoed around the forest and reverberated off the lake while Ava watched her father pace behind the windows, gesturing wildly as he talked to himself. Even alone in there he was hamming it up. Her father had somehow mistaken neediness with intensity. She felt an odd sense of loss.

She remembered those days in her youth, before he was so rich and famous, when he tried so hard to impress her, and in his best moments he was like a delighted child; and the two of them would play ridiculous board games and there was not a worry in the world. He was an overgrown boy who loved jokes and silliness and talking all night. She wished now that she could meet that father again. She wished she could sit down with him, two sturdy adults face-to-face, and she would see in his eyes that he was proud of her.

Ava stood in the kitchen with Matthew and Chris, and the three of them watched the nightly meeting take place at the other end of the banquet hall, in a circle of foldout chairs beside the staircase. The men and women were stooped forward with hands clasped, smoking heavily and mumbling. Camilla had joined them, and she was the only member sitting upright. She smoked luxuriantly, blowing out long puffs, and she talked louder than all the rest. "Oh, honey, that's a wonderful story." The older men in their fishing vests and flannels appeared charmed by her. They competed to engage her with nostalgic tales of debauchery. But the women looked resentful of her presence. Grace fretted at every word she said.

Matt whispered to Ava that she and Chris could sleep in his old room, and while the meeting was continuing, they tiptoed up the stairs. The room was spartan and clean. Matt hovered in the doorway while Ava tucked in her son and explained to him in a quiet voice about what was happening. "We're all just on a little adventure, sweetie. We're not so far away."

Later Ava returned downstairs and asked Matt for a favor. She said that Chris was afraid of something—perhaps the way the Christmas lights outside cast colored shadows against his wall—and she wanted Matt to tell him how safe everything was. So Matt clunked up the staircase again, ascending over the meeting and the wisps of smoke. Most of the women had gone home, so that there were six bald heads on opposite sides of Camilla's neatly curled hair.

Inside his room, Matt kneeled down toward Chris. "Hey, man. You can't sleep?"

"There's ghofts in the wall."

"Goats? I can't understand you."

"A ghoft!"

"I guess you wouldn't be scared of a goat. Right? I think you're just talking about the Christmas lights. But I'll tell you a secret. I could never sleep very well in here either. Of course, there *are* ghosts, but that's okay. They're not the mischievous kind. They're just lonely and lost, wandering around. Wishing they could skip some rocks in the lake. I know some of them. So don't worry. They would never hurt anybody. They just like talking about the good old days."

"But I don't like them."

"Well, you just have to get used to them. They're more scared than you are. And besides, they protect you. Ghosts are the least of our problems around here. Believe me."

"My mom said there aren' any."

"Well, I think there are. But you know me. I just think ghosts get a bad rap in the media. Whoever's here: they know you're with me. You're all set, kid. They know you're my little buddy and they're going to look after you. At most they'll just give you some bad advice. But that's all they can really do. It's the living people you have to keep your eye on."

"I'm not afraid of sarks."

"I know. So you should have no fear of ghosts. Sarks are much scarier than ghofts."

"I want to see a sark in the pool."

"Well, that's a lake. Not a pool. And we don't get too many sharks in there. But we'll come up with something tomorrow. Now promise me you're not afraid."

"Okay."

"And I'll be right outside."

———

Ava wanted to sit by the shore. Matt walked with her out of the smoke and heat of the cabin, invigorated by the cool air outside, a touch of moisture blown off the lake. He led her away from the cliffs, down a narrow path lit only by the moon. The insects were buzzing. As she followed him, Ava said, "Whatever Dad is going through, the real tragedy is how seriously he takes himself." Her voice vibrated as she took steps along the lumpy path. "It's a tragedy not to be able to laugh at yourself sometimes."

"Do you laugh at yourself?" he called out, still walking ahead of her.

"Hysterically."

They came to a rocky beach where the lake was purling against a mossy dock. The wind had died down and the moon wavered on the smooth surface of the lake. Matt threw a rock that shattered the calm and sent ripples toward both shores. "He's lucky to have so many people looking after him. I'm not altogether sure he deserves it."

Ava perched on a log with her arms hugged around her legs. She was rocking to keep warm. "I guess people don't always *have* to deserve it. He's my father and I wanted to help." She rubbed her hands on her legs. "But I also came because I was worried about you. I thought you were in over your head."

Matt sat down beside her on the log. Her legs were shivering as she straightened them. He rubbed his palm on her bare thighs covered with goose bumps. She leaned her head against his shoulder, and beneath the scent of wood smoke and her mother's cigarettes, he could smell the faint reminder of the shampoo he'd also used while at her house.

"This is the first part of your initiation into the family," she said.

He rose again and paced in front of her and Ava watched him. He was foolish to not expect something more, but he now believed that he had gone to Los Angeles and found them without considering the moments that lay beyond that initial meeting. He had expected only a scene like those from television shows in which newly reunited families hugged and sobbed on the porch of a tract house.

"I have to be honest with you," he said. He picked up a handful of rocks and began heaving them out into the water. "The speed of all this is starting to scare me a little bit. I just feel like I need to step away and think a little bit."

Ava started laughing. "I've been feeling like that for about fifteen years now."

"No offense, Ava. You say I'm being initiated into the family. But I'm a little wigged out by it. All of these allegiances and rivalries—I would need a big flow chart to figure this shit out. When it was just you and Chris and your mom, I thought you were just your average dysfunctional family. That was the time of my life. But now, you seem more like a dysfunctional *business*."

"We do all love each other, Matt. We almost need something like this. Come over here and sit down. I want to tell you something."

He sat beside her and she put her arm over his shoulder in her chummy way. "There is a lot of pressure, and I can see how confused you are. But you don't have to think all the time about what a father is supposed to be like, or what a sister is supposed to be like. Seems to me like families can get crushed by typecasting also. If Dad can clean himself up, then forget about all of that. Forget what you're *supposed* to feel about each other."

"And what about us?"

"We're friends," she said. "Any two people can be related. But friends are hard to come by."

He sat there for a while, nodding. His first true decision as an adult—to find these people—had complicated his life immeasurably, as if an earthquake had thrown all the souvenirs off his neatly arranged shelves. Abruptly he stood up and removed his shoes. "Watch this," he said. As he pulled off his T-shirt, he climbed a rocky slope and stood beside the trunk of a hemlock tree whose roots were tangled out toward the water. The water was calm beneath him, the treetops reflected shore to shore. With a howl he leaped off tucked into a cannonball. When he poked his head back up he shouted from the cold.

Ava was standing beside the tree. "You're nuts, Matthew."

He backstroked toward the center of the lake, staring up at

the clouds outlined with moonlight and spraying mouthfuls of mist into the air.

"I don't respond well to dares," said his sister.

Behind him he heard his sister splash into the water. Echoing around the forest, she squealed at the cold and shouted, "You little shit! This water is *freezing*." He trod backward and watched as her arms crawled toward him across a rippling stretch of gray water. In the distance, he heard an engine revving beside the cabin.

CHAPTER SIXTEEN

While Ava and Matt shivered under blankets beside the wood-stove, Camilla came back inside and updated them on Charlie. Grace puttered in the kitchen, opening and closing drawers loudly. Each slam of a cabinet made Camilla whisper more softly. Sloan was already asleep in one of the sheds outside.

A few of the men from the meeting, along with two orderlies and Sloan, had tried to coax Charlie out of the trailer. They circled around it in a predatory way, knocking on windows and hollering to him. Eventually Charlie came to the driver's seat and rolled down the window halfway. He would talk only to Camilla.

"He was whispering so softy, I could barely hear him," she said. "There was something he said that really troubled me. He said he needed to pay for what he'd done. Well, goodness, I said, 'That's very dramatic, Charlie. But there isn't a barter system for this kind of thing.' So he just kept on muttering that he had to pay somehow. I made him promise he wasn't going to become a Scientologist. You know, with them, you *can* pay. In any case, there we were, having this awkward little conversation, and Charlie just started up the trailer. Everybody circled around and blockaded his path, worried he was going to try to back out of there. Eventually he shut it down again and stumbled back to the bedroom. But it was a strange scene. He would've crashed that whale right into a tree."

Ava's and Matt's teeth were still chattering. Matt said, "I just left the stupid keys under the seat. I thought he was coming outside with me."

"It'll be all right, sugar. It's just that the more attention he gets, the worse the situation. He feeds off it."

Finally Grace pulled up a chair and sat behind them. She said, "He'll probably be okay in there tonight. If he's just sleeping. But tomorrow morning we are going to have to get him out any way we can."

"Why don't we just bust through the windshield?" asked Matt.

"If it comes to that," said Camilla.

"We should keep an eye on him," said Ava. "Maybe take turns staying watch."

"Well, I'll take the early-morning shift," said Camilla. "I'm the morning person around here. Wake me up. I already wanted to get up and catch the sunrise. I'm inspired by all this nature."

Camilla said good night to everyone, then took a flashlight and left the main cabin. Outside, they could see her light bobbing across the path toward the farthest shacks. Grace said good night as well, asking about sleeping arrangements and making sure everyone had enough blankets and pillows. She offered Ava another cup of tea, and told her to feel free to use the stove. "Thank you *so* much, Mrs. Ravendahl. You've been really good to us."

Grace looked away from them as she untied her apron. She said, "I suppose you're family now."

When she had gone off to bed, Matt lay down on the dusty couch and watched the fire. He fell asleep quickly. Ava touched his face lightly, then slid the blanket over him. She whispered, "I guess it's my shift, then." She checked again on Chris, who was sleeping soundly with the quilts kicked off him. With a chill in her bones, she walked with a blanket draped over her. After putting on her shoes and a robe, she headed downstairs and out into the darkness, through the cold air, to stand watch.

Charlie awakened and saw a wavering light that came off the lake. He leaned close to the windshield, his breath clouding it. Dawn was close. Shadows welled up like pools around the trees. In the clearing, he saw a flutter of movement. He stepped outside into the cold air and found a trail of socks. A blouse was snagged on a thornbush. He went to retrieve it, and across the netting of blackberry bushes and deer brush was the lake. The pattern of light upon it changed. There was a glow not from the moon or a lantern but from streaks of phosphorus on the tips of ripples, floating up and vanishing, faint as sparks. He worked his way forward through the undergrowth, cutting his arm on thorns, and saw the lights dancing upon the water.

He had run out of his hidden bottles, and he had not drank anything since afternoon. When he saw a shadow move along the length of the Christmas lights, changing colors with each bulb it passed, Charlie was frightened and fled back into his trailer, where he strapped himself to the captain's chair. He kept his eyes on the land, and his hands on the wheel.

When Ava tried to change shifts with Matt, he groaned and rose unwillingly. He found a screwdriver under the sink and took her out to the trailer. He said, "Watch this," then he opened the engine's hood and, lit only by the moon, deftly removed the distributor cap. She could see her father sleeping in the driver's seat, his head tilted to the side. "He's not going anywhere now," said Matt. "Let's go back to bed."

But Ava slept fitfully. A half hour before dawn, she saw her mother come out of a shack below, walking in her pristine camping clothes with a bandanna around her neck. She was like a catalog picture come to life. She tromped in stiff boots across the clearing. Ava dressed hastily and tiptoed down the stairs to meet her out front. The air was cold and their breath steamed. A layer of dampness had soaked into the pine needles. Dawn looked a few minutes behind the tissue of mist that now hovered upon the lake. The two women walked fast together, Ava stopping to finish tying her boots, then running to catch up as they hiked up the ridge. Camilla said, "Is somebody looking after your father?"

"The last time we checked, he was sleeping like a log."

They hustled to beat the sunrise, and when they reached the top of the embankment, they could see the lake and the campers to one side. Above them on another hill was the town, a dull glow of waking neon.

"Try not to look at all that junk back there," said Camilla. "Look at the natural part. Be an optimist."

From the driver's seat, Charlie watched the sky turn white. A lost bra was snagged on a blackberry bush, its cup inflating in the wind. He had the exhausted feeling of having bombed with an audience, a feeling of shame and humiliation. The light increased and he could see the forest behind him, split by the narrow stream, and across the undergrowth were the roofs of the shacks. For a moment he had no idea where he was, and his disorientation frightened him. But he closed his eyes and remembered Sadie, and the place was familiar again. Time had not touched it, except that she was gone. It was as if the young woman had simply been cut out of the pictures. Alarm clocks were going off around him, competing with the twittering birds. He had a painful spasm behind his rib cage and worried that it was a heart attack.

As he sat watching the sky brighten, he panicked because his head was so muddled. Being in this trailer gave him a vague sense of purpose, but he couldn't remember what it was. He was here to accomplish something, but his brain hurt from trying to concentrate. He gripped the wheel to keep his hands from shaking, and as he raised his arms a shot of pain struck his stomach so heavily that he closed his eyes and prayed. This was the stab of some indignant spirit, he believed, and it could be appeased only with the right thoughts. So in Charlie's mind a determined monologue began, and he focused with great effort on his life.

For thirty years he'd believed his failures were simple: that he had disappointed a daughter, a son, an ex-wife, a trail of lovers, perhaps some audiences. This morning he knew it was worse: he had missed half of his own life. His children were strangers, and even now he could barely understand them. He studied them during the day only for their reactions to him. He had never thought for a moment what their lives had been, who they had fallen in love with, what they dreamed of, what they longed for. Sometimes he would look at his daughter and a feeling of love would come over him briefly and intensely, and it would startle him, but almost immediately he would begin to list his injustices toward her. In his head, he would turn her into an equation of his failures and achievements, and soon he resented her for his own shortcomings. He was always confronting something from *his* life, never what she had made of her own. He understood that now, and this idea might have continued had he not become so immediately pleased with himself for seeing something clearly.

A wave of pain came again, and now it merged with the memory of that very first meeting with his son beside Ava's truck. Somehow, the kid had made the preposterous failure of Charlie's life seem complete. A son had come to defraud him. Charlie wasn't an actor. He was an insatiable liar, a con artist. He criticized Sloan, but he was really his apprentice. All his life, Charlie thought, he had been nothing but a hustler. He told everyone, gave everyone, showed everyone what they wanted. He'd given his soul for a pittance: to be recognized in restaurants, to look ten years younger. He once wanted to be worshiped, but it now seemed that being worshiped was inhuman and contradictory, like being loved without empathy or knowledge.

Out of habit Charlie began to pay attention to his emotions. He imagined using them somehow, believing that this was perhaps the purest and most beautiful self-loathing he had ever felt—far more complicated than anything he had ever portrayed on-screen. He reflected on his performances over the years. He thought about one of his earliest action films, when he had faked his own death by driving a Brinks truck into the ocean, then swam away with a tank on his back. His delirium merged with his sense of drama, and now he was willing to commit the most definitive act of his life. He wanted to see the look on his face. So he gazed into the side mirror and saw that his expression was all wrong. Lost, forlorn—he didn't look determined at all. He wanted to look like a soldier facing a firing squad. So he composed his features, and he released the parking brake.

The trailer lurched forward. Charlie slid the key into the ignition but the engine wouldn't start. He shifted into neutral. He began rolling downhill. Weeds and sunflowers bent beneath the grille. Branches slapped onto the window. He could see the lake ahead.

By the time the RV had gathered enough speed to totter over the lumps and careen toward the alder and the brush, it occurred to him that he was actually committing suicide, and not simply performing an elaborate theatrical gesture. The reality came upon him with a jolt of nausea. The trailer was pushing down saplings and carrying through like a bowling ball. Charlie started to laugh demonically.

Ava and Camilla waited but the sunrise didn't seem to come. It was blocked somewhere beyond mountains and low clouds. They watched the trailers with their lights coming on and listened to the sound of radios echoing across the valley in a medley of snooze alarms.

Suddenly Ava pointed to Charlie's trailer. It was rolling forward down the slope toward the lake.

"What is he trying to do?" said Camilla.

Charlie's trailer gathered speed. It descended at a steady pace across the mounds of grass and the stretches of weeds. Ahead was a steep hill of saplings, and beyond that a short cliff with a sharp drop into the water. Camilla stood on a log and said, "No, no, no. Ava? What is he doing?"

"Everyone is still asleep, Mom. Everybody."

"Run down there, sugar. Go!"

Camilla climbed up higher onto the log, and with all the air in her lungs, she belted out a scream so loud that all across the forest flocks of birds scattered from their nests and animals scurried up tree trunks and slumbering loggers shot upright and checked their rattling windows. She drained her lungs, and with the sudden rush of movement in the skies and on the ground, it was as if she had hurried the sun along, shouting a skip into time. The sky lightened and the nurses and patients ran from the shacks and trailers, and lights flipped on in the windows that speckled the hillsides.

Ava ran downhill, jarring her knees on the dips in the ground. She saw Matt come out of the cabin and rush toward the lake.

Charlie's trailer hit the patch of alder saplings with more speed and broke through them like a bull. Each sapling lashed the windshield before bending down and breaking under the axles, seeming to slow down the trailer with each slap. Still it fell steadily toward the ledge.

Ava was halfway down the trail when she saw the RV hit a last cluster of thin trees. They bent toward the lake until, with a whack, they broke at their bases. The trailer struck the lake with a slam that reverberated throughout the valley. It landed nose first, breaking a rift in the water, then it rose upward and floated for a few yards upright, bobbing like a cork. Matt dove into the water behind it and swam after it through the debris of branches and leaves. It surged up in the water once more, then fell to its side and began to sink slowly amid a torrent of bubbles. Ava ran until she was on level ground. She ran across the clearing—nearly decapitating herself on the cord of Christmas lights—and stopped at the shore, where she saw the last corner of the trailer sinking in a storm of bubbles. Matt appeared to be treading water, but as she looked more closely she realized he was standing on top of the trailer trying to stomp through the transom on the roof. A slick of greasy water rose and spread out on the surface.

Sloan began wading into the water in his underwear, as casual as a beachgoer.

A crowd of patients and orderlies gathered behind Ava. Camilla was stumbling downhill, winded, her face a bright shade of red. Ava yelled for her to watch after Chris, and Camilla gestured that she understood while holding her rib cage with her other arm.

When Charlie hit the water, the front windshield cracked into a web. But it held, and the green water swirling around it gave way to a last sudsy look at the shore. Everything jostled out of its place. The lake slanted on the windshield as the camper slid onto its side and began filling. The trees were erased by greenish water spun full of bubbles. The sky was swallowed. Water rushed in through every uncaulked crease, beneath the door and under windows and through the transom on the ceiling. Water pulled loose the mugs from the kitchen rack and floated them across the living quarters. Rolls of toilet paper unraveled and Ziplock bags full of air rose like jellyfish amid the shoals of butterscotch candy and stale Fig Newtons. Everything shorted out quickly, but Charlie felt an electric charge to the water.

All of his secret bottles dislodged from their hiding places, floating up with the seat cushions to bob along the surface of the murky water. Bottles spun in every corner, each like a captured bubble of air. Charlie waded toward the closet, and reached it just as the camper dropped entirely beneath the surface, the last air condensing into a mercurial layer of bubbles against the ceiling. As the trailer fell downward and glided, the water lifted rolls of paper towels. Paper plates twirled like Frisbees. Armadas of wine bottles, gin bottles, cans, tumbled along the surface; flasks shimmered and flew upward from behind fake bookcases and potted plants that now clouded the water with mud; and out of the bathroom, on a squid-ink slick of blue water, came the prescription bottles, some snugly closed and joining the other bric-a-brac, some open and shedding pills that softened and dissolved. The water was suffused with Xanax and Percodan. Orange Valium twirled like guppies toward the walls; and behind them came the oil slick of skin- and hair-care products, catching in thickets of toilet paper, the minoxidil sucked like a genie from its tube and gathering on the coats of floating kiwi. The chemical clouds spread, passing over the pornographic videos and the odd sexual paraphernalia that he had never quite figured out how to use. It merged with Barbara's protein powders until all around him was a thick porridge. Above, through the transom full of bubbles, he saw Matt stomping, the surface of the lake at his waist like a liquid sky.

It was impossible for Matt to kick hard enough in water to break through, so he walked across the top of the trailer like it was a sandbar. Sloan was shouting instructions to him from the shore, but Matt wasn't listening. All around the lake people were gathered in their robes and pajamas. Matt looked up and felt like he was on a vast stage. He knew he could hold his breath for at least thirty seconds if pressed, so he took a gasp and dove down, hoping the door was unlocked. Around the bottom there was a tangle of seaweed, and he kicked at it and lost some of his air.

He struggled toward the trailer with the pressure in his head throbbing and his cheeks bulging. To his great surprise, the front door of the RV was open, and inside—like the perfectly preserved hull of a sunken ship—there were the cabinets opened and the cushions of the couch floating loose. Fifteen seconds without a breath, he looked into the trailer. The insides had been spun loose, all the doors flapping gently in a current. The closet was open but nothing was inside. He had held his breath long enough to begin losing his hunger for oxygen. Everything had a dreamy look as he swam inside, searching the seats and the bathroom. There was a single silvery layer of oxygen shimmering on the ceiling. He drifted up to it. He pressed his mouth against the granular white ceiling and sucked a few short mouthfuls of air.

His father was gone.

The short gasps along the ceiling were not enough to sustain Matt, and he felt light-headed. The water he swallowed had the bitter taste of cough syrup. He was on the verge of fainting as he climbed back to the open doorway. The surface above was a translucent tarp, ruffled by the wind. It was perhaps only a dozen feet above him, but it seemed like miles as he sank downward into the tendrils of seaweed. He felt like he was falling into a luxuriant sleep. He had been counting in his head, but lost track at forty. He sat. The sun had come up above and was glowing on the water, sending columns of light down through the green.

He saw a figure twirling down toward him. It was just a shadow, but as it approached, he saw a long scarf unraveling behind her and the glint of skates on her feet. The light had hardened into ice around the lake. She spun downward through a single broken spot of blue sky, pretty as a postcard. The scarf uncoiled, turn by turn, as she pirouetted downward; and Matt realized it was a lifeline with the surface. She reached out her arm and Matt swam for it. He chased the scarf toward the edge of the sunlight, feeling his lungs burn, and all at once, in a rush of sound and movement, the image was gone.

He broke the surface. All around him were the hard sounds of splashing and gasping. Ava was with him in the water and she had her arms around him. She said, "Swim, Matt. Swim. Kick your legs."

Sloan grabbed his arms and helped him into a rowboat. He hoisted Ava up behind him. She leaned back, swallowing mouthfuls of air. All of the muck from the trailer was spreading out on the surface, pelted by a slow drizzle.

"He wasn't . . . in there," said Matt, gasping for air.

Sloan stared at the grease slick widening across the lake. He said, "I think he's down in there still. I think he's sitting down there somewhere, watching us."

Ava covered her face and said, "Sloan, please. You're insane."

"You're all going to have to trust me on this one. Look for bubbles. Anywhere. We've got to follow the trail of bubbles."

Just as the three of them scanned the water looking for any rupture on the surface, the rain increased and churned the water around them. Ava and Matt looked back at Sloan, confused, but still too out of breath to ask him the point of this vigil.

Down below the bow of the rowboat in silence and darkness, Charlie was struggling away. He was decked out in Sloan's scuba gear, but without the fins he dog-paddled along clumsily amid the high forest of seaweed. After clearing the regulator, he now breathed through the tank on his back. He tried to remove the water from his mask, but could release only a spit's worth of it, so he saw through a jiggling bubble over his eyes. Stretched out before him was the undulating surface of discarded bottles and cans. He was heavy in the water, and could walk more easily than swim. So he crawled through the weeds, frayed and fish-bitten.

He walked and swam all the way to the other side of the lake, and when he surfaced, he could see the people gathered at the far shore. He felt ebullient, but thought it might be from swallowing water laced with medication. For a moment, he had truly considered following through with his impulse, but now he felt cleansed of the feeling. With the trailer gone, it was as if he had disposed of his shell.

The sun had risen into thick clouds, and now the first silvery threads of rain were falling, tapping rings into the lake. Charlie left the tank on the muddy embankment and crawled upward across roots and pine needles. At the far end of the lake, fishing boats and flat-bottom barges had gathered around the debris from his trailer. No one had noticed him escape. Nestled among the trees on one shore, it looked like the local press was accumulating. Camera flashes snapped like fireworks.

Charlie's teeth were chattering and his skin was puckered. He needed to warm up, but he didn't want to stand on the shore and try to catch their attention; so he climbed through the forest, fighting through sweeps of pine branches, straight uphill to an empty road. The only structure he saw was a barn in the distance, sitting on a scalp of thick green grass. He walked along the road, his bare feet stung by the cold pavement. Beyond the trees, he heard sirens.

When he reached the farm—what looked like an abandoned dairy farm—he opened a rickety gray fence and walked on the soft grass to a dark barn. When he was within fifty yards, a door opened for him.

An old man stepped into the threshold.

"I was hoping you could help me," said Charlie. "I'm freezing and I need to make some calls."

The old man didn't seem to hear him. He said, "Well, I'll be. I thought you'd gone and fallen off the face of the earth. Come in, come in. I was hoping you'd drop by."

He led Charlie into a dark barn that was converted into a library. The place smelled like hay, but the stalls and creamery vats had been replaced with shelves and microfilm carrels and video monitors. Extension cords traversed the floor. He led Charlie to a creamery vat and told him to go inside. Charlie was bewildered, but he stooped down and crawled through the narrow opening to where he sat facing a monitor and a rack stuffed full of magazines. The old man vanished for a few moments, then brought in towels and blankets. He groaned as he came into the silo, hollow and echoing like the inside of a bottle.

"Here. Warm yourself. Must be raining hard today," said the old man. Charlie felt like he had stumbled into some hallucination. His vision had the soft edges of a dream. "You know, I've been collecting all these things for *you* all this time, and then you stopped coming around. Nobody to appreciate all of it. So, what happened to you? You still fancying yourself some kind of movie star?"

Charlie could read nothing on the old man's face. "I suppose," said Charlie.

"I could use the company," he said. "Look here. I've got all those magazines you like stacked right here. And these are some more of those videos from that actor you like so much."

With trembling hands, the man slipped a video into the slot. Onto the monitor came one of Charlie's earliest films, *The Gunman*. It began at the halfway point: the shoot-out in the abandoned tenement.

On-screen Charlie crouched down in the bathtub as a grenade clunked into the room. The explosion blew through the walls and floor and the bathtub crashed down onto a mattress in the room below, where Charlie, unscathed but for a few charcoal streaks on his face and clothes, sprang up and surprised the villains with six rapid shots.

The old man sat with him and watched, complaining the entire time. "You see what you've done to me. I can't think straight with all this mayhem around."

After the finale—in which Charlie's girlfriend hangs from a penthouse balcony as Charlie fights off goons from Cosa Nostra and the yakuza with a broken bottle and a mop handle, managing to clear himself enough space to tie a firehose to his ankle and dive off the balcony, catching his girlfriend as she falls and swinging with her straight into the mezzanine below—the old man inserted another film, this one the underappreciated *Deadly Thursday,* a fairly simple disaster film in which a tsunami devastates a quaint seaside village. The plot thickens, however, when Charlie discovers the presence of a corrupt international consortium of military contractors looking to harness the power of tsunamis to use in advance of amphibious attacks. Needless to say, Charlie thwarted this plan. They watched parts of *Hell on Ice* and *No Way Home* and *No Surrender* and *Ten Thousand Ways to Die.* They watched the Christmas movie, *Massacre on 31st Street.*

The sequences blended together in his mind into one unbroken fight scene of Charlie, sweating with a few nicks and burns, bludgeoning villains with pool cues, hurling femme fatales across the room by their high-heeled boots. He gouged and gutted and kicked and stabbed. He backed over some with his car. But soon, in all the rush of jump kicks and swinging fists, Charlie could no longer remember blocking and filming the scenes laboriously, blow by blow. As if all at once his history had been animated, he sank deeper into his chair and watched with delight. He laughed. A scrapbook was set in motion—a lifetime of gloriously over-the-top shoot-outs—and in glimpses here and there he saw something in his eyes: he was enjoying himself. "Look at what a good time I'm having!" What a likable fellow he seemed to be. He laughed and laughed at this onslaught of miraculous escapes and impossible heroics, staring at his youthful face amid all the disasters, and he was thrilled with himself. Perhaps he was no actor, but he wasn't a cutout either. Sure, there he was now, strangling a KGB agent with a phone cord, but there was lust in his eyes, the look of a boy who was heatedly playing. For so long he had believed his success to be a fluke, but he was being convinced of his own inadvertent charm. Thank God he had found this strange old man, devoted to him. When on-screen Charlie stared down the length of a rifle, about to shoot the propeller off an ascendant helicopter, Charlie laughed hysterically at how easy it all appeared.

"I go hunting sometimes," he told the old man, "and I can't hit a goddamn pheasant from six feet away." Charlie turned and hugged the old man. He said, "I can't possibly thank you enough. It's so fantastic to get away from L.A. and meet a genuine fan. It's life-affirming. You'll never know what you've done for me. I've had one ridiculous circus of a career. Oh, what a wonderfully silly business this is."

The hug surprised the old man. His arms hung limp. He squinted at Charlie's face and gave an embarrassed laugh. He said, "Well, I'll be damned. . . . You know, I don't see so well these days. You walk just like somebody else I know."

When the police found Charlie that evening, his family arrived with them. Stritmatter had called Grace and left a bizarre message that "Matt's movie star" was at his place. Sloan shouted that he had known all along and described Charlie's state-of-the-art diving gear for the entire drive to Stritmatter's farm.

Charlie's fierce laughter echoed throughout the barn. He sat inside a milk vat, and through the low trap door they could see only his feet, running in place. The vat rang with gunplay. When Stritmatter saw Matt, he looked closely. He nodded, as if satisfied. He held on to Matt's shoulder and said, "You can't take your eyes off those things. It's like watching the end of the world."

Matt and Ava leaned down and crawled into the vat. Charlie waved to them without looking away from the screen.

"You are the most selfish person I've ever known," said Ava. "You *asshole*. How could you do that to us? You just went way over the line, even for you."

"Desperate times require desperate measures," Charlie said

on-screen. He mouthed the words along with it. Then he added, "I was testing myself."

Ava leaned down and slapped him. He glanced at her, as shocked as if he'd seen a ghost. All his attention left the monitor, where Charlie the soldier, weeds in his hair and grease on his clothes, ran in slow motion from a burning village, thatched huts exploding closer and closer to him while an unlit cigar bobbed in his mouth.

"No, you were testing all of us. You're going to go and kill yourself for some stupid point? You can't scare people just to make them *prove* they care about you, Dad. This kind of idiocy is over. Hear me? Finished. Look at your son right there, Dad. He almost drowned. This kid was willing to risk his life to save *you*. Yeah, you didn't expect that, did you? You didn't expect that anyone would do anything but watch and maybe applaud. Well, you thought wrong."

Charlie glanced up at Matt, a bewildered look of admiration on his face. Matt leaned against the rounded metal wall with his arms folded over his chest. His skin had paled from the cold and he was wearing a parka over pajamas.

"That's right," said Ava, responding to his expression. "Open your eyes now. Look around. You'll go to any stupid length to show some fireworks, anything at all just to keep from looking a person in the face. It's better to lie on a train track than to trust someone or believe in them. Is that what you're telling me? Just look me in the face, Dad. Just look at your family for a few goddamn seconds. That's all there is to it. Don't give up every-thing for some moronic game. You're not a little boy playing cops and robbers. You carry on now, Dad. You get up and you snap out of it."

The flames overtook the screen with a loud detonating sound and Charlie vanished for a moment, but at last, out of the fire came a shadow, and as it approached they could see it was the hero, unscathed, the tip of his cigar now lit. But Charlie was watching his daughter's face. He stared at her, eager, expectant. She was hovering over her father with an intensity that seemed to match the chaos on the monitor.

Camilla crawled inside and fixated on Ava, at the way she leaned forward and simply stared at Charlie with a look like she'd wait endlessly for him to understand her; and so it seemed to her that her daughter was about to inherit the helm of this strange, submerged matriarchy. All her life Ava had so timidly waited for her father's approval, and now Camilla saw that she had somehow abandoned the idea of it, and was instead telling him the rules of *her* support. Ava spoke with the tone of an angry parent; she now seemed bolstered by her motherhood, the very thing she once viewed with embarrassment.

Even Matt knew there was a shift that day in the West family, though it might never be reported in the tabloids. He thought it was a shift that must happen in all families. There is a point at which everyone simply rallies around the strongest person, and on that morning Ava stepped forward and demanded the role. Matt was proud of her, feeling that he had hurried this along. Perhaps, had he never arrived, she would have forever been locked in her garage.

Charlie watched his daughter with rapt attention, thinking: *What an actress she might have been.* He grabbed her hand and put it against his bristly face. He said, "I'm finished."

To Ava's surprise, one of the cops started applauding the end of the videotape. Matt and Camilla joined in, though they seemed to be clapping more for Ava. The old man started to applaud, then Sloan outside, then Chris began to copy Matt, until a chain of applause was leading from the video monitor out to the grass covered with reporters and spectators; and in the feverish pitch of cheering, Ava leaned down to Charlie and said, "So there you go. I guess we saved the world at last."

EPILOGUE:

G O S S I P

H O U N D S

Three and a half months after the incident at the lake, Matthew came across the following article in *Gossip Hounds:*

There may be more to the Charlie West saga than initially meets the eye. Several months after the actor's alleged breakdown and suicide attempt at a drug and alcohol treatment facility, close friends now suggest that the motivation for West's actions may have been more than his imminent breakup with Barbara Hartmann and the disappointing box-office performance of *Born Ready.* "Charlie's emotional state—at that particular moment in time—was the product of many forces, good and bad, converging simultaneously," says an anonymous source close to the West family. "He simply needed a good friend—such as myself—to pull him through, show him the beauty of existence. Since the incident, Charlie has been a new man. In love with life. And convinced of the commercial viability of certain, shall we say, daring undersea ventures."

In early summer, West was helped out of the premiere of his film, suffering from a nervous breakdown. He was accompanied by a man in his late teens or early twenties. This mysterious associate became more intriguing when a tabloid bought an amateur videotape from a tourist five days later. The tape showed the young man supporting West, helping him into a nearby restaurant, and scolding him for his behavior. West's longtime publicists were quick to issue a statement claiming that the unidentified figure was "West's new personal assistant and nothing more."

But numerous sources around the Washington town of Chelan tell a different story. The young man's name is Matthew Ravendahl, born in 1980, and—sources say—the illegitimate son of the actor. He is described around his hometown as "a nice kid, kind of quiet." Another man claims, "Charlie West is his father, sure. But that's no excuse to be illiterate. I was appalled at some of the god-awful things that boy would force me to watch with him. It's the end of the world in slow motion."

Locked in bitter divorce proceedings, Barbara Hartmann commented on the situation from her vacation at a popular ranch retreat in Arizona. "My lawyers have asked me not to discuss any of the specifics of my case. It's still very up in air, you know. But I will tell you this, in a very general way: Charlie is emotionally backward. Cruel, even. He is not willing to be known. He's a block of ice. There's no *there* with Charlie. No center of gravity. And in a very generalized sort of way, yes, I believe the little sh-t is his son."

West remains unavailable for comment, refusing to leave the confines of his recently rented home. However, he did issue a statement yesterday that his daughter—Ava (28)—read aloud: "I apologize to my fans and to the American public. I have been a role model to young people throughout my life and such behavior is unacceptable. I am getting along with the healing process thanks to the people who have always cared about me. I am looking forward to spending more time with family and loved ones. I must also express my undying love and gratitude to the American public."

Ironically, while West's most recent film has been savaged by critics and audiences alike, video rentals for West's earlier films have taken a sharp rise. As further proof that any publicity is good publicity, Charlie is rumored to be close to signing a major deal with a network.

"He's as bad an actor as there is out there," said an anonymous director. "But he's like the loudest of all party crashers. People like that don't die. They just go to television."

As for Matthew Ravendahl, he could not be reached for comments.

In a corner of the garage, converted into a bedroom and partitioned off by backdrops and set facades, Matt felt almost famous. He took a highlighter and underlined each mention of his name. In the kitchen a dish broke, followed by a flurry of profanity from his sister. Chris was drumming on the wall opposite his bed, and from outside there came the faint odor of cigarette smoke. With the ashen dusk now falling over his adopted city, the garage was finally cooling. Police sirens droned as if escorting away the sun.

Matt's soup was boiling on a camping stove, but he paid no attention. He could think of nothing else. With his hands shaking and his heart racing, he smoothed out the paper. All his life was bottled into the letters of that name. He took a pair of scissors and, with patient strokes along the narrow margins, cut.